The Cat That God Sent

THE CAT THAT GOD SENT

Jim Kraus

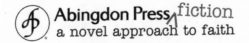

Abingdon Press fiction
a novel approach to faith

Nashville, Tennessee

The Cat That God Sent

Copyright © 2013 by Jim Kraus

ISBN-13: 978-1-4267-6561-2

Published by Abingdon Press, P.O. Box 801, Nashville, TN 37202
www.abingdonpress.com

The persons and events portrayed in this work of fiction
are the creations of the author, and any resemblance
to persons living or dead is purely coincidental.

The words to "Just As I Am, Without One Plea" were written in 1835
by Charlotte Elliott, 1789–1871.

Library of Congress Cataloging-in-Publication Data has been
requested.

Printed in the United States of America

1 2 3 4 5 6 7 8 9 10 / 17 16 15 14 13

To Petey, the noble cat who has deemed us suitable hosts.

"God made the cat in order that man might have the pleasure of caressing the tiger."
—Fernand Méry

1

Jake pulled to the side of the road, stopped the truck, then slid out into the chill of the dawn. He flexed his back, left and right, hearing the bones pop. He slowly rotated his right arm, in a windmill fashion, like a relief pitcher warming up. The muscles hurt most at the top of the arc, when it was closest to heaven.

"Think I'll get a sign today? That would be nice. Some sort of sign that this is the right move. That I'm doing the right thing. How about it? Even a little, bitty sign would be okay, too. A sign that doesn't look like a sign—okay as well."

He waited and heard nothing. He held his forced smile for a long moment. If God really were listening, he would know that Jake was only kidding—or at least mostly kidding.

"Well, the proverbial doors were open, right? That was a sign, right? An open door—or rather, an open road to Coudersport?"

The road between Kane and Coudersport remained empty with only sounds of the few birds that made north central Pennsylvania a stop on their early spring migration. To the east, the sun lit the top of a tree-covered ridge, illuminating the still-bare trees with a golden backlit glow.

"Now, here's the thing, though. Those preachers on TV get signs all the time. You talk to them. Why not me?" Jake knew he was being snarky and he was pretty sure God did not like, nor quickly answer, snarky prayers.

He took a deep breath, massaging his right shoulder with his left hand.

"Well, at least my shoulder feels better today."

He tugged on the ropes covering the tarp that held down all his earthly possessions. He checked every rope. By nature and temperament, Jake was a most careful person.

He felt a twinge.

"Almost better."

He started the engine, looked both ways twice, and pulled out onto the road. He had one more hour until he reached Coudersport.

"And that's where I'll start over. That's where I'll show everyone that I can do this. Right? Where I'll find my faith again."

He hoped the words would become his reality.

He reached into the glove compartment of the truck and pulled out one of a couple dozen eight-track tapes.

One of these days I'll get a new truck or put a CD player in this one.

He did not bother to look at the title. None were current.

Do they still sell eight-track tapes?

He popped the tape into the slot and turned up the volume. It was a compilation of Christian camp favorites. The first selection was "Onward Christian Soldiers." Jake could not help smiling and began to sing along. Loudly and off-key. Then his shoulder twinged again, sharply, as if giving him an omen of what was to come. However, the troubling thing about omens is they are open to interpretation.

The dried seed husks at the top of the tall field grass rustled together, stirred by the spring breeze with its hint of warmth. Green tendrils poked about at paw level. The cat stopped, sat down slowly, carefully, and sniffed.

A fecundity in the air.

He sniffed, his nose twitching.

I heard that word on that radio station that talks all the time and is always asking for money.

The cat would have smiled if he could have smiled. If he had the correct muscle structure.

Fecundity. That's a weird word, isn't it? Fecundity. Funny sounding. I know, I know . . . I can be a bit pedantic at times. That's where I heard that word, too. On that radio station that never plays music. They just talk. About needing money, mostly.

The feline snapped back to his task at hand and breathed in again, deeply. Not large by cat standards, perhaps the size of a football, with a thick silvery coat and black markings like a striped lynx. Gold-green eyes, wide set and deeply penetrating, a white chin and nose, and a thick feathering of white fur covering his ears. A thickly furred tail. The dark perpendicular lines scoring his forehead made it appear he was in perpetual deep thought.

I really am, most of the time.

He watched as a white truck pulled into the gravel lot. He tried not to put pressure on his right paw. He tried to ignore the agonizing tightness that raced up his forelimb when the paw scraped hard against the ground. He smoothed his whiskers with his other paw. He watched, showing no outward indication of pain. That is what cats do.

A truck. An old truck. And not very clean.

Then he crouched lower, protecting his right front paw, hidden, perfectly camouflaged in the grass, still as a rock, only his eyes, now slits in the bright sun, moving. The cat slowly tilted his head and looked up, into the pellucid sky, his vision staying on the thin clouds for a long moment. He tilted an ear toward the heavens, as if listening intently.

That looks like the man I heard God talking about. I think that's what I heard. It is hard to identify people. Most of them smell the same. A lot of them look the same. This human looks like he needs company. People need company. That's in the Bible, isn't it? A man without a cat. That's not right. He must be lonely.

The cat's eyes moved back and forth, just a little.

Well, I can say this much for sure: he needs a cat. A good cat. A smart cat. Like me. I am a good cat. I am a smart cat.

He flicked an ear, almost distracted by a soft, leafy rustle nearby. Soft and tender and whispery.

You know what? Maybe he needs a mouse. Everybody could use a fat mouse now and again. People get so excited when I bring them a mouse. They shout. They dance. People must like mice. They shoosh me away and in an instant, the mouse is gone. I guess people are always hungry. However, they are not very good at sharing their mice.

And as the cat thought about it, his stomach growled. It had been a few days since he had eaten. He stiffened, imperceptibly, hearing again the soft, furtive rustling in the grass a few body lengths to his left. He knew what small rodent made the rustle.

He would wait.

And maybe later, he would have something to give the man that would make him happy.

It's why I'm here. I need to give that lonely man a mouse. I need to help him. I am good at that. I can be a good, intelligent, helpful cat. God only uses good cats, and I am a very good cat.

The cat blinked and smiled to himself with a certain light in his eyes that gave evidence of his good humor.

The mouse dance. I really like it when humans dance the mouse dance.

———— ✺ ————

Jake Wilkerson pulled into the driveway of the church, an old church that was his new church, his new assignment, his new job—only his second real, adult job. Jake was nearing thirty, tall, thin, with a narrow face, an easy, gentle-to-arrive smile, and wide blue eyes. Some people called him striking. He did not call himself that. His unruly thatch of thick brown hair made *striking* the wrong adjective to use to describe him.

The church's exterior, weathered to a faded, chalky white, featured a scalloping of brown water stains, the residue from lawn sprinklers squirting iron-rich well water on the bottom rows of its clapboards. The building was perfectly centered in the middle of a large grassy and partially graveled two-acre lot at the southwest corner of Route 44 and Dry Run Road—a short ride south of Coudersport, Pennsylvania.

Loose gravel crunched and growled beneath the worn tires of his pickup, a slow, welcoming, rural sound, loud in the quiet of the most pleasant spring morning.

The church sign, ninety degrees to the highway, leaned a few degrees off perpendicular.

CHURCH OF THE OPEN DOOR
11:00 SUNDAY SERVICE
, PASTOR

The space before the word *Pastor* must have been recently painted over, with only a faint ghosting of the former pastor's name remaining.

Jake relaxed, stepped out of his truck, and stretched, breathing deep, twisting at the waist and rolling his shoulders. The right shoulder popped, almost audibly this time, and he felt a ripple of small creaks in his back. He tried to smooth his hair and realized that he needed to find a barber before Sunday.

This isn't so bad, is it? This is good. Really. It is.

He breathed in, filling his lungs, feeling his ribs complain. The ominous twitch in his shoulder still spoke, a hesitant pulsing.

I'm too young to feel this many aches. I need a new mattress.

He squared his shoulders.

I can do this. I can. I can make this work. I know how to do this.

He took a few small steps toward the church, stopped, then stared up at the steeple at the rear of the church roof.

Is that my imagination . . . or is the steeple tilted?

<hr />

The cat remained still, hidden in the grass, only the very tip of his tail twitching. His ears pivoted and moved, following the sounds of the man's steps on the gravel lot.

He has firm footsteps. Solid. Like he knows where he is going. Some people take little, halting steps, which mean they seldom get where they are going. Not this human.

The cat sniffed, his small nostrils flaring almost undetectably.

And I like the way he smells. Safe.

He heard the rustle again.

I have time. I will wait. Never pounce before the prey is within the space of a leap. My mother taught me that.

<hr />

Within moments of his arrival at his new job and residence, Jake watched as a pickup truck, even older than his and of an ill-defined paint color, bounced into the parking area and all but slid to a stop. The engine plinked and coughed and continued to sputter even as the driver hopped out, slammed the door, and made his way closer to Jake, his right hand extended.

"T. James Bennett," he declared, shaking Jake's hand enthusiastically. T. James Bennett looked like an inexact, off-center, tattered copy of Willard Scott—the morning weatherman who wished people happy birthday, but shorter and wider, with a genial smile. "We met back when you preached here, but you met a lot of folks that weekend, so I bet not many stand out. Am I right?"

"You are, Mr. Bennett, but I do remember you," Jake said. "I remember wondering about the 'T' in your name."

Mr. Bennett almost frowned, but didn't. "It's been T. James since I learned how to write. I hated the 'T' name, even as a little kid, and I told myself that when I grew up, I would never use it again. That's one promise that I kept to myself. Good to keep promises, you know. The problem with a bad name is all the stuff your name gets put on these days. I figured it was too much trouble to change it. People learned. And besides, they all call me Jimbo. Everyone does, including the Missus. Jimbo. Says it's a proper name for a fellow like me. Been called Jimbo since grade school."

"Well, then, Jimbo, I'm happy that you took time out of your day to meet me here. I appreciate it."

Jimbo drew a step closer. "You know why I'm the elder in charge of meeting you today?"

Jake hoped he looked puzzled. "Seniority?"

Jimbo cackled and replied, "Nope. It's 'cause I don't have a job. At least not one at the moment. Got time to burn, as they say. And I had a spare set of keys for the church. Two good reasons."

Jimbo stepped off toward the rear door of the church. "We did show you the living quarters here, didn't we? When you came and visited? The parsonage part of the church, right? Plenty of room for a single fellow like yourself."

Now a few months past, the day of his candidating had been more than a bit hectic. The drive from Butler should have taken only three hours, but Jake had been on the road for five, his sense of direction not strong. There was no direct route that led door-to-door. The trip involved multiple turns and changes in route numbers and Jake's nervous and constant referring to the map. And, being that he "auditioned" in the early winter, snow had begun to fall while he spoke that cold morning, amping up Jake's nervousness about the return trip.

"I did see it, but I didn't spend much time looking. I guess I was a tad nervous that day."

"Have to say, Pastor Jake, that I didn't think you were nervous at all. You preached good."

Jimbo pulled a fist-sized ring of keys from his coat pocket, jangling like a jailer, and thumbed through it until he found the correct one. He slipped it into the lock on the six-panel door, pulled at the handle while he turned the key, and shouldered the door open.

"Weather makes this stick sometimes," he said, then eyed his new pastor. "You handy around the house? Fixing stuck doors and all that?"

Jake lied.

"Not bad. I don't have as many tools as I would like, but I guess I'm handy enough."

The truth is, besides a hammer and a screwdriver, I don't have any tools. And if it can't be fixed with either of those tools—then it's broken.

Jimbo grinned, satisfied. "Not that this place needs much of anything . . . but the whole building is getting up there in years. Sometimes it takes a hammer to get things going."

Jake wasn't sure he knew what Jimbo meant, but nodded in earnest agreement. "Sure thing."

Jimbo slapped at the wall and switched on the light—a bright overhead lamp ensconced in a white, imitation carnival glass globe. Jake squinted for a moment. The light was much too bright for the room, but the interior was more pleasant than Jake had remembered, especially now that the soft light of spring had begun to arrive. The furnishings might have been from IKEA, even though the nearest IKEA was probably in Philadelphia: matching upholstered chairs in a gray corduroy fabric, a comfy-looking sofa, a stand for a TV. The walls were off-white, maybe a light classic gray, even. The kitchen, visible from the entry, had newer stainless steel appliances, a square wooden table by a large window, and more cabinets than Jake could possibly fill. Wide wood flooring planks. Shiny. Probably original but refinished.

"Bedroom's back there, of course. Bathroom too. That's new as of last year. New shower and tub and . . . all the other facilities as well," Jimbo said, with a guilty smirk, like saying "toilet" in front of a pastor was somewhere midway up on the list of almost-sins. "And the office is over there," he added, pointing, as if he were a lazy real estate agent.

That office Jake remembered. It was a large room, much bigger than he had been used to. Big wooden desk, well used, with great character and patina, wall of bookcases, a large wooden table (looked handcrafted) with a half-dozen chairs— for elders' meetings, no doubt. Three large windows, almost floor to ceiling, matching the Gothic style windows of the church. A smallish door led toward the church itself, buffered by a small office/anteroom that may have once held a secretary, but not in the last few years.

"You need help unloading?" Jimbo asked. "My back ain't quite up to snuff these days, but I could make a call or two."

Jake demurred. "No. I don't have much. Clothes. Books. Towels. Sheets. A few pots and pans. Mr. Coffee. Easy stuff. I'm just so glad that the parsonage is furnished. A great help for someone like me."

Jimbo fiddled three keys off his ring and handed them to Jake. One was marked FRONT DOOR, one BASEMENT DOOR, and one PARSONAGE.

"Pastor Wilkerson," Jimbo said, his words a little softer, "I gotta tell you . . . thanks for taking over here as pastor. Really, thanks a bundle. We don't have much in a small church, I know, and we're on the smallish side of small . . . but . . . well, it is what we got. Ever since Pastor Mokley quit the God business and left to sell insurance in Kane—well, we all have been without. We need a man of God, all right. An honest man. Like you."

He had to say an honest man. He had to go there. Like I'm going to be reminded of that forever. Honesty is not always the best policy. Just ask Barbara Ann. But that's water under the bridge, right?

Jimbo offered a happy grin, hoping to put the new man at ease.

"Well, it is an honor to be called," Jake replied, being totally truthful.

"So, I'll leave you be, if that's okay with you. And you remember that we got an all-church potluck this Wednesday. In the basement. Fellowship Hall, if you'd like. Folks want to meet you, see what you eat. Stuff like that. And you and the elders will meet later on. Talk things over. Answer any questions you might have."

"Should I bring anything to the potluck?" Jake asked. *Maybe pastors in small churches cook things for these occasions. Or bring the rolls or something.*

"Nope. Just yourself. One of the perks of the job. Just stay away from the Missus' Swedish Stew. She ain't Swedish and it ain't stew."

Jake stuck out his hand.

"Jimbo—forewarned is forearmed. Thanks." And as he shook the elder's hand, Jake felt that familiar twinge in the right shoulder, as if the heavens were trying to tell him that something was about to happen. Jake didn't like that twinge. The twinge was there just before he was fired from his previous church in Butler. He definitely felt it just before his former almost-fiancée-waiting-for-a-ring informed him that if he were no longer a pastor, she was no longer his girlfriend. The twinge was there when his former senior pastor and boss said there would be no letter of recommendation—"Because of all that has happened. You do understand, don't you? My niece feels terrible about all this." And he felt the twinge today—clearly and strongly.

Maybe it's a good twinge this time.

Omens.

Jake never liked omens, even though, if there was one, regardless of its portent, he would find it comforting.

The cat waited and the prey came to him. It was easy and quick. He circled around at the edge of the field. He could wait. It looked like that other man, the round man, was about to leave.

Then I'll introduce myself, the cat thought to himself. *I don't want to intrude on their conversation. If there is one thing a good cat needs to understand it's that good manners are very important. I will simply wait here until he is available for introductions.*

———⊗⊗⊗———

As they walked back outside to the trucks, Jimbo zipped up his work jacket, threadbare at the elbows and cuffs.

"You call me if you need anything. Bobby Richard—he's an elder, too, who you met, of course—got the phone connected last week, so you can call me. But maybe you have one of those new cellphones, I bet. They don't always work up here, though. Anyhow, all the elders are on the list taped to the desk—phone numbers and the like."

"I'll do that, Jimbo. But I'm sure I'll be okay."

At the far edge of the parking lot, where the gravel met the grass, sat a tall, silver-and-black cat with white accents. Jake noticed it first.

"That anybody's cat?" he asked. "Looks a little like a lynx, doesn't it? A small, skinny one."

Jimbo looked over, stared for a long moment, then snorted.

"Don't know. Never saw a lynx up here. But it's just a cat and it's not from around here. No houses nearby. Not within a mile. Maybe even farther than that. More like two miles—and that would be the Jenkinses and I know Old Man Jenkins, and well, he hates cats, so it can't belong to him. That one is just a stray. Might even be one of those feral cats. You know, raised in the wild. If that happens, they're really no good as house cats anymore. And people dump animals out here in the country all the time."

"Really? That's terrible."

"It happens," Jimbo said. "Some people got no feelings, do they?"

"I guess not," Jake replied.

"I got my shotgun in the truck. You want me to get rid of it for you?"

Jake could only manage a surprised, "Wha-what?"

"If you let it stick around, it could be a pest. And, look, it looks like it's got a lame foot there. Be a kindness to end it for it, you know?"

Jake recovered and knew he did not want to sound too surprised or shocked. What Jimbo said was probably true, but he could not cotton to a random killing of a cat—not just like that.

"No. Maybe he's just lost."

"It ain't lost. And it doesn't belong to anybody. Too skinny. It's just like getting rid of a varmint. It'll be okay."

Jake held firm.

"No. Let him be."

Jimbo looked askance, just a little, then shrugged.

"Suit yourself. But if it gets to be a pest, I'll take care of it for you."

"I'm sure he won't."

Jimbo stroked his chin and grinned. "You pastors are in the saving business, aren't you? I guess that goes with the job description, doesn't it? Saving things that are lost and lame and hurting and all that? That's a good trait for a pastor, ain't it?"

And with that, Jimbo heaved himself into his old truck; the engine sputtered to life after the third ratcheting try, and he backed out onto the main road without looking.

"See you Wednesday, if not sooner," he called out, as the truck wheezed into a forward gear and pulled away.

Jake turned back to the cat. It had not moved all the while, but instead, just stared impassively. Then it looked down at the ground beside it, and then back up to Jake. Jake thought there was an air of pride in the cat's stare, but could not imagine why.

———∞———

Please. I am not a "varmint." That was insulting. He didn't know a good cat when he saw a good cat. No time for that now. We have more important things to deal with. Like me being sent by God. That should take precedent, don't you think?

And what sort of name is Jimbo? For a grown man. We are not in the funny papers, are we?

A varmint? Really?

———∞———

Jake watched the cat watch him. Neither of them moved. Jake relented first and walked to the cat. The cat looked to his left, toward the ground.

Jake's smile dropped, replaced by a squinched expression, complete with pursed lips, a lemon-induced-lips pursed squinch.

Lying next to the cat was a mouse, a perfectly dead mouse, laid out with feline precision on the gravel.

———∞———

People are simply terrible at catching mice. I'm very good at it. I know that sharing a mouse is not what cats usually do—so that will prove to this man that I am a very good cat.

A good cat on a mission.

A mission from God.

That was in a movie, wasn't it? Where they wrecked all those cars. I saw that on television.

For some reason, and Jake was not sure what that reason was, he restrained himself from reacting like he wanted to react: dancing away in disgust and dismay and alarm. The cat all but smiled up at Jake, beaming, as if Jake had recognized the mouse, the gift, for what it was—a great sacrifice from a skinny, hungry cat.

"Is that for me?" he asked, then wondered why he asked.

The cat kept his almost-smile and offered a meow, a self-satisfied, happy meow. Almost not a meow, it was more like an explanation, or a statement of accomplishment. Not a meow. More than that. Or less. Nearly humanlike.

Why would this cat do that? Give me his . . . food?

Jake felt another strong twinge in his shoulder. Either he would have to get used to the twinges or find a chiropractor to locate the source and fix it.

"Okay, then," Jake replied. He reached into his coat pocket and pulled out a rumpled receipt from a gas station, smoothed it out, bent down, and picked up the mouse by the tail using the receipt to keep from touching the dead creature. "Thank you," he said.

The cat looked up, seemingly very satisfied that Jake received his gift with gratitude.

Jake looked down and thought he saw an expression in the cat's eyes that seemed to suggest that he expected Jake to eat the mouse then and there. Instead, Jake knelt down and petted the cat on his head, which the cat accepted gracefully, almost regally, and he said, "I'll save this for later. But thanks so much for the mouse. I appreciate it."

Jake had no idea of why he was being so solicitous of this stray, skinny, lost cat, except it felt as if it were the right thing to do. Like the cat understood somehow. The cat really appeared to understand.

Jake walked toward the main door of his new living quarters. He laid the mouse down on an exposed ledge of the building's cement foundation. He would dispose of this particular "varmint" later when the cat wasn't watching him.

Good grief. I'm worried about what a cat thinks of me? It's like being back in Butler again . . . worried about what everyone thinks. That has to stop.

Jake's stomach growled, and his first move was toward the kitchen. The cat looked famished, and Jake could use a cup of coffee. Then he stopped short and realized that there was nothing in the kitchen—no food, no instant coffee, no nothing.

"You're hungry, aren't you?" Jake said, not really expecting an answer from the cat.

The cat had followed him to the door and now meowed plaintively, low and rumbly. It was an obvious yes.

"Well, then. We both need to eat," Jake said, and again the cat meowed, softly this time, in reply.

In that brief, single moment, Jake realized he could use a cat. For company. So neither of them would be lonely. Jake had grown up in the complete absence of animals—allergies, his mother claimed he had, and from his father's side, not hers. But he was pretty sure that the absence of all things furry was simply because his mother just didn't like "wild animals."

Animals are outside for a reason, young man. Jesus didn't have a dog. And you think you're better than Jesus?

"You're not a wild animal, are you?" Jake asked the cat.

The cat meowed in return.

"You agree, right? You must be hungry. You look skinny."

He had no food in the back of his truck. When he had left Butler, he had brought no perishables—nor packed any food of any type. "There's a store just down the road. I think." He dug the keys out of his pocket and opened the door. The cat followed him to his truck.

"You have to stay here," Jake said.

The cat sat and responded with a long meow.

"Good," he replied. "I'll be back. You wait here."

He opened the door to his truck, and the cat, as agile as a squirrel, scurried and limped into the truck and settled on the passenger seat, staring at Jake, waiting for him to get in.

"You can't come in the truck," Jake said. The cat turned from facing him and looked out through the windshield. "Come on, now. Cats don't like trucks. Come on out. Come on. You go back to the house."

The cat did not move.

Maybe off-center is the way things are supposed to be today. He shrugged, and slid into the driver's seat, closed the door, put on his seatbelt, and started the truck. *No sense in struggling with a cat that may have some virulent cat disease and scratch me.* The cat did not move. If the unnamed cat was anxious or afraid, he did a wonderful job of hiding it.

⚬⚬⚬

He liked the mouse. That's a good sign. A very good sign. That has never happened to me before. He didn't dance. He just wasn't hungry for a mouse right now. He'll eat it later. That's okay. At least he liked it. He didn't dance. I miss it when they don't dance. People should dance when they get a mouse. Cats don't do that. But then again, I've never tried to dance. I would not be good at it. You need to be a human to dance. Or a dog.

The cat, who didn't call himself anything, who had no name, at least not now, sat up straight on the right side of the truck's bench seat, putting most of his weight on his left front paw. He knew something was wrong with his right paw but, as with most animals, did not consider complaining or obsessing about the pain particularly worthwhile. It was easier to ignore it and complete whatever tasks needed to be completed. The pain would take care of itself. It would go away or it wouldn't. A cat's job is to do a cat's job, regardless of pain.

The cat moved its eyes and watched the man as he drove.

That other, round, rude person—Jimbo—called him Jake. I assume that is his Christian name. Jake. That sounds nice and sturdy. A man's name. Jake. I remember a boxer called Jake. A boxer dog, not a boxer boxer—though there was that movie about a Jake who was a person and a real boxer. But the Jake I remember was a dog. Jake happened to be a very stupid dog. But he could dance, sort of. More like a St. Vitus dance. (I know. I know. You can blame the radio.) And that Jake could smile. That's an ability I envy. Only a little.

The cat saw Jake glance toward him. While animals, especially cats, hid their pain from others, people were not good at it. Not to cats, anyway.

He does look a little lost. It's his eyes. He's here—but he's not here. He knows that something is true and he won't admit that it's true. Not even to himself. A good cat can see these things. Or a smart cat. And I am both of those things. In my experience, half of all cats don't like people. The other half think they could do very well without them. But there are a few cats, like me, who are smart and are sure we can help people find their way. I am not going to speak for God, but I will help Jake see what God wants. What God wants him to do. How to be. That is my job. I will be very good at it.

The cat took his position in the world very seriously.

Humans puzzle me. They spend too much time thinking about how things should be or how they want them to be instead of seeing things as they are and accepting them. People spend too much energy trying to be something they are not. Cats never do that. A cat is a cat is a cat. I never would want to be a dog. As I said, I am a smart cat.

The cat shook his head. The man looked over, then back to the road. He appeared to be a very safe driver. That was a good thing, too.

Who would want to be a dog? Disgusting creatures. All slobbery and loose fur and burrs and snorting. Clumsy. They just don't have enough bones, I guess, and they can't even curl up into a ball. Stiff, they are, like boards. And they stink. Have you ever been near a wet dog? Even dry dogs stink.

The man slowed the truck down. The cat could see a store on the side of the road ahead. Stores meant food. The cat knew that food comes from the inside of stores. Except for mice. They come from fields. The cat took pride in his intelligence, though he tried not to show off because of it. Not too much, anyway.

Did you know that the Egyptians worshiped cats? They did. Really. They have statues of cats. I saw that on the television show that talks like the radio show but with movies and always asks for money. I can understand why those people did that, of course, but they shouldn't have done that. Cats aren't divine. We are imperial, or is the word . . . imperviable . . . impervious? Unaffected. Above the cares of the world. But we're not that, really. We're just serene. We're calm and we listen very carefully. God doesn't always shout. Jake might not know how to listen. To others. To himself. To God. That's it. Listening. Lots of people don't know how to listen to God.

He needs to hear himself—to listen to what is inside. He is exactly the way that God intended him to be—except for the sin part, of course. That's what God would say to Jake. I'm pretty sure, anyhow.

The truck stopped.

I hope they have that food in the gold square cans. I like that food. Maybe I can get Jake to buy some.

2

Jake and the cat had come to a stop three miles south of the church, just across from a shallow wideness along the Allegheny River. It was crossed by an abandoned railroad bridge that looked like it would offer good fishing. The sign read BIG DAVE'S STORE, a ramshackle gas station, bait shop, convenience store, six-pack shop—an all-in-one sort of store. Jake stopped the engine and opened the door. The plastic pennants, hung from the overhead awning by the gas pumps, flapped their plastic welcome in the breeze. He was about to tell the cat to stay put, when it bolted out of the truck and ran, limping, toward the front door, darting inside when another customer exited. Jake hurried after him. "You can't go in there."

Jake hurried inside. "I'm sorry. My . . . the cat ran in. I'll get him out. I'm sorry."

Behind the counter sat a grizzled-looking man in a red plaid shirt, with a beard looking like a swarm of bees hovering about his cheeks and chin.

"Don't worry. We sell leeches and minnows and fox pee for deer hunters. A cat won't be bothering any of my customers, for sure."

He pronounced "for sure" as "fer shore."

An old black-and-white television hung from a wall, most of the picture obscured by bands of snow and static. The clerk peered from behind the counter. The cat stared back at him and meowed loudly.

"Skinny guy. Homeless?"

Jake shrugged. "Don't know. He showed up at the church just now and followed me into the truck."

The man in the red shirt brightened. "I thought you looked familiar. You're the new pastor, right? The church on Dry Run Road?"

"Yes, I am. Jake Wilkerson," Jake said, and extended his hand.

A pastor has to be outgoing, right? I need to turn over a new leaf. And be friendly. I need to remember that. Friendly. Outgoing.

"You can call me Big Dave. That's the name on the sign out there. Actually, my Christian name is Lawrence, but when I bought the place it was named Big Dave's. Changing my name was easier than paying for a new sign. And I guess I sort of grew into the name after all this time. I've been going to your church for a couple of years. Good potlucks, for sure."

The cat began scrabbling at a lower shelf at the end of the aisle.

"The cat looks like he likes Fancy Feast. Not much of a selection. But I do got beef 'n' liver."

"I need a few cans of cat food," Jake said. "Do you have any people food as well?"

Besides the store's entire stock of cat food (six tins), Jake bought instant coffee, half-and-half, sugar, no-name Oreo-style cookies, two frozen cheese and sausage pizzas, a box of glazed donuts, a box of generic corn flakes, a small box of tea bags of a brand of which Jake had never heard, a half-gallon of milk, a loaf of white bread (fortified twelve ways), peanut butter, strawberry jam, a jar of "local" honey, and two Snickers bars.

"Your cat got a limp, you know," Big Dave announced as he rang up Jake's selections.

"I think he's got something in his paw. Any vets around here?"

Big Dave scowled, thinking.

"A couple of clinics, 'animal medical centers' they call themselves, on Route 44—east side of town. Expensive, I bet, by the looks of them. Then there's a lady vet in town . . . Emma . . . something or other. On Broad Street. Big crooked sign in front of her house. She comes in here once in a while. Really pretty. But odd. Opinionated. I think she might be one of them Democrats. Large coffee, lots of sugars, two packages of Drake's Crumb Cakes."

Jake nodded, slowly translating Big Dave's words in his head and trying not to think about how "purdy" the lady vet was. He gathered his purchases, and the cat stood up and followed him to the door.

"I'll see you Wednesday evening then, Dave?"

"It's Big Dave. And you betcha. Wouldn't miss a potluck. Good luck with your cat. Seems to be a keeper, if you ask me. Hard to find a special cat. Ordinary ones are easy."

⸙

The town of Coudersport was not that big and Broad Street was not that hard to find. Jake drove slowly, looking on both sides of the street, looking for "Emma . . . something, Vet."

And he found her, or rather, her sign. It stood in front of a large, rambling, ornate, two-story Victorian house, with large front porches on both floors that wrapped halfway around the structure, and abundantly fussy filigree work. It looked freshly painted—whites, greens, darker greens, and ochre accents.

Maybe it's the weather up here. All the signs seem to be at either more or less than ninety degrees. Freeze and thaw, perhaps?

EMMA GRAINGER, VET.

That's what the sign read—simple and declarative and tilted. There was a phone number at the bottom and nothing else. It did not indicate her political preference.

Jake looked to the cat. "Do you think she's open?"

The cat appeared to look at the sign carefully, then meowed.

"Okay. You want to walk in, or should I carry you?"

The cat stiffened at the suggestion of being carried and carefully made his way out of the truck, now lifting his paw cautiously with nearly every step.

Jake stepped up on the porch and tried the front door. The handle turned, the door opened, and a small bell sounded.

"Hello?" Jake called out modestly loud.

The cat followed him into a small reception area and stood next to Jake, holding his right paw up and close to his body.

"Be there in a second," came a voice from the back. Jake thought the voice sounded pretty.

A woman emerged, wearing a doctor's white coat. She was almost very tall, Jake thought, maybe an inch or two under six feet. Blonde hair, most likely natural, though Jake was far from expert in those matters, blue eyes, looking almost Nordic. Her hair was disheveled in a professional, careless way, with two pencils sticking out from above her left ear. She had penetrating blue eyes. Precise, sharp features—almost chiseled, yet attractive in their arrangement. Her nametag read: Emma V. Grainger, Vet.

Jake tried to offer a welcome, safe smile but wasn't sure he managed to pull it off.

"Who's sick?" Dr. Grainger asked, eyeing them both.

Jake could not think of a witty reply, or any reply at all, and instead pointed to the cat who now sat calmly a few inches from his feet.

"I think he might have something in his paw . . . or something."

Very clever.

"Name?"

"Uhh . . . Jake Wilkerson."

"Nice to meet you, Jake, but I meant the cat's name."

Jake was seldom speechless, but was almost speechless now.

"Ummm . . . I don't . . . he just showed up this morning. He looked skinny, abandoned, and he's limping, holding up his right paw."

The cat held up its right paw.

"Well, he has to have a name for me to treat him," the vet said with a medical firmness, crossing her arms and pursing her lips to one side, staring at Jake, almost testing him.

"He doesn't have a tag or a name," Jake replied.

Maybe she's just being quirky.

"I'm not good at names," he continued. "What does he look like to you?"

Emma the Vet came around the counter, a few steps closer, bent down, and stared hard at the cat. She rubbed her chin, as if this naming was a standard part of her normal examination. The cat stared back with interest.

"I would say . . . that he looks like a Petey. Or P. D. . . . P period D period. Either of those would suit him fine." She knelt down. "What do you think, big guy? P. D. or Petey?"

The cat appeared to be mulling the choice over.

"P. D.?"

The cat stayed silent.

"Petey? As in Petey, the normal name?"

And with that, the cat meowed loudly and pushed his head into the vet's knee.

The vet picked him up carefully. "From now on, this noble feline will be known as Petey. Now, follow me," she said with a doctor's authority and led Jake to a very white, very clean, very well-lit room, with a long stainless steel table and a row of cabinets on one wall.

The vet set the cat on the table, carefully, and ever so gently lifted his right paw, bent close to it, and stared for a long moment.

"It's a thorn in the pad. Imbedded pretty deep."

"Like Andromeda and the lion, right?" Jake volunteered. "You know, that old Roman fable."

The cat, now named Petey, turned to Jake and narrowed his eyes.

It's Androcles. And Aesop was Greek. I saw that on the television. It was a movie. I think. Did they make movies when Aesop was alive?

Then the cat stared up at the doctor, his eyes wide and almost pleading.

Emma the Vet kept on with her examination and simply said, "It's Androcles."

Petey the cat began to purr in agreement.

If Jake was embarrassed by his lack of knowledge, he did not show it.

"Can you hold Petey?" Emma asked Jake. "I need to give him a shot to deaden the pain. I'll need to cut the paw open, a little, to get the thorn out."

Jake held Petey while Emma administered the shot. The cat did not flinch.

Jake thought he smelled lilacs as he and the doctor stood side by side, holding onto Petey.

"Hold him like this," she instructed, and Jake did as he was told. He saw the glint of a scalpel and turned away. Jake was most unfond of needles, knives, and other unpleasant medical devices. The vet hummed as she worked. Jake heard the metallic plunk of either a scalpel or forceps. Out of the corner of his eye he saw the sewing motion of stitches being added. Then he heard the cutting of the thread.

"Stay there. He needs an antibiotic. I can administer that with a shot. Hard to give pills to a cat."

Jake did not watch that shot being given either and only turned back when he heard the hypodermic's plastic clatter when Emma laid it on the counter.

"Stay. I'll be right back."

In a moment she returned with a small bootie-shaped bandage and a roll of medical adhesive tape. She slipped the bootie on the stitched paw, then proceeded to tape it securely to the foreleg.

"You don't shave the hair?" Jake asked.

"No. Most animals hate that more than a shot. You just soak this tape in water for a while and most of it comes off easily. And a little bit of alcohol. Less trauma. And easier for me. And for Petey, too."

She stepped back to admire her handiwork.

"Let me scan him for a computer chip," she said, and waved a small wand, the size of a TV remote, around his neck and shoulders several times. "Nothing," she said. "I didn't expect it, either. Him being lost and all. Or abandoned, like you said."

She looked at the cat again. "He's neutered, too."

"You can tell that?"

Emma Grainger narrowed her eyes this time. And this time Jake did seem embarrassed, just a little.

"Oh . . . yeah."

The vet reached into a cabinet and extracted a large white plastic cone.

"I should put an Elizabethan collar on him so he won't chew off the dressing."

The cat looked up, a frantic look in his eyes. He meowed loudly, nervously. And then again, even louder. She stared back, then softened.

"But I don't think that this one will chew at it. Will you, Petey?"

Petey meowed, and anyone could tell he was in full agreement.

"If he does chew on the dressing, bring him back right away. Okay?" Emma the Vet said with a voice that made obedience all but imperative.

Jake nodded.

"I will. Promise."

Petey meowed, obviously agreeing to the terms of his care.

"He's a talker, this one."

"A talker?" Jake asked.

"Some cats are quite verbal. They meow and chatter all the time. I think Petey will be that way. It's almost as if they are actually trying to talk to you. If you listen closely, they'll repeat certain sounds, almost like a chirp, that means 'I want food,' or 'yes,' or 'I want out.' They really are quite intelligent animals. But you have to pay attention to them."

"I guess I'll be learning a new language then. Thanks for the heads-up."

Emma picked up Petey, placed him carefully on the floor, and led him and Jake back to the reception area. Petey chirped and churred as he followed her. She sat down at the computer behind the counter and began typing out the invoice.

"You new in town?" she asked. "I don't think I have ever met you, have I?"

"I am new. I'm the new pastor at the church on Dry Run Road. The little white one."

"With the crooked steeple?"

Jake leaned in. "I thought that was just me."

"Nope," the doctor answered. "Drives me nuts every time I drive past. I want to climb up there and give it a shove—either upright or off."

Emma hit PRINT.

"You don't look like one of those," she said, eyeing him carefully.

"One of those whats?" Jake replied.

"Those church people. Narrow-minded. Judgmental. Bad haircuts. Hypocritical. Wearing suits that don't fit. Like most of the people in this town—churchgoers or not. It's in the water, I think. And don't say I'm being judgmental. I grew up here. I know these people. Just haven't gotten up the gumption to leave."

Jake was almost used to getting odd, sometimes angry responses to his profession.

"Maybe I'm not like all those people. Though I do admit I need a haircut."

Emma the Vet smiled, a wry smile, knowing, almost inviting.

"We'll see. And the only barber shop worth going to is Jeff's—on Main Street. I have a cousin who goes there. And they don't butcher him."

Emma pulled the invoice from the printer.

"You married?"

If Jake was surprised by the question, he didn't show it. He was almost used to bold, intrusive questions from total strangers—or almost total strangers. "No." He didn't think the vet would be interested in how Barbara Ann Bentley broke his heart nine months ago.

"That's a surprise. I thought you church-pastor people had to be married—sort of like the reverse of Catholics."

Jake's day began off-kilter and had stayed off-kilter.

"Well, maybe in some churches. But I'm not married. The church didn't make it a condition of hiring me. So I haven't been frantically looking for a mail-order bride."

Emma folded the bill and handed it to him.

"I gave you the clergy discount. It's the same as the AARP discount. It was a slow day and you made it more interesting. Pay me when you can. My overhead is pretty low here seeing as how I live upstairs."

"Well, thanks so much. I do appreciate it. I bet Petey appreciates it, too, right, Petey?"

The cat, content to wait by the door, meowed patiently.

"Well, it's not every day that I get to name a patient," Emma said with a grin. "You knew I would have treated him without a name, right?"

"I assumed as much. It was nice to meet you, Dr. Grainger. I hope to see you again."

"Hey. It's a very small town. You will."

"Maybe at church?" Jake asked, already knowing the answer.

Friendly. Outgoing. Starts now and starts with me, right?

"Well, stranger things have happened, but I wouldn't take a bet on that, Pastor Jake."

And as he reached for the door, the twinge in his shoulder went off like an alarm clock. As they walked to the truck, Jake thought that he should have asked her if she knew of a good chiropractor.

Next time.

And she was probably a Democrat.

———⋘———

Jake pulled into the church lot. The cat stepped out of the open truck door cautiously, nursing his bandaged paw. Jake glanced to where the mouse had been. It was gone.

That's good. No disposal problems. Must be coyotes or foxes or possums around here that noticed the free meal. Or a crow. Or a hawk. Something.

He grabbed a cardboard box marked DISHES from the truck, then shouldered the door open—he hadn't bothered to lock it—and Petey followed him in. Jake had tossed his groceries from Big Dave's in the kitchen before heading to the vet, making sure the pizza was in the freezer and the milk and half-and-half were refrigerated.

He found a saucer in the box and a cereal bowl that Jake knew didn't match any of his other cereal bowls. He filled the bowl with cold water and emptied an entire tin of beef 'n' liver onto the saucer and placed them both at the far end of the cabinets, in a little alcove. The cat watched him as he prepared his meal and slowly made his way to the food. To Jake, it was obvious that the cat was famished, but it was also obvious that this cat had a special sense of dignity and decorum about mealtimes. No mad rush to the food, no caterwauling at the sound of the tin opening.

Petey walked, with deliberate steps, to the food, limping, holding his bandaged paw aloft. He sat and sniffed at the dishes for a long moment. First, he took a long drink of water, tiny little lap-lap-lap swallows. Then he set into the food, eating slowly, chewing thoroughly, taking time between bites to look around, often looking back at Jake, who was watching him eat.

"For someone who looks malnourished, you certainly have good table manners. Or floor manners, I guess."

Petey pivoted his head to face Jake and meowed in explanation, as if to say that hunger does not, or should not, supplant proper manners, or feline civility. Then he meowed again, as if to reinforce what he had just said.

Jake had first planned on baking the pizza, but that would take fifteen minutes, plus waiting for the oven to preheat, and even he couldn't eat a microwaved pizza. And he was hungry now, so he made a large cup of instant coffee and unwrapped the donuts.

Not the healthiest of lunches . . . but it will do. Just for today.

It took Jake two and a half donuts for Petey to finish his one full can of beef 'n' liver. Jake figured Petey would eat more if he put it out, but that might make him sick. A can was more than enough. No need to try and fatten him up all in one day.

Petey stepped back, sat down, and used his good paw to clean his face—but only for a few minutes. Then he rose, walked to the living room, and looked around. One large chair stood in a corner, lit by a bright shaft of afternoon sun. That was the one he chose to jump up on. He circled a few times, then coiled himself into a ring, laid his head on his good paw, and watched Jake walk about the room.

I should unpack now. It won't take long.

Instead, he sat on the couch, nursing the last of his second cup of coffee. He leaned back, trying not to wonder if the decision to move to Coudersport and assume the pastorate of this church would prove to be rash or misguided or monumentally shortsighted. He tried to put all those thoughts out of his head.

History does not have to repeat itself. It doesn't. I can do this. I can. Faith will follow works. I think somebody famous said that.

And if they didn't, they should have. Sometimes just doing good things brings about a heart change.

And that's when his shoulder did not twinge but wrenched with an intensity he had not yet encountered. Not painful, exactly, but just prominent, pronounced, and impossible to overlook—like a sore thigh muscle after a marathon.

No more shoulder omens, please. No more pain alerts, okay? Just a burning bush. Something that is easier to interpret. Maybe a letter in the mail. That would work.

Petey looked up, his head up, his ears pitched forward, as if he had heard some rustle in the distance, a prewarning.

"No. Not you, too," Jake said. "Please. No seeing things that aren't there. Okay?"

"So, Winston," Emma Grainger asked, "What did you think of Pastor Jake and his cat?"

Winston was Emma's bulldog, now eleven years old, semi-arthritic, with more than a slight weight condition, and a wicked snore that would put a chainsaw to shame. Winston must have hoped Emma was talking about food, because he began shifting his weight from side to side, anxiously anticipating some manner of sustenance that would be forthcoming. He was most fond of his cheese crunchies.

Emma, of course, who was on to his anticipatory behaviors, shook her head, "No, Winston. No food. No crunchies."

Winston appeared crestfallen and sat back, heavily, on his haunches, and snorted his disappointment.

"Winston, I have to tell you that he was the first single man I've met—in years—who wasn't wearing camouflage clothing or a stained baseball hat or chewing on a wad of tobacco. Good teeth, too. All of them right there in his mouth. That in and of itself is reason enough to swoon. And he even realized he needed a haircut. Amazing self-awareness, right, Winston?"

Winston let his tongue loll out of his mouth. Bulldogs, not the best designed dog in the canine kingdom, were chock-a-block full of idiosyncrasies that only the most tolerant owner would put up with, let alone find endearing. Emma, a lover of all things four-legged, was that sort of person. She would readily admit to being more taken with four legs than with two.

"A prime catch—that's what my mother would call him. Right, Winston?"

Emma asked Winston to agree to a lot, and Winston would do so, as long as there was a treat somewhere near the end of her questions.

Winston snorted and seemed to try to smile, which was a cross between a snarl and a grimace in a bulldog. Emma knew the dog had almost given up hope of a treat now. The longer she talked, she knew, the less likely she was to remember that he was near starvation most of the time.

"Of course, there are at least a dozen mothers of Coudersport's most eligible spinsters who will be doing the same thing, right, Winston? A man who probably doesn't have a record for petty crimes and misdemeanors. A man whose truck actually includes a functioning muffler system. And he was wearing an honest-to-goodness, real belt—not suspenders or a tool belt."

Winston let himself fall on his right side, and a rumbly woof escaped.

"I will admit that he was sort of cute. In a boyish, naive, lost sort of way."

Emma leaned back in her chair and stared out the back window. The copse of aspens at the far end of the yard had just started to green.

"But I don't know about him being a preacher. Didn't seem the type. Like he wouldn't be the type to ask hard questions. Something about him suggests that. Do pastors have to believe it *all* in order to get the job, Winston?"

Winston closed his eyes. One of his behavioral tics was the ability to fall asleep at the drop of a hat. No hats had dropped, but the bulldog was already asleep, snoring louder than a dog had a right to snore.

"Preachers are supposed to be tolerant, right? Live and let live. Accept everyone. Love and forgiveness, right? Big tent people, right?"

Emma leaned back in her chair and put her feet up on the desk. She had eight appointments this afternoon, and decided that a short rest now would give her the strength to be her normal, cheery self.

With eyes nearly closed, Petey watched Jake as he drank his coffee.

Coffee. I don't understand how anyone drinks that. Smells like a raccoon. Worse.

Petey saw Jake stare out the window and into the field beyond with a faraway look in his eyes.

He's looking for something that he can't find or doesn't know is lost. He looks like a dog. Well, like most dogs. Some dogs are better at finding things than others. But most dogs are simply simple-minded, small-brained woodland creatures. And lost much of the time.

Petey laid his jaw on his good paw and his eyes fluttered to half-closed.

He's here and doesn't know if he's here. He's in this place, but at the same time, he's not here. Humans can get that way. Dogs are always that way. Yes, I know they cover it up by being all cute and snuggly and pretending to be so loyal. They're not. They would leave one human for another human who offers better food. In a heartbeat, they would leave. Cute and innocent? It's an act. Smart? Please. Put them in a room behind a closed door and they'll whine and whimper and cry, and probably try to gnaw and claw their way through the door. Put a cat in a room and close the door—a good cat, of course—and the cat will just take a nap until you open the door again.

The cat began to vibrate softly, a purr forming in his chest. Petey wasn't sure why the purr started now, but he realized that this was the safest and most comfortable he had been in many weeks, or months, or had it been longer than that? He shook his head, just a bit.

I know that if I talked to him—that would make my job easier. But I don't do that. I know that some animals might. I recently heard a story about a dog that talked to its owner and told her all about God and what he wanted for her life.

The cat adjusted his back paws and let his tail coil around them.

To be honest, that's the most ridiculous story I've ever heard. First of all, I'm not sure if there are any dogs anywhere near intelligent enough to actually speak. I know I've never met one who is that smart. And even if the dog were smart, why would the dog bother? Humans don't learn from words; they learn by experiencing things and finding truth from that. Truth, to humans, does not come from words. I suppose I could tell Jake what God wants him to know—or what I am pretty sure God wants him to know—but that wouldn't work. Jake wouldn't believe it. He has to find the truth on his own. With some help. Obviously. From me. I am a smart cat, after all.

The very tip of Petey's tail began to twitch. It did that when he sensed something was about to happen. Either a mouse was going to show up, or something was going to happen—maybe to Jake.

I know some humans don't believe that God ever uses an animal like a cat to do things. Some cats don't believe it either. However, I am not like that. There are cats that are delusional—like they're really in charge. But I'm not a megalomaniacal cat. I'm not. I'm a good cat. I listen. I hear things. Whispered things. Almost silent nudges. Things only a good cat can hear. I heard what I was supposed to do—or more precisely, what I was needed to do, so here I am—with Jake now. I am certain that God uses small things at first, like a cat, instead of resorting to thunder and lightning first thing. I am nearly positive that I have been sent. Nearly so.

He does use cats. Good, smart cats. I'm sure he does. Cats like me.

Wouldn't it be better for a cat to lead a lost person to the truth rather than that person getting struck by a bolt of lightning tossed by God? I am not delusional. I'm not an angel—I know that—but cats can be like angels. We can help humans find the truth, and then they can feel like they found it all by themselves. It's better that way. It's the way of the cat. God uses cats because he likes cats. He protects them. He protected me. He found a way to fix my paw, didn't he? God cares for me, and he cares for Jake. Maybe I can get Jake to see that.

Petey closed his eyes but would not fall asleep just yet. The sunshine did feel wonderful on his back, and it was nice to have the pain in his leg begin to ebb, like melting snow on a warm day.

I need to be here. I don't need to talk. After all, God whispers at first—and I am just a little louder than a whisper. A heavenly cat whisper. That's me. I think. A cat sent by God.

And with that, Petey almost fell asleep, a seminap, his tail twitching every fifteen seconds or so, as if giving off a silent warning about what was soon to transpire.

—∞∞—

Jake slid into a slouched position on the couch.

Comfortable.

He balanced the empty cup on his stomach. Back in Butler, in his little apartment, there were end tables at both ends of the couch. Not here. Not even a coffee table. Jake knew he would have to buy a few pieces.

Does Coudersport have a furniture store? It is spring. That means garage sales. I guess it would be okay for a pastor to look for bargains at a garage sale.

He took a deep breath and watched the cat as he closed his eyes.

A nap. That sounds great.

But there was all that stuff in the truck. It had taken him a week to pack it up. A careful packer, he saved up a month's worth of the *Butler Eagle* newspaper and wound up using only a few issues. A careful packer, yes—but a packer with few breakable possessions.

He closed his eyes, just for a moment.

If this is the most I'll have to deal with here . . . then I'm in pretty good shape. An injured, orphaned cat. A pretty veterinarian who doesn't like church people. A sticky front door. Not bad. I can handle that. No need to call faith into question. Like I said: works can begat faith. Works will begat.

Begat. Now there's a funny word.

And the shoulder again. Sharp. A dig into the muscle.

I'm going to have to have this looked at. That much I know.

He put his hand around the empty cup.

That much I am sure of.

—∞∞—

Jimbo pulled the TV tray closer to him. If he didn't, bits of tuna fish would fall on the floor and the dog would go ape trying to find them and probably knock the tray down before Jimbo finished lunch. He didn't want that to happen. Roscoe, the dog, sat two feet away, staring at Jimbo as if he were the most beautiful creation in the entire dog universe, his dog eyes never wavering from the sandwich as it moved from plate to mouth.

Jimbo's wife, Betty, sat in the recliner catty-corner to Jimbo's. She had already eaten—in the kitchen, like a civilized person. She hated eating in the living room but refused to bring the television into the kitchen. Besides, she had argued, they would have to get a longer cable for the TV and neither of them knew how to do that. Eating lunch separately was a compromise she decided she could live with.

"It's not easy having your husband underfoot all day," Betty had complained to her neighbors, often several times a day, often when Jimbo could hear her.

Jimbo had been laid off from the Coudersport Well Drilling Company for the last seven months. New construction was down, and when construction was down, so was well drilling. The owner, Lloyd Cummins, said business looked like it was picking up, and he promised Jimbo a call as soon as he had enough work lined up. Betty was a praying woman and told everyone she prayed for Jimbo getting work every evening.

"So what's the new pastor like?"

"You met him," Jimbo replied, mid-mouthful.

"I heard him preach. I shook his hand. I wouldn't call that meeting him."

Recently, for the last seven months actually, Jimbo and Betty lived at the very edge of a permanent tussle, at the verge of a dust-up, a tiff, a spat. With spring coming, hopefully work would pick up and Jimbo could get out of the house. While she prayed for that every evening, Jimbo did the same.

"Well, he seemed nice and all that," Jimbo replied, selecting a single potato chip and chewing it noisily.

Betty winced. It was obvious she considered the way he ate potato chips to be so disconcerting that she would often have to look away, or turn up the volume on the TV, just to drown out the whole process.

"And?"

Jake remembered that their old pastor went on and on about communication between couples. That was right before he quit.

"Well," he said, picking up one more chip and examining it, "he didn't have much stuff with him. Just filled the back of a pickup truck. You know, clothes and sheets and books and stuff."

"Well, he's not married. Single men don't have much. Remember when we got married? You didn't have anything."

Jimbo chewed. "But I was living at home with my parents. I didn't need anything."

Betty crossed her arms.

"A single man. And the elders were okay with that?"

Jimbo tried not to sigh audibly.

"Yes. We all knew it. So did the whole church. You knew it. He didn't keep anything secret, you know. He said he was single when he came to visit. It was on his resumé. And the whole church voted—that means it was okay. And to be honest, since I am the church treasurer, it's much cheaper this way. Only one mouth to feed. Saves a lot on insurance, let me tell you. The old pastor and his wife—that was expensive. She seemed to get sick every week."

"But no wife means not having anyone to play the piano or teach Sunday school or anything."

"Verna Ebbert plays the organ and piano. She'd be more than a bit tussled if you tried to take that away from her."

"I'm just saying, that's all," Betty said. "You know he's from a big city? He's not used to small towns like Coudersport."

"Butler ain't a big city."

"Bigger than here. We're country folk. Simple people, you know."

Jimbo shrugged. It felt like she was trying to pick an argument, so he backed off some. He wanted to watch *Wheel of Fortune* in peace.

"All I know is that he preached a good sermon. He was funny, remember? You were laughing."

Betty uncrossed her arms.

"Okay, you got me there. He was pretty funny. I do like a preacher who can tell a joke now and again."

"Me, too," Jimbo said as he crammed the last quarter of the sandwich into his mouth. He wanted to be done eating before the show came on, and the theme music was just starting.

Jake jangled awake, tipping over his coffee cup, still on his chest, which he thankfully discovered was empty. He blinked his eyes several times and rubbed his face with his free hand. Within seconds, he realized where he was. He sat up straight and took a deep breath.

He stood up. Petey looked up, only moving his eyes.

Well, might as well unload the truck.

He left the door open and began to bring the boxes in, one by one. Clothes and sheets he took to the bedroom, books to the office, pots and pans and dishes to the kitchen. Still, he wound up with a waist-high stack of boxes that resisted an obvious destination.

Just where do knickknacks go? Does my diploma go in the office? What about my stereo—the office or living room? Fake plants? Throw rugs?

Petey stayed coiled, lying in the chair, content to watch. Apparently he knew he had plenty of time to investigate all of these things later, Jake thought. To investigate now was to run the risk of being stepped on. And for a cat with a bandaged paw, being stepped on was not a pleasant thought, Jake was sure.

As Jake hefted boxes to one room or the other, he watched the cat watching him. Never having had an animal, he could not be certain if the cat's calm observation was normal behavior or not. Jake felt pretty sure it wasn't all that normal. He also felt as if the cat were judging him, as to his possessions and his amateur unpacking technique.

During the afternoon, the phone rang three times, each time scaring Jake and causing Petey to raise his head and point his ears forward. Each time the caller was one of the church's elders, welcoming him to the area, to the church, and asking if he needed anything—anything at all. The last call was from Chester Sawicki, who nearly insisted that his wife "carry over" some stuffed cabbage rolls. Jake was pretty sure he didn't like stuffed cabbage rolls, not being certain if he had ever eaten one, but they did not sound all that appetizing, and Jake ate within a narrow range of acceptable foods. Cabbage rolls lay far outside his accepted range.

Jake lied and told him he was cooking a pizza in the oven and it was just about to come out. Chester accepted the statement as true, and Jake then felt morally obligated to turn the oven on and pull out one of his frozen pizzas—just in case Chester, or his wife, would show up, unbidden, with a casserole dish filled with cabbage and whatever it is they are stuffed with.

The bedroom was done, for now. Sheets were on the bed, clothes from the large wardrobe box were hung in the closet, each on its own separate wooden hanger. Jake liked wooden hangers. He could be precise in some areas of life.

He set up the stereo in the living room, on the large bookcase near the fireplace. He put the speakers at either end. He placed his diploma in the office. It would wait until he found his hammer and the small package of nails that he was sure he had packed in one of the boxes. The box that held his diploma also held the picture of his mother. He had no idea of what to do with that too-large picture. He placed it in the office as well, since that is the one place he was sure his mother would want to watch him.

He ate the pizza, standing at the counter, staring at the assortment of half-empty boxes between bites. His dishes were mostly unpacked. His forks, spoons, knives, and utensils were mostly unpacked. By the fourth slice, he realized that he could easily finish emptying out most of the boxes marked KITCHEN but didn't. Something felt final about emptying the last box, something that felt too permanent.

Tomorrow would be soon enough.

Even then, don't some families take weeks to fully unpack? I can take a day or two, right? I don't have a time clock to punch.

By this time, night had come to Coudersport. Jake stepped out on the front steps of the parsonage and stared up at the dark spring night sky. The heavens here in north central Pennsylvania were much darker, deeper, and encompassing than the skies in Butler. Here, no ground lights cluttered the darkness. There was no intrusion of streetlights or houses or stores. Just the stars and the dark.

He sat down and looked up.

Petey joined him on the step and stared up with him, as if the cat noticed a nocturnal bird flying by.

"Well, Petey, that's the first day. It wasn't so bad, was it? If this is a portent of things to come, then I think I'll be all right. Omens have been positive, haven't they? The people seem nice and friendly and not judgmental at all."

Petey pushed his head against Jake's arm. Jake scratched behind the cat's ears.

"This will work out, Petey. Here, I am sure I will find my faith again. I'm sure of it. It's just a dry spell for me, isn't it? Just a dry spell. I'll be okay. This will all work out. Nothing to worry about. Ebb and flow."

The cat meowed quietly.

"We'll be okay, Petey. We'll be fine."

Petey meowed in agreement.

"Petey?"

Petey meowed.

"It seems like you understand what I'm saying."

Petey meowed.

"Do you really understand?"

Petey meowed again. This time his meow was longer and lower and more nuanced, as if saying, "Of course I understand you. I am a good cat."

"Are you a good cat, Petey? Really a good cat?"

With that, Petey stood, and carefully made his way onto Jake's lap, taking care not to bang his bandaged paw. He growl-meowed.

"So I can talk to you and you'll understand?" Jake asked. Even Jake wasn't certain how serious he was.

Petey answered with a meow that sounded a lot like a yes. Or felt exactly like a yes should feel, Jake thought.

Jake petted the cat's head and scratched behind his ears. He had assumed that a cat liked that sort of attention. Petey seemed to enjoy it. After a few minutes of silence, only the early crickets sounding in the chill, Jake asked, his voice low and careful, "Petey, are you the sign I asked for? Does God do that? Send cats?"

Jake knew he was being way too snarky for north central Pennsylvania.

With that, Petey stood in Jake's lap, balancing skillfully on his back legs, and faced him, their noses only a few inches apart. Jake could smell a hint of beef 'n' liver on Petey's breath. Jake had smelled worse, but not recently.

Petey stared for a long moment, staring directly at Jake's eyes. Then he meowed, a calm, assured, songlike meow, as if telling Jake that he was absolutely correct and Petey was congratulating him for being so perceptive. Perceptive for a human, that is.

"Okay. You're the sign, Petey. Just so I have you to talk to, okay?"

Petey chirped a reply.

"Good. That's good."

And Jake smiled up at the darkness, feeling better than he had in weeks and weeks, pushing away the caustic thought that he had now sunk to the level of taking advice and comfort from a cat who brings home dead mice.

"Oh, how the mighty have fallen, right, Petey?"

Petey chirped a reply, obviously understanding Jake's misguided attempt at humor in a mostly humorless situation.

"That's assuming I was mighty in the first place."

Startled, Jake sat up straight in bed. It was the middle of the night. He must have felt something out of place, something unusual.

Petey, on the floor between the bed and the doorway, stared hard at something, in the darkness, in the hallway. His eyes fixed on it.

Jake squinted hard and did not see anything move or hear anything move. "What is it, Petey?" he whispered. "What do you see?"

Petey did not move, just kept staring at some hidden spot, lost in the darkness, just beyond human sight. He did not move. He appeared to be hardly taking a breath.

Jake tried to slow his rapidly beating heart. He did not want to get up and face whatever it was that was out there. After a long moment, Petey softened, and the tension in his shoulders appeared to melt away in an instant. He turned to face Jake, then meowed, as if to say, "What are you doing up at this hour?"

It would be the first of many such discoveries that Jake would have—learning the intricacies and the secrets of the domesticated cat. Some of them completely inexplicable to humans.

The discoveries would never end.

And Petey was far from an ordinary American domesticated cat.

3

Tassy Lambert, short for Thomasina, a name she had disliked intensely from childhood, watched the silver Camaro as it sped off northward, on Route 44, heading toward the New York state line. She would have shouted out some choice words as Randolph tore off, but he wouldn't have heard her above the static-filled din of the radio, nor did she have the energy to battle with him one more time.

"Good riddance," she muttered, then shouldered her backpack, trying to get comfortable with the weight. "Jerk."

She did not want to follow him and didn't want him to follow her. She knew that she should not have trusted him, but she had had little choice. So instead of heading north, as they had planned, through New York and maybe Niagara Falls and stopping at all the outlet malls along the way, she instead turned south and began walking. A road sign a hundred yards farther along pointed due south, with an arrow, and in bold, block letters, it read: COUDERSPORT: 5 MILES.

It's as good a place as any, she said to herself. She was used to talking to herself, since Randolph was not the most scintillating or prolific conversationalist. As she walked, she gathered her longer-than-ever mass of glowing, dark brown curls and slipped an orange scrunchy around it.

People told her she had beautiful hair—an assessment that she never agreed with. She did have deep-set, large brown eyes. Liquid. Those, she considered an asset. She hoped, one day, someone would call them "penetrating." So far, at least in the last nineteen years and four months, no one had.

A slight girl with a slight frame, she nearly bowed under the weight of her backpack, carrying with her nearly all of her earthly possessions. Hitchhiking was out of the question—especially on lonely and desolate roads of central Pennsylvania.

She would walk. Five miles was not that far.

"Maybe Coudersport will have a cheap hotel. For a day or two. To get my bearings."

Her money, all $267.45 of it, would not last all that long.

A semi whooshed past, carrying a load of TrueValue hardware. The wind pushed at her back, almost making her stumble. But she caught herself at the last moment, running for a few steps. She straightened up, readjusted her backpack, and once more, refused to cry.

Actually, she thought, *I feel really good today. And for no reason. Strong. Solid.*

She looked up to the cloudless blue pellucid spring sky. *Everything happens for a reason*, she thought, then remembered it had been Randolph who had last said that to her. And instead of crying, she smiled, beamed, almost. *He was right about that. He was right about one thing—and that may be the only thing he was ever right about.*

She hitched the backpack again, feeling it dig at her shoulders.

The jerk.

Jake woke with a start again. The room, the bed, the windows, the chest of drawers—they were all strange and new and slightly off kilter. He glanced at his watch.

What time do the stores around here open?

He shook his head, clearing the sleep from his thoughts.

And where are the grocery stores around here?

Petey stood and stretched on the bedroom chair, one of several nighttime sleeping spots.

I need to get a litter box . . . right? A cat needs a litter box.

Jake did not have a litter box, and instead, let Petey go outside. Petey slowly meandered toward the back of the graveled lot, still limping, but much improved from yesterday. Jake was certain the cat would return on his own, and in short order. While he waited, he fixed a cup of coffee and made some toast.

Maybe I'll use honey instead of jelly and peanut butter. Experiment a little. Be brave.

He wondered if there was a local morning newspaper in the area. In Butler there was the staunchly conservative *Butler Eagle* and the Pittsburgh papers if he wanted them. He followed the news, not religiously, but he wanted to know about the culture of the day. It would be important to know about cultural events, famous people, Hollywood, and the rest, if and when he encountered non-churchgoing people, so he would have some knowledge in common with them. He seldom, however, encountered non-churchgoing people, unless you counted the few people he interacted with in stores and gas stations.

He drank his instant coffee and tried to clear his thoughts. Big transitions often caused this sort of thought turmoil in Jake. The cat's insistent and loud meow moved him from his daydream. Jake opened the door. Petey was walking up the sidewalk to the kitchen door of the parsonage. The second that Petey saw Jake and the open door, the cat slowed down, as if walking through molasses. Each step carefully considered, each sniff, perfectly timed.

"Come on, Petey," Jake called, not impatient, not yet, but not willing to watch a cat walk in slow motion either.

The cat moved even slower, and Jake found it hard to imagine that Petey's slowness was nothing short of intentional.

Maybe he's trying to teach me patience.

"Come on, Petey. Get inside."

The last three steps were the slowest yet—as if the cat was part tree sloth. And once inside, Petey sauntered past, back to normal speed, meowing in a most friendly and conversational manner, almost as if he were asking, "Where is breakfast?" Jake responded by opening another can of food and letting it slop out in a single, semi-gelatinous clump onto Petey's plate. The cat made a deliberate move to first sniff at it, carefully, then to taste it with a delicate lick of his tongue, all before deciding to eat it.

Jake watched him eat and had a second cup of coffee.

When he was finished, he found a light jacket in the closest, and when he went to the door, he turned to the cat and said, "I'm going to the grocery store. You have to stay here. I'll be back in an hour."

He opened the door, and Petey set off like a scared rabbit, running fast on three legs, scrabbling at the door of the truck, waiting for Jake to open it.

"No. You have to stay here."

The cat cried, and if Jake had been asked, he would have described the cry as a practiced, pity-me cry.

He took a ride yesterday. I guess he likes riding in cars.

The cat scampered up onto the passenger seat and situated himself perfectly in the middle, with room for his tail, his four paws neatly fitting into the rounded depression in the bench seat.

Jake drove toward town. Coudersport was a small town, but it still was a town. He was certain there would be a grocery store nearby. Doug's Surplus Food looked like it was a viable business and would be open this morning. Jake told the cat to stay in the truck while he shopped.

"Maybe Big Dave will let you shop in his store, but I don't think they would be so understanding in there—you know, at a regular store."

Petey appeared content to remain truck-bound, and Jake lowered the windows enough for air circulation, but not enough to allow an escape. He didn't really think the cat would attempt to leave, but Jake was always happier being safe than sorry.

Jake grabbed a cart and headed through the automatic doors. As soon as he stepped in, he imagined himself in one of those cheap, and badly made, 1960s horror movies, where some mutant alien virus took over the townspeople and they would glare virulently at any newcomer or stranger. Virtually every person in the store pivoted to face Jake when he entered, mouths agape. The only thing they didn't do was gasp in fear and point.

Maybe I'm imagining this a little.

A short man in a green apron who stood at the first checkout lane waved at Jake.

"Pastor Jack, we wondered whose grocery store you'd go to first. And I guess we won."

Jake waved back and veered his cart a little closer.

"It's Jake . . . Pastor Jake."

"Oh, that's right. Jake. Not Jack. I have a cousin named Jack. Lives in Port Allegheny. He's on disability. Got his foot run over by a bulldozer. The two names must be confusing me. And I'm Doug. Doug Olmer. I work here. I own this place. And I work here. I guess that is pretty obvious, isn't it?"I don't go to your church, but I know a lot of people been expecting you. So welcome to Coudersport and all that."

"Thanks. Nice meeting you, Doug."

Does everyone know about me coming to town?

"And how's the cat doing? I heard you got a cat with a bum paw. Doing okay?"

Of course he would know about the cat.

"Much better. He's actually in the truck, waiting for me."

"You made a cat ride in a car? You're a brave man, Pastor Jake. I had a cousin in Smethport—Tilly, that's her name—and she tried that with her cat—Mr. Wiggles or Mr. Snuggles or Mr. Softee or something like that, and then she wound up with twenty-three stitches on her face. Twenty-three. The plastic surgeon had to work overtime to get her to look normal again. And she kept the cat. If that ain't crazy, I don't know what is."

"No, actually, this cat seems to like being in the truck. He just sits there and looks out the window."

"Don't that beat all," Doug replied, ignoring the two people who were standing in line, waiting to check out. They didn't seem to mind the wait, since they were both intently eavesdropping on the conversation.

"You're calling the cat Petey? That's what I heard. That's a good name for a cat. I had an uncle named Pete. He got killed in a car accident back in '84 down near Johnstown. Where they had the flood. He was a drunk, so everyone expected it to happen sooner or later. Ran into a concrete wall."

The two ladies waiting in line nodded at this fact. Obviously, Uncle Pete had been a well-known figure in Coudersport.

"Well, I need to get busy and buy some food. Again, nice meeting you, Doug."

"Okay. You have any trouble finding anything, let me know."

Jake headed into the first aisle, trying to compose a list in his head. He knew he should have written it down, but for a first shopping experience, whatever he purchased he would need.

He made his way through the store, and by the time he was in the next to the last aisle, his cart was near to overflowing with all manner of groceries and canned goods and paper towels and salt and pepper and crackers and condiments. He looked at the bewildering display of spices and wanted to buy a bottle of mace because it had an interesting name, but he had no idea of how to use it, so he didn't.

A tiny woman, dwarfed by a large floral scarf and a long blue coat with what might have been a fur collar at some point, stopped him between the pasta noodles and the pasta sauce, grabbing onto his forearm with a bewildered, amazed look in her eyes.

"Pastor, how do you know what to buy? You're a man."

It was mostly an amazed look. Jake had heard the question, or variations of the question, before.

"I've lived on my own for a while. I have to eat, so I learned."

The tiny woman shook her head, as if in disbelief.

"If my husband were to come to a grocery store, first off, I'd faint dead away, and second off, all he would buy is beer and pretzels."

She leaned in a little closer.

"He's not a churchgoing man. I hope that's okay with you."

Jake had not been prepared to offer dispensation so early in the morning.

"Ma'am, if you two get along and love each other, then it must be working."

The tiny woman offered a knowing smile and smirk in reply.

"Well, I'll guess that's it. Pastor, glad to see you. I go to another church in town, so I'm pretty sure I won't hear you preach. But you seem like a regular fellow. Any man who knows how to get around a grocery store is special in my book.

And you have a cat, so I've heard. And that's a good thing. I like cats. I have three of them, Daisy, Susie, and . . . and well, another Susie. They don't mind the names. Don't listen, anyhow. Like my husband."

And with that, she released his arm, grabbed her shopping cart with both hands, veered around him, banging off one side of the aisle, almost dislodging a box of mostacciolli noodles, and rattled down the aisle, past the beans and the canned fish.

———

In the few short hours Jake and Petey had been together, Jake had discovered that cats have an entire vocabulary of sounds. It was not just a simple, plain meow. There was that, of course, but much more. Jake had already heard Petey's chirps—like a mouse chirp; churrs—like the sound of a small motor; the growl—like the rumble of a small lion; a curious chattering—where his jaws would vibrate with a vibrato sort of meow; softer chirps—spoken to himself; a low meow-growl combo; a high-pitched whine—like air escaping a punctured tire; and a sharp, staccato sort of chirrup—vocalized when Petey was walking with a hurried purpose.

Jake wondered if Petey actually determined what sound fit which activity, or if he was simply toying with Jake and amusing himself.

It could easily be a little of both.

———

Tassy trudged on, estimating that she must have traveled at least five miles. Growing up in inner-city Philadelphia offered her no experience in guessing distances out in the country. Mentally, she still estimated distances in city blocks.

She was walking along the Grand Army of the Potomac Highway. Why it had that name, Tassy had no idea. The whole thing sounded old to her and history was not her favorite subject in school. On one side of the road was a small stream. Though she saw a sign reading Allegheny River Public Launch, she didn't believe it was really a river.

Rivers have to be bigger than this, don't they?

Tassy wondered where the town of Coudersport might be. She passed a few buildings and even one hotel—the Hotel Crittenden—that did not appear to be a going business. The front windows were empty and dusty. But none of what she saw and passed appeared to be a real, proper, honest-to-goodness town. She turned the corner and a few blocks down, she spotted a familiar sight: bright yellow arches. Even though she had eaten two cold strawberry Pop-Tarts this morning, Tassy felt her stomach grumble.

An Egg McMuffin sounds really good. And orange juice.

She reached for her cell phone to check the time, then remembered that it no longer functioned. The phone bills had not kept up with her travels, and even if they had, she wouldn't have had the money to pay them. She looked to the left. The sun stood halfway up the eastern sky.

It doesn't feel late. I bet they're still serving breakfast.

She hitched her backpack again, wish again that she had one with a frame instead of one that was just big. It would have made it easier to carry so much. These narrow straps were not designed to hold a heavy load. Inside she carried three pairs of jeans, two pairs of shoes (sneakers and black flats), two sweaters (one green, one black), a dozen T-shirts, a sweatshirt from the Community College of Philadelphia (which she attended an entire semester before running out of money), the second of the Twilight books (a paperback), three tubes of lipstick, an assortment of makeup, two bottles of nail polish, lip gloss, a toothbrush, a travel-size tube of Crest toothpaste, a round hair brush, a handful of underwear, a handful of socks (some matched, some did not), a down jacket scrunched tight at the bottom of the pack, a Phillies baseball cap, a knitted cap with blue and green stripes, a half-empty bottle of Paris Hilton perfume (that Randolph either bought or stole from a CVS drugstore), three long scarves, a gold necklace with a cross stored in a tightly knotted velvet bag, a small flashlight, an address book, a very wrinkled white blouse and a navy blue skirt (in case she had to interview for a job or something), a windbreaker, a short fold-up umbrella, a black polo shirt (that she bought for a quarter at a Goodwill store in Reading), $1.87 in assorted change lying loose underneath it all all, plus a half-used tube of lip balm, and two packs of Wrigley's spearmint gum.

She had a half-empty bottle of water in a side pocket and a handful of hair scrunchies and hair bands in the pocket on the other side.

Everything she owned. She pushed the thought away. No time to be sad.

She stepped inside the McDonald's and blinked. The sun was shining outside but it was twice as bright inside the restaurant. She ordered her Egg McMuffin and orange juice and was then persuaded to get the meal package "because the hash browns come with it—like you're getting them for free," the young man behind the counter said.

Tassy considered asking him about a motel in the area, but he looked all of fourteen.

He wouldn't know.

Instead, she took her tray, slid off her backpack, sat in a booth in the far corner, overlooking the street out front, and wondered what she should do next. She was hoping for some sort of sign, some sort of divine revelation as to what her next move might be. But apparently there would be no signs today. Instead, she simply ate very slowly and debated if she should also get a cup of coffee.

A cup of coffee is good for at least an hour in here. And it's a lot more comfortable than walking to someplace I don't know exists.

I should get a haircut . . . but I have frozen corn in my bag and frozen waffles . . . so maybe tomorrow.

Jake loaded up the back of the truck with his groceries, using bungee cords to hold the load in place and prevent blow-aways. He was used to doing this, not having a trunk to safely transport his purchases.

But I am sort of hungry. Maybe if I see a coffee shop . . . I could get a croissant and a latte or something. I didn't look for a Starbucks on my first visit; I hope there is one in town.

Petey sat with a contented look on his face as he watched Jake load up. Jake had purchased a litter box and litter and kibble-type cat food and a dozen extra cans of the beef 'n' liver variety, plus a few other varieties. The litter and litter box were probably more expensive than they would be in a large pet supply emporium, but Jake was more than certain that Coudersport could not boast of having a large pet supply emporium.

There's probably a lot that Coudersport doesn't have. I wonder where people go to really shop? I wonder if there is a Walmart around here? Probably in Bradford. But that's at least fifty miles away.

He backed out onto the highway.

*I'll head toward town. For just a minute. There's got to be some
sort of coffee shop.*

⚬⚬⚬

Tassy decided on a cup of coffee . . . and as she stood at the
counter, she changed her mind and ordered tea instead.

I don't even like tea. But it's like . . . healthier, right?

The purchase would guarantee her a comfortable seat for a
while longer.

*When you have nowhere to go, having a place to sit for a while
is nice.*

She opened three packets of honey and poured them into
the cup, dunked the tea bag a dozen times, up and down, and
tried to squeeze it dry with the plastic lid and without burning
her fingers.

She wondered if Randolph would come looking for her. He'd
never said he would. She did not think he would. Once done
with something, he would simply look away and move on. No,
he would not put the Camaro in reverse and come searching
for her, tears in his eyes, admitting that he had made a hideous,
stupid, jerk-faced mistake in tossing her out of the car.

No.

Randolph was not that sort of person.

She actually did not know what sort of person he was. Five
months together and she had no real idea who he was on the
inside. Most of the time, he was more blank than filled in. And
she had no choice—she had to get away from her disastrous
home life and her crazy, leering new stepfather. But she had no
money and no tuition, and Randolph just happened to show
up, with a smile and a car and an attitude that was tailor-made
for a would-be runaway.

I think if you're older than eighteen you are not a runaway. I think that it's just making a decision to leave.

And that's what they did, staying at Randolph's brother's house for a month, then at a cousin's house, and then at a house of a friend of that cousin. To Tassy, it felt nomadic and romantic and free—"like we're poets or something," she had said to Randolph's blank stare.

At their last residence, they had their own room and bathroom. At least they did until Randolph's cousin's friend went and got arrested for resisting arrest.

I think that was why he was arrested. Resisting is a great way to wind up in jail.

Randolph's story about the arrest had changed over time—from being all the cousin's fault to the current interpretation that the police just had it in for him . . . since the friend was such a free spirit, and the police hate free-spirited people, who use drugs, but only once in a while.

That meant there was no longer room in the basement for them. So Tassy packed up one more time and they headed west. "California," Randolph said. "It's warm in California. Like in that oldies song. By that group—you know the ones— that old group. With the two guys and the two chicks in it. You know the one. California something or other."

Tassy didn't know the group. But she did sort of remember that song. And Randolph did head west for a while.

Until the final argument. It had been one of many. And they had been escalating in pitch and venom.

Now Tassy, on foot and alone, had a long journey ahead of her if she ever wanted to get to the warm California sun.

As soon as I'm done with this tea. Then I'm moving on.

She watched the traffic roll past.

Maybe I'll ask for a refill. For tea, this tastes good. Maybe it's because of the honey.

⸺⸰⸺

Jake drove through town and out of it again and saw nothing that resembled a coffee shop. He noticed a restaurant or two, but no in-and-out, grab-a-latte sort of establishment.

Maybe on a side street somewhere.

On his way back toward church, he saw a McDonald's. He sighed, slowed down, and pulled in.

They do have that new coffee bar thing. Better than instant.

"You stay here, Petey," Jake warned. "I'm just getting coffee. Be back in a minute. Okay?"

Petey meowed in reply. He remained seated and calm, giving no indication that he planned on bolting for freedom at the first opportunity.

"Good cat," Jake said. Petey's face indicated he felt he warranted the compliment and perhaps had anticipated it as well.

Jake stared at the coffee menu, then ordered a medium latte.

"What flavor do you want?" the young man behind the counter asked.

"Flavor?"

"Flavor. Like hazelnut or caramel or mint or whatever. We have like a dozen of them."

"Do I have to add a flavor?"

The young man, now a bit confused, replied, "Well, I guess not. But everybody gets a flavor. It's like, free."

"But I just want the coffee . . . or latte."

"No flavor?"

"Just the coffee," Jake reassured him.

The clerk took his money, apparently quite certain that Jake was both foolish and overlooking a large dollop of free syrup to boot.

As Jake took the coffee, he heard his name called out.

"Pastor Jake."

He turned and there sat Emma the Vet with an older woman who had the remnants of an Egg McMuffin meal spread out in front of her on a smoothed-out sheet of yellow wrapper.

"How's the cat?" she asked.

"Much better," Jake replied. "He's in the truck waiting for me. Seems to like going for rides."

"Cats are most curious creatures, aren't they? It's almost like they can understand what we're saying."

"I think so, too—but this is the first cat I've ever owned."

Jake looked at the other woman, just for a second. There was a resemblance.

"Jake, this is my mother, Rebecca Grainger. Mom, this is the new pastor of the church on Dry Run, Jake Wilkerson."

Her mother smiled, a crackling of wrinkles deepening at the corners of her eyes.

"You're the single one, aren't you? Betty told me about you."

Jake ran down a quick mental list of all the folks he'd met since his first interview, searching for Betty. "Betty Bennett? Jimbo's wife?"

"The same," she replied. "Small town, you know."

"I guess. Everyone in the grocery store already knew I had a cat."

Shaking her head, Emma said, "It is so sad how starved we are for news up here. I figured the cat story would get around, but it should have taken longer than twenty-four hours."

Emma's mother almost stood, but didn't. "Emma isn't married either. You know that, Pastor Jake? Just like you."

Jake had never been good at reading people's expressions. It was a big reason he had sometimes felt inadequate as a pastor. But this was one instance where he was sure what both women were trying to say—both nonverbally as well as verbally.

Emma's mother appeared so earnest and hopeful, as though she expected Jake to ask her daughter out, right then and there.

Jake thought that Emma probably wanted to either die right then or simply melt into a puddle on the floor—of embarrassment, of course.

"I didn't know, Mrs. Grainger. But I guessed at it. Neither of us is wearing a ring."

"Mother, could you be any more obnoxious right now? Seriously. Or more embarrassing? Why don't you start measuring him for a tuxedo right now?"

Emma's mother appeared wounded.

"I was simply making conversation, honey. Pastor Jake wants to get to know people in town. Right, Pastor Jake? And I know you wouldn't mention it. Like it's a crime to tell the truth now. Put me in jail, why don't you?"

Jake could tell that it was a familiar argument or discussion between mother and daughter.

"It's okay, Dr. Grainger. Don't worry about it. But I have to get home before my waffles defrost."

And with that, he waved and stepped away.

As he did so, he heard the older woman remark, a little too loudly, "He's cute." Then she added, "What does waffles defrosting mean? Is that some sort of new slang thing?"

A perfectly nice day for a walk, Tassy thought. In the past, like even a few weeks ago, Tassy would have scoffed at the thought of walking farther than from the car to the door of the restaurant or mall. But today felt different. Today, Tassy felt energized. Maybe it was the tea. Maybe it was the honey. Maybe it was the bright sunshine on her face after several weeks of gray, end-of-winter weather. *Today feels good. I feel good. Energized. Like I could walk to California. Maybe it's because I'm free from that stupid jerk, Randolph.*

She walked another mile or so, thinking that Coudersport must lie just up ahead, or just around the next bend, unaware that she had already walked through Coudersport. The Grand Army of the Potomac Highway skirted the very southern edge of town and if you did not look closely, you would miss it all.

Tassy had not looked closely.

Up ahead, perhaps a little less than a mile away, Tassy noticed a small stand of billboards.

Maybe that's Coudersport there. I can walk that far easy.

She hitched the backpack again, adjusting the straps a bit, bunching the shoulders of her light jacket to provide more cushioning.

The air, with still a hint of chill, felt clean and Tassy thought that whatever toxins were still in her lungs from Randolph's smoking were being scrubbed out of her insides. She felt cleaner and stronger than she had felt . . . since forever, maybe.

She was on her own, with very few resources, yet she felt more whole than she had ever felt.

It's as if something is about to happen and I just have to pay attention to it. Like life is changing and I need to catch it just right. Like a surge . . . or something. A surge? Is that the right word? I think it is. A surge, like a rush.

She stopped and held onto a speed limit sign, slipped off her left shoe, and shook out a pebble.

Or something like a surge.

And as she readjusted her shoe, a truck motored past her, honked its horn, heading upriver, east, and she smiled and waved back, something she had never done . . . well, at least not since she was a little girl hoping to get a semitruck driver to honk his horn.

This time it was simply enough to wave.

It felt good.

───◈───

A second food dish had been placed in the cat's dining alcove—a deep cereal bowl that Jake filled with the "original flavor" Meow Mix kibbles.

I wonder if they made a new and improved kibble and got complaints from cats, so they had to go back to the original formula?

Petey carefully investigated the new food source and delicately chewed on a few of the newly added kibbles, making a very loud crunching noise as he ate. Jake installed the litter box in a pantry/mudroom space by the back door to the kitchen. The space would be out of sight and allow the cat a certain amount of privacy. Jake was pretty sure that cats didn't really need privacy, but he felt better about not having any of it in plain view.

Then he went to work on unpacking the groceries. Some food destinations were obvious. Perishables went into the refrigerator. Frozen whole kernel niblet corn went into the freezer. Cereal went into a tall cabinet next to the refrigerator. Pretty sure that he wouldn't remember all the locations, he tried to keep storage relegated to two cabinets and the pantry.

Jake looked at his watch.

11:30.

He had decided early that a peanut butter and jelly sandwich and a bowl of soup would be a great lunch. It took all of five minutes to prepare. He sat at the kitchen table and ate slowly. This time, Petey sat on the floor and watched him eat. Occasionally, the cat would lick a paw and comb it against his face. But mostly, the cat simply watched.

I need to come up with a sermon for this Sunday.

Jake had a file folder filled with previously given sermons, none of which now felt anywhere suitable for a first-time-as-the-pastor-in-the-pulpit sort of message.

I should start to work on it soon. It is already Tuesday afternoon, almost.

His shoulder twitched again. Sometimes carrying things made it sensitive. Perhaps the groceries were cumulatively heavier than he thought.

He put the dishes in the sink and walked into the living room, the cat a few steps behind. He sat on the couch and stretched out.

Just for a minute. I'll relax for just a minute.

———— ◦◦◦ ————

Perhaps ten minutes passed. Perhaps it was longer. Jake had not paid attention to the time when he first shut his eyes.

Petey was up, standing on the chair, eyes alert, ears back.

Why did I wake up?

Then he heard it. A soft rapping at the door. A soft feminine rapping, he imagined. He wasn't sure what a feminine knock sounded like, but somehow this knock sounded like it came from the hand of a woman. Petey carefully jumped from the chair and made his way toward the door, then sat and waited, a furry welcoming committee.

Jake pulled at the doorknob, but it stuck, just like it had for Jimbo.

Maybe there's an easy fix for this.

He used two hands and pulled harder and the door squealed open. Standing there, shouldering a very large, and apparently heavy, backpack, was a young girl—or rather, a young woman, with a thicket of wavy brown hair framing her delicate face. Sort of angelic. Pretty. Innocent and pretty.

The two eyed each other for a moment. Or, really, the three of them eyed one another. Petey walked a few steps into the living room, and peered at their visitor. His tail stood up at attention.

The young woman spoke first.

"You a preacher?"

Jake had asked himself that same question many times.

"Yes . . . I am a pastor. I'm the new pastor here. Jake Wilkerson."

If the young woman had been aware of the conflict in his response, she paid no mind.

"Hi. I'm Tassy Lambert. I heard somewhere that if you were ever in trouble, a church would be a good place to go if you needed to find your way."

Jake's agreed with her statement, but he had no idea if she was expecting a response.

She continued, "Where am I? And is there a cheap motel anywhere around here?"

And the twinge went off in Jake's shoulder once again. This time he blamed too much coffee.

"Jimbo, you have to call him and tell him Vern is coming. What if he's out buying groceries or something?"

Jimbo didn't want to call the pastor.

"No. He'll think I'm checking up on him."

"He will not," Betty insisted. "If it was me and Vern was on his way over, well, mister, I would want to know about that. Vern can be . . . cantankerous, you know."

Jimbo sighed and wished he were drilling a well right about now.

"And his wife is coming as well. Her . . . I don't like, even if she is old."

"Okay. Okay. I'll give him a heads-up. You're probably right."

And he took the phone as if it had recently been on fire and just now extinguished.

—·⚇·—

"A hotel . . ." Jake's thoughts were in a whirl.

I didn't stay overnight last time . . . the only time I've been here. I don't think I saw any hotels. There has to be one in Bradford but that's an hour away.

"You know, Miss . . ."

"Tassy."

"Tassy, you know, I don't really know. It's . . . well, it's only my second day on the job and I'm not from around here originally."

Tassy's face darkened. No, not darkened; she looked more crestfallen.

Do I invite her in? Jake wondered, his thoughts in even more of a whirl. *She's not wearing a wedding ring. I'm a pastor. This is a church. What's proper here? What do I do?*

Such decisions never reached his desk as an assistant pastor in a very large church with twenty staff members . . . His responsibilities seemed mostly to entail getting a full complement of ushers lined up for the services. This young woman posed a new problem to Jake—one he was not prepared to deal with.

Friendly. Outgoing. Works turn to faith.

Petey stepped toward the girl and rubbed against her leg, purring and meowing softly.

"What a cute kitty," she said. "What happened to his paw?"

She bent and picked him up. The cat made no effort to stop her. In fact, he more or less snuggled into her cradled arms.

"He had a thorn in it. And he showed up at church the same time I did yesterday. So I guess we've both started at the same time."

Tassy smiled.

Jake decided to err on the side of hospitality.

"Come on in. At least for a little bit. I guess I could make a few calls. Maybe there's a place in Coudersport. Would you like a cup of coffee?"

She hesitated with her answer.

"I do have some tea," he said. "I just bought it. I never heard of the brand before, but the box looks nice."

"Tea would be great," Tassy said. "Do you have any honey?"

She dropped her back pack, switching Petey between her left and right arms and took a seat at the kitchen table as Jake boiled water. He poured it into a mug, offered her a teabag, and put the honey on the table. He made himself coffee while Petey chirped, happy, content.

"There might be a hotel in Coudersport—on the east side. There are stores that way."

"Are they on this highway?" Tassy asked, pointing to the highway in front of the church. "The Grand Army of the Potomac Road."

"Yes," Jake replied.

"And is Coudersport that way?" Tassy asked, pointing in the direction she had just walked.

"Yes. If you followed the highway, then you saw the town."

Tassy sighed and put the used teabag in her spoon, with a tired, world-weary look on her face.

"Well, then Coudersport doesn't have any cheap hotels that I could see, because I walked that whole way and didn't realize that I passed through a town. And I would bet that they don't have any . . . like, homeless shelters, either."

Jake wanted to nod, but didn't. He was pretty certain that Coudersport did not see many homeless young women just walking through. But he was not positive.

"Tassy, how did you get here? This church is sort of in the middle of nowhere."

"I was with someone," she explained. "We left Philadelphia a while ago and were sort of making our way to California. We had a fight. He said, 'Out of the car.' And he called me a name I don't think preachers want to hear repeated. Several names, each worse than the other. Then he threw my backpack out on the road and drove off. I guess that was where he and I called it quits. So I started walking, ate at McDonald's, and now I'm here . . . and I don't really know what to do next."

Her bottom lip quivered, just a little, and Jake could tell that she was doing her utmost to make it stop.

———

Petey meowed softly to Tassy, then turned to Jake and stared at him—hard. He then offered a long, low, rumbly meow, almost insistent, that grew louder each second.

Jake hoped some sort of cogent answer would come to him. For a year now, maybe longer, Jake and the Almighty had not shared a common wavelength. Oh, Jake would readily admit that he was a believer and knew all about God and the Bible and all that, but never really felt at home, never really felt listened to. The gulf continued to grow wider—even as Jake pretended to be a pastor. It was hard work, pretending to be faithful without faith.

No. I wasn't pretending. I was a pastor. And I am a pastor now. That's the job I was born to do. Right? There is an ebb and flow to faith. Weak then strong. It will return. Like day follows dark.

He pursed his lips, as if in thought.

It will come back.

Remembering the start of becoming a pastor brought him back to when he was twelve-years-old and his father left without ever saying good-bye to anyone, and his mother took to running the house and his life. It was better to let her have her way than to try and construct an alternative. She wanted her only son to be a man of God and that is what she got. Inevitability. Set in stone. Immutable. As if commanded from on high. From his mother.

I have no idea what to do right now. I could call the elders. Maybe this sort of thing comes up all the time. I could call . . . who? Social Services? I bet the closest office is in Bradford. Or maybe Kane.

She needs help. I don't think she's making up her predicament. How do I help?

I know I don't have the experience that I should.

He looked up, subtly, to the heavens.

Maybe you could drop me a hint about what I should do next?

A person without faith, Jake thought to himself, had no business praying, feeling more than a bit hypocritical going through the motions. It wasn't that he was hedging his bets. It was that he felt as if he were simply pretending.

Please, Lord.

Jake had not shut his eyes while he almost prayed, and worried, a little, that not shutting eyes might invalidate the prayer or further weaken its effectiveness. His former pastor was very good at praying and often would go ten minutes without once looking at notes—just off the top of his head. Jake knew he could never do that.

His prayers all too often included a lot of "justs" and repeating what was obvious to God and everyone else in attendance.

The cat looked up at Jake and meowed. And again, it wasn't a normal cat's meow. It had more to it, like the cat was trying to tell him not to be nervous. And by meowing like he did, Petey was trying to tell Jake that Tassy was a nice person, a person to be trusted, and that something would work out.

That is what Jake thought the cat was saying.

That is what Jake hoped the cat was saying.

I'm depending on a cat for my spiritual guidance now. What next?

Well, this is a surprise. I was not expecting this person to be here. I heard nothing about a young girl with curly hair. I listened carefully. I am sure about that. No one said anything about a girl with curly hair. She has a very soft lap. Like a cat is soft. I bet she has a lot of bones. Not like a dog. Maybe she isn't supposed to be here. Maybe this is a test. For me. I'm good at tests. First, Jake helped me with my paw. Now he should help her. I could get her a mouse. There are a lot of mice in the field outside. She looks like the kind of person who would really like a mouse. Like Jake.

Jake knew he had to say or do something, but he wasn't sure of what that might be. The phone rang, saving him from thinking on his feet, an unpolished skill. A phone was mounted on the wall in the kitchen.

"Jake Wilkerson . . . Pastor Wilkerson here," he said, trying to sound like a pastor.

"Oh, hey there, Pastor Jake. This here's Jimbo calling. Jimbo Bennett."

"Hi, Jimbo. How are you? Something I can help you with?"

Jake could almost hear Jimbo thinking of how to phrase what he was about to say next.

"I'm fine. But, Pastor Jake, well . . . the Missus said I had to call. Sort of warn you."

Jake felt a coldness in his face.

Already? They've found out why I was fired. I knew it.

"I got a call from Vern. Vern Waldorf. He was—or is, I guess—like a founding member of the church. Been around forever."

And he wants to take back his vote?

He called Pastor Gust in Butler—I knew it.

"Well, last year it seems like Vern went and bought this giant RV in Bradford. It is one big unit, let me tell you. Long as a city block, or just about. We all tried to talk him out of it, but he said he wanted to see the country. But the blamed thing is, well, huge, and sort of tricky to drive, and Vern is not the best driver in the best of times, and since he had his hip replaced this winter his driving has gotten way worse. His neighbors are trying to get the city council to ban RVs in town 'cause it's on his lawn and makes it look like he's got two houses on the lot."

Jake waited.

What does this have to do with me? Or the church? He didn't call Pastor Gust?

"So Vern doesn't want to sell it or anything and he doesn't want to pay a fine or go to a city council meeting seeing as how he and the mayor don't get along at all anymore—ever since the Fourth of July fireworks fight back in '94. Holds a grudge, Vern does."

Okay. But why are you telling me this?

"Anyhow, Vern's wife called Betty to tell her to tell me, sort of warn me, and she said Vern was climbing in the RV carrying the keys and claimed he was heading to church. She says I should warn you. He wants to park it at the back of the church lot. Now, I don't think there's any harm in that. Maybe the elders have to vote on it or something. I don't know about that—the rules and the constitution and all. But I wanted to let you know he was coming . . . and I guess I'm telling you that he can park it there. At least for now. The RV, I mean."

"Well, okay, Jimbo. That's fine . . ."

"And his wife is following him in the Buick. She can't see all that well, so if she pulls in, make sure you're well out of her way, okay?"

"Will do. Vern's on his way. I'll be ready."

That's when the cat issued a low, rumbly growl, almost doglike, and stared out the small window above the kitchen sink, watching as a shadow moved across the opening, like a planet stepping in front of the sun.

The RV was as large as Jimbo said. Massive. Like a semi-truck. Maybe bigger. Jake could only see the crest of a head behind the wheel, covered with wisps of white hair, like a tiny, well-worn doll wedged into a toy truck. The unit rumbled to a stop at an angle to the church and creaked and groaned as the engine shut down. The driver's side door opened with a pneumatic swoosh, and the old man who must have been Vern shuffled out, taking each step individually, holding on to the railing with both hands.

He blinked in the bright sun. When he laid eyes on Jake, he called out, "You there—you the new guy?"

Jake said, "Yes. I'm the new pastor. Jake Wilkerson."

Vern scowled. "I know your name. Couldn't tell if you were the same fellow. You're not wearing a suit. In my day, pastors always wore suits. And ties. You don't have a tie on."

"I . . . I . . . I'm still unpacking, sort of. I arrived yesterday. Still have a lot of work to do." He didn't, really, but he hoped it was a good excuse for a pastor wearing jeans in the middle of the week in Coudersport.

Vern craned his head around and spotted the white pickup.

"And in my day, pastors drove Buicks. Or maybe a Chevy. They didn't drive trucks. You look like a carpenter driving a truck."

Jake had dealt with prickly people before. After all, he had worked at a church. He wasn't all that good at it, but he had learned that it was best to say very little and nod a lot. Jake nodded.

"Yes, sir," he said, hoping he sounded differential and not peeved.

"I told Jimbo's wife that I was parking this here. She said he said to go ahead. So here it is."

At that moment, the parsonage door opened and Petey stepped out into the shadow of the RV, graceful on three legs.

Vern heard the door and stared.

"That a cat? You got a cat? In my day, pastors didn't have money for pets. And it's not a dog."

"No, sir. And I don't really have a pet. It sort of showed up here yesterday morning."

Vern pulled his face into a grimace that was even more prunelike than what existed naturally. "Two days on the job and he's taking in strays. That's what's wrong with the church these days."

The door creaked open again and Tassy stepped out, her arms folded across her chest. She smiled at the two of them. "The cat was crying by the door. I let him out. Is that okay?"

Vern triangulated the three of them, then scowled, as only a small, white-haired old man can scowl. The scowl was nearly as big as he was.

"You're not married," Vern declared.

"No, sir, I'm not."

"Then who's that? The cleaning lady? Cats. Trucks. Blue jeans. Women. I tell you, Sonny, I don't like the looks of this one bit."

Jake remained calm, like a proper pastor should remain.

"Mr. Waldorf, that girl is Tassy—she's homeless and needs a place to stay."

"So you're taking her in?" Vern sputtered. "Sonny, you got a lot to learn about what it is that a proper, moral, law-abiding, God-fearing pastor does. Taking in women off the street is not one of them. What does that look like? Like sin, if you ask me. This church will become the laughing stock of all of Potter County. This is not the big city. Maybe big city pastors do that, but God-fearing people out here—they don't. I don't think we even have any homeless people in Potter County. They know better than to come through here."

Vern wiped at his face with a leathery hand and muttered to himself, knowing that Jake could hear him, "I knew I should have been there to vote no on this guy."

And as Vern muttered, a large, old, gray Buick, with a series of dents in both front fenders, veered off the main road and aimed itself at the parking lot. Jake could not even see the driver of this vehicle. The steering wheel eclipsed the driver. The car missed the drainage ditch by a matter of inches, bouncing through some half-hidden ruts and furrows at the edge of the gravel. Momentarily, it hissed to a stop. A very tiny, white-haired woman emerged from the car, clutching a purse that was nearly as big as she was.

"Vern!" she all but shouted. "I said I wanted to follow you, you old goat. But no, you don't listen, do you? You take off and leave me at the red light, you driving like a bat out of . . . you know where the bat is out of, Vern. I told you to drive slow!"

Vern waved his right arm in the air, palm facing her, as if it were batting away the charges of reckless driving like batting away a swarm of gnats.

"Listen, Eleanor, if I was going to make sure you were following me, we'd still be on the road. Keep up! I was shouting out the window. Keep up! But you poked along like we got all day or something. Speed limit is fifty out here. Five-oh. Not oh-five."

By this time, the tiny, angry woman was within arm's distance. An angry glower lighted her wrinkled face, her eyes flashing. Then, like switching off a light, her demeanor changed and softened to a grandmotherly glow. Deep lines formed around her eyes, as if she had spent a fair amount of her life smiling.

"Pastor Wilkerson," she said, extending her hand, "I'm Eleanor Waldorf. We met when you preached. It's a pleasure to see you again. And you have to excuse my husband, the old goat. He thinks the whole world revolves around him and him alone. I keep telling him, 'Vern,' I say, 'the world is changing and you're still stuck in 1930.' And back in 1930, he was already old and cranky."

"Glad to see you again, Mrs. Waldorf."

Eleanor caught sight of Tassy and the cat, both standing at some distance, both bathed in the bright spring sunshine. Tassy's hair illuminated her face like a thick, curly halo.

Eleanor's eyes went back and forth like she was attempting to solve a particularly difficult word jumble.

"She your girlfriend?"

"No, ma'am. She's homeless. Tassy. She just showed up at church asking if there was an inexpensive hotel in the area. She needs a place to stay. Her boyfriend tossed her out of the car and left her out here."

Vern was about to sputter again, and then Eleanor narrowed her vision to laser slits and aimed them right at her husband. "Not a word, Vern. No more. I'm tired already. I'm tired of you ranting on and on about the Democrats and Episcopalians and the mayor and the Irish. I'm done with you for now. You hear me? No more. Not a word."

Vern raised his arm as if he was about to point a jagged finger in the air, then he thought better of it, and slowly deflated. "I hear you, Eleanor. Loud and clear, okay? Like anyone in the county couldn't hear you."

The last sentence was said almost under his breath, but everyone heard it, including Eleanor, who glared in response.

She called to Tassy, "Young woman, please come here. I'm old and I don't like to walk more than I have to."

Tassy and the cat hurried closer. Tassy offered the assembly her best and most innocent smile. "Yes, ma'am," she said.

"Where are you from?"

"Philadelphia," Tassy responded.

"Did you leave home?" Eleanor asked. "Did you run away?"

"I had to leave," Tassy said, her voice just a whisper. "I couldn't stay there anymore. I have a new stepfather, and . . . well . . . I had to go. It's complicated."

Eleanor must have been a grandmother, because she reached out and took Tassy's hand. "It happens, dear. It's okay. Really."

Petey looked up at the old woman, then at Tassy, back and forth, following the questions and answers like a tennis match.

I like this old human. She smells like vanilla pudding.

⎯⎯∞∞⎯⎯

"You don't have a place to stay?"

"I don't. But I have some money. I was looking for an inexpensive hotel. For a few days. Until I figure things out."

Eleanor waved her hand in the air, a smaller, more feminine version of Vern's whole body wave of dismissal. "Nonsense child. I'd invite you to our house, but all we have is two bedrooms and one of them has all of Vern's junk piled in it, so we only have one bedroom. And no one should have to be around this old goat more than necessary."

Petey stood up and walked to the old woman and rubbed against her leg. She looked surprised and looked down. "Is the cat crippled?"

"A thorn in his paw. He'll be fine," Jake said.

"Runaways and cripples," Vern muttered. "We might as well move to Philadelphia. Fit right in. With all the other degenerates."

Eleanor hissed, "Hush, Vern."

She squeezed Tassy's hand. "Listen, honey, there's a giant RV right here that we'll never use, as in never use in a million years. I can make a few calls. The women of this church love helping out. They can get some food for you. Extra sheets and towels and the like. Maybe some clothes, if you need them."

She eyed the young woman.

Vern looked like he was doing long division in his head. "Wait a dog-blamed minute. You're saying that she can stay in my RV? Just like that? I don't know this . . . this . . . person. Maybe she's running from the law. Maybe she's a criminal—

like on those TV shows. Do you think it's smart for her to be right next to the church? We best talk to the elders. She might just drive off with my RV."

Eleanor spun around and faced her husband.

"Vern, I would be happy if she did drive off with it—but she won't. And there will be no calling the elders. She needs a place to stay and we have a place. It's settled. You go around calling the elders and trying to stir up trouble, I'll do my utmost to make the rest of your life truly miserable. You hear me? You know I can do that."

Jake could tell she was dead serious. And he could tell that this couple was inordinately accustomed to resorting to nuclear warfare with each other.

"Yeah. Okay. Okay," Vern said after a long moment of consideration. "She can use it. A couple of days. Then we'll talk."

Tassy beamed.

"You mean it? Really? I could stay there for a while? Really?"

Eleanor smiled back.

"Yes, you can. And there's an extension cord in there that you can run to the church for power. Lights and the TV and the refrigerator."

"Hunert feet," Vern said. "So you gotta park closer than a hunert feet."

"You know, honey," Eleanor said to Tassy, "we had three boys. All moved away from Coudersport a long time ago. See them once a year or so. I always wanted a little girl. Never had one. So . . . you take your time here, okay?"

"Okay," Tassy replied. "Sure."

4

As Jake made his way down the back basement steps of the church, he became enveloped in a thick scent cloud of barbeque, fried chicken, and beans, plus a breeze of aftershave and hints of cologne—the good kind from the drugstore. A battered coffee urn, the size of a small garbage can, wheezed in the corner, steam puffing out from under the lid in little snorts. Two folding tables, the long kind, covered with white plastic tablecloths, were held down firmly by a garage sale assortment of Pyrex casseroles, Tupperware containers, and almost-new square and oblong aluminum tins. Three banks of fluorescent lights beamed down, bathing everyone in a flickering glow.

Jake took the final step, the last stair creaking like a desperate bullfrog at the end of a long, flyless evening. As his foot hit the painted cement floor, like pressing a mute button, all conversation ceased, and the entire congregation simply took a slight breath, pivoted in their seats, or turned to face Jake.

The silence lasted for a long three or four heartbeats, then a tidal wave of Hellos and Howdys and Hey theres cascaded like a roll of friendly thunder.

He managed a wave and a broad smile and then was descended upon by a quartet of members of the women's auxiliary prayer group and Christian Aid Society, each bearing a special plate reserved for the pastor, each pointing out their particular specialty and whispering which ones to avoid.

"I heard that what she brought came straight from Doug's Foods. Out of a package. For a potluck. Can you believe that, Pastor?"

The quartet soon enough became a quintet. Jake trailed the anxious, plate-bearing ladies on a tour of the two tables, which were groaning with all manner of central Pennsylvania delicacies.

Jake found himself washed ashore at the head table, surrounded then by four—no, five—plates containing large servings of white and brown and red and yellow food, mostly hidden by puddles of white or brown gravies. Two glasses of iced tea appeared—one sweetened, one unsweetened. It became difficult to respond, with more than one question being asked at a time. Jake nodded a lot, smiled as much as he could while chewing, and took small bites from each colored assembly of food, smiling more broadly as he did so, then pointing to each, wordlessly, nodding in agreement with whatever it was that he was eating, giving each dish his approval. Jake knew it was not the time to show partiality—or dislike. He gave a lot of silent, smiling, thumbs-up evaluations of the cuisine.

The noise level rose as he ate.

People talk loud up here.

Bursts of laughter punctuated the eating.

Jake did wave to Big Dave, who sat with a plate of food stacked amazingly high. Big Dave pointed to his stomach, then gave a double thumbs-up back to Jake.

Immediately after Jake politely plowed through perhaps half of the food presented to him, another two plates of desserts appeared, as if materializing from the mother ship of potlucks circling overhead.

Three large slabs of cake, two cookie bars, two slices of pie, a cobbler, a pudding, and some fruit that looked like it was simply mixed with Cool Whip—blueberries, maybe. And two cups of coffee—one black, one with cream (whole milk, actually, but it was closer than the white powder that stood in a warped cardboard canister next to the urn.)

Jake managed to try a little of everything, but by this time, his taste buds had retired for the evening. The desserts might have been an epicurean delight; he truly couldn't discern.

As he finally stopped eating and sipped at his coffee, someone behind him stood up. He could feel the shadows from the fluorescent lights.

"Listen up, everyone," a man's voice crowed. "Listen up!"

Then the man put two fingers in his mouth and let out an ear-rattling whistle that came close to being aurally dangerous.

Everyone grumble-mumbled another few words, then silence enveloped the room, except for the coffee pot, which wheezed on, liquidlike.

The coffee was strong for church coffee, Jake thought.

That must be why.

"We here on the elder board want to welcome you all to this here all-church potluck."

Rudolph Keilback, an almost enormous man, as wide as he was tall, swayed back and forth on his heels as he spoke. "Let's give all the ladies a round of applause for their good food. I know I appreciated it," he said, patting at his stomach. There was a lot of territory to pat.

Jake joined in the enthusiastic response.

"Always a pleasure to break bread with the church family."

Someone toward the back shouted out an "Amen."

Jake tried to see who it was. He felt pretty certain there weren't a lot of charismatic tendencies in the church; at least when he had candidated, no one shouted out encouragement during his sermon.

Maybe they just get spiritually excited about food.

"Since this here is the first time we got Pastor Wilkerson with us, be nice if he said a few words. Maybe warn us about Sunday's sermon—or whatever. Hey, there, Pastor Jake. Get up and say hello to your new family."

Jake knew he would have to say something corporate this evening—he had thought about it all day. He stood up to a loud round of clapping, and the basement was filled with smiling, hopeful faces. Maybe it was a full stomach talking, but Jake sensed a truly warm greeting.

Afterward, he could not recall exactly what he had said. Something to the effect that it was an honor to be called to come to their church, he was happy to be here, and he looked forward to earning his place in this wonderful family. He also said he looked forward to exploring God's word with them.

And finding the truth. I should say that on a personal level . . . but not tonight.

He had practiced his remarks that afternoon and was pretty sure he sounded honest and sincere.

Whatever the words were, they went over well. Elder Keilback slapped him on the back when he finished, and the welcoming gesture nearly knocked him to the ground.

What does he do for a living? Jake wondered. *Professional wrestler? Bear wrangler?*

Jake returned to his seat where a fresh plate of new desserts awaited him. He offered a weary smile and tried to manage to at least try a forkful of each one. Off in the corner, Jake noticed Tassy sitting next to Eleanor. On the other side of Eleanor sat a very dour Vern, who apparently had a permanent scowl etched onto his face. Yet Tassy and Eleanor seemed animated, smiling and whispering to each other. It was comforting to see a stranger so accepted.

Earlier that day, Jake had talked to a few of the elders, explaining who Tassy was and how she came to be at the church. He had been right: Coudersport did not see many homeless folks passing through. The closest drop-in shelter was in Bradford, and no one had suggested that as a solution.

"Seeing as how nobody is using that RV, don't seem right to let it stay empty if there's a need for it," said Jimbo earlier that day. "We been talking and sort of said if it's okay with Vern, I guess then it's okay with us as well."

Jake noticed a few people sitting nearest to him smiling, then pointing toward the back steps. He turned and saw Petey, three steps from the bottom, almost hidden in shadow.

"Is that your new cat, Pastor Jake?" someone called out.

Jake held his hand up and most of the room grew a little quieter.

"One more thing. I forgot. Has anybody lost a cat? Or does anyone know anyone who lost a cat? Petey showed up at church on Monday, and I would like to find his real home."

Petey stared hard at Jake as he spoke, then very deliberately, without pausing, headed straight for Tassy and jumped up into her lap.

A chorus of oohs and ahhs followed.

I am not lost! I am not lost! That's even worse than being called a varmint. I am right where I am supposed to be. I know humans can be dense, but Jake—come on, now. I am supposed to be here. This is my real home.

The cat snuggled into Tassy's welcoming lap yet kept his withering gaze on Jake.

I'm doing what I am supposed to be doing . . . protecting.

Almost with a jolt, Petey sat up straight, then craned his neck backward to peer at Tassy's face. He meowed loudly. Tassy took it as a request for her to pet the cat, but that wasn't it.

Okay, okay, pet me all you want. That's fine. But I'm here to protect. I just heard that. Or felt it. Protect. That's a new task. I didn't hear anything about protecting before. But . . . what I don't get is what to protect.

Petey relaxed as Tassy scratched his neck, and then he lay down, still, forming a tidy, coiled ball.

No one said anything about protecting . . . but then who am I to argue?

He closed his eyes as she massaged his ears.

Well . . . I am a cat, after all. That's what we do sometimes.

Big Dave—Lawrence—pulled into the parking lot of his store. He lived in the attached quarters behind the store. He had four rooms and more living space than he really needed.

Charles, a wire-thin high school senior from the Coudersport High School ("Home of the Falcons") stood behind the counter, his eyes glazed from staring at the little TV. It was tuned to "Dancing with the Stars." Big Dave knew the only reason Charles was watching it was because it was the only channel that came in static-free.

"Busy tonight?" Big Dave asked.

"No. A few gas customers. A loaf of bread. Couple gallons of milk. That's about it."

Big Dave's did not get a lot of evening traffic. It would be busier after the bars closed on Friday and Saturday.

"How was the potluck?"

Big Dave patted at his stomach.

"It was real good. Real good. The new pastor guy brought out a lot more meat dishes. Three different kinds of meatloaf. One had an egg in the middle of it. I kept wonderin' how they got that egg in the middle. Did they freeze it first or what?"

Charles scratched at his chin. "Maybe it was already hard-boiled or something. That could work, couldn't it? Bake the meatloaf around it."

Big Dave liked Charles because he was smart.

"Maybe that is it. I should try that sometime. It was real good."

Charles put on his letterman's jacket—track and field, long-distance relays.

"You know, maybe you should come to the church sometime, Charles. You would enjoy it."

Charles made a face that was somewhere between like biting a lemon and stepping on a nail.

"No, thanks. Too many rules. Old guys yelling at you for having fun."

Big Dave brightened.

"No, the new guy is sort of young. No more than thirty. And he don't seem like the type that yells much."

Charles shrugged.

"Maybe. If they have like a coffee house or a dance or something. Maybe then. If there's girls there. Maybe."

Big Dave kept his smile. "Well, I'll make that suggestion to Pastor Jake. I bet he might try something like that. A coffee house, that sounds good. I'll let you know."

Jake attempted to help clean up afterward and actually managed to wash a few spoons and forks. So shocked were the women observers that they did not respond immediately. But when they did, Jake's actions had set off a small feminine tsunami: at least six women rushed to supplant him at the tub of sudsy water.

"No, no, no, Pastor. You don't wash dishes. That's our work," one of them said, scrambling to the sink.

Jake wondered how they thought the dishes in his kitchen got washed. He allowed himself to be elbowed away from the sink, though he did realize he had made the first small step in establishing a new standard of male behavior in the Coudersport religious community.

Later, Jake stood outside by the basement steps and waved as the last few cars rumbled out of the parking lot. He sighed deeply, grateful that the evening was over. His watch read 9:15.

Most of these people have jobs. No late meetings for any of them.

Tassy appeared at the basement door, Petey a few steps behind her, and she wrapped her sweatshirt around herself, crossing her arms.

"I had a good time," she said.

"I did too," Jake replied.

Petey meowed in agreement, though it sounded like he was still smarting from being called "lost."

"I haven't eaten that much in months," Tassy said.

"I have never eaten that much," Jake answered. "They all seem like nice people," he added.

"That's what Eleanor said, too, but she said that you can't always trust the first impression. She said there have been a lot of people talking about me being here. Some said they thought it was nice that I can use the RV and others said that it sets a bad . . . you know . . . a bad precedent. That only problems can come out of it. But Eleanor said not to worry. A lot of people have nothing better to do than gossip about stuff, she said."

Jake hoped she could not see the pained look on his face.

"She said that you seem like a nice pastor. And she said that you should do what God wants you to do and not listen to people who complain."

"Well . . . I try to do that, Tassy. You know . . . follow God and the Bible and all that."

"She said that was the right thing to do, Pastor Jake. She said that if you do that, everything will be fine. Once you leave that path, she said, then you'll get into trouble."

Neither spoke for a long, dark moment. Their breath frosted in puffs in the air. He could hear an owl hooting off in the woods to the east. Only a sliver of a moon could be seen, but it was as bright as a streetlight.

"Follow God," Tassy repeated. "She said that to me, too. It's just . . . well, it's just that I don't think I can do that, Pastor Jake. That's okay, isn't it? For me to stay here for a little while. I don't know about this stuff about following God or anything. That's okay, isn't it? You won't tell on me, will you?"

Jake tried to offer a reassuring smile but was pretty sure Tassy could not see his face in the dark.

"Sure, Tassy, that's okay. Take your time. Sometimes it does seem like God is far away. That's okay. That's okay."

He could see Tassy smile back at him. The moon caught her face, making her look like an angel.

"Thanks, Pastor Jake. Thanks. And good-night."

Petey meowed a good-night for both of them, then followed Jake back toward the parsonage.

94

Emma sat in her upstairs office, her face lit blue by the glow of the computer. Winston snored, sleeping on the thick rug in the hallway. There was no carpeting in the office and Winston was a glutton for comfort.

Just as well, Emma thought. *Hard enough to concentrate with him snoring out there in the hall.*

She had debated on what she was about to do for a while, first considering it intrusive, almost stalkerlike, then rationalizing it.

Looking someone up on the Internet isn't a bad thing. Why would Facebook be so popular if it was?

Emma started there. Thirty-seven Jake R. Wilkersons had accounts on Facebook, but not one of them was the Jake Wilkerson who was new to Coudersport.

"Seriously? He doesn't have a Facebook page? What decade is he living in? Even Winston has a Facebook page."

Typing Jake's name into Google returned more than a million hits.

Adding "Butler, PA" to the search narrowed it considerably.

A few more refinements in her search found Emma a short, archived article in the *Butler Eagle* records regarding Jake's hiring at the East Side Christian Church in Lyndora, a neighborhood on the east edge of Butler.

Graduate of the Bible Seminary in Hatfield. Where is Hatfield?

She looked on Google Maps.

Sort of between Allentown and Philadelphia. Never heard of it.

Then she stumbled across another article in the newspaper, written by a senior pastor, Reverend Gust, talking about preparing for marriage.

"I even have a staff member going through my marriage preparation course—Jake Wilkerson. He's not engaged yet, but he and his girlfriend, Barbara Ann Bentley, thought it would be a good idea to get off on the right foot, as it were. I think it's wise as well,

seeing as how Barbara Ann is my niece and a former second-runner up in the Miss Pennsylvania Pageant. Might as well start early," Pastor Gust declared, *"and set a healthy groundwork for the future."*

Emma did not surprise easily, but this surprised her.

He was "almost" engaged? He didn't say a word about that to me. But then . . . why would he?

She found one more puzzling bit of information. It was a small notice in the electronic version of the church newsletter of the East Side Christian Church.

We are sad to say good-bye to one of our associate pastors, Jake Wilkerson. Jake is heading off to a new opportunity. We wish him well in his new endeavor.

The dates didn't match up—that's what puzzled Emma. The newsletter notice about Jake's departure was dated more than nine months prior. If he were headed to Coudersport after leaving his position in Butler—well, it wouldn't have taken him nine months to pack.

She thought about it and came to the only conclusion that made sense: the church fired him.

Fired? Do they really fire preachers?

Leaning back in the chair, Emma exhaled loudly, causing Winston to snort and almost wake up.

"Well, Pastor Jake, I think there is more here than meets the eye."

She turned off the computer.

"Not that it's any of my business. And not that I care. Really."

She stood up.

"Do I Winston? I don't really care."

Vern parked the Buick in the garage, banging the front end, just a little, into the workbench that no longer served as a workbench in the front of the garage. A rusty gathering of old paint cans and coffee tins filled with loose nails and odd nuts and bolts rattled and jumped, but only a little. He had banged it much harder on former occasions.

"We're home," he declared, thinking that Eleanor had fallen asleep during the ten-minute ride.

"I'm awake, you old goat. Who can sleep with the way you drive, speeding and weaving like that? You make it sound like you climbed Mount Everest or something, getting us home without causing a traffic accident. That's normal, Vern, you know. Driving without dying."

He waved off her reply like he was batting at an angry moth.

It was obvious that this was a routine they had practiced for years and years, neither one really meaning what they said and neither really paying close attention to what was said in between the rehearsed lines.

"House looks so much bigger without the trailer sitting there."

"RV."

"RV, trailer, monstrosity—whatever, Vern. It just looks nicer with it gone."

Vern extended his arm for Eleanor to hold on to. In the dark, she was much less stable on her feet.

"You know what? I think I agree with you on that."

If Eleanor was surprised, she did not show it.

"You think the dead grass will come back?"

"Probably. I got some seed in the garage. I'll put it down tomorrow."

They shuffled along toward the house.

"That would be nice. Maybe we could stop at Smolka's Greenhouse and get a couple of geraniums."

Vern snorted.

"Too early. We can get a freeze up here on the Fourth of July," he grumbled. "Maybe next week, though."

Vern unlocked the deadbolt and the door lock. He was a firm proponent of never being too careful. He switched on the round fluorescent bulb in the kitchen, then helped Eleanor with her coat. "She has a bum shoulder," Vern would say to others when they saw him being chivalrous.

"So what do you think of the new guy? Seems like a kid to me. Way too young to be a pastor of a real church."

Eleanor pulled out a kitchen chair and sat heavily. Long walks tired her.

"I don't know, Vern. Seems like he's fine. But . . ."

"But what?" Vern asked. "He say something stupid that I didn't hear? The elders gunning for him already?"

Eleanor gave Vern a very familiar, peeved look, almost angry, but not quite.

"No, it's not that at all. I just get the feeling that he's not sure if he has it in him. Like he doesn't really believe that he's a pastor. That comes out, you know, Vern. Pastors have to be sure. And I don't know if he is. Of course, he's only been here a few days. Maybe he'll grow into it."

Vern took a Vernor's Ginger Ale out of the refrigerator, held it down in the sink, and pulled the opening tab on it. It hissed, just a little.

"Well, if I know the elders, he won't have that long of a honeymoon."

———∞———

Petey had not yet made up his mind where to sleep tonight. He tried the chair in the bedroom. He tried under the small table in the hall, just outside the bedroom. He tried on top of the dresser, but there was some sort of aftershave bottle there that smelled like a dead flower. And he tried the windowsill, but it was narrower than the one in Jake's office.

None of them felt just right.

He looked up at the big bed and decided he would audition that. He tried not to think about that place where he had once lived, a place where there would be punishment for a cat being on a bed.

But Jake isn't like that, Petey told himself. *God would not allow that to happen to me twice.*

So tonight, Petey waited until Jake settled into bed, then jumped up and stayed at the far corner of the bed, waiting.

"Hey, Petey," Jake said as he looked up. "You can stay up here. It's okay. It would drive my mother crazy—but I don't mind."

So Petey took him at his word.

Petey made his way to the center of his side of the bed and circled several times, then lay down, tucking his legs underneath him. He kept his eyes on Jake as he did so, not wanting to be surprised if he changed his mind.

"Good cat," Jake said, and switched off the bedside lamp.

Petey would have smiled, if he could smile, which he couldn't.

Stupid dogs have all the luck. They always get to sleep on beds.

5

Thursday.

I should have finished this sermon by now, so I'd have a couple of days to work on the delivery—and make it exceptionally good.

Jake hadn't even started his first message to his new church.

He did have a three-ring black vinyl binder—not one of the real big ones but a slim, one-inch binder—filled with his past sermons. Some of them were part of a series, a series that someone else started and then required an emergency stand-in. Most were summer sermons, when attendance was down and when the sermons were all "one-offs," nothing in a series.

Jake thumbed through the book a number of times. A few of the messages he felt proud of, but the majority, while theologically sound, did not rise to the level where the congregation would rise as one and applaud, or better yet, cheer.

Instead, he took three volumes from the bookcase behind him—three thick commentaries. An open Bible lay in the middle of the desk, waiting, almost taunting Jake.

Find something worthwhile—I dare you!

He thought he might start by looking at Romans. It was a popular book, lots written on it, lots of uplifting messages could be taken from it.

The hard parts—well, he wouldn't preach the hard parts just yet.

Get a feel for things, the lay of the land and all that. No sense stirring up deep waters first thing. Right?

Petey sauntered into Jake's office, sputtering to himself, little cat chirps, as if he were talking to himself as he walked, reminding himself that he was due for his midmorning nap. A cat person for all of three-and-a-half days, Jake had already noticed the fact that cats seem to sleep a great deal.

He looked it up on the Internet: eighteen hours wouldn't be abnormal for a house cat.

What I would give to sleep eighteen hours a day, Jake thought.

The cat walked to Jake, sniffed at his chair and then sniffed the air, and headed to the window. The window, nearly as tall as a man, featured a wide sill—wide enough to sit on, and wide enough to sleep on if you were a cat.

Petey jumped up with ease. If his bandaged paw was causing him any pain, he did not show a trace of discomfort.

"Hello, Petey," Jake said.

Petey churred a response, acknowledging the salutation.

"So, Petey, what should I preach on this week?"

Petey chirped a short reply, then looked up and hesitated a moment, jumped down from the sill and walked to the desk, and effortlessly, it seemed, launched himself to the desktop. He looked at Jake clearly, as if he had understood his question, then with feline gentleness sniffed each of the three open commentaries. Finally, he sniffed at the Bible, carefully pawed at the pages with his good paw, then looked hard at Jake and simply fell onto his side, covering, very nearly, both open pages of the open Bible.

"Well, Petey, that doesn't really help me at all. Kind of hard to see the Scriptures through a cat."

Petey responded with a low growl—not an angry growl but a warm, knowing growl, as if that was his original intention: to hide the Scriptures for now.

"Really?"

Petey rolled onto his back, inviting his stomach to be rubbed. Jake did, still mostly unsure of what a cat might be asking for. But this time he was correct. Petey responded with a loud purring and lifted his front paws as if signaling for a touchdown.

"So I don't need the Bible this time?"

Petey chirped loudly.

"Was that a yes?"

Another catlike chirp.

"Then what do I do? That's sort of my job here, isn't it? To talk about the Bible and all that? That is what pastors do, you know."

Petey responded by rolling again, stood up, and head-butted Jake's chin, purring even louder. Jake scratched behind the cat's ears.

"What? What are you trying to tell me?"

Jake knew that all of this sounded patently ridiculous, but it actually felt almost-to-sort-of normal. Expected. Like Petey knew what he was doing.

It can't hurt to ask. Maybe he does have some answers. He seems like a pretty smart cat.

Petey sat back and with his good paw, reached out, claws retracted, of course, and tapped at Jake's chin. Then the cat moved forward and butted his head into Jake's chest.

"Me? Is that it?"

Petey meowed loudly.

"Really?"

Another loud meow. And it wasn't for food, because Petey had consumed an entire can of beef 'n' liver for breakfast.

"Talk about *me*?"

Petey sat on the Bible and stared, as only a cat can stare, deeply, with conviction, as if he is seeing something, deep and hidden and hardly moving, that only a cat can see.

"I guess I could do that. Talk about how I got here. I would imagine that most of them are wondering why this church and why me. Myself included. That might work. I guess that would be a good way to start. Everyone on the same page. I could add a few verses to make it less about me and more about the Bible—but it would still be a lot about me. I think that could actually work."

Jake smoothed the fur on the cat's head. He could feel Petey move against and into his open palm as he petted him.

"I could do my testimony."

Petey stood up again and walked back to the Bible, circled three times and lay down, keeping his eyes partially open, watching Jake as he turned to the computer and started to type.

I'll just leave off the last few months.

<hr />

See. The way of the cat. Let a man discover what he needs to discover and he'll embrace it. If I told him to talk about himself, he wouldn't have believed me. It's not that God wants him to do this or that, specifically. At least not this Sunday. I would like to hear his story. I know the people in the basement would like to hear it. They like stories. Family stories. Jake should just tell his story.

Petey began to purr softly, as if he were self-congratulating a little.

That's the way cats work. Make people think it was their idea.

Symbiotic.

He closed his eyes to the sounds of Jake tapping at the keyboard.

I think that's the right word.

"Tomorrow is the day, Petey," Jake said as they both sat outside on the steps leading to the parsonage part of the church. "First sermon. First time to really start this job."

Petey meowed, obviously in a most reassuring tone.

"I know. I think the sermon is fine. It is a lot about me, but in a small town—family stories are really important."

Petey chirped.

"I know you thought of it first. Thank you, Petey. I appreciate it. A lot."

Petey rolled onto his side, purring, and gratefully accepted Jake's rubbing of his belly.

I think our relationship is starting off just fine.

Petey looked skyward.

Thank you.

Following the second hymn, as the ushers gathered, each with their offering plates at the back of the sanctuary, the door that led from the pastor's office to the platform slowly opened, just a few inches, as if by magic. Despite the small movement, it managed to catch most people's attention.

From that narrow opening, Petey slipped out onto the platform, stared for a moment at the congregation, as if he were not surprised to see them all there—but maybe a little surprised. He then looked at Pastor Jake, neat and tidy in his best suit and tie and newly polished shoes, chirped twice, and sauntered to one of the three padded high-back chairs on the right side of the platform.

Jake had wondered what the chairs were used for. None of the elders mentioned sitting on the platform with him, and so far, during his inaugural service, none had attempted to join him. The cat jumped up onto the middle chair, then sat, regally, as only cats can do, mostly staring at Jake, but keeping a cautious eye on the congregation as well.

A nervous, amused, small roll of laughter followed.

The giant-sized elder, Elder Keilback, made everyone laugh out loud when he announced from the back, "You planning to give that cat his own giving envelopes, Pastor? If he sits up there, I think you should."

Jake, at first, felt a crushing tidal wave of anxiety seeing Petey stroll in, but the laughter—good-natured, it sounded like—quickly diffused that jangly feeling.

"I might," Jake replied. "We'll see what he says about the sermon afterward. Either envelopes or I make sure that door is locked next Sunday."

Another small roll of laughter followed and in that instant, Jake felt his nervousness ebb . . . not disappear, but lessen. Now it was manageable. Earlier, Jake had worried if he would be able to get through the service without making some horrible, unforgiving gaffe.

———— ❦ ————

Well, it was a pretty good sermon, Petey thought as he watched the people slowly make their way out of the church. *Not deep, but heartfelt. That's good. And it sure looked like they all liked it as well. I only saw two people sleeping, and they were old people. I think old people sleep more than others. Like old cats. I once knew a very old cat who slept all the time. Only got up to eat, basically. And the litter box, of course. But he seemed content. Maybe I'll sleep more when I get old.*

Jake stood in the back, shaking hands with all who wanted to shake hands as they left, nodding, speaking a few words with everyone.

He seems comfortable. Petey wondered if he should wait for Jake or slip back into the parsonage and wait for him there.

Here is better. He'll want to know how he did. He'll ask right away. That's part of his problem. He should do what God says and not worry about what others think. We'll work on that. That is, if he's listening to God. I do sense that he doesn't listen all that well.

After a long interlude, Jake came back up the center aisle, loosening his tie as he walked.

When he got to the platform, he stopped.

"So how was it, Petey? Did you like it?"

Petey meowed loudly and reared up on his back legs, his front paws scrabbling in the air, as if pleading to be picked up. Jake obliged and Petey began to purr loudly.

"It was okay, then? The sermon? Do you think it went well?"

Petey could not purr much louder than he was, but he tried. He chirped once and then laid his chin on Jake's shoulder.

That should reassure him.

For now, anyhow.

In the absence of another mouse.

The rule had been written into the church constitution three decades earlier: "Pastors should have every Monday free from work and free from any particulars related to official church business, if they so prefer. Another day may be substituted for

Monday, but should not become a regular occurrence unless approved by a three-fifths vote of the elders."

Monday suited Jake just fine. He had had Mondays off at the church in Butler as well.

A few minutes past nine, Jake let Petey outside and walked to the RV. He listened and could hear the television from inside. He tapped at the door.

Tassy opened the door a crack, a pink chenille bathrobe clutched around her neck.

"The robe's from Eleanor," she said before Jake spoke a single word. "My grandmother had one exactly like this. Isn't it a scream?"

Jake wasn't sure if *scream* meant funny or tragically hip and ironic, so he nodded and smiled. "I'm going into town. You want to come along?"

Tassy shook her head. "No, I'm not feeling real well this morning. Maybe a touch of the flu. Or one of those stomach bug things. I'll stay here and have some tea."

"You need anything? Aspirin? Flu medicine?"

Tassy shook her head again. "I don't like to take medicine. I'll have tea and honey. That will help."

"Are you sure? I don't mind stopping."

"No. I'm fine. It's sweet of you to ask. Thanks."

Petey followed him to the truck and hopped up to the seat when Jake opened the door.

⊸⧢⊷

Jake didn't really need to go to town, though he was a little low on half-and-half. His coffee consumption had increased since arriving in Coudersport. And he thought he might pay a visit to Emma the Vet, so she could check on Petey's wound.

That's all. Just a checkup. No other reason than that. He was worried about the cat. As any concerned pet owner would be.

The sign outside her office appeared to be at an even steeper angle than it was a week ago. As far as Jake knew, there had been no freeze/thaw cycles in the last seven days.

Maybe someone backed into it.

He looked at the ground around the sign as he got out of the truck, but there were no recent tire marks.

Maybe some local hooligans pushed it, he thought. That's what Pastor Gust had called most everyone under the age of twenty: hooligans. He was not a man to suffer callow youths with much grace.

Petey climbed out of the truck, sniffed the air, and made his way, quite deliberately, up onto the front porch. He sat and meowed loudly. Jake hurried behind him, opened the door, and was greeted by a rumbling series of barks from the rear of the house. At least, he thought they were barks, though they sounded more like "woof-snarfle-woof-cough."

He then heard Emma's voice.

"Winston, pipe down. You keep barking at patients and we won't have any patients, and then you'll see. No more crunchies for you. Out on the street—that's where you'll be."

Emma swept into the waiting room, wearing her doctor's coat, unbuttoned, with a blue T-shirt underneath, her blonde hair pulled back into a ponytail. She may not have been wearing any makeup. The "natural" look often appeared to be totally natural, meaning Jake usually could not tell the difference between none and natural.

Back in Butler, when he was still one-half of a couple, Jake assumed that Barbara Ann Bentley always wore makeup. She would not leave her apartment without carrying a large nylon bag she called a "clutch," which seemed to be jammed with all manner of small jars and tubes and cylinders filled with powders and gels and ointments. The bag rattled when she picked it up. Barbara Ann always looked pretty, even more so when she kept Jake waiting an hour for a dinner date.

"Well, well, well. Petey and the pastor. Another injury? A barber recommendation?"

Jake reached and smoothed his hair flat. He had skipped the haircut last week, and now he was sure his hair had reached the semiscraggly stage, as Pastor Gust often described it. "Get that scraggly hair cut, Wilkerson. This is not some television church where people don't get their hair cut so they can look all hip and cool to the audience. This is a church, okay? A real church. Not some stage version of a church."

"Actually, I'm on my way for a haircut. Are they open on Monday?"

Emma scrunched up her face. "You know, I don't know. Let me call Jeff. Even if he's off, he'll open the shop for you. You are a paying customer, right? American money?"

"I am. No Canadian dollars or euros."

"Good. And I see you brought Petey with you."

Jake had almost forgotten.

"Oh, yes. Sure. Petey. Maybe you could look at his paw. The bandage is getting sort of raggedy, and I thought either it should come off or be replaced."

Emma smiled at him, as if she assumed that Petey's paw was pretty much an excuse for the visit. But Jake couldn't tell for sure, and he was pretty sure that Emma couldn't know for sure his intentions, so Jake may very well have been in the office with a semivalid reason.

"Sure. I'll take a look. C'mon Petey. You know the way."

Petey and Jake followed Emma into the same examination room as before. Petey jumped up onto the table and sat down, holding his bandaged paw up.

"A special cat you have here, Pastor Jake," she said, and took out a small pair of bandage scissors and began to snip away. She swabbed what remained of the bandage with alcohol and it slipped off with ease. She took a towel, then squirted his paw down with water. She bent to look closely at the bottom.

"Healed up very nicely. No infection. No swelling. Hardly even a scar. So if Petey wants to get into paw modeling, there won't be anything holding him back."

"He'll be relieved to know that . . . Emma. Or should I call you Dr. Grainger? What's the proper protocol?"

"Emma is fine. I have never really gotten used to being Dr. Grainger. Makes me sound stuffy. Or old. Or both."

"Okay, then. Emma."

Emma scratched Petey's neck and he began to purr.

"I hear Petey made an appearance at church this week."

Word does travel fast in a small town.

"He did. He pulled open the back door and sat on one of the chairs and watched me talk."

"I heard the congregation liked it."

"Well, they all laughed. I hope it went okay. It's hard to know if the message was appreciated or not."

"I'm sure they all loved it. Your predecessor at the church was no ball of fire, if you ask me."

"Did you ever hear him? Did you ever visit the church?"

"No. But he tried to sell me insurance just before he left town. I know insurance isn't the most exciting subject, but he even seemed bored with it. I know I was."

"Did you buy any?"

"No. I have a cousin who's an agent. Have to buy from him or I would be drummed out of the Grainger clan."

Jake stopped talking. Often, he felt at a loss for words or subjects. This was a long conversation for him, and since the other participant was an attractive woman, the right words felt more distant than ever.

Petey broke the silence with a loud meow. He then flopped onto his side and rolled onto his back.

"He does that a lot," Jake said.

"A sign of being comfortable. When a cat shows its stomach, it means that it is feeling very much at ease and there is no threat nearby. It's a sign of trust."

"So . . . he trusts me, then? Or you? Or us?"

"I guess. He does seem like a very intuitive cat."

Jake liked being trusted—even if it was by a cat.

"Jake . . . Pastor Jake . . . what do I call you? What's protocol?" Emma asked.

"Jake is fine."

"Okay, then. Jake," she said, her hand gently scratching Petey's stomach. "I know you will think this is horribly forward—and maybe it is. But would you like to see a movie this weekend? Friday? Your church doesn't have any rules against movies, does it? And please don't think I'm doing this to appease my mother—who, unfortunately, you already met."

Jake was indeed surprised, very pleasantly surprised, almost shocked, really, and he hoped that his face did not register just how surprised.

"No. No rules against it. It's like, a regular movie, right?"

"Sure. We actually have a movie theater in town. I think it's the only functioning theater within fifty miles, so you're in luck."

"Okay. That would be nice."

"Okay."

That's when Petey rolled over, stood up, meowed once, jumped off the table, and headed toward the front door, as if to say his work here was done.

"I guess we're done," Jake said as he followed the cat. "What time on Friday?"

"Every movie starts at 7:30. Come around 7:00?"

"Okay, then," Jake said, feeling a lot lighter than he did when he entered.

⊸⊷⊶

As Petey exited the examination room, he stopped, all but sliding on the polished wood floors. Standing in the middle of the waiting room was a large, snorfling, heavy-breathing, overweight bulldog with unappealing breath. Petey's nose wrinkled as he caught a good whiff of his scent, or odor, more appropriately.

Egads, dog, don't you ever bathe?

He could hear Jake and Dr. Emma talking in the room that he just left.

Are you a mean dog? Or just a stupid dog? Those are the only kinds of dogs I know.

Winston sniffed loudly, as if he had adenoid issues. He attempted to grin.

A good-natured dog. As long as you know your place—and your place is . . . out of my way.

The dog lurched backward and sat heavily on his haunches, his back legs splayed out in multiple directions, or so it seemed.

Why would an obviously intelligent woman person like Dr. Emma be associated with a . . . dog? No offense, dog, but you two do not seem to go together. She should have a cat. A good cat.

Then Petey tilted his head, as if truly puzzled.

Maybe there aren't enough "good" cats to go around. That means humans, even smart humans like Dr. Emma, have to settle for a dog. That has to be it. There are so few smart cats that there are not enough to go around.

Dr. Emma came out of the examination room first.

"Oh, I see you've met Winston."

Winston? That's much too refined a name for such a slobbery dog, Dr. Emma. Maybe something like Puddle Accident or Smells-like-Raccoon. Those would be more appropriate.

"Winston's been with me since I graduated from college. I got him just before I started veterinarian school. He had been abandoned."

No wonder.

"He's sweet and very harmless. And it seems like he and Petey get along famously."

Petey stared up at Jake and meowed. It sounded like a warning.

If you and Dr. Emma start something—like a relationship—the dog has to go. Okay? Promise?

Jake bent down and picked Petey up.

"Petey, I don't know what you want, but you're not going to stay here and play with Winston. We'll arrange a play date later, okay?"

No! You're not listening! No!

⁂

Jimbo whistled as he measured out coffee for the Mr. Coffee. He was in a good mood this morning. Lloyd Cummins had called him on Sunday afternoon and asked if he could come to work on Monday. "I got at least three or four weeks of work signed up. I can't promise anything, but I bet we'll have work through the summer, anyhow."

Betty came into the kitchen, also whistling. It appeared that she was in a better mood than her husband. She filled the toaster oven with four slices of white bread, and gathered the jelly jar and the slippery yellow tub of almost-butter from the refrigerator. "Doctor says to stay away from butter, Jimbo. You gotta listen to what he says."

Betty took two plates from the cabinet. "You make enough coffee for your Thermos?" she asked.

"I did. But the job's in town today, so I could always run to McDonald's if I run out."

"Where's the job?"

"Mondock's Garage. I guess they been losing water pressure. We're going to drill deeper and put in a new line. Couple of days."

The toaster oven dinged, and Betty spread each slice with a fat, thumb-sized glob of the almost-butter. "Doesn't taste like butter unless you use a whole lot of it," she had once declared.

The two of them sat at the kitchen table, the dog staring at Jimbo, and ate in silence.

"So did you think the new pastor did okay?"

Jimbo was reluctant to commit until he discovered how his wife felt about the sermon and the pastor's demeanor on the platform.

"Okay, I guess. The cat was funny. I got a kick out of that."

"Yeah, that was funny. But . . . I don't know. He should have locked that door or something. Shouldn't have cats in the service. I think that might start something. Like people bringing their dogs to church. You know who would bring their dog if the pastor said it was okay? Alice Kamarski. That's who. I swear she would adopt that dog legally if she could."

Jimbo narrowed his eyes, as if thinking deep and hard.

"I bet he won't say it's okay for animals to be in church. It was kind of an accident."

Betty stirred her coffee for much longer than necessary. "I don't want animals in my church. That's all I'm saying. And somebody should do something to make sure it isn't the start of something. Don't want people laughing at us. Bad enough he needed a haircut. No sense in starting up with animals. Next thing you know, we'll have drums up onstage with some sort of rock guitar music. That I can't take. That's all I'm saying."

Jimbo was just about to remark that whenever his wife said, "That's all I'm saying," it was never all she said. He looked at his watch and smiled. "I have to get going. Don't want to be late."

⸺ↂↂↂ⸺

Big Dave added three sugars to his coffee, already pale with two French Vanilla cream packets. The trio of unwrapped Drake's Crumb Cakes waited, so his breakfast was nearly complete.

The electronic bell chimed and Big Dave looked up. Carl Miller, one of his regular customers, hurried in and mixed two kinds of coffee together in a large plastic cup. He snapped on the lid and laid a five-dollar bill on the counter.

"Heard your church was interesting yesterday," Carl said as he wadded up his change and stuffed it into his pocket.

"It was kind of interesting," Big Dave said with a grin. "Never had a cat in church before. And you know what? That cat just sat in that chair during the whole sermon and looked like he was listening to every word. It was the dog-blamedest thing. Or cat-blamedest, I guess."

Carl sipped at his coffee.

"When he starts inviting dogs up front, let me know. Maybe I'll bring old Cutter with me. That dog could use a dose of manners, you know?"

"I do know that, Carl. I do. And I'll take you up on that. You should come and check it out. I bet you'd like this new guy. Seems real down-to-earth. Like a normal fellow, you know?"

"You can't be serious. Me? In church?" Carl said, his hand on the door. "Your church got insurance for getting hit by lightning?"

"I'm pretty sure we do. Let me know, and you can sit next to me. Okay? I like living dangerously."

Carl stopped, then looked back.

"Maybe. We'll see. If a cat can go. Maybe."

The field of plastic pennants flittered in the wind, a combination of hissing and crinkling, amplified by a thousand multicolored triangles. When the wind was just right, the pennants nearly blotted out the sun on the western side of the car lot.

Dan Rummel had his arm around the shoulder of a potential customer of Honest Dan's Used Kar Emporium.

"This is one honey of a car. Nearly mint. I had the new pastor of that church down on Dry Run Road come in, and he was giving it a serious once-over."

"The one with the cat?" said the customer, who might have been named Smet or Smote—Dan wasn't that sure he heard correctly.

He brightened. "One and the same, sir. I tell you, he was pretty interested in it. So if you're thinking of making an offer . . . well, no time like right now. Get a jump on the competition."

"And the cat just sat there and listened the whole time? Like he knew what was going on?"

Dan steered Mr. Smet or Smote toward the office. "He did. Like he was some sort of angel watching over things, you know? That's what I thought. Like a cat angel."

The three bells from the door sounded as Dan and Mr. Smet/Smote entered the small office.

"Would you be interested in financing or buying it outright with cash?"

⸺⸺

Petey slipped out of the parsonage and stepped into a dense layer of early morning fog. He stood for a long moment, on the top step, just sniffing.

I smell a fox. They stink worse than dogs. Must have gone through the field last night. A lot of mice there—that's why.

Jake had busied himself that morning with a third cup of coffee and buried himself in a commentary on Ephesians. Petey thought it wise of him to now focus on the Scriptures, kind of like those TV preachers do. The church now knew his background. They felt comfortable with his story. That's what Petey surmised. He wasn't a mind reader, but the people of the church appeared satisfied and happy, most of them. There were a few that Petey could not tell how they were feeling. Angry? Maybe. Concerned? Maybe.

His repaired paw remained tender but not painful.

He walked to the big house on wheels and stood on the steps that led into the middle of it. He meowed as loudly as he could while tapping at the door with his right paw—not scratching really, but tapping.

The door opened just an inch or two.

"Petey! What are you doing out there? You want to come in for a while?"

Petey chirped three times and slipped inside.

This is big. Real big. Like a house. With wheels. And a thing to steer it with. That is so cool.

⸺⸺

Tassy watched Petey as he walked around the living room. He jumped up on the sofa and stared out the window, back toward the church.

He chirped softly, looking directly at Tassy.

"I know. It's really nice, isn't it? This is the nicest place I have ever lived in. Absolutely the nicest."

She carefully carried a half-cup of tea to the sofa. She had been extra, extra careful since she first stepped foot in the RV not to spill anything, not to damage anything, and to keep everything picked up and as clean as could be. She realized this was an unforeseen opportunity and something she did not want to damage by being slothful and unkempt.

"Now, Randolph, he was a perfect slob," she said to Petey. "Never picked up anything. His idea of cleaning a room was to take a snow shovel and shovel away the empty cups and food wrappers. The jerk."

Petey waited until she was settled, with her teacup within reach. He scrambled off the back of the cushion and made his way into her lap.

She's very soft. And she has small hands. Very gentle. I like that in a person. Jake's good, but this person is better at petting.

"Aww, Petey, of course, I'll pet you."

And she commenced to doing just that as Petey settled in and closed his eyes.

I didn't anticipate this person would be here. Maybe I wasn't supposed to know about her. But she is nice. The funny thing is, every time I'm with her, I want to protect her. Not usually a cat thing. Dogs protect better. They are bigger and stupider and bark louder. But cats can do almost anything. Right?

Tassy hummed as she petted the cat, an almost tuneless melody. But a pleasant tune, nonetheless.

I wonder how I am going to do that? If that fox shows up—well, to be honest, I'm not sure I can beat a fox. They look like scrawny dogs. With big teeth. But I would try. I would have to try. That much I know.

Tassy took another sip of her tea.

"Do you think they'll let me stay here, Petey? It is awfully nice of Vern and Eleanor to let me use this. Eleanor is so nice to me. Like I wish my mother would have been. But I'm not sure about all this church stuff. I guess there is a God and all that. But if there is, he hasn't done me all that many favors. Well, that is, up 'til now. Is that what this is, Petey? Like God doing me a favor? Do you think he'll keep it up? Or will I have to . . . go to church and sing those weird songs and all of that? Does God want me to do that? I guess I could if it means staying here longer. You know, just 'til I figure things out. Does that sound normal to you, Petey?"

Petey opened his eyes and looked back at Tassy. He hadn't been paying all that much attention to what she was saying, but she seemed to calm down as she talked on.

He meowed back to her in his best reassuring cat voice.

I'm pretty sure she'll understand me. She appears to be more intuitive than most.

"You mean that, Petey?"

He chirped again.

"Well, I guess I can hope for that, then. I can hope."

Jimbo felt awkward pushing a grocery cart. He had felt awkward pushing a baby carriage—when his kids were small and that was more than twenty years ago—and a grocery cart felt the same way. He didn't like it when Betty sent him to the store. He didn't like grocery lists. He didn't like trying to remember where everything was. And to make it worse, each grocery store in Coudersport was arranged differently. So the olives in aisle four of one store would be in aisle six in another. And then if Betty just wrote down olives, Jimbo would be in a real pickle. What kind of olives? Green? Black? With those little red things in them?

Too confusing by half.

And since he was told that he had to go to Doug's, it made him even less happy. The Doug inside, Doug Olmer, who always seemed to be there, would talk his ear off. And Jimbo had heard most of the stories before.

But Betty said they needed milk—the BigValu brand, 2% type, a gallon—which she wrote down on the back of a used envelope from the bank, and cookies. She said that Jimbo could pick out the kind he wanted since she didn't eat cookies and he needed them for his lunch. Now that he was working, he went through a lot of cookies.

Doug Olmer was there in the front, leaning on a broom, when Jimbo wheeled his grocery cart inside. He thought about just carrying the groceries in his arms, but he had tried that once. It hadn't gone well at all. He'd dropped a dozen eggs on the floor, and while they didn't make him pay for them, he felt embarrassed for a long time afterward. So he had to use the cart.

Doug waved to him as he entered.

"Hey, Jimbo, the Missus send you shopping tonight?"

Jimbo tried to smile in return. "Just a couple of things. Now that I'm working again, I need to be packing lunches."

"Well, we have a sale on ham salad this week. Make it right here in the store. You should try a sample. On the house, of course."

"Maybe I will."

Jimbo couldn't remember if he liked their ham salad or not. He would have to try a sample to make sure.

"I hear your new pastor is doing well. You know he shops here, too."

"I didn't know that."

"He does. He came in the second day he was in town. Nice fellow, it seems. Personable. Very pleasant young man. He preach good?"

Jimbo wasn't a good one to evaluate preachers. He would never admit it to anyone, but he did not pay much attention to the sermons. If they told a joke or said something about themselves, that he would listen to. But once they started with the "thees" and "thous" and "shalts," well, Jimbo started to count the number of windowpanes in the sanctuary.

"He does preach good, Doug. I think so. He can be funny. I like that. He tells a good story. Keeps your attention, you know."

Doug had a faraway look in his eyes. "I wish our guy would tell a joke now and then. Liven things up."

Jimbo stopped walking. "Maybe you should come and hear him sometime."

Doug looked around, as if their conversation might be overheard. "His cat came to church, right? The one he drives around in his truck."

"I guess. Seems to like to listen to him preach."

Doug walked the few steps closer to Jimbo.

"Maybe I will. Visit your church. Just don't tell anyone, okay? Maybe I'll slip in and check it out. Like going to another grocery store to check out their specials."

"You do that? Really?"

"Sure. Every grocer does it. How else do you stay up-to-date?"

Jimbo didn't know an answer to that, and wheeled his cart away, heading straight for the deli counter and a sample of the ham salad. All of a sudden, he was hungry for a ham salad and American cheese sandwich on white bread with extra mayonnaise.

6

The second Wednesday of every month marked the official elders' meeting at the Church of the Open Door. The church had functioned under three different names since its founding in 1932, starting off as a member of a small group of Anabaptist churches, then as a member of a small group of German Reformed churches, and for the last two-plus decades, as an independent church with no affiliation to any specific denomination.

The church printed and professed a Statement of Faith, but the document was generic enough and broad enough that virtually anyone who called themselves Christian might be comfortable with it.

And Jake knew, from his time in the church in Butler, it was not the big theological statements that usually divided churches—it was the infighting about who was in control of selecting the carpet color and allowing, or not allowing, "rock-and-roll" music in church. Those were the real divisive dilemmas facing an independent church these days.

After the first seven minutes of his first-ever elders' meeting at this church, his new church, Jake realized there was a three-way power sharing, of sorts, in the church. There were three long-time church families, dating back to when the cornerstone was laid, and those families represented the majority of the church members who had at least some tangential longstanding familial relationship to one of the elders.

Jake also determined that, at least for now, there did not seem to be any simmering, mine-laden issues that would blow up and lead to fistfights at the elders' meetings. Whenever Jake read through magazines aimed at pastors, he was amazed to read of the battles in some churches—much like one is startled to see a car accident on the side of the road. Or a hot air balloon flying overhead. Or both. At the same time.

Jake also learned, at the very outset, this specific elders' meeting would not go late.

As Wilbur Brookings, head of the elder board, gaveled the meeting to order, using a metal travel-size coffee cup, he announced, "We're going to keep this short, right? Bass and trout season starts tomorrow, and I plan on getting to my spot by sunrise. Okay? Any questions about that? And no, I am not telling any of you where my secret fishing spot is. So don't ask."

Jake watched a lot of nodding and murmuring, but no one dissented, or pressed for directions.

"We have any old business?"

The rest of the elders looked back and forth at each other, as if they were expecting someone to speak up. No one did.

"Okay. Any new business? Jimbo, what about a treasurer's report?"

Jimbo squirmed a little.

"There's no report, Wil," Jimbo replied. "I left the bank stuff at home. But the last time I looked—'bout a week ago—we had nearly three thousand dollars in the bank. And the fund to fix the roof and steeple had a couple of thousand in it. Bills been paid for the month. I got the new pastor on that automatic deposit thing from First National. Don't have to make out a check or anything. Everything is okay, I guess."

"Good. Any questions?"

There were no questions.

"Hey, Pastor Jake, did you meet with the Sunday school people? They've been talking about doing some sort of summer thing out here for the kids. Been talking about it for a couple of years."

Pastor Jake cleared his throat. "We're supposed to meet tomorrow evening. I think a VBS would be something we should try. It appears that there are enough kids that age in the church."

"You take notes and let us know. We're bound to hear about it. But take notes anyhow. Okay?"

Jake nodded and scribbled a line in his notebook.

"You get the list of sick people?"

"I did," Jake said. "Nobody in the hospital, but I'll call those on the list—ask if they want a visit."

"Good. I hate visiting sick people," Wilbur announced. "They give me the willies. Coughing and shivering and all that. Old people with skin like paper. Tissues all over the floor. Yuck. You don't mind going, do you, Pastor?"

"No. I enjoy visiting. Honestly. It will give me a chance to connect with people."

"Good."

It was obvious to Jake that everyone around the table agreed with Wilbur on this one—that none of them liked being around sick people.

"You gonna let that cat come to church next Sunday?"

Jake had been ready for the question. "No. I'll make sure the door is locked. I don't know why I didn't do it last week."

"Pastor, the cat being here was okay. I heard a lot of people in town yakking about that cat during the week. I would bet, if I were a betting man, and I'm not, 'cept if the lottery gets more than $100 million, but I would bet that we get some visitors next week. I heard one lady say . . . well, it was my cousin, Irene . . . but still, Irene said that if our church was open to having a cat on the platform, it just may be worth her making a visit. And this from a woman who hasn't been inside a church since her dad passed, and that was nearly forty years ago. Some pastor said something about how her dad drank too much and she never let it go. So . . . if the cat shows up, let it show up. It would tickle her pink if she saw that. She just might come to see if it happens."

Jake took a quick glance around the table. The pro-cat sentiment looked like it was shared by three-quarters of the group. The other one-quarter looked pained, as if they were getting just about fed up with these one-man pronouncements by the head elder, and when they got elected, things would change, by George.

But in the meantime, no one said anything to the negative.

"Well, I won't chain the cat up, but I will lock the door this week."

"Okay by me, Pastor. And by the way, we all liked your sermon. Nice to know about you. You say your mom is a single mom. She still around here?"

"She lives in Meadville now, with her sister."

"Well, if she ever visits, you let us know. We'll plan a meal or something. A barbeque, maybe. She'll visit, won't she? She can travel and all that, can't she?"

"She can. And I'll let you know. She said she would wait a month or so 'til I get settled in."

"Good. I'll have a freezer full of trout by then. She like grilled trout?"

"I . . . I don't know. I do, though."

Jake wasn't sure if he'd ever eaten grilled trout before, but he was certain he had trout in a restaurant once, and he must have liked it, so grilled would be acceptable. "Well, we'll see what the weather is like when she comes. I really like grilled trout."

Wilbur sat there, his face showing that he was imagining a plate full of fresh trout, and maybe roasted corn on the cob dipped in butter.

He shook his head.

"Anything else? Anybody got anything else to talk about?"

No one spoke.

"Okay, then. Pastor, you pray and we're done. You're not one of those twenty-minute pray-ers, are you? Two pastors ago—that Green fellow—remember him? He prayed once for forty-five minutes straight."

There were smiles and murmurs of agreement.

"No. I'll be brief."

"Good man, Pastor Jake. Good man."

———— ∞ ————

Later that night, Petey lay down on the center of the bed, in his spot, with a sigh, as if he, too, were glad the evening was over. Jake reached and patted his head a few times.

"Petey, it is nice to have you here. Really nice. I never knew what having a pet was like."

Petey bristled, just a little, at the mention of the word *pet*, but settled back down again.

"So thanks for showing up," Jake said. "I appreciate it."

Petey closed his eyes.

As if you don't know who sent me.

———— ∞ ————

Petey tugged hard at the kitchen door with one paw. He'd noticed recently that most of the doors in the house didn't close all that tightly. Unless the door was slammed hard, the latch didn't really set solidly—so a hard head-butt would force open most of the inside doors. A good tug with one paw would pop open the outside ones. Jake was already up, puttering around in the kitchen, so he must not have noticed when Petey tugged the door and slipped out.

I love mornings like this. A chorus of birds, the breeze rustling leaves against each other, the scrabbling of mice in the field. A glorious creation, indeed. And since I have had my breakfast, I am most content. Jake seems to be doing fine so far. Maybe he doesn't need me as much as I thought he did. I suppose I could have been wrong. But that doesn't seem right, does it? Me being wrong, that is. That doesn't seem right.

Petey sniffed about the steps carefully.

No foxes last night.

He sniffed again.

Raccoons. Those animals I don't like. They're always fighting with each other, and their squalling gets my fur standing on end. I don't see what they have to fight about, and if they can't get along with each other, then they shouldn't travel together.

Petey made his way to the house on wheels and meowed outside the door.

He waited for a long time, then meowed again.

That's odd. She usually lets me in right away.

Petey eyed a narrow ledge under the window.

I think I can make that. Maybe.

He bent down into a crouch, wiggled his back hips a few times, mentally gauging the effort and the jump that it would take. He laid his ears flat against his head. After a moment of preparation, he pushed off mightily and landed, with inches to spare, on the narrow sill.

He meowed louder, his best let-me-in meow. He heard rustling from inside, then saw Tassy, holding her robe together with one hand and a tissue in the other.

"Okay, Petey," she said, "I heard you. Come on in."

She slid the window open and Petey hopped in, appearing a bit annoyed he had been forced to take such drastic action to visit.

Tassy sniffed and dabbed at her eyes, then sort of folded herself onto the couch, hugging her knees to her chest, offering Petey no place to sit. He jumped up beside her and sniffed at her hand.

She's crying. Women humans do that more often than men humans, I think. Cats don't cry. I know I can feel sad, but I can't cry like that. Crying. That is a very odd manifestation of emotions. I think I heard that on that radio station.

He reached up and put his paw on her forearm.

Why is she crying? Humans are so complicated. She has food and water and a place to stay. I should ask her.

He tried to form his meow as a question. He wasn't really good at asking questions, since there wasn't all that much he didn't know. But in situations like this, a question was in order. He tilted his head at the end of the meow. He had seen people do that when they were asking about things.

"I don't know, Petey. All of a sudden, everything seems to be wrong. What am I doing here? I should just go back to Philadelphia and make the best of it. No one seems to care that I'm gone, apparently. My mother sure doesn't. Randolph doesn't. No one here really knows me. So what am I doing here?"

She sniffed very loudly and wiped at her eyes with the sleeve of the pink chenille robe.

Petey moved closer and placed his front paws on her arm and extended his face closer to hers.

What would an angel do in this situation? Petey wondered. *I would imagine he would say something comforting. Or do something comforting.*

Petey tried to climb into her lap, and Tassy uncoiled herself and let the cat sit on top of her.

This always makes people feel better. A purring cat.

Tassy began to pet Petey, stroking his back and head just the way he liked it.

And they feel better when they pet a cat. That's a proven medical fact. They said it on the television. It makes blood pressure go down. I'm not sure what blood pressure is and why it should go down, but if the people in the television said so, it must be true. And they said it's a good thing.

"Petey, what am I going to do? Pastor Jake has been so nice. Eleanor has been so nice. Even Vern seems nicer."

Petey purred louder, his front paws making little kneading motions on Tassy's stomach. He was very careful not to extend his claws very far. He did not want to inadvertently hurt the young woman.

"I don't have any family here. I don't know what to do. I shouldn't stay here . . . should I?"

Petey was still mulling what it was that an angel could do that he couldn't. When he heard the pain in her voice, he simply acted and did not think about it. He stood up on his rear paws and placed his front paws on Tassy's shoulder. He then nuzzled against her neck, his cold, wet nose against her skin.

She has to hug me back. That will make her less sad.

And after a moment, Tassy did indeed hug the cat in return, and leaned her head onto his.

"Well, maybe I can stay a little while longer. But's that's all. Okay, Petey? That's all."

Petey did not move even though hugging a human was an odd position for a cat.

A little while is all I need to convince her to stay here longer.

He heard her sniff once more and then lean back. Petey also leaned back and returned to that soft spot on her lap.

There are times I really wish I could smile.

Irene gestured with a wide sweep of her left hand, the phone firmly clenched in her right.

"He said it was a CAT, Mom. Not a rat. THE PASTOR'S CAT!"

Talking with her mother, Norma Mahon, grew more and more exhausting. Norma had been a resident of the Sweden Valley Manor in Coudersport for more than a decade, but her hearing had been failing for even longer than that. She refused to even consider a hearing aid. "They make you look like an old person," she would shout back when it was suggested. Irene, at least for the first few years of Norma's fading audio abilities, would shout back, "But you *are* old!"

Irene had been attempting to tell her mother about the cat and Pastor Jake and how funny she thought it was. She was actually going to go to church there Sunday just to see if they let the cat in again.

"I would love to see that!" Irene shouted. "Maybe this pastor is a regular person. A REGULAR PERSON."

After ten minutes of shouting, Irene had gone hoarse, and told her mother that someone was at the door, just to get off the phone.

Maybe this new guy could visit her and talk some sense into her about a hearing aid. If he lets cats into church, he must be different.

Jake broke from his work on the sermon a few minutes past 11:30 a.m. He thought he had the passage well in hand, but the more he worked on it, the less comfortable he felt.

It's not because I'm not trying. And it has nothing to do with faith. It just takes work.

He decided a change of scenery would help clear his thoughts. Petey was sound asleep on the windowsill in the office and did not wake up when Jake grabbed his keys from the hook in the kitchen.

He stopped at the RV and tapped at the door.

"I'm going into town for lunch," he said. "Would you like to come along? Get out for a while."

"Where to?" Tassy asked. "I don't have a lot of money."

"I was thinking McDonald's. And I can treat you to lunch."

"No. I don't like to do that. I have enough for McDonald's. And that sounds good. But let me make the bed first. If Eleanor stopped by and saw a messy bedroom . . . well, I just wouldn't want to disappoint her like that."

Soon enough, Tassy climbed into the truck and fastened the seat belt.

"What about Petey? Doesn't he want to go?"

"He was sleeping. Let sleeping cats lie, I always say."

Tassy scrunched up her face.

"I've heard that before. What's it mean? And isn't it with dogs instead?"

Jake nodded. "It is. Usually. But I don't have a dog, so I have to use a cat. And it means that if there is possible trouble out there—like a sleeping dog—you don't wake it up to find out for sure. You just let it sleep."

"Oh. Now it makes sense."

Tassy rolled the window down and the wind tousled her hair, a hundred delicate wisps dancing around her face like a spherical halo. "Do they have a newspaper in this town?"

"They do. The *Potter Leader-Enterprise*."

"That's a funny name for a paper."

"Because of it being Potter County, I think."

"Oh. That makes sense. Does it have ads for jobs and stuff like that?" Tassy asked.

"I'm sure it does."

"Could we find a copy? I need to look for a job. I can't stay in their RV forever."

"Probably have a newspaper stand at the McDonald's," Jake said as he pulled in. Jake ordered a Big Mac meal; Tassy ordered a single burger and a small fry. Plus a cup of tea with lots of honey.

They found a booth and as Tassy unwrapped her food, she looked up at Jake. "Can I ask you a personal question?"

"Sure. I don't have any secrets," Jake responded, hoping he told the lie well.

"You're not from around here, are you? Where did you grow up?"

"No. I grew up in Pittsburgh. Not downtown, but east of the city. In Shadyside. A nice place."

"Then why are you here? This is sort of out in the middle of nowhere, isn't it? That's what you told me when we first met, wasn't it?" Tassy nibbled at each fry carefully and precisely.

"They needed a pastor."

"I bet lots of churches need pastors, don't they?"

"Maybe," Jake replied. He hoped he did not look uncomfortable. "But I guess I see this as a challenge."

"Did . . . like, God tell you to come here? I heard other people talking about how God told them to do this or that and then they do it and everything works out or they get healed or some sort of miracle happens. You know—those church pastors on television. So what I'm asking is, did God tell you to come here? To Coudersport and all that? Did you hear his voice or see a sign or have a dream or something like that?"

Jake took a large bite of hamburger and held up a finger indicating that he had to stop talking and chew. And he hoped he could come up with a coherent answer.

"Well . . . he didn't really do that. Not like a voice from the sky," Jake explained.

"Then he didn't make you come here? You picked it out on your own?"

He dragged a trio of fries through a dollop of ketchup. He shrugged. "I don't know. Though I am sure that if God didn't want me here, he wouldn't have let me come."

Tassy tilted her head, like she was hearing an odd ratcheting noise.

"Okay. I guess. I'm here because I got tossed out of a car by a really stupid ex-boyfriend. I just wonder how other people get to where they're going and how they know once they got there if it's the right place to be. Because I don't know if I'm supposed to be here or not. I can't tell. I keep thinking people will find out the truth about me and make me leave. I'm afraid of being . . . you know . . . left on my own. And without knowing what to do next. Not having hope is hard. You know what I mean, Pastor Jake?"

Jake nodded.

More than you will ever know, Tassy. More than you will ever know.

As Jake and Tassy sat in McDonald's, having a most unexpected existential discussion, in a booth across the restaurant perched a clutch of older ladies: one of them the mother of Emma Grainger, Veterinarian. Without being obvious, she kept glancing at them, noticing how the young woman ate with the delicacy of a songbird and how Jake laughed and tilted his head back when he did.

She then slipped out her old flip phone from her purse, which was resting in her lap as she ate, and dialed a familiar number. She leaned in closer to the table and turned her back to the rest of the room.

"Do you know who's having lunch at McDonald's? Yes. In the middle of the day. And do you know who's with him?"

She waited a moment.

"Well, I don't either," she said with exasperation. "That's why I'm calling you."

Wilbur Brookings sat in his office at the very back end of the Tri-County Rural Electric Cooperative. It was the biggest office in the building and the only office without a single window. Wilbur tacked up a series of outdoor posters, along with maps indicating the electrical grid as well as the major transmission lines that snaked across Potter County.

He had gotten through half the pile of incoming reports from the weekend.

As general manager, Wilbur had many job responsibilities, very few of them he actually enjoyed. He started out as a linesman, working on transmission pylons. That was a job he loved, but he was promoted out of it after only a few years.

He stirred his coffee, in a blue Tri-County Co-op mug, and stared at one of his posters—a large trout, leaping out of the water in pursuit of a small mayfly. He put his chin in his palm and his elbow on the desk.

What did Pastor Jake say Sunday? I told myself I was going to remember it. Something about working.

He wondered if his wife would remember. He wondered if Jimbo might recall it—he seemed to have a good memory. He tried to remind himself that at the next elders' meeting he should bring up the possibility of taping the sermons.

Up until now, I wouldn't have bothered. But the new guy has something to say. And I haven't taken notes since high school. But I might listen to a tape. How much could that cost? A couple hundred bucks for a tape recorder? Do they still make tape recorders? Maybe it is all on digital stuff now. So it should be even cheaper. We should look into it.

Oh, now I remember. He said it was from Matthew, I think. Something about doing small things well, with great love—and that would please God.

Well, I'm doing small things well here. I hope God is pleased with the work. Maybe I just need to change my attitude. Maybe that's what he was trying to get us to understand. Could be.

He drew in a deep breath, and then began to work through the second half of the weekly reports.

"If I get done early, I'll take a walk down to Kaytee's for lunch. That will be my reward."

Jake pulled up to the veterinarian's office a few minutes before 7:00. He prided himself on his punctuality. Actually, his on-time standard was at least ten minutes early. He had never liked to hurry, not even as a child. He would always be the first child at the bus stop for school. Always.

He was also early getting ready for this evening.

Not the most fashionable dresser, Jake spent an inordinate amount of time this evening standing in front of the mirror in the bathroom. He had tried on, and had discarded, three shirts, and had settled on a sort of quarter-zip-up sweater-shirt that Barbara Ann told him he looked good in. And he wore a pair of dark, almost-black jeans, with a relatively new pair of black slip-on shoes.

Petey had watched it all while lying in the short hallway that led to the bathroom, carefully observing Jake and his pre-date ministrations. He'd chirped softly every now and again, as if making kind but condescending comments on Jake's obsessiveness. He sat on each shirt, in succession, as Jake discarded them.

"It has been a long time since I've been on a date," Jake explained to the cat. "Even if this may not be as much of a date as most dates are. I know. I know. Emma is being friendly and knows I am new in town—so it's sort of like a Welcome Wagon date. Not a real, potentially romantic date."

Jake tried not to think about that aspect of his life. The last romance did not end well, and that brought out his cautious, anxious nature.

"You open yourself up, Petey, and bad things happen, you know? I shouldn't have been so candid with Barbara Ann. I knew it was a mistake when I started talking about all of that. But I expected her to understand, not to tell other people."

Jake had run his hand through his hair. People with thick hair didn't always need a comb or a brush. Jeff the Barber had done a good job with it, and the result was a cross between tousled and controlled—just the right amount of both.

He'd smiled at himself in the mirror.

"This is as good as it is going to get."

He parked in Emma's driveway, making sure the passenger door was even with the sidewalk.

Do I just go inside and call for her? Is there a private entrance? Do I have a cell phone number for her?

Emma appeared at the side of the house, making his worries for naught.

"Hi!" she called out as she walked toward him. "I forgot to tell you to ring the bell on the side door. Unless you have Petey along and need a quick checkup."

"No, it's just me tonight. I gave Petey the number for Domino's Pizza and a twenty-dollar bill. He should be fine."

Emma stopped and laughed with gusto. She was in jeans and some sort of silkish, white blouse, with a paisley scarf around her neck, her hair pulled back with two gold pins.

"Does Coudersport even have a Domino's?" Jake asked.

"No," Emma replied. "Closest one is in Port Allegheny, I think, and that's like forty miles from here."

Jake thought Emma looked very nice.

"So what's the movie tonight?" Jake asked. "I was going to look but forgot all about it until this evening. I wasn't sure if the theater had a website either."

"They do. And the movie . . . I forget the title. The latest explosion-filled epic about mutant machines taking over the earth. I think. Someone said there's a lot of action, and all the dialogue could be written on a three-by-five note card."

"Oh, so this is an intellectual movie? I don't like to think that much at the movies."

For a second, Emma took him seriously, but then realized he was being funny and she smiled back at him.

"Jake, you had me scared for a second. I have known guys who would have said just that without the slightest hint of irony."

Jake opened the truck door.

"And they would have no idea what *irony* meant, either," she added.

The Coudersport Theater was a small jewel box of a theater, appearing much like it must have looked back when it was built in the 1920s.

"This is amazing," Jake said as they walked to their seats. "I had no idea it was this beautiful."

"'An unexpected pleasure,' some travel critic wrote. And they use real butter on the popcorn," Emma added.

"Then it doesn't matter what the movie is," Jake replied. "You had me at 'real butter.'"

—◦◦◦—

Petey nudged hard at the kitchen door and after the third tug, it squealed open.

I wonder if I can get Jake to install one of those little doors for animals.

The door closed behind him, and Petey made his way across the graveled lot to the house on wheels. He walked slowly on the gravel; there were lots of sharp angles that hurt if he stepped hard.

He meowed at the door, and Tassy hurried to open it.

"Petey," she cried. "How did you know I needed company tonight?"

I know these things, Petey said to himself. *I am a good cat.*

Tassy retreated to the couch and patted at the cushion next to her.

"Come on. Come on up."

I'll take my time, Tassy. I like you, but there is no reason to be doglike here and rush into things. Cats are deliberate creatures, and good cats are even more deliberate.

A flat-screen television was mounted to the wall opposite the sofa, but because the RV did not get cable, the television only received a few channels and none of them very clearly. Instead of watching television, Tassy found herself reading more. She borrowed books from Pastor Jake, and Eleanor brought a paper grocery bag filled with mysteries (hers) and

Westerns (Vern's). On her last trip to town, she bought the most recent copies of *People* and *Us* magazines. Those she doled out sparingly, reading only a story or two at a time. She knew her money was extremely limited, and without a job she would have to ration out those sorts of luxury purchases. Midway through this week's *People*, she picked the issue back up and began to finish the latest story on the Kardashians.

"Suit yourself, Petey. If you don't want to be petted, that's all right with me."

With that, Petey jumped up on the sofa and headed straight for her lap.

"I could swear you actually understand me."

Petey meowed in reply. Tassy tossed the magazine to the side and began to pet Petey and he responded by purring loudly.

"Petey, can I ask you a question?"

Petey churred softly and tilted his head as if expecting a tough query.

"Well . . . here's the thing. I don't know if I should be here. I told that to Pastor Jake. He said it was okay to have questions. He said answers to some questions are long in coming, but that I should never give up hope. That sounds right, doesn't it?"

Petey meowed.

"So do I tell people the truth? Is that what they want to hear? What if the secret you have is really, really big, and sooner or later the truth will get out? What do I do then? Do I tell people?"

Petey rolled onto his back and stared up at Tassy.

I'm not sure what she is asking. And I'm not a mind reader. God sent me here, sure, but he did not give me any super powers. She's seen too many superhero movies. Or those horrid vampire ones. Gack. Who thinks a deathly pallor is attractive?

He knew he couldn't give a concise answer to a nebulous question, so he decided to take action instead.

Maybe she'll get the metaphor here.

He grabbed at her hand with his front paws, using no claws, of course, and pulled it close, then mimed biting her hand, but instead, at the last minute, licked the back of her hand, gently and tenderly.

You know . . . sometimes the fact that you can do something doesn't mean you should do something. Some things you are able to do will cause pain in others.

"I'll think about it, Petey. I'll think about it. Pastor Jake said to be truthful . . . but I don't know. I'll think about it."

Both Jake and Emma were smiling as they walked out of the Coudersport Theater.

"Not exactly at the Noel Coward level of urbane, witty dialogue," Emma remarked.

"What?" Jake almost shouted, "I couldn't hear from all the explosions."

She playfully pushed him on the shoulder.

"It was loud, wasn't it?"

"I bet there weren't more than fifteen seconds of quiet in the whole movie. Maybe when that one robot died."

Emma tucked her purse under her arm.

"No Academy Award for scriptwriting, but it was entertaining—in an explosive way."

Jake opened the truck door.

"It really was. I couldn't do a steady diet of these movies, but once in a while they are good, brainless fun."

He started the truck.

"Is there a place around here to go for coffee? or a piece of pie? or something?"

Emma smiled at him, as if relieved that he asked to continue the Welcome Wagon date past expectations.

"Sure. Head back east on Route 6—Second Street. There's a diner that's open until 11:30. Which is like four in the morning on Coudersport time."

When they arrived, they settled into opposite sides of a booth by the window.

Barbara Ann had always sat next to Jake in a four-person booth, leaving Jake a bit smothered, but he'd never told her. She was all elbows when she ate, which meant that Jake had to cede at least a quarter more of his rightful booth space. That was why he'd always asked for a table.

"They have good homemade pie. And by 'homemade' I mean they actually make it here. Not that they live here—but it isn't made in a factory."

Jake ordered cherry pie, not heated, with ice cream, and regular coffee.

Emma picked a triple berry pie with whipped cream and decaf coffee. "After I turned thirty, coffee after dark keeps me up until it's light again."

She's a little bit older than I am. A little bit. Although she didn't say how far past thirty she is. I guess it doesn't matter.

If she was watching her weight, Jake was glad it didn't spill into her dessert selection. She took a large forkful and declared her choice as "delicious."

Jake tasted his pie and nodded. "Good job. Good pick."

They didn't talk much as they ate. They exchanged a few comments about the movie, and Jake remarked how surprised he was that Coudersport still had a downtown movie house.

"I think it's a labor of love for the owners. I don't know them well, but I don't think they're getting rich off showing movies. They probably make more money off the popcorn than the tickets they sell. I sometimes just go in and get a box of popcorn without seeing the movie."

"It is good—especially with the butter."

Jake finished first and slid his plate to the side.

"So . . . you're a pastor?" she asked. Her tone was coy, lighthearted.

"I am," Jake replied.

"Did you always want to be a pastor?"

How do I answer this? Should I start being honest?

"Maybe," he said. "My father left my mother and me when I was like seven. I'm not sure of the whole story, but I haven't heard from him in more than ten years now. My mother raised me as a single mom—more or less. I don't think they ever officially divorced. My mother always wanted me to be a preacher. Her dream was to see me go to a seminary and be a famous preacher at a big church."

"Coudersport doesn't have any big churches, Jake. Or hadn't you noticed?"

"I know. But the Church of the Open Door is a legitimate church, and they needed a pastor. I needed a church."

"Your mother wanted that, Jake. But did you always want to be a pastor?"

"You want me to be honest? If I had my choice, I would be playing center field for the Pittsburgh Pirates. But that dream didn't happen. This one did."

Emma offered a knowing smile and looked like she wanted to push the question one more time, but didn't. Apparently, she would take his answers at face value.

"So, Emma, are you a 'churchgoing' woman?" Jake asked.

Emma shook her head.

"I grew up going to church. But I stopped going when I went to college. A lot of things happened, and I guess I lost faith in it all."

"What happened?"

"A lot of things."

Jake didn't push that question either.

"I'll change the subject," Emma said. "What's up with the young girl in the RV? My mother was talking about her. Tassy, right?"

"It is Tassy," Jake replied. He briefly related Tassy's story of how she came to the church and wound up living, at least temporarily, in Vern's RV.

"So he just threw her out on the side of the road? Her ex-boyfriend? A charming fellow, no doubt."

"That's what she said. And she is such an attractive young woman," Jake added. "And such a nice person. I just don't understand how someone would do that to her. She is not the sort of person who anyone would reject or abandon."

Emma almost winced, but didn't. If Jake noticed the pained look that swept past her eyes, he made no comment.

"So what does your faith say about that, Jake? I hope you don't mind me asking. As you might guess, I don't have a lot of intellectual friends in Coudersport. I have friends—good-time friends—but having an intelligent conversation? . . . Well, that doesn't happen all that much."

"No. I'm a pastor, remember? I'm supposed to handle questions like this."

He accepted a second refill on his coffee and added two sugars and cream.

"I know God is in control. Even when it seems like he isn't. Things don't always happen the way we want to happen. But it doesn't mean God isn't there. Things happened in my life I don't understand. But it is not because God turned his back."

I hope that sounds like I believe that. I'm not sure I do. But that is the party line.

"So a pretty girl like Tassy being tossed out and abandoned is all part of his plan?"

Jake narrowed his eyes, as if in deep thought. "No. Maybe. Sometimes we do stupid things and have to suffer the consequences. But God is still there. We do have free will, and sometimes our free will gets us in trouble. We do stupid things. I know that has happened to me."

"You've done stupid things?"

"Some."

"Like what?"

Jake hesitated.

Should I be honest? Should I tell the whole truth? This is way too early, right?

He looked at his hands, wrapped around his coffee cup.

"Let's just say stupid things for now. Nothing horrible. Just stupid."

Emma let him off the hook by smiling.

"I guess that could describe all of us, right?"

At that moment, Emma's cellphone came alive, warbling. She grabbed it out of her purse.

"I should take this. It could be some sort of cat emergency," she said, explaining the unexpected interruption. "Hello?"

Jake could not help overhearing. She was sitting close and the person on the other end was speaking very loudly.

"Joanne talked to Arlene and then called Betty, and she said that Arlene's son—you know, Gary, the one with the lisp—well, he was at the movies tonight and he said he saw you with that new preacher fellow. Is that true? Or is he lying again? You know how those Pipers can be."

Emma closed her eyes, as if wishing to disappear.

"Yes, Mom. It is true. He saw us there."

"So, who did the asking—him or you? You aren't getting any younger, you know."

Emma shook her head, held her hand on top of the mouthpiece, and whispered loudly to Jake, "Do not do anything in this town that you don't want everyone to know about in like fifteen minutes. Don't do anything stupid. They will hunt you down like a rabid wolverine."

She returned to the call.

"Mom, we'll talk tomorrow. I have to go."

She snapped the phone shut and watched as a wide smile spread across Jake's face.

7

Jake felt good about his take on the first chapter of Ephesians. He would plow no new theological ground, but as a basic expository sermon, it was at least okay. And he had sprinkled in a few personal anecdotes throughout. He liked hearing personal anecdotes and hoped his new congregation would as well.

Verna played through the first two hymns, mostly in tune. Jake could not be sure if it was her or the organ that went wobbly on a few verses. Jake did not study music, so anyone who could decipher the black lines and squiggles was head and shoulders above him in musical ability. Apparently Verna also taught piano on the side, so Jake blamed the warbles on the organ.

Jake—Pastor Jake—walked up to the pulpit and cleared his throat. The pulpit was on the smallish side, so Jake had to lean forward just a bit when he grabbed both sides of it.

He started with a short prayer, then launched into his sermon. Perhaps fifteen seconds into the material, he noticed a few people staring at the door to the anteroom of his office. He had locked it the night before—just in case. Petey on the platform *once* was amusing; *twice* might be seen as an affectation, and he did not want to be known as the "cat pastor." An older lady whom Jake did not recognize pointed toward the door—and not a subtle pointing, her arm raised shoulder high. Jake tried not to be obvious about it, but he looked. A silver and black, furry paw scrabbled at the bottom of the door, trying to pull it open. The door, of course, would not budge. The cat tried three more times, then the paw disappeared. Jake took a deep breath and continued.

Maybe no one other than the lady and I saw it.

Why is this door locked? It wasn't locked last week. Jake! You must have made a mistake. I get it. You locked the door by accident. I know you didn't mean to lock the door. I need to hear your sermon.

Petey scampered from the small office into Jake's bigger office. The windows were closed.

He ran into the kitchen and tried the door, but even tugging with all his might didn't open it. The door did not budge. He looked at the windows in the kitchen. All were closed tight.

How am I going to get out of here?

He ran into the bedroom. Closed windows.

Wait. I know.

He ran into the bathroom. He didn't like the bathroom. He remembered once, as a small cat, he had jumped into a tub, not knowing it was full of water. He did not like being immersed, accidentally or not.

Took me two days to dry out.

But the window in the bathroom was open—sort of.

Jake had bought one of those sliding screens with the wood frame that pop in an out of an open window. Petey made his way to that window, jumped up, and pushed. It squeaked just a little. He pushed again, and the screen went clattering to the outside. The drop was only six feet and onto grass. Petey jumped and took off to the front of the church.

How do I open those doors? If I'm supposed to be inside, there'll be an open door for me. I'm sure of that.

He ran to the front of the church and up the steps. Neither of the doors was open.

Maybe I'm not supposed to be inside. Could that be possible?

Just then, as Petey stared hard at the double doors, one side opened. Charles Hild stepped out, reaching for a rumpled pack of Chesterfields in the breast pocket of his blue sport coat.

"Well, hello there. You're the pastor's cat, right?" Charles said.

Petey meowed, a tad annoyed at having to affirm the obvious.

"You want to go in?"

Petey meowed again.

"Okay, I guess. After all, you are sort of a church cat, right?"

Charles held the door open as he pulled a lighter from his pocket.

"Something about sitting in church this long makes me really need a cigarette."

Petey chose not to run, but walked, his tail held high, and slowly made his way down the center aisle.

Jake saw him first and closed his eyes in dismay.

Don't know why he's upset. Obviously, I'm supposed to be here. There was a door open.

The rest of the congregation noticed, of course, as Petey walked past them—especially those in the aisle seats. Petey walked slowly up the steps to the platform and jumped onto the center chair—the same one he had used the previous week.

Everyone in the congregation had laughed. And for a long time. Maybe it was the exasperated expression on his face, or the calm, serene look on Petey's face, or perhaps it was the tension between the two.

Jake waited until everyone had finished.

"I guess we have a visitor again. If it's okay with you, we'll just go on. Chasing a cat around the platform isn't on my order of service today."

Most everyone agreed with a chorus of "okays." A smattering of applause indicated general approval, Jake guessed.

Petey waited for the sermon to continue, still as a statue, his eyes flickering between staring at Jake in rapt attention and with bemusement at the congregation and their smiles.

"Okay, then, back to Ephesians."

<hr />

Emma liked spring Sunday mornings. She had nothing pressing to do other than read the Sunday copy of the *Philadelphia Inquirer*, which she accomplished by 9:00. Finished with that task, she carried a cup of coffee out to the second-story porch. Winston followed her to the door but did not come out on the porch. Obviously, heights unnerved him. He realized she had not taken food with her, so he wasn't acutely disappointed. She did carry her small laptop computer with her, thinking she might catch up on e-mails.

She placed the computer on a small table and started it up. She typed in her password, then hesitated. Instead of opening her mailbox, she went to Google, and hesitated again for a long moment.

Then she shook her head and typed in: Barbara Ann Bentley.

I'm not snooping. I'm not. I'm just interested, that's all. Jake is a new friend, and I'm interested in his life before he came here. That's all.

Barbara Ann Bentley brought up more than a million hits.

Emma was not surprised. Type in "dancing pink hippos" and you'll find several million hits as well. She added "Butler" to the search and, on a whim, "beauty pageant."

Bingo.

Barbara Ann was the owner of a website that focused on beauty pageant tips and consulting on all things related to beauty pageants. Items for sale included a beauty pageant video and a book on pageant secrets, entitled, appropriately, *Beauty Pageant Secrets*. The site was very pink and very bejeweled, with many sparkles and diamonds.

It appeared that Barbara Ann no longer competed professionally but would be willing to help others in consultations, coaching and accompanying contestants with whatever pageant they entered. Barbara Ann included a picture of herself wearing a tiara and a sequined silver gown. She showed a great expanse of very white teeth.

"Well, Winston, our Pastor Jake dated a very pretty girl—if you like that style of pretty. A little artificial, if you ask me. But pretty."

Winston snorted in reply and remained standing, a few inches shy of actually crossing the threshold to the porch.

"And she has a lot of teeth."

Emma read some of the free hints provided on the site: "Always Smile—Even If It Hurts!" and some of the testimonials: "Without Barbara Ann I would have never won Miss Fayette County. From, Cindy Jones."

This is so unexpected. I never would have figured Jake as a man who would be with a woman like this. The two of them just don't add up.

She clicked on the heading of "Contact Me."

There was an e-mail and a mailing address. And there was a phone number.

Emma stared at it for a long time.

Probably an answering machine.

She looked out to the street and watched an old minivan rattle past.

Her fingers hovered over the keyboard, poised to leave the site and move on to a more intellectual news site—maybe the e-version of the *Wall Street Journal*.

Instead, she moved the cursor to the phone number, hit the copy key, and pasted the number into her contact list.

I'm not going to call her, of course. That would be wrong.

She stared at the number.

I should just erase it.

She stared a little longer. She didn't erase it.

That Sunday afternoon, Jake changed from his suit and tie and polished, uncomfortable preaching shoes into a pair of jeans and a Butler County Community College sweatshirt— "Home of the Pioneers." He once taught a course there: Comparative Religions of the World.

That seems so long ago right now.

Petey danced around him as he changed, purring and chirping and meowing.

"So, Petey," he said as he sat on the bed and laced up his sneakers, "did you enjoy today's sermon?"

Petey butted his head into Jake's shin and meowed loudly.

"You paid attention the whole time. That's a good thing. I only noticed a few sleepers today."

Petey jumped on the bed, then down again.

"So you think you're going for a walk with me? Who says I want to take a cat for a walk? And I thought cats don't do walks. Do they?"

Jake thought Petey tried to look offended and bemused at the same time.

"Well, I'm willing to try it. But you cannot run off and get lost. I already have invested a lot of money in you, between the food and the litter and the doctor's visits."

Petey lowered his head, as if he felt guilty for costing Jake actual, human money.

Spring had arrived, and then some. The breeze carried a hint of warmth, almost hot, and the trees had filled out in green during the last few weeks. Coudersport was much more rural than urban, so a walk in any direction took one into the country very quickly. The Allegheny River lay only a few hundred yards to the south of the church, though at this geographical point, was not much of a river but more like a large stream.

Jake grabbed an old Pirates baseball hat and stepped out onto the parking lot, breathing deeply. His shoulder had hardly bothered him for the past week.

No twinges, no omens. That's good. Omenless.

Tassy opened the door to the RV.

"Going for a walk? Could I come?"

"Sure. Just a short one. Down to the river."

The three of them crossed the road and headed south through an open field populated by tall grasses and milkweed plants and hundreds of butterflies that took flight as they walked.

"What kind are these?" Tassy asked. "I've seen them before, right?"

"Monarchs," Jake said. "They are pretty common. Did you know that they migrate all the way to Mexico?"

"Really? They can fly all that way?"

"I'm not sure. I think they do. Or maybe it takes a generation or two to get there. Anyhow, a place in Mexico gets hundreds

The Cat That God Sent

of thousands of them. So many at once that they can break tree limbs."

"Really?

"Well, I haven't seen it. But that's what I've heard."

Petey, following them, meowed.

The headwaters of the Allegheny River lay only fifty miles upstream, so at this point, the river was not an impressive body of water. The spring thaw muddied the water and filled the banks to their upper limit, but the river still was no more than a swollen stream.

"This is really a river?" Tassy asked as they stared at the flowing water.

"It is. It picks up volume as it goes, of course. In Pittsburgh, it joins the Monongahela River and forms the Ohio River."

"That's a big river, right? I've heard of that."

"Pretty big. I've never seen the Mississippi. That's bigger."

Tassy sat on a large stone outcropping and folded her knees up. Petey jumped to join her.

"I wish I could follow the water. Just float away. Sometimes I would love to float away from everything."

Jake tossed a few pebbles into the water.

"I know what you mean. Life gets complicated sometimes."

Tassy nodded and reached to stroke Petey's back.

Jake said, "So, have you thought more about staying, Tassy? I know you said you don't feel like you belong here. But what would make some other place better? Couldn't you start your life from here? Begin it all again?"

Tassy shrugged. "That sounds easy. But it isn't, Pastor Jake. You might have everything figured out. Like faith and God and where you're supposed to be. But I don't. And I can't even see where I would go for answers."

"Tassy, I don't have everything figured out. I don't. Just because I preach doesn't mean I have all the answers."

153

She looked at him intently, as if she heard his words but did not agree with him, yet was too polite to call him on it.

"You can stay here, Tassy. You could find a job, I bet. Make new friends. Start over. Here is as good a place as any. Maybe better. You already have a place to stay for a while."

"Maybe. I don't know. Maybe if I had faith like you did, then it would be easier. I envy you, you know? God showed you a path and all you have to do is follow it. I would really like that. To be like you. You have a church and a job and a cat. I don't have any of that. I guess I'm a little jealous."

"Tassy, you have nothing to be jealous of. Really. You can find the way. You just have to have . . ."

"Faith? Hope? Pastor Jake—that's all I had when I left home. And now where am I? Broke and lost and . . ."

They both stopped talking. Petey looked first at Tassy, as if urging her to continue, to tell the truth, to get out whatever secret she was hiding. Then he looked at Jake the same way. But neither would speak. Both simply stared at the fast-moving water, filled with sediment, making the bottom of the river a mystery.

Emma picked up the phone a dozen times and almost dialed the number once. Then she laid it back down.

No, I can't do this. What would I say? Would she even tell me about Jake? If it were me—would I?

"Winston, what would you do?"

Winston didn't answer. He lay in the middle of the hallway and snored noisily.

Emma stared at the phone.

Then she picked it up and began to tap in numbers.

———✸———

"So, Eleanor, what did you think of the new guy? Besides the cat, that is. Stupid animal. We're going to be the laughing stock around here. A pastor with a cat. That's what they're going to call us—the Cat Church."

Eleanor carried a pitcher of iced tea out to the patio and set it down carefully onto the metal table with matching metal chairs. The style would be considered retro in most settings, but these were original metal-tubed chairs from 1956. Vern religiously stored them in the garage each winter and cleaned them every spring, scraping off any rust and repainting the rusted areas with a coating of rustproof paint. They were now multicolored, but solid.

"I liked the cat being there. Did you see Irene Lindquist there? She said she would never come to a church ever again."

"She just came to laugh at the cat."

"So? She's at church. And she heard a good sermon. Maybe that's the way God works."

"With a cat?" Vern said, swatting away the idea like a pesky gnat. "God uses cats, now, does he?" He took a long swallow of tea. "Not enough sugar in this tea. Or lemon."

"Next time, fix it yourself, you old goat."

Eleanor had changed from her Sunday dress to an old housecoat. Vern didn't like her to wear a housecoat outside. "Looks like pajamas," he'd barked.

"It's just like a dress, that's all—but more comfortable," Eleanor had barked back.

They had had this discussion for more than twenty years and had not yet resolved the issue.

"Anyhow, I liked them both—the cat and the pastor. And besides Irene, I noticed a few other faces I haven't seen in years. Maybe the cat is a good thing."

"Over my dead body," Vern said. "No church I go to will start featuring a cat. Next thing you know, he'll want to have hootchie-cootchie dancers up front. That'll draw them in. What would you think about that?"

Eleanor picked up some grapes she had bought on sale at the Jubilee Foods in town.

"A cat is not a hootchie-cootchie dancer, Vern. And besides," she said as she chewed, "there's not enough room on the platform for hootchie-cootchie dancers. Maybe we could have one. What's one hootchie-cootchie called? Just a hootchie?"

Eleanor smiled to herself, knowing Vern would never find that amusing. She was right. He didn't.

"Well, he didn't talk enough about sin," Vern said with a scowl. "Needs to talk more about sin. That's what we need. Sin talk. Maybe that'll get a revival going."

Eleanor sighed.

"Sure, Vern. Let's talk more about sin. That will draw in the crowds."

"Worked in the old days. Big tent meetings. All they talked about was sin."

Eleanor was about to say, "And when was the last tent meeting in Coudersport?" but didn't. The afternoon was much too pleasant to spend arguing.

"Yes, Vern," she said quietly. "A big tent. That would do it. Crowds would come to a big tent."

Vern responded by smiling, staring at the apple tree in the backyard, and wondering when it would be the time to spray it for bugs. He enjoyed spraying things for bugs.

"NO. THE CAT WAS THERE. WITH THE PASTOR! HE CAME IN THROUGH THE FRONT DOOR."

Irene lowered herself into her plaid La-Z-Boy and raised the footrest as she listened to her mother's response. She wondered if she could teach her mother how to use e-mail. That would be so much easier and less taxing. A five-minute phone call, filled with shouting, wore Irene out.

For her first church service in decades (other than the service from the Vatican she watched on TV on Christmas Eve) this one wasn't all that bad. She had actually listened to the sermon, mostly, and had kept her eye on the cat that was paying attention to the pastor.

Verna's organ playing hadn't improved in the past years, but they had sung two hymns that she remembered from her childhood, and each brought back a tender memory of her father singing them wildly off key. Irene had managed to choke out most of the words.

"I LIKED IT. THE PASTOR IS A GOOD GUY. NO. NOT GOOD-BYE. A GOOD GUY."

And with that her mother hung up and Irene dropped the phone, nearly exhausted.

Maybe I'll go next week. Maybe. If the cat goes.

"Well," Big Dave said, smiling, "didya like it?"

Big Dave was still in his church clothes—a blue work shirt with a tie and newer jeans.

Carl swirled the coffee in his plastic cup. He was on his way home and stopped in after the service.

"Wasn't bad. The cat was pretty funny. Like he was trained to do that or something."

"Nope. Just a stray. He showed up the same day as the pastor. He came in here with him."

"Well, I gotta say I don't like sitting still for an hour like that, but it wasn't bad. Your new guy is okay. He didn't yell at all. And no lightning strike, either."

"You know, I did check the Weather Channel before I came. Just to be on the safe side."

— ❧ —

It will be an answering machine. I'll just hear her voice and then I'll hang up. No harm in that, right?

Emma dialed half the numbers and hung up eleven times, stopping and staring at the phone, debating, and then on the twelfth attempt, she dialed all the numbers and let it actually connect and ring.

And no one answers a business line on a Sunday afternoon.

It rang once, twice, then the sound of a connection.

"Hello, this is Barbara Ann Bentley. May I help you?"

Good grief! She actually answered the phone! Who does that?

"Umm . . . uhh . . . Hello," Emma's heart raced.

"Hello. Can I help you? This is Barbara Ann Bentley, of Bentley Pageant Consultants."

Get a hold of yourself, Emma. You've operated on horses and wolves. You've held the insides of animals in your hands. You can talk to a pretty woman. Talk!

"Umm . . . hello, Barbara Ann, this is Emma Grainger. You don't know me . . . but we have a mutual friend. I think he's a mutual friend."

Barbara Ann was nothing if not pert, chipper, and super-polite and positive.

"And who might that be, Ms. Grainger?"

— ❧ —

Neither Tassy nor Jake went further with the truth than they already had, much to Petey's dismay. He chirped, cried, churred, and meowed a hundred ways to Sunday, but neither of them continued to talk.

Jake thought Petey had seen some sort of larger animal—like a fox or a coyote—and was trying to warn them.

Tassy stood up hearing the word *coyote*.

"Do they eat people?" she asked, pivoting around, trying to locate the telltale movement of brush that would indicate a predator lurking nearby.

"No," Jake said, reassuring her. "They are more afraid of us than vice versa."

"I wouldn't bet on that. I've seen movies where a pack of wild dogs . . . or maybe it was wolves . . . chase these guys down and pick them off one by one. They're big animals with lots of teeth."

"I don't think we have any wolf packs in Coudersport, Tassy."

"Are you sure? This is like way out in the woods. I grew up in Philadelphia. This is like the jungle in comparison."

Jake could tell that she was more than a little frightened.

"You want to go back?"

"Yes. I do."

Petey kept hopping and chirping, as if he was trying to get them to stop walking and keep talking, but to no avail.

"Okay. Let's walk back. Petey can guard us, okay?"

Tassy offered a nervous giggle. "He wouldn't be any good at protecting me. They would eat him up in a minute. A wolf would, anyhow."

Petey offered one more meow, long and drawn out, as if expressing his resentment at being called an ineffectual guardian.

If I am going to be a snoop, might as well be honest.

"Jake Wilkerson."

"Jake Wilkerson?"

Have I made a mistake? This isn't the same Barbara Ann? This is sooo embarrassing.

"Yes. Jake Wilkerson. He's a new pastor up here in Coudersport. I thought you knew him when he was in Butler. I must be mistaken. So sorry to have bothered you on a Sunday."

Barbara Ann remained very perky. "Oh, it's no bother. I often answer the phone myself on Sunday. A lot of pageants are held on Sunday afternoon. The smaller ones. Big ones are Saturday evening. But I have some up-and-coming clients. Sometimes they are in a crisis and need some advice. Like what color eye shadow goes with a magenta gown they have to wear because their original choice got lost or torn or something. Or do I really need double-faced tape if I'm not very big . . . you know . . . up there. I always had to use it. You know what I mean?"

Emma thought she sort of knew what Barbara Ann meant, so she agreed. "I do. I guess."

"Jake Wilkerson. So you know Jake. Are you two dating or something?"

What answer does she want? I think she would rather have him brokenhearted and never dating again. After her, who could come close?

"No. He's new in town. And he brought his cat into my office. I'm a veterinarian."

"A vet? I always wanted to be vet. I would love to take care of bunnies and kitties. But I found out there is a lot of math. I'm not real good at math."

"Well, there is not as much as you might think. You could still do it, I bet. Get a math tutor if you have a hard time with it. A lot of people in my class did."

"Really?" Barbara Ann said, brightening. "Wow. Maybe I could. Could I do this pageant consulting while I went to vet school? I really like helping girls be beautiful and win prizes and stuff."

"Well, I don't see why not," Emma replied. "Anything is possible."

Emma heard an atonal hum, then Barbara Ann said, "Jake Wilkerson. Yes, Ms. Grainger. I know Jake. Very well."

Tassy retreated into the RV, waved good-bye to Jake and Petey, and closed the door behind her. Jake heard the lock bolt securely.

Jake felt a little guilty about scaring Tassy, but he really thought Petey might have seen or smelled a coyote. Why else would the cat be making all that racket.

The two of them went into the parsonage. After preaching, even though it was only a single sermon, Jake went into what he called his "shut-down" mode. He put a disc in his stereo—some soft jazz music. He had a dozen such discs and he could never really tell them apart. He switched on the TV, found a basketball game between two teams he did not care much about, put it on mute, and laid down on the couch, with a scrunched-up pillow under his head. He would spend the next few hours there, alternating between watching and listening and napping. Such remains of a Sunday afternoon were the most delicious times of the week.

Petey sat in the middle of the room, keeping an eye on Jake, and watched him fall asleep.

So that's all he's going to do this afternoon? Petey thought. *I knew that being able to talk would come in handy sometimes. Like today by the river. They both need to open up. They should have figured out what I was trying to say. I made it as obvious as the noses on their faces.*

Petey sniffed loudly, licked his paw a bit, wiped off his face—both sides—and sauntered to his favorite chair.

If he can sleep, so can I.

In his thoughts, Petey smiled.

Jake is entitled to take a nap once in a while.

He circled the chair cushion several times until he found the most perfect spot in which to lie.

I shouldn't be hard on them. I don't like to think about my past either. I try not to think about it. I don't know why those humans acted like they did. Hurtful. And those people seemed like normal humans. But . . . God saved me from that, didn't he?

He lay his head down and closed his eyes.

Maybe I'll think about that some other time. Maybe.

———❦———

"You do?" Emma replied. "Did you go to his church?"

"Yes. But it wasn't *his* church. He was an associate there. That's all. Not a senior anything."

Emma wanted to come out bluntly and ask the questions she really wanted answered, but was pretty sure that blunt would not work with Barbara Ann.

"So the two of you went to the same church."

"We did. Or he did. I was there first. My uncle—he's the senior pastor there. Has been there for years and years."

"Is it a big church? The church Jake is at now is really sort of tiny."

Emma thought she heard more than a note of smugness in Barbara Ann's reply, "I knew it. He didn't tell anyone where it was. I just knew it would be tiny. I figured the church would be a little desperate. And yes, my uncle's church is big. It is the biggest church in Butler. And has been the biggest for years and years."

"Barbara Ann, I hope you don't mind me being direct. But if you would, maybe you could tell me about the particulars. You know—what happened. Girl-to-girl, you know?"

Emma heard a long sigh.

"I will, Ms. Grainger. As a warning. Okay?"

"Sure."

"Jake and I dated for like forever. A year, I think. We even talked about getting engaged. Just talked about it. That's all."

"This was while he was on staff?" Emma wasn't sure why she was so intently curious, but she was, and having found a person willing to offer an explanation, she was determined not to let it go to waste.

"Yep. My uncle liked him at first. I did, too. Jake is a nice guy. Really he is."

"Did he do something bad? What?"

Another deep breath and a sigh.

"Not bad in a bad way. But bad enough. Bad for a pastor. We were taking this thing—a seminar or whatever—that my uncle taught for couples, on how to talk about stuff, how to be honest—all that sort of stuff."

"Sure, like premarital counseling."

"Except that we were definitely not premarital. We were dating, that's all. My uncle said it would be a fun thing to do as a couple. So we went. One of the exercises was to be totally honest about something we had hidden inside of us. I told him—and I am kind of embarrassed even now—that I used to touch up my hair color in high school. Not now. It's totally blonde all by itself now."

"Your picture on your website looks very pretty, Barbara Ann. Very pretty."

Emma could tell that Barbara was beaming.

"Why, thank you, Ms. Grainger. That's very kind of you. Anyhow, when it was Jake's turn, he started telling me some really disturbing stuff."

"Disturbing?" Emma braced herself.

"Yes. Disturbing. He told me he was having doubts about being a pastor. He even admitted to having doubts about God and faith—like maybe God wasn't always there helping us. Like maybe he's just watching and not saving us and doing good stuff for us."

"Really?" Emma replied, hoping that she sounded as shocked as Barbara Ann sounded, all the while thinking that such feelings of doubt sounded pretty normal to her.

"Yes. For a pastor to say that—that's just not right. So I told my uncle and my uncle confronted him and asked if it were true and Jake had to say it was and then my uncle had to fire him. He couldn't have a pastor who didn't believe in God."

"Did Jake really say he didn't believe in God?"

"Not exactly. But close enough. If you think God is just watching—that's like not believing in him."

"Wow," Emma replied, not really meaning she was surprised or shocked, but that she was just amazed at the whole incident.

"Wow, exactly. So I had to tell Jake that if he wasn't going to be a pastor, we weren't going to be a couple. I intend on marrying someone who can be the pastor of a church someday. That's important to me. I have an image to be concerned about. I couldn't go around dating an atheist, could I? Who would use a half-atheist beauty pageant consultant?"

"Nobody?"

"Exactly."

Emma inhaled deeply this time. After a moment, Barbara Ann posed a question. "You said Jake has a cat?"

"I did. Petey. A very special cat, if you ask me."

"Now, that is amazing," Barbara Ann said. "Him having a cat. I take it his mother doesn't know about it."

"I'm not sure. Maybe."

"She doesn't, Ms. Grainger. I am sure of that. She is a very controlling person. I am sure she would not go for him having a cat. Not at all. It's a good thing she lives all the way in Meadville. If she lived close . . . well, I am not sure what would have happened."

"Barbara Ann, I have to thank you so much for being honest with me. This explains a lot."

"So, you asked me for the truth—girl-to-girl. Now it's your turn to tell me the truth, Ms. Grainger: Are you two dating? Girl-to-girl."

"Okay. I'll be honest. We went out once. Just to the movies."

"At least now you're prepared. I don't know about you, but dating an atheist would be a big no-no to me. I talk about this in my video. If you don't believe you can win a beauty pageant, then you shouldn't enter. You have to have faith in yourself. If Jake didn't have faith, then he should have steered clear of the ministry—and me. Would have saved me a whole year of dating the wrong person."

"Well, Barbara, again, thanks so much."

"You're welcome, Ms. Grainger. By the way, Ms. Grainger, would you like a copy of my video? I have a lot of VHS ones. They don't sell very well these days."

"I would love one, but seeing how as my veterinarian job takes most of my time, I don't think I'll be entering any pageants."

"Oh, that's okay. It's got loads of good advice on beauty and self-confidence and all sorts of good, positive things. I'll send you one for free. Okay? Seeing as how we both know Jake. Okay."

"Okay, if you insist. That would be very kind of you," Emma said, wondering if she still owned a VCR that would play a VHS tape.

8

Jake walked out of Jubilee Foods with two bags of groceries. His cat food supply was already low. *Petey must be making up for lost time of not having enough food to eat for so long by eating a full can of tinned food every day, plus nibbling on dry kibbles all day.* Jake thought that level of consumption was a lot. He made a mental note to ask Emma about the proper amount to feed a cat the next time he saw her.

He loaded the groceries in the front of the truck. Petey had stayed at home this morning, barely raising his head from his morning nap position on the chair in the living room. It was his first stop on a standard rotation: morning nap—living room chair; midmorning nap—windowsill in office; after lunch nap—sofa in living room; predinner nap—the unused pillow on Jake's bed; and prebedtime nap—one of the kitchen chairs. The variety of sleeping spots Petey selected and how quickly he fell asleep and woke up fascinated Jake. And how varied his sleeping positions were: the prone cat, the cat on his back, the cat curled into an impossibly tight ball, the cat with his head upright and eyes closed, the cat with his head on his paws, the cat with a paw on his face, and the cat stretched out to twice his length.

As Jake walked around his car with his groceries, he spotted a tall, very thin, younger man walking toward him, with very long blond straight hair, worn well past his shoulders. A full beard flowed around his face and chin—a long beard, full and bushy, a bandana covered his head. He also wore torn jeans and a very tattered jean jacket. It appeared that he was coming straight at Jake. Granted, Coudersport was out in the country—well out in the country. And there were folks who lived even farther out in the country—miles away from even a small town and miles off any main road, and some, miles off even a bad, semi-paved road. Almost off the grid, if the truth be told.

One of these wilderness-looking men attended Jake's church. He heard him referred to as a "mountain man," a person who simply wasn't comfortable living in close proximity to anyone. He lived in a small cabin deep in the nearby Susquehannock State Forest, virtually hidden from view. His name was Mylon Fedders, and he slipped into church as it started and exited as they sang the final hymn.

The man approaching him was not Mylon but apparently went to the same barber and clothing store as the church's mountain man.

"Hey there, you the new pastor fellow, right?"

Jake extended his hand. "I am. Jake Wilkerson."

"Yeah, that's it. I saw you with Doc Grainger the other night."

"At the movies?"

"Naw. I got no use for movies. I was heading out of town and saw you walking. Me and Doc Grainger go way back. We went to high school together. She was real smart back then. Well, I guess she still is. Sorry. Let me introduce myself. Where are my manners? They call me Speedy Davis. Don't ask my real name. Doc Grainger may remember it, but I hope she don't. Anyhow, I hear tell you let a cat come to church. That right?"

If Jake was worried about becoming the "cat pastor," this may have confirmed it.

"I guess. The cat, my cat . . . yes, he did show up in church the last two Sundays. Apparently he likes to hear me talk."

"Don't that beat all? Animals—they do have a special sense, you know. They understand things. They know. I sort of live out there in the woods. Animals all around. Deer. Raccoons. A couple a bears, recently. Spiritual creatures, them bears."

Speedy pushed his hair behind his ears, using both hands, then shook his head to straighten the flowing locks on his shoulders.

"Anyhows, Pastor Jake, I was wondering."

Jake waited.

"I don't do church. I don't like being inside with all those people. Get real nervous, you know. Miracle I made it through school, you know?"

"I can understand that, Speedy. Really."

"But that don't mean I ain't interested in God and all that. But I was wondering. Maybe sometime you and I could talk. Not here in town. I'm sort of already itchy and I only been here a few minutes. Maybe you could come out to my place and we could talk. I got questions, and them bears—well, they do have a spirit, but they ain't much help with my questions."

He was asking for a pastoral visit?

"Well, sure. I could do that."

Speedy looked like he had just dropped a large weight onto the ground.

"Okay, then. I'll mail you a map. You couldn't find me without a map. Hey, even I have trouble finding home sometimes."

"Sure," Jake replied. "I would like a chance to talk. Anytime."

"That's righteous. Any man who preaches to a cat . . . well, that's a righteous man, you know?"

Jake didn't know, but for today, he took Speedy at his word.

Jake moved quietly in the kitchen. After years of apartment living, he kept his morning footfalls soft and the clatter of cups and coffeepots to a minimum. He knew he did not need to worry now—since Petey nearly always woke with him—but old habits and tendencies, deeply ingrained, are hard to ignore.

He stood at the kitchen sink, finishing his first cup of coffee, and saw headlights swing into the church parking lot.

"Maybe they're lost or turning around," Jake said aloud, as if Petey had been interested, which apparently he wasn't, being occupied by the half-filled bowl of kibbles at his feeding station. Jake had learned that Petey did not like his canned food early in the day. That meal should be served at lunch. Kibbles were enough for a morning snack.

But the car in the lot did not turn around or back out. The lights came closer to the church, the car stopped, the lights switched off. It was a truck, not a car. And the lumbering form that exited looked familiar. As it came closer to the light above the steps, Jake recognized his very early morning visitor.

"Jimbo Bennett," Jake said with some cheer as he opened the door. "What brings you here so early? Is there a predawn elders' meeting that no one told me about?"

"If there is, I make two people who haven't heard about it."

"Come on in. Want some coffee?"

"Sure. I pulled in just to see if your light was on. If it wasn't on, I wasn't going to stop. But I'm headed out to do a little fishing. No work today. One of the hydraulic lines on the drill unit we use busted yesterday and it won't be 'til tomorrow that we get the right part to fix it. I could have gone in and swept up the shop or something, but Lloyd—he's the owner, Lloyd Cummins—well, he said it was fine if I took off. So I've tossed my fishing poles in the truck and thought I would drown a few worms this morning. And the Missus is always saying how I don't have any men friends, so I thought I would ask if you wanted to come with."

Jimbo looked near exhausted after his dissertation. Jake had never heard him use that many words at one time before.

Jake ran through a quick mental calculation. He had never been fishing. He was pretty sure that he wouldn't like fishing. He was pretty sure that he would not like the feel of a real fish, slimy and flopping and jumping, in his hands. But he was also just as certain that this was probably a huge decision for Jimbo.

"Sure. If you have a pole for me, I'd love to go."

"Really?"

"Sure."

Petey looked up and meowed very loudly.

"You want to go, Mr. Petey?" Jimbo asked.

Petey meowed again, the same insistent tone.

"Can he?" Jimbo asked. "Maybe you don't want him to go with us."

"No. It's fine. He likes riding in a truck. Seems to like being by the river. We walk down there a lot. He sits and looks at the water. So, if you don't mind, he can go."

"Never had a cat in my truck before. Never had a pastor in my truck before. A lot of first times today."

Petey sat in the middle of the bench seat, though it was obvious he wanted the window seat instead. He complained loudly when Jake picked him up and plopped him down in the middle, moving a tackle box to make room for him.

Petey sniffed at the orange plastic box and wrinkled his nose, in obvious distress at the long-lasting odor of fish and worms and whatever else Jimbo handled when he picked up his tackle.

They drove a few miles past Big Dave's.

"There's a bend in the river here. Easy to get to. Lots of rocks for fish to hide in. Current isn't too strong. Usually a good spot."

Jimbo pulled off into the field and into the scrub grass and brush for one hundred yards or so, bouncing and rattling as they went. Even sure-footed Petey lurched back and forth a few times when the truck came upon bigger ruts.

"Right here. Shady spot, too. Should be good fishing today."

Jake accepted the pole Jimbo offered him.

"You want worms or a lure?"

Jake answered in a hurry. "A lure."

"I got a couple of Red Devils that always do well. I'll set it up for you."

"Thanks." Jake really meant it.

Jimbo showed him how to cast out, to hold the release just so and to let it go at the top of the cast, and where there might be fish beneath the silvery water.

"I'll use some fake worms. They say fish don't know the difference."

Petey climbed out of the truck with them, watched intently as Jimbo set up the rod and reels, and when Jake first cast into the water, almost made a jump after the lure.

"No, Petey. We're not playing catch. This is for fish."

Obviously disappointed, the cat sat glumly on a small rock at the river's edge.

The sun peaked above the small ridge that bordered the river valley, the water glistening red and gold.

For a long time, the only sound was the rippled water, and the occasional sounds of either Jake or Jimbo casting again, the whir of the reel and the hiss of the line and a small, indistinct splash when the lure hit the water's surface.

"Any bites?" Jimbo asked.

"I don't think so. I can sort of feel the lure move a little, but that's probably just the flow of the river."

"Probably. A fish bite is a sharp, little tug. Sometimes they hit it and spit it out. Sometimes they taste it first. That's what they say, anyhow. Never seen a fish eat, so I go by what they say on the fishing shows on TV."

"You do a lot of fishing?" Jake asked as he cast once more.

"Some. Not as much as some of the other guys. I like fish okay. I am not too crazy about chopping them up and all that. Most of the time I just toss 'em back in."

"I've heard that. Catch and release, right? The fun is the catching."

"Yep," Jimbo replied. "You know what kind of fish I really like to eat?"

"Trout?"

"Yuck. No. I really like them fish sandwiches at McDonald's. If I could catch those out here, I'd be here every day."

Jake laughed in reply.

After another longer period of silence, and after Jimbo cast out again, he spoke, his words measured.

"This is nice, isn't it? Gives you time to think. That's what I like about fishing. You don't have to pay attention all the time. Hunting, now, with a loaded gun and all—you have to be alert. Fishing, not so much."

"I have never been hunting. But I'll take your word for it."

"Yeah, I like fishing. I like sitting out here, by myself," Jimbo said. "Not that being with you is bad, Pastor Jake, but you know what I mean."

"I do."

"I can think about things out here. Like what's going to happen in the future. What we'll do when we retire. Stuff like that. Where I would want to go if I didn't have to work anymore."

"Where would you go?"

"Beats me. I like it here fine. The Missus wants to move to Florida. Or Hawaii. I don't think that would happen. Maybe Florida. I guess I could swing that for a week or two—but I'm not sure if I could move there."

Jimbo cast again. Petey flinched as he did, wanting to chase the worm.

"Where would you go, Pastor Jake? To retire."

Jake shrugged.

"Haven't thought about it. I have more than a few years until I need to answer that question."

"You pastor guys have all the luck," Jimbo said. "I know you're busy all week with sermons and meetings and visiting people and stuff like that—and everybody is happy to see you. You have a lot of connections. Us regular guys, not so much. I like the guys at work all right, and at church, but there aren't many that I would want to take fishing with me. I always feel like I'm being evaluated. Or judged. Like I'm not the smartest guy. I know that, but still."

"I don't think they're doing that, Jimbo. Not at church anyhow. Everyone seems to like you fine."

Jimbo brightened.

"Really? You think so?"

Jake could hear the insecurity in his voice.

"Sure. You're the church treasurer, right? That's a hard job. They wouldn't give that to you if they thought you couldn't handle it."

Jimbo tilted his head, considering the thought.

"I guess that's right. Maybe I'm just being . . . I don't know . . . too sensitive or something. Maybe it's because of the way I was brought up."

"How's that?"

"I was the last of four. Everyone had real good grades in school. I didn't. I couldn't seem to concentrate. So I got laughed at a lot. Funny, I don't think I ever told this to anyone before. Not even Betty."

Jake cast again.

"That's good. To talk about things. You ever want to talk, I'm here."

Jimbo stopped reeling in his plastic worm.

"Why, thanks, Pastor Jake. Thanks a lot."

———∞∞∞———

Wednesday found Jake polishing his second sermon from the book of Ephesians. Later on in that book there are problematic verses on submission and obeying and wives and husbands and slaves. Jake was pretty set on their meaning and implications, but many pastors regarded that section of Scripture as a live hand grenade. Regardless of the interpretation, somebody was bound to be a bit ruffled at the end.

Jake did not mind ruffling people when they needed ruffling, but as a realist, he knew that a few weeks into his position as a senior pastor—or only pastor—might not be the best time to start pulling the pins on theological hand grenades. *Time enough for that*, he thought. *Let me focus on the things we can all agree on first.*

The phone rang. Jake did not bother looking at the number on caller ID. He was a pastor, assigned to serve, and that meant answering the phone when it rang. It was the least he could do, rather than let calls disappear into a voice mail abyss.

"Pastor Jake Wilkerson here. How may I help you?"

Pastor Wilkerson . . . it is still hard to get used to answering that way.

"Well, Pastor Wilkerson, you could start by calling your mother more often than once a week. That's for starters."

Jake sat up straighter.

"Hello, Mother. You surprised me. You never call during the day. You always call in the evening. You say it's cheaper at night."

"Well, Mr. Smartypants, you are not the only one who is 'with it.' Your aunt said it doesn't matter when I call. They don't have evening rates anymore, with all these cellphones and crazy new gizmos. She said I can you anytime at all."

Jake winced, just a little.

"So, to what do I owe the honor of this call?"

"Jake, do not take that tone with your mother."

"I'm not. I just asked what you want."

"And I can't call just to talk to my only son? Is that so wrong now?"

"No, Mother. Not at all. It is not wrong to call. I'm happy you called. I am always happy to talk to you."

Jake's mother paused for a very long time before she responded.

"I am calling to let you know that your aunt has graciously offered to drive me from Meadville the whole way to Coudersport. That's a five-hour drive, Jakey. I offered to pay for gas, of course."

"Mother, the drive should only take three hours. I looked it up on MapQuest."

"MapQuest? That's smarter than your aunt now? Your aunt said five. She knows these things. You have to respect your elders, Jakey. She's been driving a long time."

Jake felt a small headache forming at the base of his neck, working its way up, tiny little fingers of tension clutching at him.

"Okay, Mother. Five hours."

Neither spoke for a long time.

"When were you planning to come?"

"Well, that's just it, Jakey. I would like to see your new church. Next week is just terrible, your aunt says. She has a hair appointment on Tuesday and a doctor's appointment on Friday, and I have my Lady's Circle on Thursday morning and I can't miss that, of course, and your Aunt Harriet doesn't like to drive that far on Mondays. She says there are too many trucks on the road trying to get back to work or something. So that doesn't leave us a lot of options. Saturday is out. And Sunday . . . well, of course, we cannot drive on Sunday. Other than to church, of course. And maybe to a restaurant. So, we don't have a lot of options, as you can plainly see. And the rest of the month is even worse. Next month, Harriet has a cruise planned—so it's out, of course."

"Yes, Mother, I understand."

"So we're coming tomorrow."

Jake shut his eyes. Hard. And pressed his thumb and forefinger on the bridge of his nose. He had hoped her first visit would not take place for a few months. This was early on Jake's radar. Very early.

"Okay," he replied. "Tomorrow is good. My sermon is almost done. I'll have plenty of time to spend with you."

"Well, won't that be nice," she said, though Jake did not believe she meant a word of it. "We can only stay for an hour or two. Your aunt doesn't like to drive after dark. So we'll leave at first light, get to Coudersport at noon. Is there a restaurant in Coudersport?"

"Of course there is, Mother."

"Then we can have lunch. We'll pay for our own meals, Jakey. You don't have to worry about that."

No sense in arguing about this now. Plenty of time for that . . . tomorrow.

"Sure, Mother. That sounds great. I'll expect you at the church at noon?"

"Okay, Jakey. Your aunt has one of those cellphones. So we will call when we're halfway there. Okay? So you can wait for us. Okay?"

"That would be great, Mother. Just great."

And Jake hoped that all traces of sarcasm were gone from his voice.

Jake sat still for a long time. Petey looked up from his perch on the windowsill. He jumped off the sill, hurried to the desk, and jumped up into Jake's lap. He started to knead his paws against Jake's thigh, purring loudly.

"Thanks, Petey. Thanks for understanding."

Petey meowed in reply.

Jake looked around the room with a critical eye. *What do I have to do before she gets here? The parsonage is clean. I'll do all the dishes, of course. Make the bed. With tight corners. Sweep. Dust?*

Jake did not dust often.

I have coffee and half-and-half. I could buy donuts. Except she won't eat them. Too fattening, she will say. That is, unless she buys them for herself.

He sighed as he petted Petey's head.

What about Tassy?

A pained look came across his face. He narrowed his eyes.

Nothing I can do about that, short of driving the RV down to Big Dave's for the day.

Petey chirped loudly.

But I will have to warn her about my mother's visit. At least it gives me something else to think about. Worry about, that is.

The clock ticked slowly, the last few minutes before noon seeming to take an hour to pass. His mother had called as they passed through Warren. There was no direct route from Meadville to Coudersport—no freeway, no single route. There were many ways to make the trip, all of them involving at least three route changes.

Maybe they'll get lost, turn around, and just go home.

The thought streaked through Jake's mind and he tried not to smile when it did.

At noon, he took his cellphone and walked outside. The church was not easy to miss; it was easy to find, but he would put nothing past his aunt or his mother. At ten minutes past noon, he caught a glimpse of his aunt's maroon Buick Electra slowly coming down the road, doing all of thirty-five miles per hour.

Maybe the trip did take a full five hours, Jake thought.

The car began slowing a quarter mile away, and Jake moved closer to the road so they would know they were in the right place. It kept slowing until it reached the driveway, traveling at perhaps three miles per hour, made a wide turn into the lot, and nearly circled it until it turned completely around, facing the road again. Jake was pretty sure his aunt did not like to go in reverse, so this circuitous parking procedure negated any requirement of backing up.

The car stopped and neither woman exited for at least thirty seconds.

I would ask why they are waiting . . . but Jake thought better of it and stood between the car and the church, a wide smile affixed to his face.

His mother exited the automobile first, dragging and pulling herself upright. "I thought we would never get here. This place might as well be on the moon, Jakey, it's so far away."

Jake's mother was a much shorter, older, feminine version of Jake—more wide than tall, with perfectly coiffed mousy brown hair and sensible shoes. She wore glasses, much larger than what was currently in style, in pale brown, that rode low on her nose.

"Hello, Mother, Aunt Harriet. Did you have a nice trip?"

Aunt Harriet held on to the car as she made her way forward. "Are we still in Pennsylvania?"

"You are. Almost in the middle of the state," Jake replied, hoping he could keep his vow of maintaining a level, calm discourse today. Even though he promised himself he could do it, he knew that he really couldn't. Not for a full two hours.

"This is in the middle of nowhere, Jakey," his mother said. "When you said senior pastor, I had no idea you meant it was so far away."

Jake didn't follow her logic. *But then, I seldom do.*

"Come on in. Let me show you around."

"And you live here, too? There's no separate parsonage?"

"I told you the living quarters are attached, Mother. It's a small church."

She harrumphed quietly and followed Jake to the front door of his house.

They both remained quiet as he gave them a quick tour of the kitchen, living room, office, sanctuary, and finished up by going back through the office and into the bedroom.

Petey was sitting in the middle of the bed. Apparently he had revised his nap schedule, given the coming of the special visitors. As they came in, he yawned broadly and meowed a greeting.

"Jakey! There's a wild animal on your bed!" Jake's mother said, retreating three steps back into the hallway.

"It's not a wild animal. That's Petey. He's a cat. He sort of adopted me on my first day here."

"Jakey! There's a cat on your bed. You have to get rid of it. You'll get a disease from it. He's on your bed. Where you sleep."

Petey lowered his head and offered a lower, rumbly growl-meow-growl. That was a new sound to Jake. Petey made dozens of different sounds, but his growl-meow-growl had been kept hidden until now.

"Mother, the cat is very nice. Very tame. And he was checked out by a veterinarian in town. He has a clean bill of health."

Petey made the same growl-meow again, as if perturbed at having his pedigree and health status discussed by strangers.

"And you plan on keeping it? A cat? Remember what I said about having wild animals?"

Jake sighed. "You did say Jesus never had a dog or a cat." Jake was sorely tempted to add, "As far as we know," but refrained.

"That too. But animals are cesspools of vermin and disease," his mother replied. His aunt covered her mouth, as if warding off some manner of infectious disease.

"Well, Petey's going to stay, Mother. He and I get along very well."

Petey meowed. Proudly and loudly, Jake imagined.

Jake's mother appeared stunned. "What?"

"The cat is going to stay."

My goodness. That felt so good to say. The cat stays. Wow.

"Jakey, I'm very sorry, but no. You have to get rid of the cat. You have to listen to your mother. The Bible says children have to obey."

Jake's aunt nodded vigorously, all the while eyeing Petey with suspicion.

Jake had read ahead in Ephesians. He'd compared at least six commentaries. "Mother, it says *children* have to obey. That means when a child is in their parent's house. Then it says to *honor* them. That's different than obey. Much different."

His mother narrowed her eyes. Her shoulders appeared to tighten and tense.

"Okay, Mr. Seminary Degree. That I paid for, may I remind you. Obey. Honor. To me, they are the same thing. Right, Harriet?"

"That's right. The same thing," Harriet added, taking one more step in retreat.

"Sorry, Mother. But they are not the same."

Goodness, that does feel good. Have I ever done that before?

His mother appeared on the verge of extending the argument. But Petey meowed loudly again, this time a friendlier meow, and jumped off the bed. Both Aunt Harriet and Jake's mother retreated farther and headed to the front door.

"I'm not agreeing with you at all, Jakey. But your aunt and I are hungry. I think we want to eat now, don't we, Harriet?"

"We do."

Petey must have had the good sense to stay in the bedroom, catching the morning sun on the floor. He did not follow them to the door as Jake thought he might.

Jake shouldered the door; it still grew balky on certain days. It squealed open. The three of them exited, blinking, in the bright noon sun.

At that moment, the door to the RV hissed open and Tassy made her way outside. She had been taking long walks each day. She said the exercise felt wonderful and she could not imagine why she had not done this before.

"Well, it was because of Randolph. He hated to do anything physical. Like walking," she had told Jake.

Tassy waved to Jake, smiling broadly. "Hey, Pastor Jake. Good morning."

Jake's mother stopped. Harriet almost ran into her.

"And who is that? And what is that monstrosity there?"

Might as well see everything at once, Jake thought.

"That's Tassy. She didn't have any place to stay, and a nice couple from church are letting her use their RV until she gets on her feet. She's looking for a job."

Jake's mother turned to face her son.

"And she lives there?"

"She does."

"And you live there?" she asked, pointing at the church.

"I do." Jake wanted to add, "with a cat," but he didn't.

"Jakey, that's not right. She has to leave. This doesn't look right. Not at all. You have to get rid of her. People will talk. They'll talk, won't they, Harriet?"

"They would talk in Meadville. That's for certain."

"Well, Mother, we are not in Meadville. This is my church and the elders are fine with her there."

Jake's mother drew in a sharp breath and held it for a long moment.

"Jakey, you have changed. I don't like it one bit. Do I, Harriet?"

"I don't think you do."

"God can't use you in this church, Jakey. It's too small. And you have a cat and a young woman living next door. God can't look past those things. And I would really tell you how I feel, Jakey, but Harriet is hungry. We need to eat lunch. Then we'll talk. When we all can think clearer. Right, Harriet?"

"That's right. We're hungry now, Jakey."

∞

Jakey—or Jake—survived lunch with his mother and aunt. Almost. Barely.

No one changed their minds or opinions about Tassy, the cat, or God, for that matter, but everyone ate their fill. Jake took them to Kaytee's Family Restaurant in the small downtown area of Coudersport. Kaytee's was not the most expensive place in town, nor was it the least expensive. They featured comfort food and real waitresses, and the owner went to Jake's church. Kaytee, the owner, extended a warm greeting to Jake and his party as they entered, made a fuss after finding out that he was with his mother and his aunt, and took them to their "best" table, which, in reality, was no different than any other table in the room. Perhaps it was being closer to the window that made it better.

Jake ordered the meatloaf platter special. His mother and Aunt Harriet debated for at least fifteen minutes the merits of the meatloaf platter versus the meatloaf open-faced sandwich versus a chicken salad sandwich, including a "free" cup of soup, versus the All-American KT Burger with fries and cole-slaw. Jake had given up being interested in the discussion and afterward was not able to recall what it was that either of his two guests actually consumed.

Kaytee had brought them each a piece of apple pie for dessert—"on the house."

Jake's mother had not been impressed with the church, but she was impressed with a free dessert.

Jake drove them back to the church in their car and Aunt Harriet insisted that they leave immediately because darkness falls quickly in the late spring in central Pennsylvania. Jake knew there was no scientific basis for such a claim but was not sad to see them hurry off so soon after lunch.

He stood at the edge of the road and waved until Aunt Harriet's car slowly disappeared into the horizon. He took a deep breath, felt the tension in his shoulder slowly unwind, and turned back to his new home.

Today was the first time I stood up to her—in any way. I know it wasn't that important—owning a cat. Or living with a cat, I guess. I don't think Petey would say I "own" him. And Tassy and the small church and everything else. And you know what? It wasn't all that bad. She didn't collapse into tears. She was shocked. She would love to see Tassy and the cat disappear. But when she left it seemed like she might have actually been a bit resigned to them both.

He heard Petey howling on the other side of the door. The cat darted out when Jake shouldered it open, his eyes searching for the strangers, crying softly when he did not see anything other than Jake's old white pickup truck on the gravel of the church lot. Petey looked up at Jake and meowed loudly.

"They're gone, Petey. They went home."

Petey meowed again.

"No. They didn't like you. Or Tassy."

Petey offered his odd growl-meow in reply.

"But I told them . . . I told my mother that both of you are staying. She didn't like it. But I told her."

Petey meowed again, this time with his head tilted to the side.

"Yes, Petey. It did feel good. Really good. Healthy, almost."

Petey stretched up and put his front paws on Jake's knee. Jake picked him up and held him, sort of like a fullback holds a football. Petey meowed.

"I know. I feel good. I feel really good."

The two of them went back into the parsonage.

"And now I could really use a stiff cup of coffee."

9

The old Buick rattled and knocked as it came to a stop in the parking lot. Jake was outside, pulling weeds around the front steps of the church. One of the church members came in once a week with a large lawn tractor and cut all the grass but did not do weeding and primping. And Jake did not feel it proper of him to point out the weeds that he'd missed. Plus, he liked basic, manual labor. Weeding offered the opportunity to start a job, finish a job, and see the results of the job in short order.

Jake stood and waved to the driver, dropped the weeds he had just pulled into the large pile, and came over to offer his greetings.

"Vern, what brings you here today? On a Friday." Jake asked.

Vern clambered out of the car, fighting with the seat belt, muttering "Infernal contraption" under his breath. Once freed, he nearly tumbled out, and Jake made a move to stabilize him.

"I'm fine. I'm fine," Vern replied, all but brushing Jake away. "I have always hated this rattletrap of a car. I thought Buicks were good cars, but I'll never buy another one. General Motors, my foot."

Jake nodded.

The car is probably twenty-five years old. I think he's gotten his money's worth out of it.

Vern glared at Jake. Jake realized that this look was a permanent feature of Vern's and not to be taken seriously.

"I got food in the back for the girl. Eleanor had to get her hair done today. Why on Friday, I have no idea. Should be Saturday so it's all set for Sunday, but no, she says. Friday is her regular day and I got nothing to do all morning. So I went to Doug's and bought some food."

"You went grocery shopping?" Jake replied. There were four bags of groceries on the backseat.

"With the prices they charge, the owner should be wearing a mask and carrying a gun. Almost three dollars for a gallon of milk. That's just robbery. A young girl like Tassy can't afford that."

Jake thought he saw something in Vern's face, or his eyes, soften, but just for a moment. A very fleeting moment.

"So, Sonny, make yourself useful and carry some of this inside. She in there now?"

"I'm sure she is. Said that her stomach has been bothering her."

"Yeah, I heard. Bought some of that Eye-talian tea that's good for that. Made out of flowers—cammo something or other. Probably an old wives' tale. But it couldn't hurt, I guess."

Jake shouldered three bags, and Vern barely managed to lift the last one.

"She should be getting a job; that's what she should be doing. Can't live in the RV forever, you know. Eleanor wouldn't mind her staying, but come winter—well, she needs her own place."

"She's looking, Vern," Jake said. "I know that. Looking through the newspaper. Not much there."

"Maybe I'll ask around. People in this town owe me some favors."

"Well, Vern, that would be very kind of you."

Vern snorted.

"Just don't tell her, okay? I don't want any special thanks or nothing. Okay?"

Jake tapped at the RV door.

"Sure thing, Vern. Sure thing."

Jake discovered a hidden talent in his new feline companion: Petey loved playing fetch. Jake had been in the office, and after a particularly troubling attempt at summing up the sermon, he'd snatched the last page of the sermon, wadded it up into a ball, and tossed it at the small trash can in the corner. Of course, he'd missed, and the ball had bounced back onto the floor. Petey watched this intently from his perch on the windowsill, then took off like a rabbit as the crumpled paper ball rolled toward the bookcases. He grabbed it in his mouth, shook it once, then trotted back to Jake and proudly dropped it at his feet, staring up at him with a great sense of accomplishment. Jake threw it again, and Petey chased it again and returned it to him just as promptly. They kept the game up for several minutes, until the phone rang.

This morning, Saturday morning, Jake sat on his front steps, enjoying the bright sunshine. He took a badly dented Ping-Pong ball he'd found in one of his boxes (how it got there he had no clue, as he had not played Ping-Pong since high school) and tossed it into the soft grass beside the church. Petey tore off like a cheetah, little clumps of grass kicking up from his rear paws as his nails dug into the turf. The dented ball had enough odd, flat surfaces that Petey could get his teeth on so it made retrieving easy. A dozen times, Jake threw the ball, and even though Ping-Pong balls don't travel all that far when thrown, Petey would watch the ball leave his hand and take off like a shot, following the arc as intently as a real cheetah might watch a fleeing antelope.

By the end, Petey began to pant a little, and at the last throw, he dropped the ball a few feet out of Jake's grasp, as if to say, "I'm done chasing for now. Let's take a breather."

It was at that moment that a car pulled into the church lot. Jake thought he recognized the driver, but the sun made it difficult to see.

"Hello, Pastor Jake, Petey. Just the two people I wanted to see."

"Hi, Emma . . . Dr. Grainger."

She wore her official doctor's coat and was carrying her official veterinarian's black leather satchel. The outfit and equipment may not have been actually official, but to Jake, they looked official enough.

"I know. It's Emma. But right now, you look like a doctor."

Petey ran up to her and rubbed against her leg.

"You know they do this to sort of mark the humans they lay claim to?" she said.

"Really? I just thought he liked me when he did that."

Emma smiled. "Well, that's what *The Big Golden Book of Vet Knowledge* said. What do books know, anyhow?"

Emma looked up toward the sky.

"You fix the steeple yet?"

Jake turned to look up as well.

"No. But it is crooked. That's been confirmed. A member of the church who said he knew all about steeples installed it twenty years ago. Turned out that he didn't, and no one wanted to offend him while he was still alive by going up there and fixing his mistake."

"How's his health now?" Emma said in a furtive whisper.

"Oh, he died seven years ago. But no one has formed the right committee to fix it. Money issues. Time. Energy. Now we're the church with the crooked steeple and the cat in the congregation."

Emma bent down and picked Petey up. He appeared to enjoy Emma's attention.

"I've heard. Someone said that the newspaper might want to do a story on it. You've got the town talking about your church, Pastor Jake."

Jake hoped his expression was that of happiness or surprise or glee, but that was not how he truly felt. His shoulder twinged again, sharply this time, as if he were expending a lot of energy to keep something hidden. He was used to that feeling. And he was getting used to the twinge.

"Well, I guess there are worse things that could happen. So, what brings you out here? On a Saturday. You don't have office hours on Saturday, do you?"

"Just in the morning. Some people can't get in during the week. But I came to give Petey a s-h-o-t. I completely forgot about it when I worked on his paw. No way of knowing what sort of vaccines he had before."

At the word *vaccine*, Petey squirmed a bit. Emma held on tight.

"Can we go inside? Just in case he knows what a vaccine is?"

Jake shouldered the door open. "The fellow who built the steeple installed the door as well."

Emma gave Petey to Jake, then opened her bag. She took out a small vial and a hypodermic. "He needs a rabies shot. And a booster shot. I'm nearly certain he would have had the standard vaccinations when he was a kitten."

She filled the hypodermic. Petey obviously saw what was coming and while he meowed loudly and pitifully, he did not try to squirm away. She poked once and injected the vaccine. She quickly grabbed the other and injected it into the other hip. Again, Petey yowled loudly but did not try to claw free.

"There. Now he is up-to-date. Legal and healthy."

Jake carefully put Petey on the floor. He looked up at both of them, meowed once more, in an angry tone this time, and stalked out of the kitchen, his tail held high, obviously more than a bit peeved at both humans.

"Both spots will be a little sore for a day or two. No playing tackle football, okay?"

"You said that he probably had shots as a kitten. How could you tell?"

"Shy of running elaborate blood work—and very expensive blood work—you can't. But Petey looks like a Siberian mix. Maybe with Maine coon. I looked it up to make sure, and he's got breed characteristics for both. Thick, nonshedding coat, right color, right body structure, right face. Siberians, even mixed, are not that common—I've never had one in my practice yet. Full blooded ones are still rather rare—and expensive. Around $1,000 a cat."

Jake whistled his surprise.

"Wow. I had no idea. You can get cats for free."

"Then you're lucky, aren't you? A thousand-dollar cat picked you. Oh, yes, and the breed is said to be almost dog-like in some of its behaviors."

"I could vouch for that. We were playing fetch-the-Ping-Pong-ball when you came. He loves retrieving things."

"Funny he doesn't have a microchip, though. Expensive cats usually do. But not all of them," Emma said. Then she looked around. "Nice place. I wouldn't have imagined this from outside."

Jake nodded. "It is nice. Very comfortable. And almost stylish."

Emma narrowed her eyes. "You know, this could be a wormhole in space and time and we've been teleported into another dimension. Somewhere far away from Coudersport."

"You're a science fiction fan?"

Emma picked up the two used hypodermic needles.

"I like some of it. I'm a sucker for the *Dr. Who* reruns on PBS."

Jake nodded again.

She is easy to talk with.

"Listen, Emma . . . if you're not busy . . . or don't have other arrangements . . . how about coffee or dessert or dinner or something . . . Sunday evening?"

Emma's eyebrows rose in surprise.

"This Sunday? Can you do that on a Sunday?"

"I'm . . . I'm pretty sure. The church hasn't had Sunday evening services for a decade. So, sure. I can go out on a Sunday evening."

Emma shrugged.

"Sure. I have nothing on my calendar. How about 6:00? Closing time in Coudersport on Sunday evenings is even earlier than during the week."

"Sure. That would be great. I'll see you then."

From the living room came the low, rumbling yowl from Petey, as if saying, "Good riddance."

"And tell Petey I'm sorry for the shots," Emma said as she walked out.

I do smell lilacs. Must be her soap. Or disinfectant. Or something.

The two elders, Bobby Richard and Rudolph Keilback, stood in the back of the church as the service started—the official ushers of the day. Ushers in a small church did not have many functions. They handed out bulletins that listed the hymn numbers, the sermon title and Scripture reference, the upcoming meetings, the year-to-date finances, and the weekly attendance figures.

Rudolph fanned himself with his stack of bulletins. The organist started to play the first hymn and most everyone who regularly attended were in their seats.

"You read this yet?" Bobby asked, his voice low and elderlike.

"Nope. Not yet."

"You see the attendance number?"

"Nope."

"Last Sunday, we were up twenty more than last year. That's as high as we been in . . . well . . . in years."

Rudolph wiped at his face with his other hand. The weather carried only a hint of warmth, and already, Rudolph was sweating. Summer and high temperatures were not kind to big men like Elder Keilback.

"I guess we made the right decision when we hired Pastor Jake."

"Think we did, too," Bobby added with a smile.

"The cat don't hurt, either. Got people talking."

Bobby craned his head.

"Is he here yet? Didn't see him come in."

"Yep. He's up there, sitting on his normal chair. Just waiting."

"Don't that beat all," Bobby replied.

"We made a good call on letting the cat stay, too."

"That we did, Brother Keilback. That we did."

"I guess it shouldn't matter why the new people are here, just that they're here is a good thing."

Jake pulled into the drive and hurried out of his car. Emma called out from the second-story porch. "I'll be right down, Jake. Give me just a minute."

Jake leaned against his truck. He had washed it that after-noon—getting it mostly clean. He'd even vacuumed the interior, though it was already fairly clean. He was not one of those people who use their vehicle as a mobile recycling bin. The mats, however, had needed the cleaning, and he'd even taken Windex to the truck's windows—inside and out.

Emma came out in a rush and tossed a white sweater around her shoulders. She wore a simple blue blouse and jeans, but they looked nearly elegant to Jake.

The lilac smell is stronger now. Must be the soap. I like it.

Both settled in the truck.

"Where to?" Jake asked. "You have me at a disadvantage. I only know how to get from the church to Doug's Foods. And the movie theater. And maybe to Kaytee's."

"Oh, yes. Kaytee's. I heard about your mom and aunt visiting."

"Does anything happen in town that everyone doesn't know about the next day?"

"Nope. And remember that in Coudersport, you're almost a celebrity."

"What? A celebrity? Get out," Jake replied, surprised.

"No. Really. You'll be one of the better-known people in town. Already are, kind of. Me too. A sort-of celebrity. Not as much as you. I'm a doctor—of animals—so I'm a little lower than a real doctor. I'm a woman—makes the doctor thing unusual. I'm from here, so I have known many of the people in town all my life. I meet lots of people during the course of a week. It all adds up. We may not be the Hollywood sort of celebrities, but there's no escaping it. Like I said, don't do any-thing foolish here. They'll find you out."

Jake stopped at the stop sign at the end of the block.

Emma finally snapped her seat belt closed. "Are you hungry? Like let's-eat-right-now sort of hungry?"

Jake looked both ways and shrugged. "Not so much. A little. I don't know. After preaching, I stay sort of a little jangled the rest of the day. At home, I usually wind up just picking at things. Chips. Pickles. Popsicles. I don't know."

"You want to drive a little? Around town? I can point out the famous spots. And where people live. We have enough light for an hour's tour. Then, if we're hungry, we can split a milkshake at the malt shop."

"Really? You have a malt shop in Coudersport?"

"Of course not," laughed Emma. "Back in the fifties, we did—I think. Now we have McDonald's. Not the same, but it's what we have."

Jake liked being in the truck with Emma. He liked how easy she was to talk with. He liked that she laughed easily. That she was smart and witty. He recalled his time with Barbara Ann. It was so different. Even though he knew he shouldn't compare the two, and of course not this early, because he didn't really know if this was the start of a relationship or not (though he hoped it was), being with Emma felt better. Easier.

"Sure. Let's do the Coudersport tour. I'm up for that."

For the next hour, Jake and Emma drove slowly through town, and out and back again. She showed him the high school and the elementary school, and the homes of nearly all of his elder board, the organist, and the Sunday school superintendent. She showed him where she grew up and a good place to fish. She gave him the pros and cons of the supermarkets in town and told him which doctor—the human kind—she considered to be the best. "I'm still auditioning dentists. Haven't settled on one yet. But I inherited good teeth, so I don't have to rush."

She does have good teeth. Very nice smile.

When darkness came, Emma suggested that a trip to McDonald's might just be the proper end to an evening of cruising the town. "It's what we did in high school," she declared.

They both ordered Big Mac meals and sat inside the very bright restaurant and used too much ketchup on their fries. Jake ordered a small vanilla shake, Emma chose chocolate. They drank them as he drove back to her house. He pulled into the driveway.

He was about to turn the truck off.

"Leave it on, Jake. I'm going to run in and this way no one will see what I'm about to do. The porch light is too bright and I have curious neighbors." She held the shake in her right hand, undid her seat belt, and leaned toward him, closer and closer. Then she brushed his lips, cold from the vanilla shake, with hers, cold from chocolate. More than a brush, it was closer than that, and a little longer. It was a nearly chaste, chilly, longish peck, but earnest at the same time.

"I had a ball, Pastor Jake. We should do this again sometime."

He was still blinking as she slipped out and the bright dome light of the cab came on.

"See, too much light."

All he could say before she closed the door to the truck was, "Thanks. I had a great time, too." And she waved and disappeared up the stairs and into the darkness.

Jake arrived home, after dark, and Petey sat in the middle of the kitchen floor, almost at attention, and meowed loudly when he came in, obviously upset at being left alone. His stare could be deadly.

"Hey, Petey, cut me some slack, would you?" Jake said as he tossed his truck keys in the blue porcelain bowl on the counter. "I was with Dr. Emma. You know, Winston's mom."

Petey narrowed his eyes.

She is NOT his mother. They cohabitate. Please. I am not stupid like that dog is. And tell her to give him a bath more often. Dogs are simply horrid at keeping themselves clean.

Jake walked over to his new coffeepot/machine, which used little plastic pods to whoosh out a single cup of coffee. Petey watched him as he stored away an armful of different boxes filled with pods and fussed with the machine, pressing buttons, seemingly at random.

He makes a big to-do about each cup—so he must like it. Still smells like an old raccoon, if you ask me.

Jake poured half-and-half into the freshly brewed cup of coffee and opened the kitchen door.

"You want to come out for a while? Get a breath of fresh air?"

He sounds downright chipper this evening. Why is that? And isn't chipper *an odd word? I wonder where that comes from.*

Jake took his usual spot on one of the lawn chairs. Petey sniffed about for a while, then joined him in the other lawn chair. Jake had found a round, metal table at a garage sale that he had placed between the chairs. That's where he put his coffee cup. The breeze carried the smell to Petey's face and the cat wrinkled his nose in reaction.

"We went for a long ride around town. We had fun. She is really easy to talk to—and funny."

Petey meowed in reply, a cautious meow.

"I know she is not a churchgoer. But we're talking about it."

Petey chirped.

"Well . . . we will talk about it. I bet she's open to discuss it."

Petey waited a moment, then replied with a low, rumbling meow.

"She's nice, Petey. She listens to me. And it's not serious. We're friends. That's all."

Petey looked the other way, thinking he heard movement by the back door.

"Well . . . "

Petey spun around and chirped again.

"She did kiss me goodnight. That was different."

Petey sat up straighter. He stared harder.

"Just an innocent peck. That's all. Between friends."

Petey narrowed his eyes. Even though it was dark, he was sure Jake could see his reaction.

"I'll be careful, Petey. I know. I know. I'll be careful."

10

Tassy put on her good sneakers and started to walk. This time, toward town.

Pastor Jake said he checked the odometer of the truck and from the church to McDonald's was only four miles. That's not so far. And he said Kaytee's was only a few blocks farther. He said their food was better. And not expensive at all. I'll see how long four miles actually is.

Staying inside the RV all day was making her a little claustrophobic. Tassy cleaned every morning, washed every dirty dish, made the bed, did not allow any clutter to form anywhere, but doing all of that did not take long. She read the employment ads in the paper and, so far, had found nothing she was qualified to do. And there were very few employment ads to begin with. A couple of them she asked Jake about—selling from home, working from home, and the like—and he had assured her that all of them were simply scams and would cost her money to sign up.

So, today she decided to wear her relatively good clothes, with sneakers for walking, and head into town to put in applications at whatever business would take them. She knew that Jake would drive her there, or she could call Vern or Eleanor, but she wanted to do this on her own. And Pastor Jake said a brisk walk is at least three to four miles per hour. So it would only take her an hour to get there. If she was really tired, she could always head back to Vern and Eleanor's house to arrange a ride back to the RV.

Four miles did not prove to be an insurmountable distance. Almost before she knew it, she was down the street from the McDonald's. She had eaten breakfast, a couple of crackers and some ginger ale, and the walk seemed to settle her stomach, which remained a little sensitive and a little nervous. She thought a single cheeseburger might be okay, with a Sprite or something clear. Maybe even a cup of hot tea. In the past few weeks, she had developed a fondness for tea laced with honey.

She ordered her food and looked around. There were no empty single seats or empty tables. The restaurant wasn't large and it was a bit too cool to try and sit outside. So Tassy held the bag in her hand, her cup of tea in the other, and waited off to the side.

Someone will get up soon.

In the corner, a tallish blonde woman, older than Tassy but not really old, motioned her over.

"You can sit here. No sense in waiting. Your food will get cold."

Tassy smiled. "You sure? I don't want to intrude."

"No. I'm by myself. It's fine. I'm Emma," she said, and gestured for Tassy to sit.

"And I'm Tassy."

Emma offered the most puzzled look.

"Tassy from Pastor Jake's church?"

Tassy removed the single cheeseburger and laid it on a napkin.

"I am. Well, I live right next to it. In Vern's big RV. Until I find a job. They're letting me stay for a while. They're nice people. Vern and Eleanor. And Pastor Jake, too."

Emma shook her head in what looked like amazement.

"And I'm Emma Grainger. The veterinarian. I fixed Petey's paw when Pastor Jake first showed up in town."

Tassy could not help from grinning. She leaned in closer and whispered. "He took you out on a date last night."

Emma whispered back. "I know. I was there."

Then they both giggled.

"Small world, isn't it?" Tassy said.

"Well, Tassy, I don't know how small the world is—but Coudersport is a very small town."

Tassy wondered if Emma would ask her if Pastor Jake said anything about their "date," but she didn't.

Maybe old people don't care as much.

"Did Pastor Jake bring you?" Emma asked, looking out into the parking lot, scanning for Jake's white pickup.

Tassy chewed slowly, making sure her stomach was ready for the food.

"No. He would have if I asked. But it's not a bad walk. Good exercise."

"Walk four miles for a McDonald's burger? You must be hungry," Emma said.

"You know, I'm not. But I want to look for a job. I thought I might put in applications around town. Maybe here, too."

Emma took a drink and appeared to be thinking something important. Tassy couldn't tell for sure. Older people often puzzled her. Like Vern, who always looked angry but was actually very nice.

"Tassy, what kind of job are you looking for?"

"Anything, I guess. I don't have much experience. I was in school before. The Community College of Philadelphia. I was just taking general studies. But now I'm looking for any sort of job. I don't mind working hard."

"Do you like animals?" Emma asked.

"I do," she replied, brightening. "I love Petey. He comes to visit in the morning if I don't feel good. He seems to want to take care of me."

"And you don't mind cleaning? Sweeping and mopping and that sort of thing?"

"No. I don't. I'm sort of a neat person. I like things tidy."

Emma looked away for a long moment. Her face grew serious.

"Would you consider working in my practice?"

"In a vet's office? That would be great. You mean it? What would I do?"

"I could use someone to do the cleaning, because I don't have the energy to do it at the end of a long day. Keep the supply cabinet up-to-date. Maybe answer the phone when I'm with a patient. Fill out patient charts. Send vaccination reminders. It's all on the computer. I could offer four days a week. I can't pay a lot, but it would be more than you would make at McDonald's. And it would all be daylight hours."

"Could I do all that? Is your phone system complicated?"

"Just two lines with one button each."

"I could do that. I could. I would love to do that. And be around animals all day. Wow. That would be super."

"Well, why don't we finish our lunch, then I'll take you over and we can talk about hours and pay and all of it. Does that sound good?"

"Doctor Grainger, it sounds like a miracle. It truly does."

Jake tapped at Tassy's door. She did not answer.

"Must be out for a walk, Petey. Did you see where she went?"

Petey chirped a reply and looked up at Jake with a quizzical look.

"Well . . . you want to walk by the river?"

Petey remained sitting, his tail wrapped around his rear paws. Usually whenever Jake said "walk," Petey was up and circling his legs, ready and excited to be walking anywhere.

"What about that way?" Jake asked, pointing to the west. The woods grew thick just past the church. Jake had yet to explore that part of the neighborhood. Petey just sat.

"You want to go for a ride?"

With that Petey jumped and ran toward Jake's truck, turning every few feet, looking back at Jake, making sure he was following.

"Okay, then. A ride. There's no one on the church's sick/must-visit list. I guess a ride would be okay. It gives me time to think, right, Petey? Being in charge of a church brings up a lot of things that I never had to deal with before."

Petey meowed loudly and scratched at the door on his side of the truck. Jake opened it and Petey hopped up, assuming his standard position. Jake drove toward town and then through town, waving at a few people he passed.

A celebrity. That's what she called me.

After the fourth honk and wave, Jake smiled to himself.

Maybe I am . . . a little.

He drove east until the town receded and only road and woods and fields remained.

Of course, they may be waving at Petey, and not me.

He drove on, not fast, watching the scenery roll past. North central Pennsylvania offered wonderful, natural vistas. Once outside of town, the landscape became nearly uninhabited. He drove east on Route 6 until he reached Denton Hills State

Park. He pulled into the large parking lot and looked up at the labyrinth of ski trails, now covered in green.

Petey meowed.

"We're not stopping. Just turning around, that's all. I could come here next winter. I could take up skiing."

Petey meowed loudly.

"No? You don't think I would be any good at it?"

He meowed again, as if to say, "No, you wouldn't be."

"Okay. We'll head back."

Midway between the empty ski runs and Coudersport, Jake saw a canted sign, the sun catching it just so, almost illuminating it, the sign almost lost in the foliage, covered with a tangle of vines. In a week or so, the sign would be hidden beneath the full greening of summer vegetation.

"Coudersport Ice Mine. Nature's Amazing Curiosity."

He pulled to the side of the road and stared at it.

"Petey, what's an ice mine?"

Petey chirped.

"Don't know, do you?"

Jake knew that farmers cut ice from lakes and rivers and stored the ice blocks under straw for the summer. But there were no large bodies of water nearby, from what Jake could see. A small stream lay on the other side of the highway, but that could not produce enough ice to furnish an ice mine, or to call it an ice mine.

He thought about taking a picture of it, but didn't have his good camera with him and his phone's camera would not do it justice. He looked around and tried to make himself remember the location, though much of the road looked like every other part of the road.

"Who would I ask about an old ice mine?"

Petey looked at him and chirped.

"Well, Emma might know. I could try."

He looked back to the road. There wasn't a car to be seen. He pulled out and headed back to Coudersport.

Ice mine? Ice mine?

He pulled into a service station.

"I need gas, Petey, okay?"

Petey sat, implacable, silent, and simply looked around at the other cars.

Jake went inside to pay.

"Have you ever heard of an ice mine around here?" he asked the clerk. "I saw an old sign along the road back a ways."

"The Coudersport Ice Mine? Sure. The road there is Ice Mine Road. Used to be famous, I guess. And aren't you that new pastor in town? The one with the cat? The cat that comes to church?"

"Jake Wilkerson," he said, and held out his hand. "The cat's waiting for me in the truck. Petey."

"Bailey Stewart. Don't go to your church, but I heard people talking about it. Mind if I come out and say hello to Petey? I'm more of a dog person, but cats are all right."

He followed Jake out to the truck. Jake opened the door on the passenger side.

"That's Petey."

"That's a pretty cat," Bailey said. "Can I pet him?"

"Sure. I guess. He doesn't get ruffled by much."

Bailey reached and stroked the top of Petey's head. Petey meowed softly in response.

"That's a handsome cat. Beautiful coat. And he likes going for rides?"

"Seems to," Jake said. "But what about the Ice Mine?"

Bailey stood there petting Petey. "Oh, yeah. It was the darndest thing. Been closed for, I don't know, years now. People say way back when, Indians had found a silver mine in these parts. That's the story. Some early settler or farmer thought he knew where it was and dug this mineshaft to get at the silver. Never found a trace of it. Wound up with a big hole in the ground. What happened was the mineshaft would be clear of ice all winter. But come spring and summer, giant icicles would form all along the roof. Like it didn't know what season it was—or like a hole opened onto the other side of the world or something. For a long time, they used to charge a quarter to go inside. But everybody is playing video games now, and hardly anyone came anymore, so they closed it down. The mine is just down this road, maybe ten miles."

"Ice in the summer—and not in the winter?" Jake said. "That doesn't make sense."

"Some professor from Penn State or somewhere came to look at it. Somehow the water in the rocks freezes during the winter, he said, and traps cold air in the rocks. When spring comes, the cold air gets loose and starts to freeze what water is dripping. He said it made sense. And he was a doctor of something or other."

Jake thanked him for the information.

"Say, there, Pastor. What time is your church? Maybe I'll take a Sunday and come see the cat. Would that be okay? Just to visit?"

"Sure," Jake said. "We would love to have you visit. Service is at 11:00. Petey would like to see you there as well."

"Okay, then. Maybe I'll see you some Sunday, then. Bye, Petey."

Petey looked at him and meowed a farewell.

"Don't that beat all?" Bailey said.

Jake headed back to town.

Freezing in the summer, empty in the winter. The exact opposite of how things should be. And there's always some logical explanation for those curious quirks of nature. Sounds like me—sort of. Full of

*faith when it didn't matter and now that I should have faith . . . I
don't, really. Icicles in the summer. Paradoxical, isn't it?*

The sun had turned velvet purple as Jake pulled into the
church parking lot.

Quite the paradox.

Jake stopped in at Kaytee's for a tuna fish salad sandwich.
He liked tuna fish salad, but every time he tried to make it at
home, it never tasted just right.

*Easier—and better—to get it at a restaurant. They must use
special ingredients.*

Petey was at home this noon, so Jake had the luxury of a
slow lunch, complete with coffee and pie afterward. He ate too
many meals standing up in his kitchen.

The sandwich was great, the coffee was hearty, and the
blackberry pie was more than delicious. He ate with deliberateness, slowly.

A man came and waved. His face was familiar—probably
attended the church—but Jake could not put a name with the
face.

"Dan Rummel, Pastor. I've been at your church. Once, any-
ways, since you've been here. Not a regular church person, I
admit. I hope that's okay. I hope it's okay that you can be seen
talking to a non-churchgoer in a public place."

Jake waved him to sit down.

"Of course we can talk. When a pastor can't talk to a person
who doesn't go to church, well, that would be a sad day."

"Good. Thanks. Like I said, I'm Dan. Dan Rummel. I run
Honest Dan's Used Kar Emporium on Sixth. That's *car* spelled
with a K. People stop and tell me its spelled wrong."

"Do they really?"

"Well . . . no. Not yet. But they might. I've seen you drive by a few times. You've got a white pickup, right? A '87 F-150, right?"

" '86."

"Honest mistake. Not much difference between those two model years. You think of upgrading to a newer vehicle? I've got a couple of great late model truck deals just waiting for you."

Jake shook his head. "Not right now, Dan. The old truck is running fine. Maybe before winter. We'll see."

Dan pulled out a card from the breast pocket of his yellow sport coat.

"See, it's a magnet, too. You can put it on your refrigerator to hold shopping lists or pictures of the kids. Oh, wait, you're not married, right? Someone said that."

"No. Still single."

"Footloose and fancy-free. That's the way to be. Although for a pastor there may be a different definition of footloose and fancy-free, am I right?"

"I think you are correct. For me, anyhow."

Dan suddenly grew serious. The grin left his face. He pulled his chair closer to the table. Jake was glad he had finished his pie. If not, he would have faced the dilemma of eating in front of someone or not eating and waiting until they left.

"I've got a question, Pastor. You mind if I call you 'Pastor'? You're not exactly *my* pastor, but then again, you are *a* pastor, so the title should still be good, right?"

" 'Pastor' is fine. Whatever you're comfortable with, really."

"Okay. I have a church sort of question. Been bugging me for years."

"Go ahead," Jake said, as he tried to put a studious, serious look on his face.

"So, when I was a kid, the family went to a loud church—lots of arm waving and shouting. Nothing wrong with it, I suppose. Baptized when I was ten. Like I really knew what I was doing at that age—sure. But here's the problem. Since getting out of high school, I don't go to church all that much. Couple of times a year. But I was baptized. So that should be enough, right? Do I still have to go to church? Should I feel guilty about not going? Because I really do, and I don't like feeling guilty."

Jake waited to respond.

"The Bible does say that we should not give up on gathering together."

"Does it give the number of times a year we have to do it?" Dan asked.

Jake had encountered such questions before.

"The Bible doesn't give you a calendar or a checklist of things you must accomplish. It does say that we need to be in fellowship, Dan. That's important."

Dan appeared to grow even more serious.

"But what happens if I stop having faith? Does my baptism make up for that? Because I can't say I believe much about religion anymore."

Jake drew in a breath.

"Dan, you need to have faith. Without it, there is no hope, no salvation."

I am such a hypocrite. I'm telling him what someone should be telling me. No faith means no hope.

"You sure about that, Pastor? Really sure?"

I should tell him the truth. But I can't.

"I am."

"Do you let people in church who don't believe? Isn't there some sort of test these days?"

"No tests, Dan."

"So it's okay to have doubts? You sure about that, Pastor?"

"Yes. I am sure, Dan. Tell you what. You think about it. And come see me in a week or so. Call me. We can meet here. Or I can come to the lot and look at the trucks you have."

"Really? You want to look at the inventory? Okay, then. I'll think about it. And you have to promise me that you'll think about a new truck. Okay?"

"Dan, we have a deal."

Petey growled and stared at the door. Jake came out from his office. "Did someone knock?"

Petey meowed and stared at the kitchen door. This time, Jake did hear it. A soft rapping.

"Tassy," he said as he opened the door. "How are you today?"

She had her arms folded across her chest. The skies had been cloudy and gray since morning and a wind came down from New York, almost cold and biting. Tassy wore a black, hooded sweatshirt. Her nose was a little red.

"Come on in. Do you want some tea?"

She bent down, petted Petey, then picked him up and he began to purr loudly.

"No. Not today. I've had some. But I need to ask a favor."

"Sure. I'll help if I can."

"I need to buy a bicycle."

"A bike?"

"I need to be able to get to work."

"Tassy, I could take you. What about when it rains . . . wait, did you say you need to get to work? Did you find a job?"

Her face nearly disappeared behind her grin.

"I did. Or it found me, sort of. Emma—your Emma, the lady veterinarian—hired me to help clean and answer phones and stuff. It's only four days a week, but I can save up and maybe find a place of my own and a car and stuff. But I need a bike right now. It takes too long to walk to town from here."

"Emma . . . Dr. Grainger hired you?"

"I was waiting for a table at McDonald's and she invited me to sit with her, and we introduced ourselves and talked and she knew who I was, and I said I was looking for a job and she said she needed help with cleaning stuff, so we talked and now I have a job starting Monday morning. That's like a miracle, isn't it, Pastor Jake? A little miracle. Not like being cured of cancer or anything. But still."

"I guess it is, Tassy." *And why does the word* miracle *sound so hollow and false to me? It is the truth, right? Or it could be, I guess. A little miracle. Just not my miracle.*

"So I thought I could buy a used bike. Do they have, like, a resale shop in Coudersport?"

Jake squinched up his face.

"I . . . I don't think they do. But it's Friday. Most garage sales start today. There's always someone selling a used bike. We could go look."

"Can we? Do you have time? That would be super."

"Tassy, I can make time."

Petey stood by the truck's passenger side door and hopped up when Jake opened it. He took his normal position on the seat and then stared at Tassy as she attempted to enter, as if wondering where she was planning on sitting.

"Petey, move to the middle. Tassy has to sit down."

Petey meow-growled, one of his doglike behaviors, and reluctantly gave ground, edging over only a few inches to make way for Tassy.

Before Jake started the truck, he pulled Petey more toward the middle.

"It won't kill you to give up your spot, Petey. Be a gentleman, okay?"

Petey meowed loudly, in protest, but settled himself in the center of the bench seat, obviously unhappy at being usurped from his rightful seating choice.

They drove through downtown and headed off into the residential area. On the first block they saw two garage sales with cardboard signs and streamers announcing the sale. Jake slowly cruised past, waved at the people sitting in folding lawn chairs, looking for a bike in the assemblage of stuff displayed on the driveways.

"No bikes here," he said after looking at both sales. "We'll keep driving. I'm sure there'll be one."

Two blocks over, there was a giant sheet of cardboard with the badly drawn words BIG HUGE GARAGE SALE written with a fading black marker hung at an angle on a telephone pole.

"This looks promising," Jake said, and pulled to the curb. In the shade of the garage stood a tangle of used bikes. Tassy got out, excited, and Petey followed her, meowing the whole way.

Someone called out, "Hey! There's Petey!"

A woman in a very snug Coudersport Falcons sweatshirt bent down to the cat. "Aren't you the sweetest thing ever? I just love it when I see you in church. You're just so pretty."

She looked up to Jake. "I'm Millie LeGran. We come to church, on and off. Sort of mostly off, 'cause my husband says Sunday is the only day he gets to sleep in. But I've been coming since I heard about the cat. Really. He's such a cutie."

Petey sat back on his haunches, apparently drinking in the affection like a thirsty man.

"Well, that's good," Jake replied, trying to be sincere.

I am sincere. Aren't I? They're coming. Fellowship. Hear the word. What more could I ask?

"Do you have any bikes for sale? Tassy—you know, the young girl living in Vern's RV— is looking for one."

"I do. I do have bikes. When all five kids are grown and gone, they leave a lot of stuff behind. Like a dozen bikes of different sizes. I've been saving them, thinking that they'll come back and get them, but Bud says they're never coming back for an old bike, so I should just sell them along with all their other junk. He's not very sentimental, my Bud. So, they're all for sale. Tassy, what kind of bike do you want? A red one? The blue one is nice. I think this one has different speeds on it or something. Try it out. I had Bud pump up all the tires this week."

Tassy pulled out a blue one with gears, a girl's bike, that seemed to be her size. She climbed on top and road it down the driveway and began pedaling as she got to the street.

"I got helmets to go with that, too, Pastor Jake."

Petey watched Tassy ride away and meowed loudly. He ran to the end of the driveway, watching her. He called out again, a very loud meow this time, the loudest Jake had heard yet.

He didn't think Tassy heard but she turned around and pedaled back, coasting into the driveway. Petey ran and sniffed at her and then sniffed at the bike.

"What do you think? Does it ride good?"

"It does. Real nice. Fits me perfectly. This will be great."

Tassy got off the bike, put out the kickstand, and stepped back.

"How much?"

Millie sighed.

"I was going to ask $20 for each bike—and then, you know, haggle some. Bud said they're worth more, but this is a garage sale. But since you're with Pastor Jake and Petey . . . tell you what—I'll make this a donation to the church. Can I do that, Pastor Jake? I don't really care about the money. I just want to get rid of things. Just take it. And take one of these helmets. Try 'em on. Find one that fits. Okay?"

Tassy smiled like a child on Christmas morning.

"You mean it? This is so nice of you. But I should pay you something for this."

"Tell you what: you put a couple of extra dollars in the collection plate next Sunday and we'll call it even."

She picked Petey up.

"Especially since you brought Mr. Petey with you. I'm glad I had a chance to meet him personally. He's as nice as I thought he would be."

Jake could have sworn Petey's next meow smacked of smugness, as did his wincing expression as Mrs. LeGran gave him an extra special, long hug of farewell.

11

Emma, this is Jake. I don't want you to think that I do everything at the last minute—because I don't. Normally, I'm much more organized and scripted. I was supposed to join our Woman's Guild and Assistance Society meeting tonight, which has been cancelled since both chairwomen have come down with something and neither wanted the committee to meet without them. So I have the evening free. Rather than the two of us eating alone, would you like to share a table at Kaytee's?"

Emma, at that specific moment, was holding a frozen lasagna dinner that promised great taste with "only 375 delicious calories!"

"I would love to," she said as she stuffed the box back into the already overpacked freezer. "What time? And will this be formal?"

"Yes. I am wearing tails. And would 6:00 be too late? Or early?"

"6:00 is great. See you there."

Petey was staring at Jake during the entire conversation.

"Hey, Petey. It's just for dinner. No milkshake kisses after this meal, since we're driving separately."

Petey shut his eyes in response, as if trying not to think of what a milkshake kiss might be.

"I'll be home early."

⸺✳⸺

Jake walked into the restaurant and saw Emma waving from a booth in the far corner.

"Hey."

"Hey, yourself. I bet the rest of the committee was disappointed that they wouldn't have you all to themselves."

Jake's face showed his total puzzlement.

"Jake, you can't be serious. You're a single fellow, reasonably attractive, and the talk of the religious circuit around here. Or the society circuit—at least as much as anything in Coudersport could be considered 'society.' Don't you think that the ladies-in-waiting would have wanted to have the meeting—regardless of the lack of leadership?"

"You think so?" Jake seemed both oblivious and surprised.

"Yes, really," Emma said, shaking her head in mock amazement at Jake's naiveté. "I thought pastors had to be perceptive."

"I am perceptive. Sort of. Maybe. Aren't I?"

"No, Jake, you're not. But that in itself is charming. It's why the ladies of the Women's Guild love you and are so disappointed."

A waitress came up to the table.

"Hey, Pastor Jake. Nice to see you tonight. How are you? How's Petey?" She turned her head toward Emma and added, dryly, "Dr. Grainger."

Jake saw something in Emma's eyes, and in the waitress's, but wasn't totally sure of what it was, except it made him a little uncomfortable.

"I'm fine. Petey is fine. And how are you, MaryBeth?"

Jake could have cheated and looked at her nametag, but MaryBeth went to his church and was the cousin or the niece or the next-door neighbor of the owner of Kaytee's.

"I'm fine, Pastor Jake. Thanks for asking. Since there's always a crowd around you on Sundays, I just wanted to tell you how happy I am that you came to our church. I love to hear you talk. And you make so much sense. And you're not old. And I really, really love little Petey."

"Why, thank you, MaryBeth. I'll be sure to tell Petey. He will be happy to hear it."

MaryBeth giggled in reply.

"You guys know what you want to order? Pastor Jake?"

Jake looked at Emma, who offered the barest hint of a shrug and an arched eyebrow.

Jake wasn't sure what that meant. He paused, then ordered. "The deluxe cheeseburger. Medium is fine. Fries are fine. A diet whatever-you-have would be fine."

MaryBeth turned, finally, to Emma, "And you, Dr. Grainger?" MaryBeth's words bordered on frosty.

"I'll have exactly the same. Makes it easy, right?"

"Sure," MaryBeth said, and spun away, heading toward the kitchen.

It was Jake's turn to shrug and offer a very sheepish expression.

"I didn't start that," he said, defending himself.

"I know," Emma said. "But that's why the Ladies Auxiliary is so disappointed."

"Women's Guild."

"Whatever. Just be assured that they are."

Jake took a long drink of water. "They never taught this in seminary."

"Just like they never taught me in vet's school how to deal with a pet owner who collapsed in tears—literally collapsed on the floor—when I suggested that an eighteen-year-old, blind, arthritic, half-paralyzed dog might be ready to go. Never touched on the human aspect of a vet's job."

"It is funny. Both of us have to deal with serious people problems sometimes—and we got very little training for it."

Emma rearranged the salt and pepper shakers. "Some people are good at it. Some aren't. I don't think it's a skill you can learn. Either you have it—empathy and understanding—or you don't."

Jake looked out the window for a moment.

"Jake, what is it you're good at? Knowing what a pastor does—really does during the week—is not something I'm too knowledgeable about."

Jake appeared pleased, for once, to talk about his role as pastor.

She really is interested. In me. I think.

"You know, the funny part of church and pastors is that a lot of people think all you have to do is really know the Bible. That's important, but what's more important is making what's in there understandable to people in the pews. And that's not easy. Some of it is confusing. Some of it will remain a mystery. So . . . making the Bible understandable—and keeping the church supplied with coffee. Those are the two most important things a pastor does."

MaryBeth brought the cheeseburgers and served Jake first.

"You guys enjoy. You need anything, Pastor Jake, just whistle, okay?"

"I will."

"One more church question," Emma said. "Then we can start complaining about the weather or something."

"Shoot."

"Okay—a pastor tells Bible stories. I get that. I did spend most of my youth in youth groups and Sunday school. So I have an idea of the general layout. Here's my question: Does a pastor, or do all pastors, or whatever, do they really and truly believe in everything they preach about? Or can they have some doubts about some of it? Is that something that never happens or sometimes happens or always happens?"

Emma took a very healthy bite of her cheeseburger and chewed thoughtfully as Jake scrunched up his face in thought.

How much do I tell her? And . . . why is she asking this? It almost feels like . . . like Butler revisited. Did someone call her? Or did she call someone? But she wouldn't do that. Would she?

"I'm sure it happens. And I think every pastor encounters things he can't explain. But doubts? Maybe some do."

"Do you?"

Jake looked out the window for a moment, trying to think of the right answer.

"No. Well, no. A few. A while ago. But everyone goes through ups and downs. It was just a down stretch."

Emma appeared as if she were about to offer a follow-up question. Instead, she just took another bite of her cheeseburger.

"This is pretty good, isn't it?"

Jake nodded. And he hoped his expression did not give away his anxiety.

Tassy practiced the bike ride to her new job on the Sunday before she started. She knew Pastor Jake would have given her a ride, but she did not want to ask him for help more than necessary. The bike ride took only fifteen minutes. It took even less on the way home, since there was a long stretch that was mostly downhill.

She washed her bike the day before, too, taking time to clean each wheel spoke individually. She washed her good jeans and her sneakers that Dr. Emma said would be acceptable to wear. She woke early that Monday and was on the road at least twenty minutes before she needed to be. She did not want to be late on the first day of her first real job.

Dr. Grainger had ordered several tunic tops with Tassy's name stitched on the breast pocket. Tassy had volunteered to help pay for them when Dr. Grainger asked her size, but Dr. Grainger assured her that a good animal clinic provided uniforms for their staff.

Tassy had just sat down behind the counter in the reception area when the front door banged open and a giant Great Dane lunged and clamored into the room, eyes wide, paws nearly akimbo, with a smallish woman clutching on to the dog's leash. Dr. Grainger must have heard the commotion and came out from the first examination room.

"Dangerfield, how are you?" Dr. Grainger said as she petted the very large dog, attempting to settle him down and only being partially successful. The small woman at the end of the leash put her hands on her knees and took a deep breath.

"Mrs. Linhart, how are you?"

"Desperate. Let's just get the shots done."

Upon hearing the word *shot*, Dangerfield looked back, with some nervousness, at the human at the end of his leash, but other than the anxious look, he did not react.

"All right, Dangerfield," Dr. Grainger said with firmness. "Let's go in here and I'll give you a treat."

Dangerfield perked up at the word *treat* and followed the doctor and Mrs. Linhart into the examination room.

Tassy waited and listened. She was pretty sure he was not supposed to come in to offer help but the dog was really, really big.

After a moment, Tassy heard one high-pitched yelp. She expected a deeper bass yelp. Then another, louder this time, and the door banged open, with Dangerfield semiwild-eyed, barging for the door, and Mrs. Linhart hanging on.

"I think he wants to go home now. Send me the bill."

Dr. Grainger followed them out to the porch and called out, "I will! And good luck!"

Tassy waited behind the counter.

"Vaccine and booster. Send the bill to Ruth Linhart on Niles Hill Road. She's in the database. The one I showed you. Remember?"

"I do, Dr. Grainger. And here it is."

Dr. Grainger shook her head and said, "Why she ever bought such an unruly dog, I will never know."

"Maybe her husband likes big dogs," Tassy volunteered.

"Maybe. But he also likes twenty-five-year-old secretaries. They divorced years ago. She lives by herself. Well, almost. With Dangerfield."

Tassy printed off the invoice, addressed the envelope, answered three phone calls, met two more patients—one an older man with a large, beautiful iridescent parrot on his shoulder—all before noon. She asked if she could pet the parrot, but the man explained that the bird—named Billy—wasn't the most pleasant parrot around. "He bites. And not little nips. Like cracking a Brazil nut."

Tassy wasn't sure if she had ever eaten a Brazil nut, but imagined they had pretty thick shells.

During the first morning of work, the unpleasant feelings in Tassy's stomach seemed to have diminished, but they returned, hard and sharp, on her second day.

Even Dr. Grainger noticed.

"You look pale, Tassy. Are you feeling well?"

Tassy had anticipated the question.

"I'm okay, Dr. Grainger. Just happens once in a while. Pastor Jake said it might be the water. He said some people are just very sensitive to changes in their water, and he said that Coudersport is on well water and I'm pretty sure we didn't have well water in Philadelphia. So I usually have tea in the morning—with honey—and that helps sometimes. Not always but sometimes."

Dr. Grainger looked concerned. Tassy felt it was very kind of her to be concerned.

"I do have a guest bedroom upstairs. Actually, I have several of them. If you ever feel ill, you can take a break and lie down for a few minutes."

"That's kind of you, Dr. Grainger. But I'll be all right. It passes."

⁊⁊⁊

The Church of the Open Door often lived up to its name and left the doors open during the service. Never a wealthy congregation—far from it, really—air conditioning was a luxury beyond their limited reach. Windows were opened when the weather grew hot. The quartet of ceiling fans was switched on when it grew very hot. One of the fans produced an almost inaudible, shrill whir, so using them was a last resort.

Spring in Coudersport could turn warm, and on this Sunday, the elders decided to lift the large windows, propping each of them up with a one-foot stick. During the summer, a basket in a far corner at the back of the church held an assembly of sticks of various sizes, all painted white. One-foot sticks were for warm days. Two-foot sticks were for slightly hotter days. Three-foot sticks were used only when a heat wave gripped the area.

Even Petey seemed affected by the heat. Normally, he remained in a seated position the entire sermon. This time he lay down, still paying attention.

The elders had placed the church's entire supply of hand fans in the pew racks. Some of them dated back twenty years, when the Jones Brothers Funeral Home was still in business. Some were simple, generic, green paddle-shaped fans. When Jake preached that morning, it was like gazing out on a field of corn dappled by a stiff breeze.

At least it is helping keep the air moving.

The elders informed Jake that when it got too warm, the pastor could preach without a suit coat. When it got extra warm, ties could be undone and top collar buttons unbuttoned. Jake wondered how warm it would have to be to wear shorts in the pulpit.

A few degrees less than hell, I imagine, Jake thought, then scolded himself for being petty.

The energy level in the congregation felt low, even sluggish—probably because of the heat. Even so, he thought the sermon had gone over well. Not too many people appeared to be dozing.

Jake dismissed everyone with a benediction, wished them a good week, and walked to the outside door to shake hands. He noticed that Petey had as many visitors as he did. There seemed to be, as of recent Sundays, a pool of people gathering around the cat, petting him, asking how he was doing, laughing at his inability to shed his fur coat in the summer.

Not everyone said much as they made their way outside. Sometimes it was "Good preaching, Pastor," or "Liked it a lot," or "Spoke to me today, Pastor." Today, he heard, five times, "Start up an air conditioning fund," and "Do it while it's hot," and "People will give more while it's hot outside."

Jake made a mental note to bring up air conditioning for discussion at the next elder's meeting.

The church had already grown some since he had become its pastor. Some of the faces could just be people coming back to their home church after such a long absence of a senior pastor, but some were entirely new faces—people who had never come to a church, and those who had not darkened the door of one for years.

If we want to keep them, we need to make everyone feel comfortable.

And it was at that moment Jake felt most uncomfortable.

Comfortable. Like that's what I need to work on. Like the Bible needs to have an air-conditioned audience.

Jake scolded himself again.

Just who am I to be so self-righteous Mr. Empty Inside.

One of the newer attendees at church, Glenda Davis, waited until everyone else had departed or at least had left the building. Usually, since Jake had been preaching, there would be one person, or a couple, or a family, who would hang back, waiting until everyone left. That's when they would come and present their problem or ask for a prayer or lay out an improbable, or unsavory, situation they hoped a pastor could deal with and make better.

Jake's seminary training now seemed terribly light and trivial considering the small number of interpersonal counseling classes required in a four-year course of study.

Maybe Emma was right. Some people are good at it. Some aren't.

Jake obviously did not consider himself a skilled counselor or mediator or problem solver.

Good problem solvers solve their own problems first.

"Pastor Jake, I'm Glenda Davis."

"Hi. I remember you. You introduced yourself a few Sundays ago. It is so nice to have you with us."

Glenda appeared flustered, as if she hadn't imagined that any pastor would have taken the time or effort to remember her name—an occasional visitor.

By this time, Petey had grown impatient, jumped down from his chair, and slowly walked down the aisle, chirping to himself, apparently complaining to himself about the heat.

"I love that Petey is coming to church. Gives me hope, you know?"

Jake waited. He did not know.

"I like the way you tell stories. And the way you listen, Pastor Jake. You listen a lot for a preacher. In the past, all they did was talk at me. But you seem to listen real good."

"Why, thank you, Glenda. I appreciate that."

"You met my son. That means a lot to me, too."

"Your son? Was he here this morning?"

Glenda's face showed happy and sad at the same moment.

"No. But he talked to you in town a while ago."

Jake screwed up his face, puzzled.

"Speedy Davis. He said you promised to talk to him. He told me in a letter. He doesn't have a phone."

"Oh, sure. I remember. I got his map in the mail yesterday. He asked if I would come next Friday. He didn't have a return address, but I plan on going."

Glenda put her hand on Jake's forearm.

"Thank you, Pastor Jake. Sidney—or Speedy—really needs help, Pastor. He's just . . . well . . . he's lost. His father was arrested ten years ago last February. He's in prison down at LaBelle. Attempted murder. It was the alcohol that did it. Since he left, Sidney went off the deep end. Lives out in the woods all by himself. Does odd jobs now and then. He might even be growing some weed for all I know. You know—marijuana. But when his father left, it was like a light went out inside, and he's been hiding out by himself ever since. I know you don't promise miracles, but the fact that he found you means a lot. Maybe he's coming back."

Petey circled Glenda's legs in a figure eight. She bent down to pick him up, obviously used to having a cat around.

"And thank you, Petey. I bet Sidney heard about you and figured Pastor Jake was a good man. Right?"

Petey meowed in the affirmative.

"Anyhow, Pastor Jake, I just wanted to thank you for listening. And for helping my Sidney."

Sometimes, more often than not, it seemed, Jake had nothing to say that fit the moment.

Petey spoke instead, offering a long, low, rumbling meow, followed by a loud purring.

Glenda's smile indicated that a cat's purr was enough.

Emma clipped the leash on Winston, who did not to want to go for a walk.

"It's not that warm, Winston. You need the exercise."

And obviously Winston disagreed with her assessment, since once they were both on the driveway outside the house, he sat down heavily, with an audible "worf," and looked as if he had completed his required exercise by simply waddling down the stairs.

"No, Winston. Not enough. We're walking to the river. Maybe to Mitchell Park."

Winston groaned as he stood.

"It's no more than a mile. You can do a mile. Right?"

The dog snorted, not agreeing with the good doctor, not at all.

Emma walked slowly because of Winston's short legs, poor condition, and general aversion to anything remotely athletic.

Traffic in Coudersport on a Sunday remained light. The main road carried some traffic, but Emma and Winston stayed on the sidewalks and took three short breaks on their trip to the park.

Once there, she walked to the river's edge, found a nice grassy spot shaded by trees, and sat. Winston sat next to her, then rolled onto his side as if exhausted, his tongue lolling out, his eyes closed.

"Good acting, Winston. It was only twenty minutes. A dog your age should be able to run for an hour without problems."

Emma could have sworn that Winston closed his eyes even tighter, as if not wanting to hear what she just said.

"You can rest for a while. I don't mind sitting here. It's a nice day and this is a nice view."

The view featured a wide area on the yet-small river with smooth, clear water. The park was nearly empty and the flowing water produced a pleasant, calming sound.

I might as well spend some time thinking about it. Since I've been avoiding the thought all week. So here it is: I like Jake. I think he likes me.

Emma grinned at herself.

It's like I'm in ninth grade again, isn't it? I should start writing his name on the cover of my notebook.

"What do you think, Winston? You have a say in this as well. Remember Petey? The cat with the thorn in his paw? Did you like him? Think you could get along with him? Do you like Petey the cat?"

Winston responded with a snort. Emma thought it sounded dismissive, but Winston had never been a deep-thinking, intuitive dog. Some dogs were, Emma had discovered in her practice. And cats as well. Cats like Petey. If she asked Petey that same question, she would get an answer that was clear and decisive.

Some animals have a sense about things. You can tell what they're thinking. Winston, not so much. Of course, it might just be that he doesn't think at all.

She watched a duck glide down, quacking furiously as he landed, not very gracefully, on the river.

Winston is like a very young child. Sleep. Eat. Sleep. That's all he thinks about.

She stretched her legs out, kicked off her sneakers, and touched the water with her toes. Despite the warmth of the air, the water felt chilled—cold, actually.

"Winston, I know more about Jake than I should, I think. And what do I do with this information? It all has to do with faith, right? He doesn't have it. I don't think I ever had it. The big difference is that Jake probably had faith and lost it. I don't think I ever believed, and now . . . well, I guess I still don't. We both have questions. We both have doubts. That's a good reason to be together, isn't it?"

As she said the words out loud, she realized that it was a truly foolish reason to be together.

Having faith—or belief—would probably be a good thing. Maybe not having it will draw us together—both of us looking for the same thing. Maybe.

Emma reclined back, cradling her head in her arms crossed behind her, staring at the sky.

Well, he would be looking for it. Me, not so much.

"Do I tell him what I know? What Barbara Ann said about him? Do I tell him that I don't mind that 'he doesn't believe'? Would that make it easier for him?" Her face tightened in response to her own questions.

"Maybe that's it. We cancel out each other's doubts."

She closed her eyes.

That doesn't make sense either. But what do I do next? What do I do?

Jake had all but decided that he would buy a window air conditioning unit. But he would have to wait until tomorrow and take the drive to Bradford—the closest town with a Walmart Superstore, and the closest town with an inexpensive air conditioner.

"Hey, Petey, let's go for a walk."

Petey raised his head. He enjoyed being in a deep sleep on the living room chair, stretched out on his stomach, his back and front legs splayed out. He opened his eyes and blinked. *Give me a second to wake up, okay?*

He watched Jake lace up his shoes, and noticed that Jake would always carefully make sure the tension on each lace was the same as the other. He stood up and checked the fit and the tension.

"Okay, let's go. We'll go down to the river. It's cooler down there."

Once they entered the field, the air actually grew hotter, still, almost as if an invisible cloak of hot air had been drawn over the area. He listened and heard only the sporadic call of a bird or two. There were no avian squabbles this afternoon, no territorial battles. Jake forged ahead, Petey a few steps behind him, placing his paws down with care.

Once they arrived at the river's edge, Jake picked up a handful of smooth pebbles and began tossing them into the middle of the stream. The first time, Petey charged toward the edge of the water, giving chase to what Jake had thrown.

"No, Petey. These are not for retrieving. I just like to see the little splashes they make."

Petey stared up at him. *What? Watching splashes? What sort of fun is that?*

Petey sniffed at the water and gently nicked at it with his right paw. Then he splashed a bit deeper, drawing his paw back and licking at it, testing the water, as it were. He then retreated and jumped up on a smooth, flat rock, shielded from the sun by a large willow.

Jake remained until his handful of rocks was gone, tossing them in at random, his eyes set on the far southern horizon. He made his way toward the cat and joined him on an adjacent rock. He did not speak, just sat, with his legs extended out toward the river, leaning back on his palms, his face turned upward to the heavens.

Jake . . .

At these moments, and only at these moments, Petey wished he had been born with the ability to form words, to speak. He seldom wanted that ability during the course of any regular day, since he had discovered, early on, that speech often served only to get in the way of real feelings. People, and cats, for that matter, often did things they found hard to explain, and if they tried, they would simply use the wrong words to do so. Ask a guilty-looking cat why they shredded the drapes and you would not ever receive the real, truthful, soul-honest answer. And maybe there wasn't a real answer. Maybe they acted on pure instinct or pure impulse. But today, it was obvious to Petey that Jake had issues on his mind. It was obvious that Jake needed to talk things through.

Petey meowed, not loudly, not insistently, but inquiring, observant.

After a moment, Jake looked over.

"I don't know, Petey. Maybe it's just life that is bothering me."

Well, that worked pretty well. Maybe he's beginning to understand "cat."

"I know you don't understand, Petey. But it feels too good to imagine that you do."

I do understand. Most of the time, anyway.

"So, why do I talk to you?"

Because you need to.

"I guess when I say these things out loud, they get more real. They become . . . something I can deal with, rather than hide from. Maybe that's it."

Of course, that's it. People need to talk. Cats need to act. Good cats need to listen. And I am a good cat.

Petey meowed, hoping to sound quite understanding and aware.

"I know you would like to help, Petey. But maybe you can't."

I can, too. Why else would God have sent me? He did *send me. That's why I am here. To help you.*

"I'm a pastor of a church. Not as big a church as my mother wanted me to have. But I am a pastor."

I didn't like your mother, Jake. That may be terrible of me to say. But I don't think she was a very nice person. She thought I was a wild animal. Imagine that. Me. A wild animal. Preposterous, right? Is that the right word? Preposterous?

"When she visited . . . I don't know . . . things seemed to fall into place. Kind of. Maybe."

Things? What sort of things?

"When my father left, I was still pretty young. And it hurt, Petey. It hurt, even though my mother said we would be better off without him. I don't have many memories of him anymore. It's even hard for me to picture his face in my mind. It's like I see a form without a face. And he's always getting smaller when I think of him. He is fading away. The memories are. Disappearing."

That is sad, Jake. Cats don't grow up with fathers. And they don't spend a lot of time with their mothers, either. I remember my mother. She was very nice and very smart and she was a good hunter, and I bet she could catch more mice than anyone. She was a very nice mother.

Petey looked away from Jake and stared at the river, swallowing a few times.

"So my mother had my life planned out for me. Be a pastor. That's what she always wanted, Petey. And that's what I did. I became a pastor. She never asked me if I believed. Not really. I went to catechism and youth group and all that. I looked like I believed. And . . . even in seminary, deep down I was never really sure. Was I there for *me*? Or for God? Or did I go just for my mother? You know, Petey, I'm not sure anymore. My mother really struggled raising me. She always worked hard and we never had a lot and she always told me how much she sacrificed to raise me and send me to school. I felt obligated to pay her back. To do what would make her happy—to make her life have some shred of joy. And it worked. Me being a pastor gave her hope. I think it did, anyway. She was happy when she told other people I was a 'man of God.' That was the only time I remember her being truly happy."

You didn't want to be a pastor? I thought all pastors wanted to be pastors. Why else would anyone take the job?

"I wanted to do it—for her. Not for me. What does any seventeen-year-old know? Do any of them have any idea? Take Tassy. She's young. What does she want with her life? Get a tattoo? Find an apartment and a new boyfriend and start the whole stupid thing all over again? I don't know anymore. I just don't."

Petey meowed.

"I know you don't understand."

But I do.

"It's just . . . not having a dad . . . it's complicated. How do I have faith in something that I can't see? That's what I tried to tell Barbara Ann. And you can see where that got me. How do I have faith? In God the Father? What about *my* father? My mother never had a good word to say about him. It's not that she always said bad things, but she never said good things, either. It was like he wasn't even part of the equation. And then, I tell Barbara Ann some of my 'deep feelings' and that blows up. Better to keep deep feelings deep and hidden. Does no good to tell people what you really feel. That just gets you in trouble. I can do this job and not believe all of it. Right, Petey? Right?"

I never met that Barbara Ann person but I am sure I don't like her. I bet she had a bed full of stuffed animals, too. That is just creepy. You can have a real animal. Why bother with inanimate animals? Wait . . . you do need to talk about how you feel, Jake. That's important.

"So here I am, Petey. I am pastor of a church that is growing—and it's because of you."

I can't take all the credit.

"I don't have faith. Maybe I never had faith. Maybe I never really believed. I've read that boys who grow up without fathers struggle with this. And I'm struggling, Petey. Just like the books say."

Petey looked at Jake and Jake stared back, almost as if they both understood.

"I don't know, Petey. I don't know if I can keep doing this. Being hypocritical like this. Not really believing what it is I'm preaching. Is anyone really being affected or changed? Or do they simply show up to see a cat in church?"

That seems a little . . . harsh, Jake.

"Who has really been changed by what I'm doing? Whose life is better because of me being here?"

And with that, without waiting for Petey's response, Jake got up in a hurry and started walking back toward church.

Petey waited just a minute, wondering what it was he should do now. Then he got up, stretched, and set out following him.

This is a hard thing. I don't know what it will take to get Jake to really see.

Petey heard a mouse rustle a few feet away.

Something big, I bet. I wonder if I can come up with something big. And soon.

12

Tassy set off for her second Monday on the job, the start of her second week. This morning had not been a good one. She had been awake for hours before dawn. She had a few crackers and the last of a large bottle of diet ginger ale that she bought at the Speedy-Mart in town. Neither ingredient seemed to do the trick, and during the entire bike ride she felt her stomach roll and twist as she pedaled.

The water here must really be horrible, Tassy thought. And I don't think I even drank that much. The water I did drink, I boiled for tea—so that should make it safe. That's what Jake said. He said he learned that in Cub Scouts. I can't see him in a Cub Scout uniform with a little yellow scarf and all that. He doesn't seem the type. And now that he's all grown and handsome, he seems so far from being a little boy.

Her stomach twisted again. She stopped pedaling for a long time, coasting to a stop until the curving and knotting in her gut stopped.

Good thing I left early. This trip is taking twice as long as usual.

She had planned to stop at McDonald's but didn't. The thought of a second cup of tea was nearly enough to make her stop pedaling again. Now she was down to seven minutes until

Dr. Grainger expected to see her come through the door. But when Tassy finally arrived—on time—and unlocked the front door with her key, she found herself in an empty waiting room.

"Dr. Grainger?" she called out softly. She went to the foot of the steps and called up again. "Dr. Grainger?"

She heard Winston scuffle about and saw his chubby face at the top of the stairs, with a grin, knowing that Tassy's presence meant a treat. He clomped down the steps in a furious snorling rush.

"Good morning, Winston. Want a treat?"

Of course Winston wanted a treat and tried to jump but mostly just raised his shoulders a bit.

Tassy gave him a dog biscuit as a reward, which he ate noisily.

"Is Dr. Emma up, Winston?"

She heard hurried footsteps on the hall upstairs.

"I'll be down in a minute, Tassy. I overslept. Can you believe it? The first time I've done this in years."

After a moment, Tassy heard the sound of water running.

Good thing we don't have any early appointments today.

Tassy rubbed at her stomach, hoping the nausea would soon pass.

A very good thing.

On Monday morning, Jake decided against the air conditioner. He had a fan and that had been enough.

"I'm a bit worried that an air conditioner might be seen as excessive by some people in the church. What do you think, Petey?"

Petey chirped.

"I thought you would say that."

Instead of Kane or Bradford, which Jake had already visited or driven through on his day off, he decided to travel in a different direction. He pulled out his worn road atlas and peered intently at it while he had his second cup of coffee of the day.

"Emporium. Let's drive there."

Petey just looked at Jake, and it seemed as if he would have shrugged if he could shrug, but he couldn't.

Jake disappeared into the office but returned after a moment. "The Internet says that Emporium is a pretty little town out in the middle of nowhere. In a valley, I guess. It is supposed to be quite scenic. That sounds like a good ride, doesn't it?"

Petey stared. He did not seem to care one way or the other. Jake knew he simply liked riding in the truck.

With his nose close to the page, Jake peered at the atlas, muttering to himself. He traced one route with his finger, then another.

"I guess it doesn't matter how you get there—so I'll try this way. Come on, Petey. Let's take a ride."

Petey did not hurry to the truck but did not walk at slow cat speed either.

"See, Petey, we drive west a little bit and take the first road south. Regardless of what road we take, we'll get there. Sort of a metaphor for life, don't you think?"

Petey seemed unimpressed by metaphors and simply turned to stare out the passenger side window.

As he drove, Jake noticed that the area between here and there became sparsely populated, a few homes and farms dotted the hills, bucolic, pastoral.

"This is nice, right, Petey? Pretty landscapes."

Petey chirped his response.

If you like this sort of thing. I think I like towns better. There's more to look at.

They drove in silence through several small clusters of houses huddled by the side of the road: Inez, then Austin, and Sizerville. In Sizerville, Jake saw a road sign that said: EMPORIUM 5 MILES.

"See, I told you all roads led to Emporium."

Jake drove into the small town, agreeing with the Internet's assessment of the picturesque nature of the place. And it was indeed "in the middle of nowhere," nestled in a bucolic valley, hidden, as it were, from the rest of the world. The Pennsylvania version of Brigadoon. That isolated part of the description began to appeal to Jake more and more, a place even further removed from the pressures of society and culture.

"Wouldn't it be nice to live out here, Petey? Far from the madding crowds. That's a title of a book or a poem or something."

Far from the Madding Crowd . . . by Thomas Hardy. It's about a shepherd. You know, I don't think I like sheep either. They stink, too. Not like foxes or skunks or dogs, but they do really smell. Anyhow, it's a book title.

Jake drove down the main street.

"You want some coffee, Petey?"

Not a disdainful cat by nature, Petey turned slowly to face Jake, with a tight, restricted look in his eyes.

Go ahead. You don't function all that well without multiple cups of the horrid drink. I'll be fine all by myself, left alone in the car. I'll be fine.

Jake pulled to the curb.

"Another nice thing about small towns is that you generally can find parking spaces. Where I grew up, you could drive around for an hour to find a free spot. See how nice this is?"

I have heard that before, Jake. You are repeating yourself.

⊸☙⊸

Jake rolled down both windows nearly halfway. The temperature had been predicted not to climb out of the 60s today, so Jake felt more than comfortable leaving Petey alone in the truck. He knew him well enough to know that he would stay put until he returned. And besides Petey, there was nothing of value in the truck to tempt a thief.

The Cabin Kitchen, a basic storefront restaurant, featured handwritten breakfast specials taped to the front window, along with signs for church bazaars, garage sales, rummage sales, bake sales, and free car washes—all bordering the bottom of the front window like an edging of mismatched flowers.

"A community place," Jake said to himself as he walked in. A clustering of patrons occupied the tables: some couples, some single gentlemen, all of them older, some with newspapers, all with coffee cups in front of them.

A waitress called out from the far end of the counter, "Sit anywhere. Take your pick. I'll find you."

Jake selected a stool at the counter. He liked stools at counters, perhaps since his mother never let him sit at a stool at any counter, in any restaurant, claiming that stools and counters looked too much like a tavern for her sensibilities. "What if Jesus came and saw you sitting on a stool like one at a bar and thought you were drinking a beer or a whiskey? He would pass you by, Jakey. You can't take that chance." Jake had always wanted to ask why, if Jesus were truly omniscient, he wouldn't already know that no alcohol was being ingested. But Jake, even at a tender age, knew better than to ask "foolish, devil-inspired" questions like that.

So he sat at the counter and slipped a menu out of the rack at its edge. Now seated, and noticing the smell of pancakes and toast, he decided that he might be hungry, as well as thirsty.

Dr. Emma came down the steps in a hurry, her hair still wet. Winston had gone back up the steps and now followed her back down, lagging a full five steps behind, his back legs flumping on each step as he descended.

"So sorry," she exclaimed in a rush. "That's what having a back-up does to you, I guess. Makes you sleep in. I've never had that luxury before—having someone cover for me like this."

Tassy smiled back, or tried to. She was not successful.

"Are you not feeling well, Tassy? You look a little pale."

"No. I'm fine. I am. Just a passing morning thing. I think my stomach is still getting used to the water up here. Seems that I'm a bit sensitive, I guess."

She smoothed her hair from her face and hoped that she appeared healthy.

"Are you sure, Tassy? You can lie down for a few minutes . . . upstairs. I have four extra bedrooms, you know. Those old Victorians had a lot of kids, I guess. Or servants. When a single woman goes into a furniture store and asks for five mattress sets, you get odd looks, let me tell you."

Tassy tried to smile.

"Are you sure you're okay?"

Tassy grimaced, just a little, then nodded.

"I am. It will pass. It always does. And it only happens in the morning. That's the funny thing about it."

Dr. Emma stopped moving, stopped looking at the clip chart listing today's appointments, stopped looking at the order form for medicines that she had to sign, and stared at Tassy.

"Just in the morning?"

"Yes. Usually, if I have some tea and toast, or a couple of crackers, it goes away. By lunchtime, I'm good to go. Just getting used to the water. That's what Pastor Jake suggested. He said that some stomachs are sensitive. He said his mother was sick for a month when she moved to Meadville, and Meadville was only like an hour away from where she used to live. And Philadelphia is a lot farther than that. So . . . I'll be fine. It'll pass."

Dr. Grainger put the clipboard on the counter.

"And it is just feeling sick to your stomach? No other symptoms?"

Tassy pursed her lips.

"Yeah, that's it. Maybe . . . well, I'm thinking it's because of riding the bicycle and all . . . but there are some areas of my body . . . you know . . . that are more sensitive now than they have ever been. I don't know what the water would have to do with that. But I guess I'm just being overly dramatic. Right? A little neurotic, maybe. Or being a hypochondriac—that's what it's called, isn't it? When you always think you have some disease? Hypochondria?"

Dr. Grainger pulled up the chair next to Tassy and sat, putting her arm on Tassy's forearm.

"That's what it's called, but that's not what you are. I don't think you're being dramatic. And I don't think it's the water."

"Coffee, hon?"

Beverly, according to the nametag on her uniform, sidled up to the counter where Jake sat, carrying a half-full glass carafe of coffee.

"Sure. Regular."

"That's the only kind to drink," she replied as she sloshed the coffee into a thick mug. "Decaf is like drinking bad-tasting water. Seriously. Why bother?"

She took her order pad from a pocket.

"You ordering anything?"

Jake looked down at the menu in his hands.

"Do you have sweet rolls? I don't see them listed."

"We do. I have a couple of cinnamon rolls left, but if I were you," she said in a stage whisper, "I would order a toasted pecan roll. We actually make them here and they are very good."

"Okay. I'll have one of those, then."

"Wise choice."

Then Beverly stopped and stepped back a step or two, and leaned backward, as if studying an odd work of art.

"Do I know you?" she asked.

"I don't think so. This is the first time I've been to Emporium."

"No. Well, maybe that's true. I'm not questioning your veracity. But I have seen you somewhere."

Beverly turned to one of the couples seated at a nearby table.

"Dolores—doesn't he look familiar?"

Jake felt obligated to turn and look in return.

The woman who obviously was Dolores leaned forward and squinted at Jake.

"I don't think so. Henry? What about you?"

Henry lowered his newspaper. "Nope. Maybe you could just ask him who he is and how he got here and his Social Security number and his mother's maiden name so you could do a background check on him. How's that sound? Or get a skin sample for a DNA test."

Dolores dismissed her husband's caustic reply with a wave of her hand.

"Don't mind him. He's antisocial."

Beverly brightened.

"I know where I saw you. You're that pastor—the one with the cat. Right?"

Even though surprised, Jake had to nod in agreement.

"Jake Wilkerson. Church of the Open Door in Coudersport."

"That's it. My cousin e-mailed me a picture. Were you in the newspaper?" Beverly asked.

"When I first got to town. I think the church sent a notice to the paper. The *Potter Leader Enterprise*, right?"

Beverly shrugged. "Could be. I don't read newspapers anymore. I get all the news from the Internet. Dinosaurs like Henry—they still read the newspapers. But that's because he's too cheap to buy an iPad."

Henry lowered his paper and glared at her.

"Just because you're my older sister doesn't give you the right to criticize."

"Of course it does," Beverly replied. "Dolores said I could. Right, Dolores?"

"She is your only sister, Henry. You should be nice to her."

Jake watched as the family comedy unfolded before him. Beverly stopped, then turned back to Jake. "Where's the cat? You leave him home alone this morning?"

Jake figured the question was coming.

"No. Actually, he likes riding in trucks. He's in the truck waiting for me now."

"Get out! Really? Bring him in. Can we meet him?"

Jake hesitated.

"Oh sure, like the Health Department is waiting outside to do a sting operation on us for illegally serving cats in here." Beverly responded, noticing Jake's reluctance. "It's okay. For a minute. Anyone mind if the pastor brings his cat in?"

Weak choruses of "No" and "Okay with me" were the votes from the current pool of patrons.

"Okay. I'll get him."

Be careful what you do. You're a celebrity in these parts.

Jake went outside, walked to the truck, and opened the door. Petey sat up, obviously having been napping.

"You have fans who want to meet you. You want to do a meet 'n greet?"

Petey stood, stretched, arching his back, yawned, shook his head, as if clearing his thoughts, and then jumped down from the truck, almost like he was looking to see where his fans might be gathered.

"Over here," Jake said. "Follow me."

Dr. Grainger slid her chair closer.

"Tassy, I know I am an animal doctor, but I know a little about people medicine as well. Some of it transfers, I guess."

Tassy nodded.

"You're only sick in the morning? Nauseous, right?"

"That's about it."

"And it's usually gone by the afternoon?"

Tassy nodded.

"Tassy, I am not one to pry. And I don't have any right to ask—as an employer, and all."

"I know . . . I guess."

"I guess the only way to ask this question is to ask it: Do you think you might be pregnant?"

Tassy leaned back, as if she had planned on that specific reaction.

"No. No. I couldn't be. Really, I couldn't be," as if Tassy was trying to convince herself of the fact.

Dr. Grainger gripped Tassy's arm a little tighter—not hard, but firm, insistent.

"No. Really. I . . . Randolph has been gone for . . . It couldn't be. Really. It couldn't."

Dr. Grainger looked hard at her new employee, hard and long.

"No. No. No."

"Tassy, could it be true?"

"No."

"Tassy."

Tassy's face softened, her eyes went wavery, and her shoulders slumped.

"Maybe. I don't know. Maybe."

"Have you taken a test, Tassy? You know, the kind they sell at the drugstore?"

Tassy shook her head emphatically.

"No. I couldn't. I couldn't buy one because the man who runs the store knows Eleanor and if I bought one, he would find out, and then Eleanor would find out, and I couldn't do that to her. She has been so nice to me—letting me stay in the RV. Vern even bought me groceries. If they thought I was pregnant, what would it do to them? I just couldn't do that— disappoint them like that."

Dr. Grainger stopped. Her back stiffened. A harsh look came on her face.

"Jake . . . Pastor Jake isn't involved, is he? You're not protecting him, are you?"

Tassy appeared shocked—very, very shocked.

"Pastor Jake? No! No! Of course not. Pastor Jake, he's like a church person. He couldn't do that, even if he wanted to. And sure, he's cute and all that, but he's like, old. Not real old, like a grandfather or anything. But he's old. No, nothing to do with Pastor Jake. He's just been so sweet to me, too. He always asks if he can get me anything when he goes to town. Of if I need anything fixed. Or whatever. No, Pastor Jake. No."

Dr. Grainger appeared relieved.

"I had to ask, Tassy."

"I know. But, Pastor Jake? Heavens no."

She looked down at the floor, avoiding Dr. Grainger's concerned expression.

"I have been worried about this since I got here. Sort of. Like I've been nervous thinking that maybe I am."

Jake opened the door and Petey sauntered inside, sniffing and looking about, taking it all in with great deliberateness.

"He is just like she described him," Beverly said. "A perfect gentleman. She said he sits through the whole service like it's the most important thing he's ever heard."

"He is awfully cute for a cat—and I'm not a cat person," Dolores said. "But he does look like a good cat."

"He started coming the first Sunday I preached. I guess I was upset at first, but now, he makes it his business to be on the platform Sunday morning."

"And your church people don't mind?" Henry asked. "The elders or deacons or whatever you have?"

Both women turned to stare at Henry.

"I was just curious."

They pivoted back to Jake.

"No. The elders said that if Petey comes to church, it's okay with them. Actually, it turns out that more than a few new people have started attending since Petey's been coming."

Henry folded his newspaper and laid it on the table.

"Interesting. Sounds like you got an interesting church there. Pretty liberal, right? Gays and all that? Not that I'm being judgmental or anything."

Jake shook his head.

"No. If anything the church has a history of being very traditional, very conservative. Very. Fought for years over singing any hymn written later than 1890. So . . . it's traditional, more or less. We're traditional, and then some."

It took a long moment until Henry's face softened and a very small smile came, but a smile nonetheless.

"Might be worth checking out some Sunday. What do you think, Dolores?"

Both women pivoted back and stared at Henry.

Beverly spoke first.

"Henry here said that all church and God stuff is a bunch of hooey. He said that a lot. For a few decades, right? He always used a different word than *hooey*, but I have respect for having a preacher in here. This is *big*."

Dolores sputtered, "You mean it?"

Henry shrugged, trying his best not to appear anything other than normal.

"Sure. A cat in a church. That's interesting. Makes it more normal, I guess. More human—although that's a contradiction, isn't it? Down to earth. I don't know. Interesting, you know. I'd be willing to give up a Sunday morning to see that."

Beverly picked Petey up and held him in her arms. He meowed, enjoying the attention.

"Henry said it would take an act of God to get him to go back to church. Apparently, your cat, Petey, is an act of God."

Petey jumped down and walked to Henry, placed his front paws on his knee, and stared hard at the man's face.

"We have service at 11:00," Jake said. "It's a nice ride to Coudersport."

Henry patted the cat's head.

"Maybe. This Sunday. If the weather is nice. Or if I don't have anything better to do."

Petey the cat began to purr.

"I said maybe, cat. Not for sure."

———— ∞ ————

"It's positive, Tassy," Dr. Grainger said as she examined the test. "We probably need to get a doctor to confirm that."

Tassy appeared to be at the edge of tears.

"I can't afford that, Dr. Grainger. I just started working here and if I do see a doctor . . . somebody will find out. I just couldn't do that to Eleanor. Or Pastor Jake. They trusted me."

Dr. Grainger and Tassy sat upstairs from her office, in her small, tidy, very modern kitchen. Dr. Grainger made whole-wheat toast and a cup of tea—the only food Tassy said she was capable of eating.

Tassy nibbled at one end of a piece of toast, like a mouse nibbling on a cracker, taking cautious, careful bites.

"We don't have to do anything today," Dr. Grainger said. "And I do mean 'we.' I won't let you go through this by yourself. Okay? I want you to know that, Tassy. You're not alone here."

Tassy managed a small smile.

"Thanks, Dr. Grainger."

"We have at least a month to handle this. You can't be that far along. We still have time. So we don't have to do anything today."

Tassy nodded, like a small child nods when dealing with something much, much bigger than she is.

"Okay. And thanks. Like a weight off my shoulders. Knowing for sure."

Dr. Grainger put her arm around Tassy's shoulder and squeezed.

"I know how you feel. And for now, Tassy, let's keep this a secret. It is nearly impossible to keep any secret in a small town, but let's keep this just between you and me. Okay?"

"Okay. Okay. Okay. Okay."

Each word grew smaller and softer until it was no more than a whisper escaping from Tassy's mouth.

"This is not something that needs to ruin your life, Tassy. You're young. You can start a new life. But not like this. This is not the way to do it. A child needs a family, Tassy. You don't want it to happen like this, do you?"

Tassy waited, then shook her head, signifying no, but a reluctant, hesitant no.

"One mistake does not have to ruin your life. And this would. You know it would. We can correct this. We can handle this, Tassy. Right?"

She mouthed the word *right*, but she produced no sound.

"Good. Then we'll think about it. But we know what we need to decide, right?"

Tassy nodded again, smaller this time, and she said not a single word, just nodded.

And for Dr. Grainger, that was enough.

For now.

<hr />

Jake drove back toward Coudersport, the church, and his home. He did not speak for much of the trip. Petey sat, as was his custom, in the middle of the seat, staring straight ahead. Both appeared to be lost in their thoughts.

"Petey, I have to tell you that I'm really puzzled."

Petey faced him and meowed in response.

"If Henry said he was going to come to church because of me, I might feel good. Maybe. I don't know. But he didn't. He said he would come because of *you*."

Petey churred a reply.

"I know. It couldn't be because of me. I know that. I don't feel particularly close to God. And that's an understatement. I'm not even in the same county."

Petey chirped.

"Or the same country, for that matter. I'm puzzled because of what will happen when they show up. The people who are coming to see you are hearing me talk. And I feel like a counterfeit preacher up there. Am I really a man of faith? No. So that means then, that all of what I do is just some sort of show. Like a sideshow, or a carnival attraction. Is anyone really encountering the truth? Not from me. Maybe it's even worse than that. Maybe I'm even worse than a charlatan. Maybe this is all . . . not divine at all. Maybe it's all pretend. Maybe I'll wind up hurting a lot of people. Or damaging their faith. I don't know what to do now, Petey. What should I do? I've been lying to everyone since I got here. They think I have faith. I don't."

Petey did not like to walk about while the truck was in motion, but after hearing this, he stood up and tried to climb into Jake's lap.

Jake pushed him away, gently, but firmly.

"Dangerous to do that, Petey. But thanks for the support. What do you think? Do you think it could be a test to see if my faith comes back? Do you think it will happen, Petey? Can a person force faith to come back? Can I make it come back?"

Petey rammed his head into Jake's side, as if to tell him to stay with it, to keep searching, to keep trying, and to listen, to listen to that small voice calling for him to return.

⚬⚬⚬

Late that afternoon, after Dr. Grainger insisted on driving Tassy back to her RV, she hurried out of the church parking lot without stopping. She did not want Jake to come out. She did not want to talk to Jake. She didn't want to see Petey or Jake. She did not want to speak to anyone.

She drove past Big Dave's store, driving faster than she should have on the narrow, two-lane road. She snapped off the radio and drove in silence, the wind coughing in the open windows, loud, whining.

She stopped paying attention to where she was and just drove west, until the surroundings became more and more unfamiliar. She looked down at the speedometer and realized that she was not only breaking the law—by a lot—but also being really, really foolish. Even on straight, wide roads, with a clear head, Emma was not the best of drivers and became easily distracted.

Her thoughts were in a swirl, and she had never once envisioned her final moments on earth as flying off the road and slamming into a tree. She slowed down to the legal limit, and a few miles later, pulled off the road onto a wide shoulder overlooking a small valley and a rock-filled stream. She got out of the car and walked to the hood and leaned against it, wishing that she still smoked—a brief aberration in college— so that she had something to do with her hands at a moment like this. Instead, she crossed her arms, shut her eyes, and listened. The engine began to ping and creak as it cooled, birds called out, the breeze ruffled the branches. She heard her own breathing, coming faster than it should, as it always did when she was angry, impatient, and hurt.

She tried to fend off the flood of memories that the events of today had brought to the forefront. She knew, from the first moment of her encounter with Tassy, that those memories would come and it would be of no use to attempt to hide from them. Hiding would do no good. Drinking would do no good. She had tried that before and it just made for horrid mornings after. She knew she should simply let them happen, let them build and wash over her and then they would be forgotten—at least for a while. Not forgotten really, but put away. Hidden. For a little while.

This specific set of memories started during the summer between the end of her undergraduate career and the start of veterinary school. She was young, pretty, energetic, and vivacious in a way that drew attention from the most eligible of the eligible young men heading off to graduate school or medical school or to work in their father's companies.

Emma Grainger felt—no, knew—that she was at the center of many young men's desire.

And for Emma, Josh Cummings was her first and only choice. A premed student headed to Vanderbilt, Josh had met Emma in a math class during their junior year at Penn State. They were a cute couple, by all standards, and appeared destined to marry and have very handsome children.

But all of that would wait, of course, since medical school was in both of their futures.

And then it all changed when Emma discovered that she was pregnant, using a pregnancy test kit, much like the one Tassy had just used.

Emma squeezed her eyes tighter, hoping somehow the past would magically change and the path to today would alter and shift and become . . . different.

It did not happen today. It never happened. The past remains unchanged. Like always.

Josh had been sweet and supportive when she'd told him, almost excited. In retrospect, Emma saw his actions as practiced, as if acting out "this is how a man has to act when being told of an unplanned pregnancy: be supportive, be caring, but do not commit to *anything*." That is how it had seemed. For the first few days, he had held Emma and had whispered that everything would work out fine, that things were just a little confusing right now, and that they would soon deal with this after having thought it through, using logic and clear thinking.

A week after the announcement, that's when "the talk" occurred.

The question was: "Whose career gets put on hold for this?"

Josh had to become a doctor. It was his parents' dream. Emma had to become a veterinarian. It was her dream.

"A baby is going to make this very, very complicated. One of us will have to give up on their dream . . . if we go through with it. This . . . situation."

It had become a "situation" and not a pregnancy. Not a life, not a baby.

Emma had known what he meant. The thought had crossed her mind without his prompting. A baby would create a massive upheaval in their well-crafted plans for the future. It would add one more hurdle, a huge hurdle, to achieving their dreams.

"We need to think this through, that's all. It doesn't affect the way I feel about you. But we have to face reality. We have to think of our careers. Don't you agree?"

Emma had agreed. What choice did she have?

And Josh had driven her to the facility to "handle it." He'd driven her home afterward. He'd stayed with her that night, bringing her hot compresses for the cramps, and brewing herbal tea. He'd stayed part of the next day.

And life went on. For Emma, the colors of her world had changed. They had become muted, burnt sienna instead of red. Life was a bit askew. Sounds were different. Every smile felt forced.

And one month, to the day, after Emma had "handled it," Josh had sat in the driver's seat of his Volvo, after a dinner of pizza and beer, and had told Emma, dispassionately, "This just isn't working for me. I think we both need some space here. We both need to find our own way. You feel it, too, don't you, Emma?"

Emma had not felt it but had seen her new reality in Josh's hopeful face, only hopeful because he was jettisoning unwanted baggage from his life.

Emma was that baggage.

The rest of the summer, and for much of her first year of veterinary school, Emma simply had gone through the motions. She did not hear from Josh at all that year, though a friend said he was dating again—a perky, red-haired, second-year medical student from Syracuse. Emma had felt nothing. She had felt empty.

And during a routine medical checkup some nine months after "handling it," the doctor had become more interested than usual in certain things, and had ordered more tests than usual, and afterward, had given her the news that it looked like, to him, at this date, that Emma would probably not be able to have children in the future. Something about scarring. Something about seeing this with some regularity in women who had "handled" things.

And since then, Emma did her best to hide the guilt and the shame and the anger that "handling it" had caused. For the most part, she was successful. She was not often reminded of the past. Her friends who married and had children were no longer her closest friends, really—drifting apart because of different interests, of course, so her chance of seeing a happy mother and child had grown increasingly slim with each passing month.

And Emma went on with her life.

She seldom thought of the word *murderer*.

It was not murder.

It was simply handling a problem.

She had "handled it."

She got her life back. Josh went on with his life.

No one murdered anything.

She'd pursued her dream, achieved it, and in that she could take cold comfort.

And her life went on.

And she told herself the decision had been correct, even it was painful. And it had been.

Painful but necessary.

Not murder. Not murder at all.

And Tassy would see the truth in that. Eventually. She would.

13

Jake picked up the phone in his kitchen and dialed a now-familiar number.

"Hey, this is Jake. You up for a ride to Port Allegheny? One of the church folk said there is an Italian restaurant there that's actually pretty good. And I haven't had good Italian food for weeks. Want to go for dinner? My treat."

The phone had rung a number of times, almost to the point of the call automatically going to voice mail. First, Jake wondered if Emma was home, and then he wondered if she had been debating on whether or not to answer his call—based on the caller ID, of course. Jake looked at the caller ID and made those "answer/don't answer" decisions all the time.

"Jake, thanks so much for thinking of me, but can I take a rain check on this? I'm . . . I guess I'm just not in the mood for it right now. Maybe some other time, okay?"

Obviously, her answer took him by surprise, at least a little.

"Oh. Okay. Maybe some other time, then."

As he hung up, he wondered if "some other time" meant something more than just "some other time." Was Emma trying to tell him that she no longer wanted to see him? Or that she had better things to do than go out to dinner with a pastor who didn't believe that he should be a pastor? Or that she simply did not really like him at all and was trying to find an easy, safe, nonconfrontational way to let him know?

———— ⚉ ————

Petey sat on the desk and watched as Jake dialed the phone and held it up to his ear, with an odd, nearly goofy look on his face. He stared intently as Jake spoke, and noticed Jake's eyes as he hung up the phone. The expression had changed. Dramatically.

He meowed as if to ask about the problem.

"She said she wanted a rain check."

Petey tilted his head.

"That's a nice way to say no."

Petey meowed again.

"Hey, she's allowed to say no. We've only been out a few times. No one said anything about long-term. No one is suggesting that we're . . . you know . . . dating. It's okay, Petey. She's nice, but she isn't the only person in the world, you know."

Petey simply stared back, watching Jake's eyes.

"Yes, I know. But I don't think God has anyone preordained for another person and we have to search until we find that one person. It doesn't work that way."

Petey remained silent.

"Okay. I get it. I shouldn't be talking about God's plan for my dating life, since I'm pretty sure he doesn't have plans for my spiritual life. Right? That is what you're thinking, isn't it? Why would he want me to find a special person when I'm lost myself? That's it, isn't it?"

And with that, Jake stood up quickly, nearly tipping the chair over, and stomped, or almost stomped, out of the room.

Petey watched him go.

I just wanted to know what a rain check meant. I never heard that before. Why do they say a "rain check" when they mean "no"? Wouldn't a "no" be much simpler and easier?

He licked his paw and wiped his face three times on both sides.

Human are so confusing, aren't they?

⬥⬥⬥

The tattered envelope, apparently a reused direct mail solicitation for a credit card, with a new address taped over the old, had arrived in the mail to the church. Jake almost threw it away, but took a second and a third look at it and realized what it was and who had sent it.

Speedy had sent the map, an intricately drawn map, complete with an index and a map key in the bottom right corner. He had labeled route numbers and street names, indicated Jake's church, Dr. Grainger's office, the movie theater, Kaytee's, and the route to take out of town heading east into the Susquehannock Forest. He had drawn the road to turn off into the forest, and the road to turn off the road that he turned off on, and what stand of trees to look for, and the exact mileage between forks in the road, and included the notation "Rough road, drive slow and watch for badgers."

On the top of the map was a handwritten note, done in tiny, precise letters, all capitals, in blue ink.

Can you come to visit on the twenty-first? I will be home that morning. Until noon. Then I will be gone until three. (I don't have a watch, but I am pretty good at telling the time from the sun.) Promptness would be appreciated. If you are not there, I will assume that you are not coming. Perhaps if that happens, we can set another time. If you are not there, I will write again. But please save this map. You can use it if you come at another time. Thank you. Speedy Davis. (Dr. Grainger did not tell you my real first name, did she? Did she remember? It is Sidney. Isn't that a horrible name? I have never liked it. Speedy is much better. Thank you again. Speedy Davis.

Jake took Speedy's map and compared it with his well-used atlas. The route would be easy to follow. Speedy was a competent, if obtuse, cartographer.

He placed the atlas and the hand-drawn map on the truck seat. He had asked if Petey wanted to accompany him, but the cat did not budge from his chair that morning, only raising his head in response, and blinking his eyes, as if not willing to be roused.

I can't go today, Jake. I can't. Something tells me that I have to stay here and protect things. I'm not sure what I have to protect or from what.

But I sure hope it is not from foxes.

I am hoping, and praying, that if I am asked to protect Tassy I can do as asked, and I will be successful.

Just no foxes, God. I don't think I can win against a fox.

Petey stood up and stretched.

But you know I would try my best, whatever happens, right? I would try my best to do my job.

Whatever that job might be. Whatever the task. I will try.

Jake left Petey at rest and drove through town and out again, heading east, deeper into the dark green forests of north central Pennsylvania and the stands of century-old lumber and moss and deep, almost nighttime shade, and clean mountain streams filled with bears and badgers, apparently.

He spotted his first turnoff easily. He stopped the truck and looked carefully at the speedometer.

"4.3 miles."

He did the math in his head and drove south, along what must have been a former logging trail, filled with ruts, rocks, and small fallen trees. Rough, but not impassable.

At 4.2 miles he slowed further, and scanned the east side of the road for the second cutoff and the stand of old pines that formed an "X" of sorts, flanked by a grove of black cherry trees.

"That must be it there," Jake said as he slowed and then turned into a thickness of brush—brush that all but covered a set of tire tracks. The truck protested a little but climbed and bounced and rocked and then came out on a small meadow filled with wildflowers and Queen Anne's lace. The rough track led around the meadow. At the far end was a small cabin with a tin roof and a curl of smoke coming from a stone chimney. As Jake got closer, he saw a figure come out of the house, waving.

"Hey, Pastor Jake, you found me! Good job. Not everyone can follow a road map that well. You know, you gotta trust the mapmaker when you go off road. If you don't trust the map-maker, then you're just lost, right? And you must have trusted me. That's a good thing. Reassuring."

Jake stopped, felt his kidneys settle back into their proper place from the jostling of the washboard road, and stepped out.

"It looked like you've drawn the map before. I figured you had directed people here before me."

Speedy looked alarmed.

"Good heavens, Pastor Jake. No. I never did. You're the first person I ever invited here. The very first. You won't tell anyone where I live, will you? I'm pretty sure I'm on state land here and they might not take kindly to me living here, rent-free and all."

Jake extended his hand.

"Speedy, no one will ever ask. But if they do, I will have forgotten all about the map. I promise."

Speedy looked greatly relieved. His face relaxed. He let a smile return. He wiped his hands on his shirt, then looked around as if expecting a few more people to show up.

"You hungry, Pastor Jake? I got some awesome squirrel jerky. And I got a pitcher of cool sassafras tea. And it's sweetened with real honey that's from a hive 'bout a mile from here."

Jake followed Speedy up onto the porch and took a seat on what looked like the middle seat from an old VW van.

"The tea sounds good, Speedy. I'll pass on the squirrel. I had a big breakfast."

"Sure thing."

Speedy returned after a moment with two metal cups filled with amber liquid.

"I like these metal glasses, 'cause they can't break. I don't wear shoes inside the house, so glass slivers can be dangerous."

Jake tried not to hesitate when he took his first sip. The tea was cool, not cold, and tasted earthy and sweet and healthy and not poisonous at all.

"Good," he said.

Speedy beamed as if he had just been given an award.

"Music to my ears, Pastor Jake. I like a man who likes his sassafras tea."

Emma tapped in her request for information on the Internet. She waited a fraction of a second and the result popped up.

She scanned down the first page and saw the link she needed. Another tap and the website popped up. It posted the hours. Then a list of frequently asked questions. She scrolled down the list. Answers to her three questions were there within the first ten. She slowed and read them carefully.

"We'll have everything we need. No problem there."

She looked at her watch.

"Plenty of time."

She turned the OPEN sign on the front door of the clinic to CLOSED and called up the stairs.

"I'll be back in a few hours, Winston. You're in charge until then."

She heard a muted "worf" in response.

She drove out of town, pulled into the parking lot of the Church of the Open Door, and stopped close to the front door of Vern's RV. She tapped at the door.

Tassy appeared, a little pale, and let Emma inside.

"Hi, Dr. Grainger. I'm sorry I'm not at work. But I just don't think I could make the bike ride today."

"Tassy, like I said before, that's not a problem."

She laid her car keys on the coffee table and sat on the couch opposite Tassy. They both turned to hear a scrabbling at the window. Tassy smiled weakly, rose, and slid the window open. Petey jumped down and meowed loudly, looking at Tassy first, then turning his stare to Dr. Grainger.

"Petey, I'm not here for you today. I'm here for Tassy. Don't have to worry at all. Okay, buddy?"

Petey chirped a reply.

Dr. Grainger looked small and tight, her arms almost folded in front of her, her hands clasped together.

"I know we've both been thinking a lot, right? About what we discovered. About your condition."

Tassy nodded, glum and unsmiling.

"And I think we probably have come to the same decision."

"I don't know. Maybe," Tassy said, her words small, snaillike.

"You don't have to go through this, Tassy. You're young and this is not the time for a burden like this. It's unplanned, right? You don't want to complicate your life anymore than it already is."

Tassy looked up. Petey walked into her lap.

"You're right, Dr. Grainger. You're right. I'm sure you're right."

The cat appeared confused, or concerned. He looked at Tassy, then Dr. Grainger, and then back at Tassy.

"We can handle this today. There is a clinic just across the state line, up in New York. It will take us forty-five minutes to get there. It's the closest clinic—other than driving to Philadelphia. The procedure is short—maybe thirty minutes. We can be back here by dinnertime. And then your life will start over—from that point. You can make a fresh start that way. It's . . . it's really the only logical way. And we have to look at this logically."

Had Tassy been more intuitive, more sensitive to the subtle nuances of long-delayed guilt and anger, she might have picked up on why Dr. Grainger was so sure. She might have understood that by following the path already walked on by a young Emma Grainger, it would somehow alleviate, or ameliorate, the pain Emma carried inside, carried every day, the secret carried and hidden. Pain is manageable when divided and shared. With this decision, neither Tassy nor Emma would feel totally alone—ever again. They would be connected by this shared pain. Emma would not be unique or alone or the only woman she knew that carried this sort of secret burden, this invisible pain. Pain shared is pain halved. Emma did not want to see another woman follow a different path and make it through unscathed.

No.

No, Emma knew that for her to heal, the pain had to be shared. Tassy must endure what she did. Theirs had to be a shared story, a shared history.

It was the only way. Blood for blood. Sacrifice for sacrifice. Biblical.

"So, you believe in God—right, Pastor Jake?"

Now is not the time for total self-disclosure.

"Yes, I do, Speedy. I believe there is a God."

Speedy looked at his hands.

"I been thinking about one thing, Pastor Jake. Could you call me Sidney? Just for today? I don't think that Speedy is the right name to use when God is listening. Like I'm trying to hide something. And I don't have anything to hide. I want to make sure God knows that. Okay?"

"Sure. Sidney it will be, for today, if you want. But I think that both names would be fine with God. I am certain he doesn't spend his nights worried about our nicknames, no matter how inappropriate."

"You think?" Sidney replied. "That's a relief."

"So Sidney . . . you said you had questions. I am not sure if I am the person who has all the answers, but I will try. I will try my best."

Sidney took a deep breath as he closed his eyes.

"Man, that's all I can ask, right? Try to find the answer. Try to find the truth. That's righteous."

"Can I pray for you . . . and us, to get us started?"

"You sure can. Don't think anybody's ever prayed for me before, 'cept maybe my mom."

Jake folded his hands together. He bowed his head. He closed his eyes.

"Dear Lord, I'm asking for your help today. For Sidney. For me. Help us find you. Help us find faith again. Help us see you. It's a simple prayer, God. It's a simple request."

Jake sniffed loudly. His throat had grown tight, but he coughed and continued.

This prayer might have been the first prayer—ever—in which Jake had actually asked God to help him find his faith, his belief, his center. Up until this moment, Jake knew it was up to him, and him alone, to find his faith. As he'd heard all his life, he knew God rewarded those who were seeking faith.

"I don't know what questions Sidney has for you. But I know the questions I have for you, God. Questions like . . . why did you abandon me as a child? Why did my life turn out the way my mother wanted and not the way I wanted? Why did I pretend to have faith all my life . . . when it was never really there?"

Now Jake felt the tears form behind his closed eyes.

"Lord, help Sidney. Help me. Please help me, God. Help me find faith . . . help me know what faith is. Help Sidney find faith, God. Help him right now. Enter his heart, God. Give him the gift of faith. Fill us with your Spirit. Fill us with faith. Help us know, without doubt, that you will never abandon us. You have never abandoned us."

He took a deep breath. He opened his eyes. He looked up.

"Amen."

He looked at Sidney, who had fallen to his knees while Jake prayed, and whose face, too, was wet with tears.

"Amen, man. Amen. It's like you looked inside me and knew what I needed. Faith. And then there it was. God heard you, man, loud and clear."

Petey's meow turned into a soft, gravely growl as he stared at Dr. Grainger, his eyes narrow as if he were facing some loud, hidden, dangerous noise.

"Today?" Tassy asked.

"We don't have much time, Tassy. If we wait, they won't be able to handle it. It will get more complicated. There is a time limit. Let it go too long and it becomes much more difficult. It might even be impossible then. And we don't want that, do we?"

"Today?"

"Yes. Waiting will only make it harder."

The fur on Petey's neck began to grow stiff and expand, making the small animal appear bigger, more ferocious, more protective. He growled again, low, rumbling, threatening.

"Petey," Tassy said sharply, almost scolding him. "Settle down. There's nothing for you to be angry about."

He jumped from her lap and stood between Tassy and Dr. Grainger. He arched his back.

"Petey!" Dr. Grainger snapped. "Enough. Stop it or get out."

Protect her. That's what I have to do. I'm not sure what they're talking about, but Tassy has to stay here. Nothing good can happen if she goes to New York. I don't know where that is, but it is not where she should go. Right? Right?

His breathing quickened, his ears folded back, his fur on edge, his back arched.

This is why I'm here, isn't it? To protect someone who is helpless? You sent me to do this, didn't you? You did, right?

He took a step forward, toward Dr. Grainger, keeping his eyes locked on hers.

That's what you do to danger. You stare it down. You can't let them look away.

That's what my mother taught me.

He arched his back higher and for the first time in many months, Petey hissed, as loudly as he could and with his right paw, the one that Dr. Grainger had repaired, he swung out, claws extended, swiping at the air, letting everyone know just how serious and dangerous he could be.

Especially when called on to protect someone helpless.

"Is that what you need, Sidney? To find faith?"

Sidney pushed his long hair behind his ears and shook his head as if to clear his thoughts.

"No. I mean, yes. But, like, Pastor Jake, I think I've found it. No. That's not it. I *know* I found it."

"You mean now?"

Sidney shrugged, sheepish.

"Yeah, I guess."

"Just like that?"

Sidney shrugged again. He shrugged a lot, Jake observed.

"How long should it take?"

Jake had no quick answer for that.

"I'm . . . I'm not sure."

"Ain't faith like a switch—on . . . or off? Not much in between, is there? And you asked God, and he . . . I guess he gave it to me. Or let me see it. And let me know what it felt like. It got switched from off to on. Inside me. Faith. It's on now. That faith switch. It's on. I can see."

That's it? That's all it took? All that seminary training, and all it took was a thirty-second prayer? And not a very good prayer at that.

Sidney sat back on his rickety wooden chair with fingers of the frayed wicker seat poking out under his jeans. He looked about, as if seeing his world for the first time, smiling, beatifically, graciously accepting whatever it was Jake helped him find.

"You want to pray, Sidney?" Jake said, almost secretly hoping that Sidney had not found faith—because if he had, and if it were that simple, then Jake's wandering in the wilderness for these past years would have been rendered implausible and self-indulgent and foolish and childish—and more—and worse . . .

Sidney doesn't understand faith. I'm betting he has no idea what he's talking about. A person who is lost does not get found just like that. It takes time. It takes effort . . . a lot of personal effort. It takes . . . work. And Sidney has not worked at all. Faith does not snap on like a light switch. It doesn't work that way.

He waited, the crickets or spring peepers or katydids chorusing at the far edge of the meadow.

If Sidney can find faith like flipping a switch . . . then what about me? What's wrong with me?

Sidney closed his eyes.

"Hey, God. Thanks. I guess it took Pastor Jake to help open my eyes. Thank you for sending him to me. Thanks for giving me faith. I can feel it. Like I know that everything comes from you and that I came from you and I owe everything to you. I have that faith. I do. And like, God, if Jake needs something, could you show him the way? That would be righteous, man. I guess . . . amen. Amen. Is that right? Amen."

"Yes, Sidney, that's right. Amen."

———∞∞∞———

Petey appeared to quickly cycle through all the alternatives and choices he had before him. He could attack. He could defend. He could do battle. He was obviously ready to do any and all of them.

But at the moment, when his back was arched highest and his ears laid flattest, he saw the glint of shiny metal, a glistening of a key.

He knew that those metal things, keys, started cars and trucks.

Without them, no one could go to New York.

Houses on wheels, he was not sure of. Perhaps it was a different system. But he did not think Dr. Grainger would drive the house with wheels.

From the couch, he launched himself at the coffee table, sliding when he landed, his head down, his mouth open, growling as he bent down, close to the surface, and closed his jaws around Dr. Grainger's keys—all on a ring with a short but thick leather lanyard. He grabbed the lanyard in his mouth and launched himself toward the open window. There was not a large landing space there, on the inside, but there was the merest hint of a ledge, of a sill. The weight and the heft of the keys almost took him off balance, but his front paw landed just right, and rather than perch there for a second, he just pulled harder on the thin ledge of the window and propelled himself through the still-open window and down to the ground.

The drop was at least six feet onto hard, sharp gravel.

The keys jangled and fell when he hit the ground.

The RV door slammed open.

"Petey! Petey! Put them down! Now!"

Dr. Grainger ran at him.

Though his paw hurt, a lot—the one that had been fixed—
he still scrabbled as fast as he could, as efficiently as he could,
and got hold of the leather lanyard just as Dr. Grainger reached
him. He jumped to the left and ran, with the keys in his mouth,
banging against his chest with each step, running as fast as he
had ever run, straight toward the open field beyond and then
to the tree line beyond that. He ran, hearing the heavy footfalls
of Dr. Grainger behind him.

"Petey! Drop that! Now! Drop it!"

He ran harder and faster, darting to the left, around and
under a thickness of brambles and blackberry bushes, and
then under a pine that had branches low to the ground. He ran
farther. Dr. Grainger's voice became quieter, but no less urgent.

"Petey! Come back here with those! Now!"

He ran into the cool shade of the trees and did not stop running until he jumped a half-rotted fallen tree. There he turned
around, panting.

There was no one following him. Then he saw Dr. Grainger
at the edge of the woods, the field and the church behind her.
She looked small from that distance.

"Petey? Petey? Where are you?"

Petey let the keys drop. The leather hurt to bite. It felt as
solid as wood and tasted of salt and grease.

He tried to still his panting. He knew it was loud and he
knew he could have heard it if he were the one doing the
looking.

But Dr. Grainger did not see him. She obviously did not
hear him. He flattened himself as much as he could, only a
thin sliver of his eyes visible from behind the fallen tree.

Tassy joined Dr. Grainger and they both called out to him.

It hurt not to answer, because he was a good cat, after all,
but he had done what he had to do. He was not sure why he
had done it. All he knew was, in that moment, it had to be

done, and he was the only one left to protect Tassy. He was the only one available. He had to act. He knew that beyond the shadow of any feline doubt.

Sometimes a good cat has to do a bad thing.

The two women called and tromped about at the edge of the woods for several more minutes. Petey watched as they both turned and headed back toward the church and the big house on wheels where Tassy lived.

He looked down at the keys. He looked at the trees around him and paid close attention to what this smelled like. He stood up and looked about, carefully and slowly, breathing in the environment carefully.

He would remember this. He would.

And then he began to walk back to the edge of the woods. He would remain in the shadows until Jake returned. Jake would know what to do. Then he would bring the keys back.

He would wait.

After all, he was a good cat. He was a smart cat.

14

Listen, I know it's a smart key. Do you have another one at the dealership?"

Emma paced in the small living room of the RV, holding her cellphone to her ear.

"Well, when is Frank coming back from lunch?"

She pivoted on her heel, obviously becoming more upset and anxious by the minute.

"Could you call his cellphone, please? This is important."

She lowered her head and half-cradled it in her free hand, her eyes shut tight.

"Well, then, do you know where he went for lunch? Come on, this is not that hard, Marjorie."

She stopped, tapped her foot, then shook her head.

"Okay. Okay. He's incommunicado for the moment. Okay. I get it. But he will be back by 1:00? Are you sure?"

Dr. Grainger snapped her phone shut.

"Only one person at the dealership who can access the records needed to program new keys. That is, if they have any spare keys on hand. What I wouldn't give to live in a city inhabited by people other than incompetent bumpkins," she hissed.

Tassy sat on the couch, holding herself tightly, making small rocking motions, almost imperceptible.

"Tassy, you don't know where Pastor Jake is, do you?"

"He didn't stop by when he left this morning. He usually does. But he didn't today."

Emma stabbed at his cellphone numbers again.

Even Tassy could hear the automatic "No Service" recording.

"Okay. Okay. What now?" Emma said, as if there was no one else in the room.

Dr. Grainger drew in a deep breath and exhaled loudly.

"Okay, I know," she said, answering herself.

Dr. Grainger slipped her cellphone in her pocket. She zipped up her light jacket.

"Tassy, how long does it take you to bike to town from here?"

"Fifteen minutes. Maybe a little longer, if I don't push as hard."

"Okay. I'm taking your bike. I'll ride into town and to the dealership and I'll be there when Frank gets back from lunch, and he'll get me a new key and I'll be back by 1:30. That still leaves us enough time. Okay?"

Tassy looked up, her eyes only a few moments from tears, and nodded.

"Okay, Dr. Grainger. Okay."

She did not say thank you as Emma thought she might.

Emma got on the bike and wobbled out of the parking lot. She began pedaling as fast as her legs would allow. It had been a number of years since she had been on a bike, and she knew that she would pay for it with stiff and sore muscles the following day.

"Well, can you hot-wire it—or whatever they do on TV? Seems like a pretty simple operation."

Frank, a short man in a formerly white short-sleeved shirt and a short tie, shook his head. He appeared to be sad.

"No, Dr. Grainger. I bet Harlan in the back could do it. He's from up toward Shinglehouse—and I think they teach that in shop class up there."

Frank smiled as he said that, then frowned again.

"But that would void your warranty. And since I know about your predicament, well, I would have to hold you to it. Voided. That's not good. Not good at all. And you don't want to void a warranty. Your car is only a year old. Not worth it at all. We'll have a new key tomorrow morning, Dr. Grainger. Of course, if you have a dog or cat emergency, I'd be happy to drive you there."

Dr. Grainger inhaled, obviously exasperated.

"And no loaners? No rentals?"

Frank shook his head.

"What if I take a test drive in a new car and bring it back by dinnertime?"

Frank's laugh was short, choppy, and hacked.

"Dr. Grainger, you are a kidder, aren't you? Like I said, I'll be happy to take you anywhere now. But our two loaners are out. And the owner of the dealership is gone until late—some sales meeting in Kane. Or was it Bradford? I'm not sure. I could check. Anyhow, so I don't have anything available right now. This evening, I'll have one of them loaners back. Six, I think he said. Would that help?"

Emma shook her head no.

"I wish them smart keys never got invented," Frank said. "People lose 'em and it's real expensive to replace 'em. Can't just go to the hardware store to cut a new one anymore."

Dr. Grainger had misplaced one set of keys already. The set that Petey made off with was her second, emergency set. Her mother didn't own a car anymore. She could call a friend, or one of her cousins—but how would she explain that she needed to take Tassy to New York and why they were going? No . . . that would not work. Anything other than using her own car would simply be too risky and too fraught with someone insisting to hear the reason for the trip. That would mean one untruthful explanation piled onto another, and Emma was certain that it would all fall apart. It would force her to tell her secret, which was something she vowed never to share with anyone.

"Can't you take your trip tomorrow, Dr. Grainger?"

Her shoulders slumped.

"Maybe. Maybe I can. You're sure the key will be in tomorrow morning?"

"Yep. I just called the parts warehouse and the key will be in our shipment. Stanley always gets here by 9:00 in the morning. He comes all the way from McKeesport, but he leaves real early. He'll be here, all right."

Well . . . if we have to wait one more day . . . we can do that. One more day won't change anything.

Petey remained hidden under a thick laurel bush. He would wait for Jake to return. Jake would know what to do.

While he waited, he remembered.

He had hidden beneath bushes before.

It was a time he did not want to recall.

His first memories were pleasant. He remembered his mother and how sweet she smelled. He remembered a young woman with blonde hair selecting him and taking him to live with her. He remembered her name but refused to bring the name into his awareness. It was better not to remember. Petey was happy there. He had another name then, but he chose not to remember it, even though he could if needed.

She was a nice person. When she left for work in the morning, she left the radio on for Petey. Sometimes she left the television on instead. That was the reason—one of the reasons—that Petey was now so smart. He watched the house from the windows. She did not let him outside. Petey did not mind not going outside. He did not like the birds that flittered about in the trees. He did not like the squirrels; they seemed to be rude and inconsiderate. But those problems were not insurmountable. Petey imagined that every cat had some problems in their life. His did not seem that bad.

The woman really, really liked Petey and let him sleep on her bed every night. He made sure there were no birds or squirrels in her room.

When that man came into their lives, everything changed.

Petey did not like him, even at the first meeting. He seemed harsh, tall and harsh.

The man and the woman seemed happy at first, but some time later they began to argue and fight. The woman would cry sometimes, and Petey tried his best to cheer her up. This was before he knew about God. He learned about God on the radio.

One time they were arguing, and the man kicked Petey. He hit the wall—hard. The woman ran to pick him up. He was fine, but very, very sore. The man never apologized.

It happened again. But this time, the man hit the woman and threw her against a wall. When Petey tried to step in between them, the man kicked him again.

Three days later, the woman took Petey in her car and they drove for a long time. She stopped the car, opened the door, and pushed Petey outside. She was crying. He did not hear what she said, but she was crying very hard.

Then she closed her door and drove away.

Petey spent two days at that spot, waiting for her to return. She did not return.

He knew now he had to fend for himself. God helped. Petey found mice and water and safe places to sleep. He walked and walked. He lived on his own for a long time. He could not remember how long it was. But it was a long time. And then, one day, he heard where he must go and who he must find.

And that's when he found Jake. And Tassy.

It seems we all are abandoned.

Except by God.

Petey must have dozed off. He awoke to see Tassy and Jake in the parking lot. Tassy was speaking, then she gestured in Petey's direction. Jake stared and squinted. Petey felt sure Jake could not see him, but Jake started to walk toward him.

And he began to call out his name.

When he was a few dozen yards away, Petey came out from under the bush, meowing loudly. Jake stopped.

"What did you do, Petey?" His words were very harsh. He sounded like that man who Petey did not like to think about.

Petey stood and walked away from Jake, very deliberately, into the woods—not running, but walking fast, looking over his shoulder, making sure that Jake was following, making sure that Jake saw where he was going, keeping yards between them.

He came to the fallen tree and jumped, and turned to face Jake, sitting just behind Dr. Grainger's car keys, his front paws almost touching the thick, leather lanyard.

"Petey! What are you . . ."

Jake stopped talking when he saw the keys.

"What? Why did you bring them here?"

Petey meowed, trying to explain. It was obvious that it was a more complicated situation than a cat could easily talk through.

"You brought them here?"

Petey chirped. That usually meant yes.

"You hid them from Emma?"

Another chirp.

"Why?"

Petey remained silent.

"Does Tassy know why?"

Petey chirped once, then once more, then one final time. Then he got up, waited until Jake picked up the keys, and started walking back to the house with wheels on it.

Of course, as Petey imagined he would, Jake followed, walking fast. Muttering to himself.

Tassy was waiting outside the RV, her arms crossed over her chest, a worried look in her eyes, her hair pulled back into a severe ponytail.

"Tassy, what happened here? Where is Emma? Where is Dr. Grainger?"

"We . . . we were talking and Petey came in and stole her keys, and then she had to take my bike to town to try and get a new car key."

"Petey took her keys? Why?"

Tassy shrugged.

"I don't . . . I don't know."

Jake looked down at the cat.

"Why did you take the keys, Petey?"

Petey meowed and stared back at Jake. Then he looked at Tassy and refused to look away, even when she looked away and even when she stepped backward a step. His eyes followed her as she turned and walked back inside the house with wheels.

"Petey?"

⊸⊶

"Jake!"

Jake looked up and watched as Emma coasted the bike across the parking lot. She came to a stop and simply let the bike fall to its side.

"Did you hear what your stupid cat did? He stole my keys. My very expensive-to-replace keys."

Jake held out the keys Petey had led him to.

"These keys?"

Emma snatched them from Jake.

"Where did you find them? He took off like a rabbit into the woods. We didn't even see what direction he took once he hit the tree line."

"He led me right to them," Jake answered. "Like he was proud of having taken them but didn't know what to do with them once he had them."

"Stupid cat. You should really train him better. Or keep him out of Tassy's place. It was like he was possessed or something."

Emma thumbed through her keys, counting them, as if she thought maybe Petey took one off the ring and hid it somewhere else in the woods.

"What were you here for, Emma? I thought Tassy wasn't feeling well today."

Emma glared back.

"That's really none of your business, is it?" she said, her tone sharp and brittle.

If Jake had been surprised by her attitude, he did not show it. He had learned how to stand up to his mother. He could stand up to Emma.

"It is my business. A little. She goes to this church. I'm her pastor. I'm concerned about her, that's all."

Emma's face went cold, like ice forming on a pond.

"Yeah, you're a pastor, all right. You're a pastor."

Jake stepped back a half step.

"What do you mean by that? What brought this on?"

Emma stepped forward, leading with her chin.

"Listen . . . Jake. I talked to your ex-girlfriend. Your former fiancée, Barbara Ann Bentley. Remember her? You never said anything about her, did you?"

Jake did not retreat. "What does she have to do with any of this?"

"I called her, Jake. I was interested in how you wound up in this backwater, here in isolated Coudersport. Well, Jake, she told me that you were fired from your church in Butler. Something about not having any faith. That ring a bell?"

"She called you?"

"She didn't call me, Jake. Come on, now. I called her. I wanted to know more about you. Why you're here, for one."

"And she told you?"

"She did. And you call yourself Tassy's pastor? Please, Jake. Let's not kid ourselves. You say you don't even have faith in God. How can you be anyone's pastor? Really, now."

"You don't know what you're talking about, Emma."

"I do, too. My question is what are you doing—pretending you're a pastor if you don't believe any of it? Petey probably has more faith than you do."

And with that, Emma ended the argument. She jumped into her car, slammed the door, and started the car. Tassy must have heard them arguing and stepped out of the RV.

"I'll send you the bill for my new keys I had to order because of your stupid cat. And no clergy discount this time, Jake."

Her tires spun and roared and a cascade of gravel bounced off the side of the RV.

The three of them—Tassy, Jake, and Petey—watched Emma drive off, watched her fishtail out of the parking lot with squealing tires, and speed onto the two-lane road back toward Coudersport. No one said anything for a few moments. Petey was the first. He meowed loudly.

It was obvious, to Jake at least, that he was confused.

"I don't know, Petey."

Jake turned to Tassy.

"Do you have any idea of what's going on?"

And with that, Tassy ran back into the RV, leaving the door open. Jake was fairly sure she was crying as she ran. They both followed her inside. She had collapsed onto the couch and curled herself into a ball, her head hidden in her knees, her arms wrapped around her legs.

She was crying.

Petey jumped on the couch and butted against her side, chirping and meowing. Eventually, she uncoiled, and he climbed into her lap, purring so loudly that Jake could hear him. Jake sat in the chair opposite.

"Tassy," he said with care, "something is going on. I would like to be able to help. Please let me help."

"You can't help, Pastor Jake. It's beyond anybody's help. Really."

Petey meowed, loudly, as if he understood, but disagreed with her.

"Tassy, Petey is right. Nothing is beyond God's help."

She sniffed loudly and wiped her face with her sleeve. She stared at Jake, not in anger, exactly, but more in supplication. Angry supplication, perhaps.

"I'm pregnant. Can you help that, Pastor Jake?"

Her words were indeed tinged with anger.

Jake resisted the urge to answer right away, to say the first thing that came to mind, to be blunt or bold or inconsiderate or unfeeling. He waited. He tried to allow the meaning of the words to sink in, to be assimilated fully before he spoke.

Petey spoke first, with a long, low, rumbly meow and purr combination.

Jake had not heard that before.

He tried out one response in his head, and then another, and another, and none of them sounded correct, sensitive, or pastoral enough. Then he remembered Sidney's smiling face.

"First, Tassy, you have to remember that no matter what—God loves you. He will always love you. You cannot do anything that will change his love for you. I promise."

Jake was now talking to her as well as himself.

"God is constant. We may change and get angry and make mistakes . . . but God will always be there, waiting for us, with open arms."

Tassy stared back at him. Jake was not sure if she believed a word of what he said. But the words had to be spoken.

"And it doesn't matter if we understand it or not . . . it's true. That's where faith comes in. We just have to believe in the truth. It's pretty simple, actually. Just believe."

Jake listened to his own words. Most of the time, he didn't. But this time he did—and he found himself thinking, *That makes a lot of sense. Just believe. Don't complicate it with how it should be or how others think it should be—just believe. Faith. Belief. Just accept it.*

"Maybe," Tassy said.

She did not look convinced, but she appeared less angry.

"Why was Emma here?" Jake asked.

Tassy shook her head and said nothing.

"Tassy . . . why was Emma here?"

Tassy began to pet Petey.

"We were . . . we were going to . . . 'handle it.' You know. Take care of it. She said that having a baby now would complicate my life too much and it wouldn't be right and if I handled it, I could just start over again. Sometimes things happen and you have to take care of it. This was a mistake I needed to fix. That's all. I was going to take care of it."

She started to cry again halfway through, and the tears began to course down her cheeks and fall on Petey's head and back. He did not attempt to move away.

"That's when Petey took her keys. That's when he ran off with them."

Jake waited a long time until he spoke again. "Tassy, I know that things seem dark right now . . . but what you were considering . . . well, that wasn't the answer. If you had done that, you would live with that regret and that pain, every single day, for the rest of your life."

She nodded.

"Whatever happens from here on in . . . I'll support you however I can. The church will support you. I know they will."

She nodded. "Do I have to go to church every Sunday?"

"If you want to, yes. If you don't, then no."

Her voice grew small. "I'll probably go. But not if I don't feel well."

"I understand."

"But I'll probably go. Petey goes all the time. I guess I can go, too."

Jake sat with Tassy and Petey until they both fell asleep on the couch, and then he silently slipped out. He knew where he had to go and what he had to say. He didn't want to have to ask, but he knew he had to. The church was bigger than he was. He did not want people hurt. He did not want new faith damaged.

He would ask. But he remained unsure of what the answer might be.

He carefully got into his truck and closed the door as silently as he could. He let it roll to the edge of the parking lot before he started it up. He drove to Coudersport, always keeping the truck well below the speed limit.

He pulled up to Dr. Grainger's office and drew in a deep breath. He closed his eyes, still trying to come up with what he might say that would help to keep others from peril, or damage.

He rang the bell on the side of the house. He heard footsteps and a series of rumbling barks. He waited. After a long time, he saw Emma's feet first, descending the long staircase.

There was no welcome in her eyes as she propped the door open halfway, then crossed her arms over her chest.

"What?"

Jake threw away whatever practiced words he had formulated. "Listen, Emma. I . . . I want to apologize to you. I should have been truthful from the very beginning. And I wasn't."

"Okay. You're sorry. Good. You're still a fraud."

Obviously, looking at Jake's face, one could tell that the words stung.

"Maybe. Maybe I was. But not now."

Emma offered a twisted smile in reply. "Just saying it doesn't make it so, Jake. Words are cheap."

Jake stood firm and did not look away. "You're right. They are. Coming here, I was thinking how I could ask you not to say anything about Barbara Ann to anyone. And not to say anything to anyone about why I was fired from the church in Butler. But right now, this very minute, I decided that I couldn't do that. It would be a lie. And I'm tired of lying—to others, as well as myself. So . . . I just want to say I'm sorry. For everything, I guess."

"Good. You're sorry. Anything else?"

Jake took a deep breath. "Emma, I am going to stand by Tassy. Whatever she needs to have this baby and to raise this child, I am going to do my best to supply that. Whatever it takes. I am not going to abandon her."

Emma smirked. "Listen, Jake, we have all been abandoned. Me, you, Tassy, Petey. We are all abandoned. By someone. God, former boyfriends, parents—whomever. All abandoned. It's the way of the world, Jake. You should be the first to realize the truth of that."

Jake shook his head. "That's where you're wrong, Emma. I just found out this morning. God never left me. He was always there. I may have moved away, but God did not abandon me. And he sent me Petey. God must have done that."

Emma's caustic, brittle laughter gave every indication that she considered Jake to be delusional.

"No. I am serious. If Petey had not been there, you and Tassy would have 'handled it.' And that would have scarred her, Emma. She would have to live with that forever. God knew what Petey was doing. God was saving me—and protecting an unborn life."

"Okay, Jake. Sure. I believe that. God sends cats to save people. Right. And we're done here, okay? We're done."

Jake saw in Emma's face something hidden and painful and lost. "Emma?"

"We're done. See you around, Pastor Jake. Maybe. See what happens this Sunday when people find out what sort of fraud you are. See what happens then. Abandoned? You'll see, Jake. You'll see."

Emma closed the door.

"I'll be back, Emma. God did not abandon me. I won't abandon you, either."

She spun around on her heel.

"Hey, don't bother with any special treatment for me, okay? Once people find out, you won't be around anymore. So don't bother."

And all Jake saw was the heels of her feet, hurrying up the steps and out of view.

15

Jake spent all of Friday and all of Saturday in his study.

He stopped at the RV several times, checking. Tassy did not work on Fridays and she said she felt a little better. Jake insisted she make an appointment at the county health department in Coudersport for a prenatal checkup, which she did.

Other than making coffee in the morning, Jake spent the majority of both days working on his message. By Saturday evening, he thought that his sermon was in good shape. Not spectacular—but good.

On Sunday morning, he woke up at 4:00, well before the sun rose, and walked into the office. He picked up his packet of sermon notes. By the time he read through the second point, he realized, beyond a shadow of a doubt, it was a sermon he could not deliver. Not now. Maybe not ever.

He tossed the notes back onto his desk.

Petey walked in, meowing to himself.

"What do I say, Petey? What do I say? Emma must have said something about all this to at least one person . . . so the whole town knows about everything, by now. So what do I say?"

Petey jumped up on the desk in one fluid motion and then flopped onto his side, purring loudly. Jake petted his side.

"I don't know what you want," he said.

Petey purred louder.

"Lord . . . what do I say? What do I tell these people? How I betrayed them? How I found you? What?"

Jake held the hymnal for the first two songs of the Sunday service and pretended to sing, just mouthing the words, just moving his lips. Elder Keilback presented the announcements for the day—the upcoming all-church picnic, the status of the steeple fund. There might have been others, but Jake hardly heard a word of it.

He glanced down at the bulletin. The sermon would immediately follow the announcements.

Jake swallowed hard, stood up, and walked to the pulpit.

Petey was already in his usual chair, sitting, precise and attentive. The church was full. Jake had read all the studies that indicated if a church wanted to grow in attendance, it needed to have 10 percent of its seating capacity unfilled. Fewer open seats than that meant newcomers would feel uncomfortable and not return. Perhaps another ten people could fit in the church, if others scooted down a little bit. They had enough room to place folding chairs in the aisles, something the elders had talked about but had not yet scheduled. It would add another thirty spots.

"We're always down a little during summer anyhow," one of them said. "Let's table the extra chair discussion until the fall. Then we'll see."

A building program . . . well, there had never been a building program at the Church of the Open Door, so none of the elders had experience holding on to the idea. They had never once needed to consider an expansion of their facilities.

Until the cat showed up, that is.

Along with Pastor Jake.

Jake took hold of both sides of the pulpit. They had raised it six inches a few weeks earlier, at Jake's request. The carpentry work was not elegant, nor seamless, but the pulpit now stood higher and was more comfortable for the pastor.

Jake normally took his notes, which he always folded precisely, lengthwise, out of his breast pocket.

This morning, he did not take out his notes. He had no notes. This morning, he realized, something different would be required. There was no need for a prepared sermon.

Jake took off his sport coat and laid it on one of the chairs next to Petey.

That was not unusual. When the temperature rose, the church people cared less about style. The pastor could preach in a shirt, without a tie, when the thermometer rose past eighty degrees.

But today, the temperature hovered in the mid-seventies, with low humidity.

Jake looked out on the congregation. He knew almost all of them, at least by first name, maybe not all intimately yet, but he knew them all. And they knew him. He could not go to downtown Coudersport without running into someone from the church, or someone related to someone from the church.

Coudersport was a small town, but people already knew Jake . . . and perhaps even respected him, a little.

He looked at their faces. He tried to decipher what they were thinking. He attempted to gauge how many had heard the secret Emma held—the secret Emma said she was going to unleash on Coudersport.

He did not see incredulity or anger or disbelief or suspicion.

He saw the same earnest, hardworking, honest (for the most part), genuine people he saw the very first time he spoke

in this church. He saw Jimbo and his wife. He saw Eleanor and
Vern. He saw Tassy sitting next to them, her face more radiant
today than ever before. He saw Sidney's mother, beaming. He
had told her about his meeting and prayer with Sidney. He saw
people expecting to hear from God that day—not hoping, not
wishing but expecting. This is the day when God would speak
to them most clearly.

They knew God was everywhere, and all the time. They
knew that. But they also knew—no, felt—God spoke to them
most clearly and directly in church. That is how it worked in
their lives. God speaks most clearly when they are behind the
church doors and under the cross on the steeple.

Jake cleared his throat.

He said a very short and very concise prayer—silently, to
himself.

Help me.

And he concluded it very concisely.

Thank you.

He cleared his throat again. It was a nervous tic, and he
knew it, and he did his best to keep the throat-clearing under
control. He did not want to be that pastor who every teenage
boy in the youth group could imitate with startling clarity, and
all they would have to do is clear their throats a few dozen
times before speaking.

"Friends," he began.

*And they are my friends. For the first time in my church career,
I have friends in the church.*

"I have to share something with you today. I never intended
on sharing this with you. But I have to. I always knew, eventually,
the truth would come out. And the truth will be better now
than waiting until later. That's when truth turns bitter."

Now he noticed a shift in the attitude of those listening. They had noticed he had not started off the sermon with a joke or a personal story, or something he had read in the newspaper.

Today felt real and serious.

Several people leaned forward. Some people appeared to be bracing themselves, as if they were about to embark on some roller-coaster thrill ride at Kennywood Park.

"I am going to tell you something about myself that I hoped I would keep forever hidden. But there is no secret that can remain a secret forever. All secrets get told, eventually. No confidence is forever confidential."

Now, everyone was listening—even the few older men who always fell asleep during the first two minutes of Jake's sermons.

"When I came to this church, when you invited me to this church to become your pastor . . . I am sure—no, positive—you all expected me to have this strong faith and a resolute, bedrock trust in the Almighty. You expected me to have no doubts as to the center of the Christian life. You expected, and you deserved, a man who had a solid, sure, positive, long-time, deep-seated, forever sort of faith."

He took a breath. The rest of the congregation seemed to breathe in with him. A great deal of fresh air left the sanctuary with one assembled breath.

"I was not that person. I had doubts. Serious doubts. When I was a pastor in Butler . . . at the church where I served before I came here, I told a woman I was dating I just wasn't sure about my relationship with God. I told her I wasn't sure if God was really watching me and directing my life. I was honest when I told her I just didn't have . . . I didn't have faith anymore."

Jake stopped for a moment.

The congregation did not seem to be incensed or angry or to be thinking about getting out their pitchforks and torches.

They did seem as if they were intent on hearing this story play out, however. Very intent.

"When I told her, this woman I was dating, that information, that secret was no longer a secret, and it got back to the senior pastor of the church. I know. I know. It was bound to happen. That's why I said that no secret ever stays a secret long if more than one person knows it."

Jake walked away from the pulpit. There was a microphone on the pulpit, and a small amplifier, but the sanctuary was not large. Anything spoken aloud, with some power, even a little power, was loud enough for everyone to hear. Jake made sure he spoke loudly and clearly.

"So my boss, the senior pastor, asked me if it was true—me admitting to this woman that I had lost my faith. I could have lied and said she had been mistaken."

Jake paused.

"Did I mention this young woman was the senior pastor's niece?"

There was a smattering of nervous laughter, and those who laughed quickly realized it was not a laugh line and immediately ended their smiles and laughter.

"I could have lied and blamed this woman for 'misinterpreting' what I had said in confidence. But even I couldn't do that. I told him it was the truth. That what she had said was true."

Jake sat down in the chair next to Petey. Petey meowed as Jake sat, as if to say his actions were most unusual and did he really know what he was doing this morning?

"He fired me. He had to. He had no choice. You can't have a pastor—someone in charge of the spiritual well-being of hundreds of people—who doesn't have faith. An oxymoron."

Jake wasn't sure if a majority of people sitting in front of him knew what an oxymoron was.

"Like jumbo shrimp. That's an oxymoron. Is it jumbo or is it small?"

He grinned at them. "He fired me and I can't blame him one bit for doing that. A pastor who no longer has faith may be acceptable in some churches, but not a church that really believes in the Bible and everything it teaches. A pastor without faith."

He stood. "An oxymoron."

He walked back to the pulpit, carefully choosing each step.

"So I started here as a pastor without faith. And I think I was doing okay. Even though I thought God had abandoned me. I've told you about my childhood. I've told you my father left us. He abandoned us. I intimately knew that feeling—the feeling of being alone. What I felt about my father's leaving, well, I thought God had done the same thing to me. And when my father left, I pretended to be brave and strong. I thought if I did everything right and went to seminary and became a pastor, then everything would be fine and dandy. It wasn't. It caught up to me. A few days ago, I was praying with a young man who was looking for faith. And he found it—just like that. He was filled with faith and the Holy Spirit. Immediately."

Jake snapped his fingers. It sounded loud in the still church. He looked out and saw Glenda Davis, near the back, tears in her eyes.

"Just like that. Amazing. Here I was struggling and working and striving to regain my faith—and this young man just lays down his arms, stops battling, and accepts. And there it was."

He walked to the other side if the platform.

"This is what I discovered. This is what I learned. God never left me. He was always there. I wandered off. God didn't. And he sent me a cat. He sent this church a cat. Petey. How many people are here today because Petey is here?"

A number of people—a large number of people—raised their hands.

"God cares about you. Enough to send a cat—because He knew that is what would work. That is what would draw you inside a church. He brought you all here."

Jake sat down on the steps of the raised platform.

"But I've lied to you. I have been a fraud. I have said I was a man of God . . . but until a few days ago, I was lying. I'm sorry. So, so sorry. You need someone better. You deserve someone better. You do. This church deserves the truth."

Jake clasped his hands together, loosely, and sat still for a moment, not speaking.

What happened next surprised Jake. Really, really surprised him.

The massive elder, Rudolph Keilback, stood up in the pew. He made his way to the center aisle, people parting to let him pass, like Moses and the Red Sea. He turned to face Jake and marched up the center aisle. Jake looked up at his face. Rudolph wiped his cheeks with the back of his hand. He might have been crying.

"Listen. I don't want to be up here. I don't do well in front. You all know that. But . . . Pastor Jake . . . you can't leave us. I . . . said I believed when I was a little kid. But you want to know the secret I kept for the past forty years? I never did believe. I don't think I did. I went to church. I went to church for years. I'm an elder. But I never knew . . ."

He held the pulpit with both meaty hands and gripped it so hard Jake was sure he'd hear wood splintering.

"Not until Pastor Jake showed up did I know what it was to believe. And not until today did I ever think anyone else had that problem or that secret. If you think you have to leave, Pastor Jake, then so do I."

Quiet filled the sanctuary like a tidal wave.

After at least a full two minutes of silence, with Elder Keilback at the pulpit and Pastor Jake sitting on the platform, another man rose. He was in the middle of the row, seven rows back.

"I never believed either. Until right now. I've been pretending. Thank you, Pastor Jake, for making it okay for me to . . . cry with you. And to find faith with you."

A woman stood up on the other side of the aisle.

"I've been head deaconess longer than a lot of you have been alive. Today I believe. Today I have faith. Today it all became real. Today my real life with God starts."

Jimbo stood up. His wife, at his side, was in tears.

"I know I could be a better husband. I could listen more. I don't know what I would do without . . . Betty here. I would be lost—totally and utterly lost."

Jimbo had begun to tear up as well.

"Family. That's what matters. This family."

Tassy stood up. She was holding on to Eleanor's hand. Jake could see that their grips were tight, white-knuckle tight, perhaps.

"You here are all my family. This church is my family. And I have a secret I need to share with you all. I'm going to have a baby. And before today, I was planning on running away because I felt like you would all be disappointed with me. I almost had an abortion. I came within minutes of it. Petey saved me. It's a long story. God led me here—to this church and to Pastor Jake and to Petey. He has protected me. And now you're my family. And I promise I will do my best to make the faith you have in me worth it. I promise."

Eleanor stood up and put her arm around the young girl's shoulder. Vern stood up as well, his eyes and face wet, and embraced them both.

And people began to cry and to pray and to hug and to embrace.

Jake saw a few people standing in the back. One of them was Speedy . . . Sidney Davis. His mother was crying harder now.

And that's when the church organist, Verna Ebbert, walked up to the platform, switched on the organ with an audible pop, and began to play a warbly, off-tempo rendition of "Just as I Am."

Just as I am, without one plea,
but that thy blood was shed for me,
and that thou bidst me come to thee,
O Lamb of God, I come, I come.

Just as I am, and waiting not
to rid my soul of one dark blot,
to thee whose blood can cleanse each spot,
O Lamb of God, I come, I come.

Just as I am, though tossed about
with many a conflict, many a doubt,
fightings and fears within, without,
O Lamb of God, I come, I come.

Just as I am, poor, wretched, blind;
sight, riches, healing of the mind,
yea, all I need in thee to find,
O Lamb of God, I come, I come.

Just as I am, thou wilt receive,
wilt welcome, pardon, cleanse, relieve;
because thy promise I believe,
O Lamb of God, I come, I come.

Just as I am, thy love unknown
hath broken every barrier down;
now, to be thine, yea, thine alone,
O Lamb of God, I come, I come.

To Jake, it was the most beautiful song he had ever heard, better than a celestial choir of a thousand angels.

Much, much better.

———

Sunday service ran long that day.

There was a lot of singing. There was a lot of sharing, a lot of asking for forgiveness. There was more hugging in the church this Sunday than there had been in the last decade. Perhaps two decades.

At a few minutes past 2:00, a few people decided they were really hungry, or they had children who were really, really hungry, so the crowd started to slowly disassemble. By 3:00, the sanctuary was empty, save for Pastor Jake and Petey.

Jake could not help smiling. It was not a smug smile, or a self-satisfied smile, but a smile warmed by gratitude and amazement.

"God showed up, didn't he, Petey?"

Petey meowed contentedly.

"I know you thought you had it all figured out . . . but I sure didn't. I never expected any of this to happen. Never in a million years."

Jake was sitting on the platform steps, and Petey lay down next to him and rolled on his side. Jake petted his stomach and Petey rolled his head back and forth, purring loudly, content, happy.

"There is probably one more person I need to deal with today."

Petey looked up.

"Emma. Dr. Grainger."

Petey meowed in agreement.

"I should go now. She might think she destroyed my career. But in reality, she started it."

Jake stood and pulled out his truck keys.

"Want to come?"

Petey stayed exactly where he was.

"Okay. I'll leave the office door open. Okay?"

The cat chirped a reply.

A few minutes later, Jake stood outside Dr. Grainger's door—the side door, her private entrance. He was not frightened or anxious or nervous or intimidated. All that had apparently disappeared with a number of Jake's other fears and phobias.

He saw the curtain move in an upstairs window. She had to have seen his truck in the drive. A moment later, he heard footsteps—slow, methodical, as if each step down was a harder step to take.

She turned the inside latch and opened the door, only a quarter of the way. Jake was pretty sure he saw fear in her face.

"Emma, I want to apologize to you again. I should have been honest with you from the very beginning. I wasn't. I led a lot of people to believe I was something much more good and noble than I really was. But all that has changed."

Emma's face did not show a smile or a frown or any emotion at all. She had become a cipher, neutral.

"I spent all of Friday and Saturday trying to figure out how to spin what happened, how to make people believe that what happened didn't happen the way it happened. But then, this morning, I realized I could no longer pretend. I stood up and confessed everything to the church. And no one condemned me. They forgave me."

Now Emma looked surprised.

"Others stood up alongside me and confessed to have the same doubts. People began to cry and hug one another and forgive one another for past transgressions. It was the most amazing church service I have ever been part of. And you know . . . when I was praying with Speedy—rather, Sidney—Davis, praying for his faith . . . that's when my faith welled up inside of me. I had spent so much time working, trying to find it and to cultivate it . . . and all I had to do was accept it. You taught me a valuable lesson, Emma. And I want to thank you for that."

Emma remained surprised. Her eyes were wider than they had been.

"You're . . . you're welcome, I guess," she said.

"Thanks for helping me finally see the truth. Thank you so much."

Jake left her standing in her doorway and walked back to his truck, feeling lighter and clearer and more solid than he had ever felt in his entire life.

16

Three weeks later, Jake had a meeting with Wilbur Brookings, the head of the elder board. The meeting was a small one—just Jake and Wilbur—with coffee and donuts at Kaytee's. Several donuts, actually. Kaytee's made very good donuts.

Wilbur wanted the meeting to stay confidential, at least temporarily.

"You said it yourself, Pastor. A secret is compromised the second another person hears it. So I'm trusting you to hold this one under your hat for a while. Since you're an honest man and all."

Jake promised that he would, and then braced himself for what might be coming.

"We need to start a building committee," Wilbur said in a whisper. "The church is packed and it's summer, and no one comes in the summer. We're putting chairs in the aisles and that's not enough—or comfortable. So my question is, how do you go about starting a building committee? We've never done this before. I've never done this before."

Jake was taken aback, for a little bit. He was expecting something darker, more personal. Building onto the church was neither of those. Jake had never started a building campaign either but had a shelf of books in his office that described the process and the parameters and the pitfalls.

"I'll look at them and get you the two best ones. That will be our start. And I promise not a word will escape my lips until you say so."

Wilbur sighed deeply, and it was a happy sigh, if sighs can have happy connotations.

"I blame that stupid cat, you know. And you, too, Pastor Jake. We could have stayed small and happy if it weren't for you two."

He paused for effect, then smiled.

"I'm kidding. But you knew that, right?"

Jake sat at Kaytee's by himself after Wilbur left.

He was simply happy to sit there with his coffee and one more small chocolate donut . . . until Emma Grainger walked in. She saw him and hesitated, then seemed to shrug to herself, and walked to his table.

He was pretty sure that the waitresses knew what had gone on between them. No—he was not just pretty sure. He was positive. News that delicious does not remain untasted, especially in a town this small.

"We should probably talk, Jake."

Jake bore no anger or grudge. He liked Emma. He liked her a lot. And he was willing to let her walk away from a relationship with him if that was her choice. And it certainly appeared to be her choice.

"Sure," Jake replied. "Anytime."

Emma pulled a chair out and sat down.

"How about now?"

"Now is fine," Jake said. *Now* did surprise him a little. He thought she might give him some time to prepare. Or give herself time to build up courage or whatever she needed. But no, it would be now.

"First off, I need to tell you that I didn't mention your . . . 'situation' with Barbara Ann to anyone in town. I wanted to. I really wanted to hurt you badly. But I didn't say anything."

Jake wanted to take her hand and squeeze it in a reassuring way but did not.

"I know," he replied. "Some of our more . . . attentive church members, the ones that are more plugged in, if you know what I mean, asked me later why I'd said anything at all. And I told them I figured they had all heard about Barbara Ann and what happened. But no one had heard a word before I brought it up that Sunday. I see now I easily could have kept that secret a secret. But I am so grateful I didn't. And I'm glad you didn't say anything to anyone. That's a lot to feel responsible for."

"I wanted to tell everyone, Jake. I did. More than you can imagine."

Jake nodded to the waitress who came by with a coffeepot. He waited until she poured the coffee and left.

"Emma, you don't owe me any explanation. And I may be out of line for asking. But . . . I'll ask anyway. Why? Why did you want to see me hurt?"

Emma looked pale and drawn, as if she had not slept well the past few weeks.

"You talked about honesty. I suspect I need be honest about this as well. Hiding it all these years hasn't done me much good."

Jake waited. Tassy had suggested a possible reason for Emma's anger, but Jake wasn't sure. For the last few weeks, Tassy said Dr. Grainger had been strictly professional in the office. Not cold or hostile or angry, just a chilly sort of professionalism. Tassy did not mind, but she did feel bad for Dr. Grainger. It appeared to her that Dr. Grainger was not enjoying anything.

"It started just before I headed off to vet school. The summer before."

Emma looked down at her hands, folded in her lap.

"Do you want some tea, Emma? or coffee? or toast?" Jake asked.

She looked up, offered him a weak smile.

"No. Maybe water. I'll drink yours if I need it. You've had your shots, right?"

They both smiled.

"I have my papers," Jake said. "Me and Petey both."

He waited.

"I got pregnant," Emma said. "He said he would take care of me. He made it sound like everything would work out. I loved him. I loved him a lot. We were perfect for each other. He would be a doctor and I would be a vet. Perfect."

She looked out the window and watched a TrueValue hardware truck make its way, carefully, down the narrow street.

Jake had learned that being attentive and silent was often all that was required of a good listener.

"Then he said one of us would have to give up their dream. If I 'went through with this.' He said we had to be adult about it. He said we needed to 'handle it.' He said nothing would change afterward. He promised me nothing would change— after we handled it."

She took in several deep breaths, trying not to choke up, trying not to cry.

"He promised."

She looked down, away from Jake's eyes.

"We handled it. It was hard, but he was with me. It would be okay. He promised. And then he left. He never talked to me again. He's married now, to another doctor. They live in Dallas. I handled it for him. So we could both keep our dreams. No one would get hurt."

Jake waited. Emma did not cry. But she did not look up, either.

"I murdered my first child," Emma said. "My only child. I live with that every day, Jake. There's not a day that goes by that I don't think about my baby, a baby I had killed. It's hard. It is very, very hard. Some days I just do not know what to do with the truth."

She looked away for a long time and Jake let the silence be.

"And when Tassy found out she was pregnant—all that anger came back. Here was a young girl who was in the same situation I was in. I was cheated, Jake. I was cheated out of a child. And abandoned. I'll never have children now. That's what the doctors have told me. And I didn't want anyone else to have what I can't have anymore, either. That's why I tried to get Tassy to an abortion clinic."

Now she started to cry.

"I am so sorry, Jake. I am so sorry for what I almost did to her. I feel like the worst person in the world. She comes to the office in the morning, and I see her all radiant and growing and happy—and I don't know how I will get through the day without being reminded every second of what I almost forced her to do."

She grabbed a thickness of napkins from the chrome dispenser on the table. She wiped her eyes and her cheeks.

"How do I do this, Jake? How do I move on from here? How do I move on from murder?"

This time, Jake followed his instinct and took one of her hands. From the corner of his eye, he could see the waitress in the far corner, by the coffee service, put her hand up to her mouth as he did that.

There are no secrets, especially in a small town.

"Emma. We can start over. Your life can start anew right now."

Emma sniffed.

"What I tried to do was horrible. To her. To you."

"You want it to be forgiven? I forgive you. Tassy loves you like she would love an older sister. She would forgive, even though she knows there is nothing to forgive. You acted out of pain. And what is bigger than her or me is the fact that God loves you, Emma. And he will never leave you. There is nothing we can do that will strip God's love for us. Nothing, Emma. That is true. And that is faith. He will never leave you."

She looked up, tears streaking down her face.

To Jake, she looked beautiful.

"Can you show me what I need to see? What I need to feel? Can you show me this faith you have?"

"I can try," he said. "I can try."

⟨∞⟩

Tassy handed the keys to the RV to Jake.

"I'll miss living here. I'll miss having you to talk to. I'll miss Petey."

Petey stood at Tassy's side, meowing, rubbing his face against her shin, then meowing again. There was a suitcase on her other side, and Petey knew what suitcases meant. They meant good-byes, and Petey did not like good-byes.

No one said anything about her leaving.

He jumped up on the suitcase and stared at them both, Jake and Tassy, with defiance in his eyes.

She can't leave now. Not with me on the suitcase. She'll have to stay here forever and ever.

Tassy leaned into Pastor Jake and hugged him with a fierceness.

"I'll be here for you. Anytime you want me, I'll be here. And I know you won't have Petey to talk to—but you'll have Winston."

What!? Winston is leaving, too? That doesn't make any sense.

"I'm happy for you and happy for Emma. She does have a lot of spare bedrooms. One will make a great nursery."

"That's what she said. She wants it all pink and frilly. I was thinking something a little more hard rock and edgy."

She's moving in with Dr. Grainger? Why doesn't anyone tell me anything important? First, I find out the house with wheels has to be moved. Then they tell me a new building is going to start soon. And now Tassy is leaving. You take a few naps, and the world passes you by. I don't get it.

"And I guess I'll see you there as well . . . sometimes. Right?"

Jake tried not to grin.

"We are taking things very slow. Emma needs to let her faith grow without me holding her hand. So we're moving slow."

"But steady."

"Okay—slow but steady. No heavy lifting at the moment."

Tassy laughed. "Speaking of lifting, how's your shoulder? Dr. Grainger said she knows a great chiropractor. She knows the best of everything around here. She knew the best obstetrician—and Dr. Hallis has been so sweet to me."

"My shoulder is fine. For the most part. That's just me getting old in front of your eyes."

An old Buick with dented front fenders bounced into the parking lot.

"You're not getting old. Now, Mr. Waldorf—he's getting old. But he's my ride today. He and Eleanor insisted."

Jake waved. Vern almost waved back. Eleanor did.

Tassy stood on her tiptoes and kissed Jake's cheek.

"I love you, Pastor Jake."

Hey! What about me? I'm the one who saved you. Petey meowed and nearly stood erect, swatting at Tassy's side.

"And you, too, Petey," she said as she gave him a dainty kiss on his forehead. "I love you most of all."

Epilogue

Early autumn is a most beautiful time in Coudersport. The oaks and cherry trees start to redden and yellow and the hills are aflame with fall colors, the sort of colors an artist could never hope to truly capture.

The air grows neat with a chill, just the hint of chill, and a scent of apples and of harvested corn and pumpkins fills the valleys.

Petey took to lying on the concrete steps to the old sanctuary, catching the afternoon sun.

He sat up, adjusted himself with great care, and looked up at the heavens.

This was where I was supposed to be. Jake was the man I was sent to help. This has happened like it was supposed to happen. Like I said on that first day. I am really pretty certain I am the only cat that could have done this. I am a smart cat, aren't I? I am a good cat.

While he sat, still as a statue, he heard a rustling, then saw a nervous dart of gray and brown. A field mouse scurried across the bottom step, oblivious to Petey, since he had not moved in some minutes. Petey flinched, just the merest fraction of an inch.

No. No one here needs a mouse right now. Maybe later. But I don't need one now. Not today. I have too much already.

He watched the mouse disappear under a thickness of dried leaves.

I am a good cat, aren't I?

A good cat and a smart cat.

Discussion Questions

1. Come on now, a cat? Really? A cat who thinks he talks to God and is following God's instructions? Seriously though, do you think that God could, or would, use such a method as that to reach a person who is lost?

2. In a sense, Jake Wilkerson assumes the position of pastor of the small Church of the Open Door under false pretenses: he is pretending to have faith and be spiritually mature. Do you think God can use a broken person in such a way, or do you think Jake was being deceptive? Why would God choose such a person to lead others?

3. Besides his feeling lost, what other obstacles does Jake face in his return to the pulpit and to faith?

4. Perhaps Vern Waldorf is simply being honest when he grows angry over the idea of letting Tassie live in his RV. Perhaps he is simply mirroring the views of some of the "upstanding Christians" in the community. How might we be guilty of the same sort of attitude if we try to separate ourselves from someone who seems to be sinning?

5. Suppose Jake is only thinking that Petey is manipulating him into certain situations? In what ways can that sort of "perceived manipulation" be the sort of nudge we need to turn back to God? And could the nudge from a manipulating cat be of a divine nature?

6. Dr. Emma Grainger lets her past actions define who she is—even if she is not aware of it. Do you agree with that statement? Are there things in your life that are defined by what you have done in the past? Is that always a bad or negative thing?

7. Tassie is nearly convinced to have an abortion because of the strident urgings of Dr. Grainger, a person she

greatly respects. The doctor uses her position to attempt to get Tassie to do what she says. Is using our position to get people to act in a certain way or to do certain things always a negative? Have you ever used your position or standing to get someone to conform to your way of thinking?

8. Many people get stuck in a situation or an emotion because of a tragedy or dramatic event in their life. What sort of advice would you have given Emma? Would that advice change over time—would the advice you offered a month after the abortion be dramatically different than the advice offered a year after the abortion?

9. As an outsider, and a stranger, and an unwed mother-to-be, Tassie faces some immense challenges in her life. Do you think she handles them well? Do you think she listens to others too much? What would you have done in the same situation?

10. Petey the cat seems to draw a lot of people to the church—perhaps only because of the novelty of it all. Do you think it is wise of the elders to condone such an action? Do you think that simply preaching the word should have been enough? Do you think that the cat on the platform with the preacher is simply a gimmick—and that God never uses "gimmicks" to attract people to the truth?

11. When Dr. Grainger learns the truth about Jake's past church experience and his past relationship experience with Barbara Ann Bentley, she truly wants to use that information to damage Jake's reputation and to hurt him. Has anyone ever hurt you using "the truth" as a weapon? When is it okay to leave secrets secret? Is it always necessary to tell the "whole" truth?

12. Jake's mother is terribly controlling—or at least tries to be—all with good intentions. She wants Jake to do well, wants him to be free of scandal, she wants the best for her son. Have you ever felt overwhelmed by the crush of "good intentions" from someone who was just trying to do good? Is there a way to gently tell people that they have gone too far in their efforts at helping you?

13. Do you think that Jake and Dr. Emma eventually get married? Do you think the story would be satisfying if they didn't? Why or why not?

14. Do you think that Emma will eventually find faith? Is it proper for a pastor to "see" someone who is not a believer—yet—but seems to be well on their way to finding faith? How would that be received at your church?

If you missed Jim Kraus's first adventure, check out this sample chapter

———— ∞ ————

The Dog That Talked to God

1

Born in the wealthy enclave of Barrington, Illinois, in late autumn, Rufus was the smallest pup in a litter of four—black with white highlights, white eyebrows and chest. The breeder, a precise woman with a lazy eye, said that as an adult, he would most likely remain on the smallish side. That's a good trait for a miniature schnauzer. He had the look, even as a seven-week-old, of a polished, professional dog, holding a practiced dog show stance—legs back, chest forward, eyes alert—all inherited traits, genetics at its best.

But she said nothing about Rufus talking. Not just talking, but talking to God. In dog prayers, I imagine.

Though, in her defense, I would guess that she was unaware of this unusual talent.

And, also in her defense, if she knew of his abilities and had mentioned, "Oh yes, Mrs. Fassler, and the runt of the litter—the dog you want—well, he talks, and he claims he talks to God." I mean, honestly, if she had said that, or anything remotely like that, then odds are that the good dog Rufus would not be sitting in the chair opposite me right now, watching me type.

Perhaps if Rufus had been adopted into another home—a home with an owner who wasn't lost and confused and didn't need to be returned to the awareness of the existence of God— he would not have bothered speaking at all, except to bark at the door to be let out. Even Rufus is not sure of that possibility.

"I don't ask foolish questions, Mary," Rufus answered when I asked him about the odds of him spending his life with me, rather than some other, more spiritually healthy person.

But I digress.

I did not mean to cavalierly hurry past the most compelling element of this story: the fact that Rufus talks to God. And he talks to me—Rufus, that is, not God. Sometimes.

It's hard to be nonchalant or blasé about such an ability, I know. But I cannot leap into this tale without returning to the beginning. You need to know how all this came about. You need to know the origins of the story. After all, what would the Bible be without Genesis and the garden of Eden? Confusing, to say the least, and most likely incomprehensible. Imagine the Bible as a movie you walk into during the middle. You can make up your own backstory, but it would all be just a guess. Admit it: without that opening scene, not much of the rest would contain any internal logic.

As a child, I used to do that—walk into a movie theater whenever, and watch the film, sit through the ending, and wait for the opening reel to start again until I would say to myself, "This is where I came in." It was easier years ago, before the age of googolplexes and corporate theater chains. Back in the day, each theater had one screen and would play the same movie over and over, with only a cartoon and previews to separate one screening from another. Once I got to that point of having seen a particular scene before, I would leave, satisfied that I had seen the entire story. I remember doing that to *The Time Machine* with Rod Taylor, a movie star without much reason to be a star. Seems ludicrous to me now. I had constructed my own narrative as to how Rod got to whatever point in the future he started at, which then altered my imagined story as the true narrative unfolded. With that movie, I was close to guessing the actual story and plot. Close, but, as they say, no cigar.

As a child, reconstructing a complicated narrative was child's play.

It is not so easy today.

Throughout my youth, my family owned pets. Owned, I suspect, is now a pejorative term. I mean, do we really own a dog? Or do we merely cohabit in the same spaces? The latter, I am now certain. My father, an impetuous man with a generous heart, once bought a squirrel monkey from Gimbels Department Store in Pittsburgh, Pennsylvania—when department stores, I surmise, could sell squirrel monkeys.

A monkey proved to be a pretty interesting pet, but if you fed it something it did not like, it would simply heave it out of the cage. Neatness is not any monkey's most endearing trait.

I remember growing up with a mutt, the family dog, a loyal animal who became as much a member of the family as I. As a teenager, I stood beside her in the vet's office when he administered the oh-so-humane and oh-so-lethal injection to a lame, sick, dying dog. I remember her eyes, just as they went dark. I remember weeping all night over that loss.

In my forties (midway, if I am feeling honest) I found myself alone again. I was pretty certain I needed a dog. Christmas was coming and I did not want to be alone.

Before—well, before my current losses and tragedies—the parameters of a dog purchase became the topic of long conversations among Jacob, John, and me. It had been decided that hypoallergenic was a necessity; preferably nonshedding, small, with minimal genetic health concerns, loyal, good with children, non-nippy, benevolent, artistic, and kind. Just kidding about the last three, but we did have a pretty substantial list of preferences. The miniature schnauzer breed met all of our qualifications.

But we, as a family, never had a chance to fulfill that dream.

Alone, now, I decided to take action—and taking action was something I did not do lightly. Unlike me, the schnauzer, according to the breed books, had decisiveness bred into its genes. A good watchdog, the books insisted. A barker, but not a biter. Since I live in a relatively safe suburb, a barker would be sufficient.

I made a few calls; I looked on the Internet.

A friend advised against getting any dog. "They're all the same—stupid, hairy, and only interested in food. Trust me," she had said. "You will get companionship, but it will be stupid companionship. Like a blind date who you find out later cheated to get his GED, and who is five inches shorter than he claimed."

She owned an Irish setter, a truly small-brained animal. I say she owned it since she did all the dog upkeep in her family—feeding, walking, feeding, letting out, letting in, feeding, washing the muck off of it. The rest of the household liked the dog, but as is often usual for families, the mother remained stuck with all the dog duties. And to complicate things, her dog could not be described as smart—not even close to smart.

It ran into the same glass sliding door every morning of its life. Like a chicken, it appeared to wake up to a new world every dawn. A pleasant dog, for certain, but, as noted, not very smart. And it often smelled wet. Most of us know that musty, yeasty, heady, nearly unpleasant aroma of a wet dog. Like wet newspaper. What they have in common is beyond me.

"But I'm looking at a smaller dog. Something that I can pick up if I have to," I told her.

It took two people to lift my friend's Irish setter, or a single person using a hospital patient lift—and where was one of those when needed?

"Jacob always wanted a schnauzer. Sort of like fulfilling a promise, you know?" I added.

My friend shrugged, apparently resigned to my choice, to my fate.

After all, how do you argue with one of the last wishes of a dead man?

There were a few AKC breeders near where I live who specialized in miniature schnauzers.

And when I was ready, only one breeder—the precise lady in Barrington with the lazy eye—had a litter with an unspoken-for puppy.

"I have a litter of four. The two females are spoken for. The larger male is going to another breeder in Florida. That leaves one male puppy. He's the runt of the litter. But he's healthy."

I attempted to make arrangements to complete the purchase.

"It's not that simple," she said, a slight note of caution in her voice. "Before you come, I have some questions. Save you a trip. I don't sell my dogs to just anyone."

"Of course not," I said, thinking it was a poor method of marketing puppies, but I played along. "I completely understand."

"Do you live in a house or an apartment?"

"A house. It's too big for me," I said, telling this stranger more than she needed to know. "I plan on selling in a year or two, and moving to a smaller house. More manageable. But a house. A house, yes, not an apartment or a condo. I don't think I would do well in an apartment anymore. Odd noises and someone is always cooking with too much curry. So, yes, I have a house. I will have a house. Now. And in the future."

"Does the house have a yard? Will the new house have a yard?"

Don't all houses have yards?

"It does. And the back is fenced. It's pretty big. The landscapers bill me $40 a week to cut it . . . so there's a lot of room for a dog to run. And if I do move, that house will have a fenced yard. Keeps out the riffraff dogs, if you know what I mean."

Her silence probably meant that she didn't.

"Do you work?"

No . . . I thought I might pay for the puppy with food stamps.

Sorry. That's just me being snarky. Sorry.

"Yes."

"Are you gone all day? Will the dog be alone all day?"

Oh . . . now I see why you're asking.

"No. I work from home. I write books. And I edit some. And I publish a newsletter for writers. But I'm home 95 percent of most weekdays. I do go out to Starbucks sometimes to write. There's something about having to block out other people's conversations that makes me concentrate more effectively. But that's only once a week. Maybe twice, if I'm stumped by something."

The precise lady waited, then spoke carefully.

"I wouldn't sell this dog to a single person who worked outside the home all day. These puppies need companionship.

They'll get neurotic without a person—or people—around. Nothing worse than a neurotic dog."

She said nothing about dogs that had delusions of grandeur. Would I describe Rufus as . . . delusional? Or would that just be me?

"Any small children in the home?"

I waited a heartbeat, as I have done now for these last few years, until that small scud of darkness passed.

"No. No one else. It's just me."

The precise lady must have been thinking "divorced," or "widowed," or "never married." I did not volunteer further information. She did not ask. Often, when even thinking about the past, even to myself—still—I would get teary. Buying a dog is no time to get teary.

"Well, why don't you come up this Saturday? The puppy won't be ready to leave for at least another three weeks. You can see how you'll get on with him. We can talk."

I hung up the phone thinking that I need to make a good impression on this woman, or else I'll have to find another breeder and the next closest—with puppies available—was in Ohio. I did not want to drive to Ohio. Not just yet. Maybe not ever.

I arrived at the breeder's home early—a lifelong trait. To me, being on time is fifteen minutes early. The setting was not exactly rural, but I estimated that I was a good ten minutes from the nearest Starbucks—or a Texaco station selling chilled bottles of Starbucks Iced Coffee. So I sat in the drive and waited. I would have really liked a coffee. Caffeine settles my nerves.

I rattled in the car, more than a little nervous.

The breeder was exactly as I had pictured: precise, wore her hair short, trim, with practical glasses clipped to a gold chain around her neck; with that one eye slightly off-kilter to the other. She may have been wearing Earth Shoes. I was unaware if they had made a comeback; hers looked sensible and organic with a leather strap. I admit that I am far from being style-conscious. I buy good clothes, good outfits, designed to last. I haven't purchased a new outfit in years . . . well . . . since before the accident, I guess.

She extended her hand for a firm handshake, and escorted me to the basement. I could hear scuffling and yipping as we descended. In a large, airy room, with French doors leading to the outside, now closed, two adult schnauzers were in a large pen with what appeared to be a large, single mass of wiggling puppy. The room smelled of dog—but that inviting new-dog smell.

"Sit down," she said, and for that second I was not sure if the breeder meant me or the dogs. I realized that I should sit.

I sat on a plastic chair—one of two in the enclosure.

The two adult dogs sniffed the air, not in fear, but in exploration, in greeting. The larger one trotted over to me, placed its front paws on my knees, and stared hard into my eyes.

Schnauzer eyes are dark, or mostly dark, so the iris in their eyes is all but indistinguishable. They are like cartoon eyes—all one color—so it is difficult to see emotion in them. And schnauzers are not smilers. Some dogs—like labs, for example—can pull their lips back and offer a grin, with a lolling tongue. (I have since discovered that labs aren't that happy. They are simply manipulative.)

The larger dog, apparently satisfied with what it was looking for, hopped down.

The smaller dog walked toward me, with what I took to be deliberate steps. It too placed its paws on my knees and stared.

"That's the mom," the breeder said, not using the word *mom*, but the breeder word for a female dog—a word, incidentally, that I have never liked using, either in anger or in scientific dog-calling. She was Rufus's mother after all, though the name Rufus would not be decided for a few weeks.

She stared deeply, as deeply as a dog can stare, without being distracted by the yelping of one puppy or the whine of another. She stared, just stared, for the longest of moments. Longer than most dogs stare at anything, with the possible exception of an empty food bowl. (This I have learned recently as well.)

I didn't know what to do, so I gently covered her paws with my hands—like offering a manner of assurance that I was a good person who would treat her offspring well.

After what seemed to be a long time, she sort of gave a nod, like she approved, or found me acceptable, or knew her one special offspring was exactly the puppy I needed, then dropped back to the ground, sniffed my leg and shoe for a moment, and walked back to the big ball of puppies in the corner. This was not her first litter, so she obviously knew the routine. Puppies grow up and move on in the wild, and they do the same if they reside in urban domesticity.

The breeder walked over, reached in, and extracted a small furry lump of wiggle, mostly black, with some white. She handed it to me.

"This one will be yours if you want."

I held the small wriggling bud of puppy cupped in my two hands with plenty of room to spare.

"The pup can't see real well yet, so all it sees is your hands."

I stroked the little face with a finger, gentle, but not overly gentle. It was a boy puppy, after all. The puppy seemed to like that and promptly fell asleep in my hands.

"That's a good sign. Some dogs just stay all riled up—being picked up, carried, strange scents—they'll struggle to get away. Apparently, he thinks you're a safe place."

He was the most beautiful puppy I had ever seen.
And he fell asleep. My heart began to sing, just a little. After such a long silence, it startled me at its ability to do so.
This was indeed the puppy that I needed to have in my life.
More surprises came later.

⸺●⸺

The breeder gave me a list of things to do, and to have them all accomplished in the three weeks between the initial meeting and the final handoff—Rufus's adoption, as it was. The list was not extensive, but it was twice as long as I had anticipated.

"I can't visit your house, so you have to give me your word that all of it gets done. Okay?"

It was a command that I could not say no to.

"Of course."

I could see why she was good at training dogs. I really wanted to please her.

A dog crate; dog carrier for the car ride home; puppy food—one of two preferred brands—a water dish; collar, two leashes; one retractable, one a strong tether; the name of the dog's veterinarian; a picture of the fenced yard; an appointment set for a puppy class. The list ran on for nearly a full page.

Obtaining all the necessary documentation and supplies was not that difficult. The cage—sorry, the *crate*—fit into the alcove of a desk built into the kitchen layout. (I had been told that *cage* was pejorative, crate was preferred by most breeders.) I never used the kitchen desk, except as a temporary storehouse for receipts, mail, and magazines waiting to be evaluated before becoming recyclables. The top drawer held in the neighborhood of a thousand pens and pencils, all halfway to being thrown away because none of them worked, forcing me to take telephone notes with a huge felt-tipped sign marker on legal pads, the ink soaking through four sheets at a time.

I have to get better organized. I mean it this time.

The cage—rather, the crate—fit snugly in the kneehole of the desk. I added two sleeping pads, the top one a leopard print, to ensure a soft rest. I took a picture of it. I would show the breeder all my preparations.

No one prints pictures anymore. All they do is show others the back of their camera or cellphones. I miss passing actual snapshots around, but I didn't think I needed a permanent record of a dog crate and food bowls and the like, so I carried my camera with me.

I'll probably never delete them from the memory stick, though.

I wasn't sure about the crate situation. I never had a crated dog before. The family dog had the run of the house. Looking back, I don't remember where the dog slept. Did we have a dog bed somewhere? My mother, the sole surviving parent, resided in a nursing home, and while she had only begun to wade into the shallow, yet troubled waters of dementia, for now she would resent being asked inconsequential questions like "Where did the dog sleep?"

She would become agitated a little, and wave the question off as if it were a pesky mosquito. "How I am expected to remember foolish things like that?" she would snap, prickly as she had ever been. Some things do not change over the decades.

I would want to say that I did not expect her to recall the details, but that we were simply making conversation. Instead of asking a follow-up question about how the family had decided on a dog name, I would instead sit back, and watch

Wheel of Fortune with my mother. She could not hear worth beans and had no use for gadgets like hearing aids, so the volume would be turned up to a painful level. Virtually every television in the Ligonier Valley Nursing Unit remained turned to the same level. I don't understand how the nurses and aides tolerated it. It would be like working in a tavern that featured heavy metal music. Or working in a steel mill. Here, all televisions, except the one in the main visiting lounge, had to be turned off by eight in the evening. Then silence rolled down the halls like a tsunami.

The breeder said that the prehistoric dogs lived in dens, so a crate, which she was careful to call a crate, fulfills their ancestral urges of being covered, protected, and easily defended. I draped a thin blanket over the top and sides. I planned to swap the thin one out for a heavier one in colder weather. The door latched easily. The crate provided plenty of turnaround area. The padding looked, and felt, pretty comfortable as well.

I had not purchased the Kuranda Dog Bed—patented, orthopedic, and chew proof. It certainly looked comfortable in the pet store, nearly as expensive as the new mattress I had purchased for myself eighteen months earlier. That was a necessary purchase; a deluxe dog bed could not be considered in the same category.

I had an assortment of puppy food, puppy chews, puppy toys, and assorted puppy diversions.

Even before I handed the breeder a check, this dog purchase had become expensive.

Do friends ever give puppy showers? My initial reaction was a strong no, with a wishful yes right behind.

I was ready. I was prepared.

Yet nothing could prepare me, really and truly, for what was to happen in a few short months.

The breeder actually looked at every picture I took of my purchases, my preparations, my supplies, my complete photo essay of my backyard. She even checked the photocopy of the medical license of my intended veterinarian.

"I've never heard of him," she said, "but he went to Cornell. Best vet school in the country."

"She. She went. The B. T. stands for Barbara something or other," I answered.

The breeder brightened.

"Good. I've always found female vets to be more compassionate—and intuitive. Good choice."

I felt proud of what I had accomplished. It was a feeling I had missed in recent months.

She presented me with the puppy's papers and AKC registration—a thick packet of documents that displayed his lineage back to the *Mayflower*, apparently. I had assured her that I had no interest in showing the puppy, or dog, as it grew. I promised to have him neutered; perhaps breeders do not want more competition from unskilled amateurs like me. "Neutered makes for better pets," she declared. I knew, for certain, that his papers would be filed in my office at home, and then lost in less than six months.

I'm not going to sell the dog for a profit, like flipping a fore-closed house. He's not going to procreate. Why would I need to know his great-great-great-grandfather?

I handed her the check. The dog was now mine.

"What are you going to name him?" the breeder asked.

I shrugged, apologetically.

"I'm not good with names . . . or book titles. I let my publisher pick titles. But with the dog, I thought I might see what sort of name fits him after a day or two."

"Don't wait too long. Puppies get imprinted with whatever you call it—especially if you use it a lot when they're young."

He lay down in the middle of the pet carrier, not frantically trying to escape or cowering in the corner. But in the middle, like that is where he was supposed to be. It did make it easier to carry, since the weight was evenly distributed.

I had been nervous concerning the ride home, worried about a whining, yelping puppy carrying on so much that I would have to stop. I'd imagined him chewing wildly at the door, scrabbling to escape his new and probably evil owner. But there were no histrionics, no puppy on the edge of puppy craziness. Just a very calm puppy, supine, staring out through the wire mesh door.

I pulled into the garage, stopped the car, and carefully took the carrier from the car.

"Show him his bed, his food, and the door you'll use to take him outside. Take him out on a leash right away and start his bathroom training," the breeder instructed, touching on the three most important elements in a puppy's small world.

I followed her instructions to the letter.

He dutifully sniffed at his crate, stepped inside, sniffing, looking at the cushion, then up at the top of the crate—like people do on all the HGTV shows when they enter a new room. I have noted that potential homebuyers invariably look at the ceiling, as if to make sure the house has one. Why do people do that? It's a plain ceiling. Look to see how big the closets are first, and if you have good water pressure. No one checks the water pressure on those shows. I have yet to see a single buyer flush a toilet. There might be a lot fewer home sales if people flushed toilets or ran showers.

The puppy completed his examination of the crate. I led him to his food dish and water bowl—both filled with fresh supplies.

He sniffed at both.

I snapped a leash onto his collar and led him to the . . .

Wait. What door am I going to use?

The back door led to a back deck, a second-story affair. A puppy this small would not yet be able to climb stairs.

I'll have to use the front door.

We stepped outside through the main door, and his sniffing became a bit more earnest. It took him fifteen minutes to sniff his way around the front yard. I was cold by the time he completed his inspection. There were other dogs in the neighborhood, so he took some time getting acquainted with their calling cards.

I am told that dogs can tell the size and sex and temperament of other dogs by the scent they leave. Seems a crude way of doing it—but if you can't talk or write, I suspect it is the only way.

He actually relieved himself out there, by a bush toward the side of the house—a bush I didn't really like, so if his ministrations killed it, I would not be upset. It was some sort of weedy looking shrub that had been billed as the bearer of fragrant flowers. The flowers lasted all of three days; the rest of the time it simply looked weedy. I praised him, as I had been told to do.

We walked back into the house. I unclipped his leash.

"Keep him in the kitchen at first. He'll be overwhelmed if he has too much space to explore."

Two doorways led into the kitchen: one a pocket door to the dining room, easily closed off; the other archway could be cut off by opening the basement door, leaving a gap of only an inch or two. The bigger problem was the wide arch between the kitchen and the family room.

The puppy seemed to be a cautious type, so my initial solution employed two lengths of white clothesline rope, strung at two inches off the floor, and the other at six inches, and affixed to the molding with adhesive-backed Velcro. If the puppy ran into them at full force, which he gave no indication of doing, the ropes would give way. More important, if I ran into them, stumbling toward the sunroom with the first coffee of the day and with my typical morning slit-eyes, then I would dislodge them as easily, without tumbling down and scalding myself with hot coffee.

The puppy sniffed the ropes, and made no attempt to cross the barrier.

It appeared effective. Maybe I could market this idea.

The puppy stared up at me.

No. How hard would it be to duplicate this? Not very.

I sat on the floor, my back to the wall, and invited the puppy to play. He slithered over with a wiggle. I imagined that he looked happy. I couldn't tell. This was the start of a long process, learning how to read the moods of this small animal.

He crawled into my hands and began a gentle nibbling on my fingers. His breath smelled healthy, like milk.

"Don't let him bite you," the breeder had scolded me. "Bad habit for a dog to have—biting."

But chewing is what a puppy does. As long as he did not bite in anger, I would tolerate a dog-to-owner chew every now and again.

After thirty minutes, the puppy crawled down from my leg and sat on his haunches, looking as tired as a . . . well, a puppy.

"Go into your crate," I directed and pointed at the open door to his den.

The puppy stared at my finger for a moment, as if my finger was the object he should focus on. "No," I said, as I pushed my finger forward into the air, gesturing toward the door. The puppy appeared to scowl, or furrow his brow as if in thought, then turned his head toward the crate. He lifted himself off the floor and walked with a surprising deliberateness toward his den, his crate, climbed over the two-inch frame, walked in, circled three times, then lay down, his head on his paws, his eyes facing me.

"Tired?"

He blinked, and let his head fall farther onto his paws.

"Can I get some coffee? Will I keep you awake?"

He did not answer. I am not sure, in the retelling of this episode, if he understood me at that young age, and simply waited to speak until the right time, or if he was in the process of trying to understand my speech. I think the latter, though I have not asked him. It doesn't seem to be that pertinent a question, in retrospect.

I sat in the upholstered chair in the bay window in the kitchen, sat with my coffee, watching The Weather Channel with the sound muted, sipping as quietly as I could manage, watching the puppy fall into a deep, untroubled sleep.

Want to learn more about author
Jim Kraus and check out other great
fiction from Abingdon Press?

Sign up for our fiction newsletter at
www.AbingdonPress.com
to read interviews with your favorite authors, find tips
for starting a reading group, and stay posted on what
new titles are on the horizon. It's a place to connect
with other fiction readers or post a
comment about this book.

Be sure to visit Jim online!

www.jimkraus.com

Discover Fiction from Abingdon Press

BOOKLIST 2010

Top 10 Inspirational Fiction award

ROMANTIC TIMES 2010

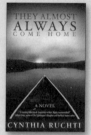

Reviewers Choice Awards
Book of the Year nominee

BLACK CHRISTIAN BOOK LIST

#1 for two consecutive months,
2010 Black Christian Book
national bestseller list;
ACFW Book of the Month, Nov/Dec 2010

CAROL AWARDS 2010

(ACFW) Contemporary
Fiction nominee

INSPY AWARD NOMINEES

Suspense   General Fiction   Contemporary Fiction

Abingdon Press fiction
a novel approach to faith
AbingdonPress.com | 800.251.3320

FBM112220001 PACP01002597-01

What They're Saying About...

The Glory of Green, by Judy Christie
"Once again, Christie draws her readers into the town, the life, the humor, and the drama in Green. *The Glory of Green* is a wonderful narrative of small-town America, pulling together in tragedy. A great read!"
—Ane Mulligan, editor of *Novel Journey*

Always the Baker, Never the Bride, by Sandra Bricker
"[It] had just the right touch of humor, and I loved the characters. Emma Rae is a character who will stay with me. Highly recommended!"
—Colleen Coble, author of *The Lightkeeper's Daughter* and the *Rock Harbor* series

Diagnosis Death, by Richard Mabry
"Realistic medical flavor graces a story rich with characters I loved and with enough twists and turns to keep the sleuth in me off-center. Keep 'em coming!"—Dr. Harry Krauss, author of *Salty Like Blood* and *The Six-Liter Club*

Sweet Baklava, by Debby Mayne
"A sweet romance, a feel-good ending, and a surprise cache of yummy Greek recipes at the book's end? I'm sold!"—**Trish Perry, author of** *Unforgettable* and *Tea for Two*

The Dead Saint, by Marilyn Brown Oden
"An intriguing story of international espionage with just the right amount of inspirational seasoning."—*Fresh Fiction*

Shrouded in Silence, by Robert L. Wise
"It's a story fraught with death, danger, and deception—of never knowing whom to trust, and with a twist of an ending I didn't see coming. Great read!"—Sharon Sala, author of *The Searcher's Trilogy: Blood Stains, Blood Ties,* and *Blood Trails*.

Delivered with Love, by Sherry Kyle
"Sherry Kyle has created an engaging story of forgiveness, sweet romance, and faith reawakened—and I looked forward to every page. A fun and charming debut!"—Julie Carobini, author of *A Shore Thing* and *Fade to Blue.*

Abingdon Press fiction
a novel approach to faith

AbingdonPress.com | 800.251.3320